By Matt Hilton

DEAD MEN'S DUST

Forthcoming

JUDGMENT AND WRATH

DEAD MEN'S DUST

MATT HILTON

HARPER

An Imprint of HarperCollinsPublishers

This book is a work of fiction. References to real people, events, establishments, organizations, or locales are intended only to provide a sense of authenticity, and are used fictitiously. All other characters, and all incidents and dialogue, are drawn from the author's imagination and are not to be construed as real.

HARPER

An Imprint of HarperCollins*Publishers*
10 East 53rd Street
New York, New York 10022-5299

Copyright © 2009 by Matt Hilton
Excerpt from *Judgment and Wrath* copyright © 2010 by Matt Hilton
ISBN 978-0-06-171719-2

First Harper paperback printing: May 2010
First William Morrow hardcover printing: June 2009

HarperCollins® and Harper® are registered trademarks of Harper-Collins Publishers.

Printed in the United States of America

Visit Harper paperbacks on the World Wide Web
at www.harpercollins.com

10 9 8 7 6 5 4 3 2 1

THIS BOOK IS DEDICATED IN SAD MEMORY to my beautiful girl, Megan Rose Hilton (1989-2006). My first and foremost fan and critic. I miss you dearly, Megs. Your energy, I know, goes on. When the time is right, I will see you again.

DEAD MEN'S DUST

Prologue

JUBAL'S HOLLOW.

Sounds nice, doesn't it? Like one of those gentle Appalachian towns with timber-framed houses and split-rail fences. Where life takes a leisurely pace: where people actually sit on their sun-dappled porches beside a pitcher of homemade lemonade with beads of condensation. Can you almost hear the rustle of branches overhanging slow-moving rivers, the shuffle of wildlife in the long grass?

Nice, huh?

The vision couldn't be further from the truth.

Try this instead.

Nothing but scrub, sand, and more sand. Blistering midday sun, unbearable cold at night. Harsh rock formations surrounded by a blasted earthscape. Nothing lives here.

Death is the only resident. Ever present. Waiting, waiting.

Look closely. Bones litter the sand, some the petrified remains of creatures that lived in the mud of prehistoric swamps, but some are more recent. There are the bones of birds and small animals that limped here searching for non-existent water.

Occasionally the sand will cast up bones recognizably human.

Supposedly, a troop of Confederate soldiers fled here to the western desert when they were split from the forces of Jubal Anderson Early as he fought the Yankees at Waynesboro, Georgia. Rumor is that it's their bones that are occasionally stripped bare, left exposed by the wind.

There's another myth behind the hollow's name. In the Old Testament, blind-eyed Lamech had a son by the name of Jubal Cain, father of all who handle the harp and pipe. Jubal was said to be the first musician. This is a fitting place to carry his legacy.

Jubal's Hollow, a natural amphitheater, is noted for its strange acoustics. Wind can make it moan like a dirge of funeral pipes. It is a preternatural music of the dead.

But it is not the only connection to Jubal.

Jubal had a brother named Tubal, and if legend is true, he was the first metalworker. It was he who forged the first knife. But today it is another Tubal Cain who fills this place with the bones of men.

1

PAIN AND FEAR TRANSCEND EVERYTHING, AND know no boundaries. It doesn't matter where you are. You could be in any metropolis in the world—New York, London, Paris, Moscow—and the parallels would remain consistent. There are differences in culture, in law, in language, but at their most basic level, civilizations share one undeniable truth: the scream of a victim sounds the same the world over.

Stepping off an airplane into the sticky heat following a Florida thunderstorm, the screams of my past were ringing in my ears. Somehow I knew that the hunt for John Telfer would add further memories of pain and anguish to my already full heart.

My quest had begun two days previously and an ocean's breadth away in England. There were screams then, too.

It was just like the old days. I was back doing what I was good at. Where I crouched, broken glass and rubbish littered the floor. Nearby, a train rattled past and last week's front-page news fluttered in the service alley. It wasn't all that stirred; the stench was terrible, a mix of urine and filth.

It chilled me.

Jennifer Telfer's curtains twitched inside her apartment.

She was scared. And that was to be expected. She knew why I was there, on the street, watching her place.

It wasn't me she was afraid of.

Some people call me a vigilante. That's their prerogative.

I prefer to think of myself as a problem-fixer. When you're a single mother whose children have been threatened by violent men, you send for Joe Hunter.

A black BMW slowed at the end of the street.

"Here we go."

It halted in front of the apartment building. There were three men inside: the harsh and aggressive men I'd been expecting.

First to step out was a large bald-headed man, busy pulling on leather gloves. From the back came a man equally tall. Unlike the first, his frame was lanky and thin. Together, they moved toward Jennifer's place.

The idling engine covered my approach. So did the blaring radio. The first the driver knew of my presence was when I tugged open the door.

"What the—" was all he got out before I hit him.

I aimed for the carotid sinus and struck the bull's-eye. Such a blow could prove fatal. Call me compassionate—I chopped him just hard enough to knock him out.

Leaning over him, I grabbed at the seat belt. It made a good noose. The remainder of the belt looped around the headrest and jammed into the door frame made it even better.

I caught up with the other two before they'd reached the apartments.

With a bent back, a cap pulled down over my hair, I moved toward them. I might as well have been invisible.

I straightened up and thrust the V of my thumb and index finger into the bald man's windpipe. As his hands went to his damaged throat, I slammed my clenched fist into his solar plexus and he folded over my arm. Breath exploded from his lungs as he performed a slow dive, meeting my lifted knee midway. He hit the floor hard, but it didn't matter: he was already oblivious.

There was no time for taking satisfaction from my work: Skinny was already going for something inside his jacket. Could be a gun.

Grasping his wrist and tugging his hand out of his jacket, I saw that he held a knife.

"Now isn't that just typical of you, Shank?" I flexed his wrist, hearing bone grating on bone. Made it easy to pluck the knife from his fingers.

His name was Peter Ramsey, an idiot who began his criminal career stealing lunch money from the other kids at school. But—like all third-rate gangsters—he loved his nickname. He favored a knife when threatening desperate mothers. Shank should be a scary handle for someone wielding a blade. I thought it was pathetic.

I took a fistful of Shank's hair and pressed my knuckles against his skull.

"Listen closely," I growled. "One thing, and one thing only." I snatched his head forward, meeting him eye to eye. "Jennifer Telfer is off your books. *Permanently.* You hear that?"

"Jennifer Telfer? Who the—"

I slapped him hard.

"You know who I mean."

Wagging the knife at him, I said, "Tell me you weren't thinking of cutting her." I lifted the blade. Sharp edge beneath his nose. His breath misted the steel. "You know something, Shank? Just thinking of that makes my blood run cold."

"I wasn't gonna cut anybody," Shank said.

"Good. You won't be wanting this back then." I dropped the knife into my coat pocket. "If I see you around here again, I'll hurt you bad."

"What have I ever done to you?"

"Messed with the wrong person," I told him. "That's what."

To punctuate the point I backhanded him across the face. "When you walk out of here, you keep on going. If you as much as look back, I'll be all over you like a bad case of hives. You got that?"

"Yeah, man, I get you."

"See you, then."

"Not if I see you first," he said, turning quickly away. "Psycho!"

"Believe me," I said, "if there is a next time, you won't see me coming."

2

"COME IN, JOE. QUICK."

Jack and Beatrice huddled in front of a television. A cartoon vied for their attention and they barely gave me a glance.

In a hurry, Jennifer shut the door. Behind me came the clink of a security chain, the ratchet of a dead bolt.

"You won't need as many locks in the future, Jenny." I pulled off the hat and jacket. "Shank won't be paying you any more visits."

Jennifer hugged herself. Barely above a whisper, she said, "There's worse out there than Shank to worry about."

Fourteen years working as a counterterrorism agent had already convinced me of that. If I required reminding, all I had to do was look at the kids. Only six and four years old, they already had the look of the infinitely wise about them. "Hi, kids, what're you watching? Cartoons?"

"SpongeBob," Jack said matter-of-factly.

"He's got square pants," Beatrice added.

"Interesting," I said. I gave her a lifted eyebrow. She was too young to know who The Rock was, but she appreciated the effort. Her giggle was like soft music. A baby again. The resilience of children never fails to amaze the cynic in me.

Her mother wasn't so easily calmed. My hand on her shoulder was waved off with a gesture. Jenny took my coat and hat, abandoned them on the arm of a settee, then walked across the room. Perched on a chair next to a battle-scarred table, she had the look of a condemned prisoner.

"You can quit worrying. I guarantee you, Shank'll look somewhere else for his cash."

She plucked at a pack of cigarettes next to an ashtray overflowing with half-smoked butts. The ashtray was testament to prolonged worry.

"For now," she said. "But what about when you leave? What's to stop them coming back?"

"I'm only a phone call away."

Jennifer hacked out a cough. She stabbed the cigarette into her mouth.

"What about when I can't pay you, Joe? Are you still going to come running then?"

"You think I did this for money? I helped you because I wanted to. You needed help. All of you."

"But you don't work for free, Joe. Didn't you tell your brother John that? Why didn't you help John? If you had, then maybe he'd still be here . . ." I saw fresh tears on her lashes. "Why didn't you help us then, huh? I'll tell you why, should I? It was about the *money*."

I didn't answer.

She brought a light to her cigarette and went at it as if it were a lifeline. She glared at me. "You wouldn't help John when he needed it. I can't pay any more than he could."

I had to say something. First, I settled in opposite her. "Jenny, you don't really understand what happened between me and John. It had nothing to do with whether he could pay me."

She snorted, sucked on the cigarette.

"I don't know what he told you, but I guess it wasn't the truth," I said.

Her eyes pierced me.

"What are you saying, Joe?"

I sighed. "It's water under the bridge, Jenny. Forget it, okay?"

She shrugged, flicked an ash that missed the ashtray. "Suit yourself."

Silence hung in the air between us, mingling with her blue smoke exhalations.

Once, I watched a heron spearing trout from a stream. Jennifer's hand made similar stabbing motions to douse her cigarette. Then, like the greedy heron, she reached for another. I gently laid a hand on top of hers. She met my eyes. Hope flickered beyond the dullness but only for a second. She pulled her hand away, drew the pack to her. She lit up and took a long gasp. Through a haze of smoke, she said, "I want you to find John." She reached out and twined her fingers in mine. "I want you to find your brother and bring him home."

"That might not be as easy as it sounds. He's not in the country anymore."

"No, he isn't. He's in America," Jenny said.

"You've heard from him?"

Searching in her pocket, Jenny pulled out an envelope and held it to her breast. After a moment, she placed the envelope before me. I looked up at her, but she was looking over at the kids. "You two, go into your room while me and Uncle Joe are talking. You can watch TV in there." Before they could argue, she hurried over, took them by their elbows, and ushered them into their bedroom. Closing the door, she said, "I don't want them listening. After all's said and done, John's still their dad."

Nodding, I concentrated on the envelope. It was standard white and dated more than two weeks ago. It was stamped *Little Rock, AK*.

"Arkansas?" I asked.

"Where else?"

The tattered edge of the envelope produced two sheets of paper. On first inspection, it looked like the kind of note you scrawl and leave in a prominent position when you have to leave in a hurry. Only longer. A *Dear John* letter. Or in this case a *Dear Jenny*? But it wasn't my brother's handwriting.

I sought Jenny's face. "Go ahead. Read it," she said.

I did.
It read:

> *Jenny,*
>
> *I probably have no right writing you like this. No doubt you hate me, but I hope you'll listen to what I have to say.*
>
> *John has gone, and I don't know what to do. Don't get me wrong, he hasn't just left me as he did with you. When I say he's gone, I mean vanished.*
>
> *Maybe you don't care, maybe you think I deserve everything I get, that John definitely deserves it, but I don't think you're that kind of person. John has got himself in some kind of trouble. He was jumpy for two or three days before he disappeared. He was frightened. I think something terrible has happened. And that's why I'm writing to you now.*

I placed the first sheet of paper on the table and looked across at Jenny. She'd retreated to the opposite end of the room, staring vacantly into space. The letter was my problem now.

> *John said that he's got a half-brother over in England. Someone he called Hunter. I know they didn't get along that well, but John said once that if anything ever happened to him I had to send for Hunter because he would know what to do. So I'm asking, I'm begging, please do this for me. And if you won't do it for me, do it for John. Send for his brother.*
>
> *Please. L.*

"This woman," I asked, "who is she?"

Jenny returned to stub out her cigarette. Her words held more vehemence up close. "John's bitch."

"Is she American?"

"No. She's English."

"What's her name?"

"Louise Blake."

"How did John meet her?"

"She worked for the same company as him." She gave me a pointed stare. I just watched her, and Jennifer added, "By all accounts they were seeing each other for six months before he left me." She gave me the pointed look again. "Everyone knew but me."

"I didn't."

She wiped at her mouth with the back of a hand. "Well, you're about the only one who didn't." Her words became softer as she recalled the betrayal. "Louise stole my husband from me, Joe. Now she wants help to find him. What does she want me to do, hand him right back to her?"

"Have you ever met her?"

"Not formally. I saw her a couple times where John worked." Jenny laughed. "When I think about it, I suppose you'd say she's a younger version of me. Without the baggage around the waist from carrying two kids. Basically John traded me in for a younger model."

"But you still want me to find him?"

She sighed. Her gaze flickered toward the bedroom. The kids were very quiet and I wondered if they had their ears to the door.

"He's still their dad, Joe. He should be doing more to support them."

Yes. A sad fact. But not something I was about to put into words.

Jenny said, "Probably Louise is right: John does deserve everything he gets. But my kids shouldn't be made to suffer, should they?" She could look all she wanted but she wouldn't see any sign of disagreement from me. After a few seconds she asked, "So . . . what do you think? Is there anything you can do?"

"There is," I promised her.

And I meant it.

3

WHEN WORKING, I DON'T USE A VEHICLE THAT I care about. I use an old car I picked up at an auction. That way, when the disgruntled dig a key into the length of the paintwork, I don't get too upset. The car has many scars. The only concession I make to roadworthiness is to have the engine regularly overhauled and tires of the puncture-proof variety. Both have proved invaluable in the past.

Before setting up the takedown on Shank, I had parked the old Ford a couple of streets away. Okay, I wasn't that protective of it, but neither was I going to make my wheels a sitting duck. I was approaching the car when the BMW swung into the street behind me. To be fair, I thought I'd seen the last of Peter Ramsey, yet here he was, back for more.

Maybe I should've done a better number on him the first time. My fault, but as I said, I can be a compassionate guy.

"This time . . . no messing about," I promised.

In an effort at stealth, the music volume had been turned down. Still, the thud-thud rhythm sounded like the heartbeat of a predator coiling for the death lunge. Thick tires whistled on tarmac. The engine growled. Even without looking, I'd have known they were coming.

It was like patrolling in-country all over again. Only then I was an inexperienced rookie, immortal in my battle fatigues and holding a submachine gun. Unprepared for what happened, I hadn't even realized I'd been shot until I surfaced through a morphine haze the following day and blinked up at my nurse.

You don't hear the bullet that kills you. Which meant the two bullets Shank fired at me missed their mark. Good job I'd leaped forward at the right time. The sidewalk was a little unforgiving, but a scraped elbow and knee were the least of my worries.

The BMW was a sleek black shark, as dangerous as the .38 Shank aimed at me. It made sense that the driver swung the BMW onto the sidewalk. A half-ton of metal on my head would finish me as quickly as a slug in the heart.

"Get that son of a bitch!"

Even as I rolled away from the car, I had to smile at Shank's determination.

The BMW bumped down off the curb, knocking value off the alloys. I rose up behind them. From beneath my shirttails, I drew my own gun, a SIG-Sauer P226. Unlike these cretins, I had a full load. In addition, I knew how to shoot. One round into a rear tire, two into the trunk, and one through the back windshield for good measure. More than the deflated tire, panic spun the car across the road and drove it into my parked car.

In this part of town, gunfire would ensure that witnesses kept their heads down. On the other hand, a good old-fashioned car wreck would bring the ghouls running.

"Out of the car," I shouted. "Now!"

The driver was slumped over the steering wheel, blood frothing from both nostrils. Sound asleep for the second time that evening. Shank wasn't in much better shape. Half out the window when the car collided with my Ford, he was now on the road, crying like a baby and cradling a busted elbow. His gun had slid harmlessly beneath my car. Only the third guy, the big baldy, posed any threat.

"I said, *Out of the damn car.*"

Staring down the barrel of a SIG is enough to motivate most men. He was surprisingly sprightly when offered the correct form of stimulation. His hands went up. "Okay! Easy, man, easy."

His gloves were gone. Heavy gold rings made a rich man's

brass knuckles on his right hand. Fancied himself a pugilist.

"Pick Shank up," I told him.

Conditioned to taking commands, he didn't object. He quickly stooped down and lifted Shank to his feet.

"Up the alley."

Opposite us was a narrow alleyway between a vacant lot and a video rental store that was closed for the night. Maybe the store had closed for many nights, judging by the faded posters.

I knew what was going through the big guy's mind. He thought the ignominious alley was where he was going to end his days. Give him his due; I think he was braver than he was stupid.

"You aren't taking us up there to shoot us."

"I'm not?"

"If you're going to do it, do it now. Out here in the open."

"Okay," I said.

Not so keen, Shank whimpered.

Baldy gave his boss a look that suggested there were going to be changes in their arrangement—if they managed to get out of this alive. Shank was left swaying as the big man stepped away from him.

"Go on," he challenged. "I don't think you've got what it takes."

I gave him my saddest smile.

The big man took that as a sign of weakness. He snatched at a gun tucked into his waistband.

I caressed the trigger and his right kneecap disintegrated.

He collapsed to the floor, and despite his bravado he screamed.

"What about you, Shank? Do you think I haven't got it in me to do you?" I aimed the SIG at a point directly between his eyes. "After you tried to shoot me?"

Think of an air-raid siren and you'll imagine the sound that Shank made.

"You know something, Shank? You should have listened to me."

I pulled the trigger again.

Shank fell next to his friend, clutching at his own shattered knee.

"Next time I will kill you," I promised.

4

HE HAD THE DESIRE AND THE PASSION. HE CERtainly had the ability. But that wasn't everything. Tubal Cain also had an agenda.

Right now he was short on materials.

There wasn't much hope of acquiring what he needed here, but for these cretins, he'd make the effort.

"You know something? You should all be damned straight to hell!"

There weren't too many things that got him riled, but these pigs on wheels were the exception. Motor homes! These monstrosities of engineering were a blight on the landscape. Colossal steel bullets fired from the devil's cannon to cause woe and destruction wherever they landed.

Without their intrusion, this oasis turnoff beside Route I-10 in Southern California had its own beauty. A semicircular drive ran up to an artesian well, and trees had been artfully arranged to block the view of the interstate. Laurel trees made a pretty silhouette against the star-filled sky, but not when a goddamn Winnebago hunkered beneath them, square, unnatural, and spewing light from a cabin the size of the flight deck of the USS *Enterprise*.

"It's enough to make you sick," Tubal Cain said.

Neither Mabel nor George *or whatever the hell they were called* argued the point. George was equivocal on the entire subject. However, that could be expected. Speaking could be difficult with a gash the width of your thumb parting your trachea.

For her part, Mabel was pretty verbal, but nothing she'd said up until now would change his opinion. She was too intent on screaming for her unheeding husband. Another thing: she wasn't giving any clues to George's actual name. She'd only refer to him as Daddy. She was obscene, like a wrinkly Lolita.

"Aw, for crying out loud!" Cain said. "Put a lid on it, will you? How do you expect me to work with all that racket you're making?"

Mabel hunkered down in the kitchen compartment. She was a hunched package stuffed beneath a fold-down counter, looking like the garbage sack George had been about to drop into the bushes when Cain surprised him.

"Daddy, Daddy! Help me, Daddy!" she screamed for about the hundredth time.

"Daddy's not interested," Cain pointed out. "So you might as well shut up."

Daddy sat in the driving seat, surrounded by the luxury of leather and walnut. But he was of no mind to point out the lushness of his surroundings. The elderly man was currently preoccupied with trying to stem the tide of blood flowing down the front of his pullover. Chalk white, his features showed he was losing the battle.

"Daddeeee . . ."

Cain took the man's hands away from the wound, guiding them to the steering wheel. His final earthly experience would be gripping the wheel as though with the intention of taking the Winnebago through the Pearly Gates with him.

The knife snicked through tendons and gristle, the old man's death grip loosened, and his hands flopped onto his thighs. Sans thumbs, his hands looked like dead squid.

Moving toward the woman's hiding place, Cain slipped the thumbs into a sandwich bag and dropped them in a pocket.

"People have to learn to take their trash home with them, Mabel." If there was anything that got his goat even more than motor homes it was the irresponsible and harmful littering George had been engaged in. Bad enough that he destroyed the picturesque beauty of the desert with this huge beast—but then he deposited its shit before he left. "Maybe if George wasn't so indiscriminate with his garbage, I wouldn't have had to call on you and teach you such a valuable lesson."

"You killed Daddy because there were no trash cans?"

"Yes. And for his ridiculous taste in vehicles."

"You're insane!" Mabel shrieked.

"No, Mabel. I'm angry."

"You killed Daddy!"

"Yes."

He stooped down, pulled her from beneath the counter. She slid out as boneless as an oyster from the shell. Cain didn't like oysters. Didn't like anything boneless.

He rapped a knuckle on her head. Just to be sure. The clunk was only partway reassuring.

"How old are you, Mabel? Seventy? Eighty?"

Her turquoise-framed spectacles lent an extra dimension to her incredulous blink. Confusion reigned, terror tamped down by befuddlement. Her mouth drooped. At least she'd stopped screaming.

"I wouldn't ask, but it is pertinent," Cain said.

"Eighty-three." Saliva popped at the back of her throat.

"Hmmm. Quite elderly." Cain gripped her shoulder. He kneaded with a masseur's skill. "Frail under all that padding. I bet you suffer from arthritis, eh?"

She showed him her misshapen knuckles.

"Thought that might be the case." His sigh sounded genuinely remorseful. "What about osteoporosis?"

He was offering hope, and she wasn't so distraught that she didn't recognize it. Even after such a long life, when faced with dismemberment, an octogenarian can still desire further years. "I'm riddled with it. I only have to sneeze and I can break a rib."

"Doesn't bode well."

"What do you want from us?"

"Nothing."

"You cut off Daddy's thumbs . . ."

"I did, Mabel. I have a purpose for them. But you needn't fear. You have nothing that I want."

"Thank the good Lord!" Mabel sobbed.

"But only for small mercies," Cain concluded as he slipped the knife back in his pocket. He didn't require a knife when dealing with an invertebrate. The heel of his shoe would be all he'd need.

Ten minutes later he was back on the road.

The Mercedes SUV he drove made a fine chariot. Interstate 10 stretched out before him, an umbilical cord drawing him ever westward, toward the fertile stalking-grounds of Los Angeles.

Billy Joel was cranked high on the SUV's CD player. A window open so that the warm breeze ruffled Cain's fair hair. He was a happy man. Beside him on the passenger seat were the tools of his trade, flagrantly displayed in total disregard of law or common sense. If someone saw them, well, so what? A cop died as easy as any man did.

With that thought in mind, he reached over and lifted the flap of the pouch. Inside was an array of knives, scalpels, and other cutting utensils. *Tap, tap, tap.* He danced a finger over the dozen or so hilts. *Tap.* Rested momentarily on the sturdy hilt of a Bowie knife.

"Ah, sweet baby," he said. Such fond memories.

A would-be knife fighter back east in Jacksonville had bestowed the knife upon him. What unashamed southern generosity. Such a polite man, too.

"You're going to have to take it from me first, sir," he'd offered.

"Gladly," Tubal Cain had agreed.

The blade was broad and easily a foot long. Whenever it was thrust into flesh, it made a satisfying *thunk!* A firm favorite for instilling fear in the hearts of his victims. Sadly, it lacked finesse. If carnage was your only desire, then fine. Ever the artist, he preferred a little more delicacy to his cutting.

Now this was more to his liking. Black plastic hilt, slim

and unadorned. Grasping it lightly, he teased out the cutting edge. Muted moonbeams played on a curved, very utilitarian blade backed by saw-toothed serrations. Beautiful in its simplicity. It was a fish-scaling knife acquired during a northern foray to Nova Scotia. The blade had seen employment on a number of occasions since, but never on anything so mundane as trout or salmon.

Happy with his choice, he pulled the scaling knife free and held it up for closer inspection. With a thumb, he tested its keenness. "As keen as I am, eh?"

The knife went into an inside pocket of his sports jacket.

Billy Joel was winding down, Christie Brinkley demanding his full attention. The CDs spread over the passenger seat beckoned. Cain selected a Robbie Williams disc: Stoke-on-Trent's best-known export doing his best to capture the cool of Sinatra and not doing a half-bad job. He changed the CD, then bobbed his head along with the tempo swinging from the speakers.

"My kind of music," he whispered. An aptly named track—a cover of "Mack the Knife." He cut lazy figures of eight into the air with his right hand. Like conducting a big band, but instead of a bandleader's baton he imagined a blade in his hand. With each swing of the music, he cut another strip of meat from a faceless victim.

"Swing while you're sinning." He grinned. A nod toward the title of the album.

5

THAT EVENING, AFTER THE EPISODE WITH SHANK, I returned home to a house in darkness. Nothing new there. It's been like that since Diane and I divorced.

The auction car wasn't registered to me, so I was happy to leave it in place. A cab took me to the lock-up garage I used, so it was my other car, an Audi A6, I parked on the tree-lined street. My two dogs, Hector and Paris, were inside the house, and I could just make out their forms as they pressed their noses to the glass doors leading to the patio. I must have made an indistinct shadow against the deeper night. Hector, largest of my German shepherds, huffed once, then I watched as the two dogs became animated.

I was conscious of disturbing my neighbors, but it was pointless trying to be quiet; Hector and Paris were making enough racket to wake the neighborhood. I pushed open the patio door. Instantly I was assaulted by twin black-and-tan whirlwinds. We went through a round of play fighting before the dogs would obey my command to sit.

As always, the TV cabinet became a receptacle for my car keys and wallet. It was a habit my ex-wife used to frown upon. It was only one of the many things that annoyed her before our split. Probably the very least of them.

Sometimes I wished Diane were still there to keep me right, but she wasn't. As soon as I tendered my resignation from the army, the death knell for our marriage was rung.

Probably she understood me in a way that I never could. Physically I'd resigned, but mentally?

"Married men can't just rush off, placing themselves in life-threatening situations all the time," Diane told me the night she left.

"So you want me to sit at home and die of boredom?" I demanded.

"No, Joe." She'd shaken her head sadly. "I just don't want to be the one who has to bury you."

Diane wanted someone she could grow old with. Understandable, but it wasn't something I could promise her. I'm way too impulsive for that. My promise to Jenny was nagging at me to get going. I wanted to make a start with some phone calls.

The clock on the wall had to be telling lies. Not too late, though, I decided. Hector and Paris ran out into the backyard. I followed them, pulling out my cell phone. Four years on, I still had Diane's number on speed dial.

"Hello?"

"Hi, Simon," I said, concealing any trace of jealousy. "Can I speak to Diane?"

Diane's very safe, office-bound husband grunted, muttered something unintelligible, but handed over the phone.

"What do you want, Joe?"

"I'm going away," I told her.

There was a momentary hitch in her voice. "So why are you telling me?"

"Thought you might want to wave me off at the airport."

I heard her sigh. "I already did that. Too many times."

It was my turn to sigh.

"Can you take the dogs for me for a few days?"

"Simon has allergies," she said.

"Shit," I said. "Isn't it a good job we never had kids?"

Her silence said everything.

"I'm sorry, Diane. I shouldn't have said that."

"No, Joe. You shouldn't have." In the background, Simon

was whispering something. "Simon said we can take them, but they'll have to stay in the shed."

My dogs were gamboling around the yard, play fighting among the rhododendrons. Full of life.

"So long as they're exercised they'll be fine," I said.

"Okay, then."

"I'll drop them off in the morning," I said.

"No," Diane said, way too quickly for my liking. "I'll come there with Simon."

Then she hung up.

With the dogs sorted, I returned indoors, settled into an armchair, and dialed a number in Tampa, Florida.

"Hey, Hunter, what's up?"

Jared Rington's voice is a rich southern drawl that always reminds me of that guitar-playing wedding suitor in the John Wayne movie *The Searchers*. He has the honky-tonk twang of a country-and-western singer, which always surprises people; it's a strange anomaly coming from a mixed parentage of Japanese mother and Scottish father.

"You busy with anything, Rink?"

"Got my heel planted on a weasel as we speak," Rink said.

"I take it you're speaking metaphorically?"

"Uh-huh," Rink said. "I just gotta finish up a little one-on-one business with my client, then I'm all yours."

"So what's the deal? Anything exciting?"

"Nothing startling. Guy paid me to do a little eyeball on his wife. He grew suspicious when she started doing too much overtime at work. Thought she could be playin' away from home."

"Maybe she was just after more money," I offered.

"Yeah, you might say she was after a raise." Rink chuckled. "I got the goods on her last night. Filmed her giving head to her boss in the back of his limousine."

"So you just have to hand over the evidence and that's you finished?" I asked.

"More or less, yeah. Anyways, what's up?" Rink asked. "You haven't rung for the sake of idle chitchat. That's not the Joe Hunter I know and love."

"I've got a job for you . . . if you're interested?"

"Uh-huh." It could've been agreement, but more likely he was waiting for more.

"Could be a long story," I told him.

"Fire away, it's your dime."

It was so still I could have been in a mausoleum. But habit caused a quick over-the-shoulder glance to make sure I was alone.

"I'm going to be coming out there," I told him.

"Out here? As in Florida?"

"Well, yeah, I was thinking of stopping over a day or so, but then I have to get myself to Little Rock, Arkansas."

"My old stomping ground?"

"It's why you're the man for the job."

"You think I'm a tour guide all of a sudden? Get yourself a map." Good-natured sarcasm was rich in his drawl. How anyone could dislike Rink is a mystery. What's not to like about a sarcastic curmudgeon?

"Local knowledge is half the battle," I told him.

"I ain't been home in eight years, Hunter. Don't know how up to date my local knowledge'll be."

"How much can Arkansas have changed in eight years?" I asked. "It's not like it's the center of American culture."

"Yeah, but it's not like it's simply rednecks in pickup trucks, either," Rink said, sounding exactly like a redneck in a pickup truck. "They're as cultured as anyplace else, Hunter. They know the difference between Paris, France, and Paris Hilton."

"It'll do you good to get yourself back there, then."

Rink chuckled. "So what's the deal?"

"Missing person," I said.

"That all? I thought it was going to be something exciting."

"There's more. The missing person is my brother."

"You mean John?"

"Yeah. He's finally surfaced, only to drop off the face of the earth again." I gripped the phone tight. "I'm worried, Rink."

"You know what guys are like. He's probably gotten himself drunk, picked up a coupla hookers, an' is holed up in a motel someplace," Rink said. "Give him a day or two an' he'll be home with his tail between his legs."

"Maybe," I agreed. "And with John it wouldn't be the first time."

"You guys had a big falling out. Why you lookin' for him now?"

"He's in trouble," I said.

"Always was."

"I'm not doing this for him," I lied. "My sister-in-law asked me to find him. I promised her I would."

"Figures." Seems like Diane wasn't the only one who could read me from a thousand paces. Rink asked, "So is he skipping out on the alimony?"

"He has for years," I said. "But that's not what this is about. Yeah, there're kids involved, but it all goes a lot deeper than that."

"Pray tell," Rink said. It sounded like a car engine burst into life, the sound only slightly muffled by the intervening thousands of miles.

"You driving, Rink?"

"Just setting off. But you can keep on talking; I got a twenty-minute drive. Just ignore me if my language gets foul, but the I-75's a bitch even at this hour."

Rink maneuvered his Porsche through the Florida traffic. My run-in with Shank and his goons was just another war story to us. The creative use of a seat belt as a noose won me kudos. So did the fact that two major assholes would be walking with crutches for a while.

I got around to the note from John's current girlfriend and the plea made by Jennifer. My promise to help.

"You always were a soft touch, Hunter," Rink said. "Never could turn down a damsel in distress."

"She's also my sister-in-law," I reminded him.

"Sister nothing. If you'd never met her before, you'd still be coming out here."

"Now you're starting to sound like Diane," I said.

"Your lady was right in a lot of respects," he pointed out.

"Even Diane would understand this time. It is my brother we're talking about."

"No argument from me, Hunter."

Even if I didn't crave the kind of action that keeps me alive, I couldn't turn my back on my brother. For all that the last time we spoke, I threatened to punch his face.

"You've missed him, huh?"

"Like a hole in the head."

It was a good place to lighten the conversation. "So how's the Sunshine State?"

"A contradiction in terms, my man. Rain's coming down in torrents. Third day in a row. They sure don't show that on no 'Come to sunny Florida' TV ads, do they?"

"I'll pack for the weather, Rink. But can you set me up with the necessaries?" Mentioning a key word—particularly *gun*—over the telephone is never a good idea. Especially since 9/11. Conspiracy theories aside, all kinds of enigmatic government establishments known for their acronyms are tapping phones for just such words. I know. I've been there. Last thing I wanted was to land in Florida, then get a one-way trip to Guantánamo Bay.

Rink said, "Leave it to me. You want I get you a couple of day passes to Universal Studios?"

"Best you do. Hopefully I'll have a little time for sightseeing; I don't want to be wasting time queuing." More code. *Universal* was a cipher. It meant the entire package: passport, Social Security number, driving documents, credit cards, the business.

"Sounds like we could be in for some fun, Hunter."

"Fun isn't the half of it," I said.

6

TUBAL CAIN WAS IN HIS ELEMENT. DRIVING A FLASHY car in the dark with the highway all to himself.

Interstate 10 was one of his all-time favorite places, stretching all the way from Jacksonville, Florida, in the east to Santa Monica, California, in the west. A transcontinental artery with no less than three of the largest cities in the United States straddling its route. Houston, Phoenix, and Los Angeles were all ground he knew. But what appealed to him more than the cities was the transcontinental highway itself. It was a popular backpacking avenue across the states. Throughout its length there wasn't that great an elevation change, and even in winter the daytime temperatures were generally warm. He could almost guarantee a year-long stock of wandering lambs.

George and Mabel—or whatever they were really called— were good examples of what could be achieved by one as enterprising as himself. Okay, he'd only gained a couple of thumbs for his collection, but consolation was his in the form of the scorched motor home he'd left behind.

He'd spent some time in all the major tourist centers along the way, sampling the atmosphere of each before moving on. He'd thoroughly enjoyed the vibrancy of New Orleans, the Cajun flamboyancy of Lafayette, the history of San Antonio, where he'd used his Bowie knife in tribute to Colonel James Bowie, who'd met his death there. He'd sampled the culture, the music, and the southwest flavor of Tucson while hunting students in its universities. Forging westward to Santa

Monica, he'd found easy pickings amid the crowds jiggling for elbow space on the world-famous pier.

Then there was Los Angeles itself, his current destination. A city he found best suited his way of life, where he could ply his trade and fear little consequence. What with all the gangs shooting and hacking each other up, his two previous victims gleaned from South Central L.A. had barely raised more than an eyebrow.

His return was overdue. He intended executing a series of atrocities that would force even the jaundiced eyes of the LAPD to take note. If he could achieve that, then he would be cementing the foundations of his notoriety.

But that didn't mean a little fun along the way wasn't allowed.

Arriving in L.A. a few hours later than originally planned was no time at all to quibble over. Not for one whose name was destined to last an eternity.

He flicked on the turn signal, politely showing his intention to pull onto the wide shoulder, even though there was no traffic behind him. Politeness was a virtue Tubal Cain believed he held in abundance. The man waving for assistance by the side of the road would never guess that such a gracious driver could be so dangerous.

"Boy, is this your lucky day," Cain said. The wing mirror made a fine TV screen for the man jogging up to his SUV. Road Runner kicking up a plume of trail dust as he charged into Wile E. Coyote's trap.

Cain noted the possibility of trouble. Though harassed and worn down by the attempt to resurrect a dead engine, the man appeared moderately young and fit. Might put up a bit of a fight if not taken carefully, he concluded. Best not to give the game away. Quickly he concealed his knives under the passenger seat. He stepped out, tasting the silicone tang of the desert.

Cain wasn't the only one acting here. Conscious that few people would even stop to pick up hitchhikers, the man was careful to show that he was harmless. His gait was amiable, boyish, friendly. As fake as Tubal Cain's smile.

"Having a little trouble, mister?" Cain asked.

"Yeah, car's broken down and I can't get it going again." Pushing an oil-smeared palm down a trouser leg gave him the look of a bumbler, but to Cain the act seemed premeditated. His offer of a hand was no more believable.

"You're not from around here, are you?" said Cain. "Here on vacation?"

The stranded driver shook his head. "It's been no vacation, believe me."

Cain studied the man's eyes. Beyond deliberate innocence, a certain amount of deceit shone through. He was hiding something, but that was all right. Everyone had something to hide.

"Not the best of places to break down," Cain noted. The Mojave nightscape demanded their attention. "Pretty barren."

Nothing much more than sand and gravel and sparse vegetation, offering neither shade nor protection from the extremes of the weather, surrounded them.

Concealment of a crime could be difficult here.

"No place is a good place to break down, mister," the man said, "but you're right about this desert. I'm only happy that it's nighttime and I'm not stranded in a hundred degrees plus."

"Yeah, things do get warm around here when the sun's up. It's a bitch having to walk any distance, believe me."

"Oh, I believe you," the driver said. He nodded toward the SUV. "I bet that beauty's reliable."

"Has been for as long as I've had it," Cain agreed. That he'd only had it for eighteen hours was academic. "You want me to take a look at your car for you? I know a thing or two about engines."

A shake of the head toward his abandoned vehicle. With its hood raised to the star-filled heavens, it looked like a lizard attempting to swallow the distant moon. "It's done. Blown a cylinder, I think."

"Let's take a look." Cain brushed past. Shoulders touched

briefly. There was strength hidden beneath the man's denim shirt. Reasonably young, fit, and *apparently* strong. Could be trouble. Cain slipped his hand inside his sports jacket, caressing the hilt of the scaling knife.

"There's really no need," the man said. "A lift out of here'll be fine."

Cain turned around slowly. Was that a demand? Am I supposed to be obliged? "Let me take a look at the car first. If I can't get it going, then fine, I'll give you a ride."

"You're wasting your time." The man shifted his hands to his hips, inclined his chin at the broken-down vehicle. "Piece of crap won't be going anywhere."

"Let me take a look," Cain said again.

"Suit yourself . . . but it won't go," the driver said. Subtle words concealing an equally subtle action. His scratch at an itch on his side wasn't as mechanical as it seemed.

"I insist," said Cain.

Practice makes perfect. Cain had practiced this maneuver a thousand times. He pulled the blade free of his pocket, held it braced along his wrist, took a quick step forward . . .

And met the barrel of a semiautomatic pistol aimed directly at his face.

A short laugh broke unbidden from his throat. It was neither shock nor fear. His laughter was self-deprecating. Looked like a little more practice could be in order. Not least, the resheathing of his knife. Hidden from the man's view, he slipped the blade into an outer pocket of his jacket.

"No," the man said. "I insist."

Cain shook his head sadly. "You know, I can't believe you've gone and pulled a gun on me, when all I want to do is help."

"I appreciate your concern, mister, but I don't need your help. All I need is your car." A jerk of the gun was an invitation for a walk in the desert.

Casting his eye over the terrain, Cain saw a deep arroyo. It was steep-sided, the bottom choked with rocks and stunted sagebrush. A good place to hide a crime after all.

"So . . . you're going to shoot me?"

The driver sucked air through his teeth.

"You're going to put me down in that hole for the coyotes to find?" Cain shrugged his shoulders. It wasn't as if he hadn't done the very same thing to many others.

"I'll only shoot you if I have to," said the driver.

Was that so? BIG MISTAKE. Rule one: Never show weakness to your enemy.

"You're no killer."

"I will be a killer if I have to be," the man said. The new edge to his voice held a tremor. Fear or anticipation—either could cause a nervous man to pull the trigger. "Climb down in that ditch and kneel down. I'm warning you, mister, if you don't do as I say, I will use this gun."

Cain lifted his hands in supplication.

"Come on, man. You can't do this to a Good Samaritan."

"I can and I will." The man jerked the gun again. "Get moving. Down in the ditch."

"I'm not dressed for climbing."

"Well, jump."

Cain started toward the arroyo. "You think you could let me get something from my car? You're going to leave me out here in the middle of nowhere; at least let me get a bottle of water."

"In the ditch."

"It's called an arroyo."

"Well, get in the damn *arroyo*. If you don't, I'll put a bullet in your head and then throw you the hell in."

Cain shook his head again. No urgency to his tread. "Easy now, I'm going."

The man watched him clamber down the embankment. Cain turned and peered up at him. His face was a spectral gray in the starlight. A blob of silver that would prove an easy target for a gunman. "Turn around and face away from me, kneel down, and put your hands on your head."

"Why the amateur dramatics?" Cain asked. "You're going to take my car. There's no way I can climb out and stop you, so why do you want me to kneel down?"

"Because I said so," the man answered.

"It's going to ruin a perfectly good pair of slacks," Cain said in a singsong voice, choirboy sweet. He turned and knelt in the gravel as though at a pew.

"Okay, stay right there," the man said.

The scuff of shoes through sand marked the man's progress. Fetching something from his own abandoned vehicle, Cain surmised. The unmistakable thud of a hood being slammed. Then the sound of footsteps returning to the brim of the arroyo. Glancing over his shoulder, he saw the man outlined against the stars. In his hand he carried a backpack. He delved in the bag, pulled something out, and cast it down.

Cain's assumption was justified. Definitely not a killer. A plastic bottle three-quarters full of water settled against a boulder ten feet in front of him.

"Don't say I'm not grateful for your help," the man called down. Then he turned to go.

"Wait!" Cain shouted.

"What?"

"I'll do you a trade."

"There's nothing you have that I want."

"You sure?"

"Positive."

"How's about the keys to my car?"

That got his attention.

"Throw them up here."

"No."

"Throw them up here or I'll shoot you."

"No. Like I said, I'll do you a trade."

"Just throw the damn things here or I'll put a bullet in you."

"You do that and you won't find the keys. While you were off gallivanting, I hid them. Fair enough, they're not too far away, but it'll take you a while to find them. Are you sure you want to waste precious time looking for them for the sake of one little request? You know, you could kill me, but what if someone was to come along while you were still searching for the keys? Are you prepared to kill them as well? Could even be a cop."

The man swore impolitely.

Cain grunted in amusement. "One little request," he repeated.

"All right, but you give me the keys first."

"No. You get something from my car first."

More profanity. Then, "So what the hell's so important?"

"Look under the front passenger seat. You'll find a utility belt. Bring it to me, please."

"Okay, but then you give me the keys. And no messing around."

"Deal." Cain lifted one hand off his head and gave the driver a thumbs-up.

What could the man do but acquiesce?

"Don't move. I'll go and get your utility belt. But if I come back and you've moved as much as an inch I'm going to kill you."

"Deal." This time he put up two thumbs.

He knelt in the gravel, ignoring the sharp edges of rocks against his knees like a monk in penance. He attained Zen tranquility through the mantra of "Mack the Knife" hummed to himself.

"You liar." The man's voice broke the trance. "The keys were in the car all along."

Without looking around Cain shrugged.

"I've got a good mind not to give you your bloody bag for that," the man said.

"It's no good to you," Cain pointed out. "You may as well leave it."

"I took a look in your bag, mister. Hope you don't mind, but I wanted to check there wasn't a gun inside. Didn't want you chasing me up the road taking potshots at me."

"Well, now you know there's no gun. Just leave it there for me, please."

"What's with all the knives?"

"Just a passion of mine."

"They don't look expensive. Not the kind of thing anyone would collect."

"I use them in my work, that's all. And you're right, they're not expensive. So it'd be pointless stealing them."

"What the hell's so important about them if they aren't expensive? You were prepared to risk a bullet for the sake of a few old knives?"

"Just call it sentimental value. I've had them a long time. They hold a lot of memories." Cain turned and peered over his shoulder. He held the gaze of the driver. "Indulge me, will you?"

The man dropped the utility belt on the ground, kicked it down into the arroyo. "Don't climb up from there until you hear me driving away. I'll be watching."

A wink. "Understood."

"Good."

As he was commanded, Cain waited until he heard the SUV grumble to life, then recede into the distance. What would be the good of rushing? A footrace with a 4x4 wouldn't offer good odds.

First, he retrieved the bottle of water. It felt tepid against his palm. Then he picked up his belt. He didn't need to make an inventory of its contents. He could tell merely by its weight that something was missing.

"You thieving asshole!" He tore open the pouch. His Bowie knife was gone.

This changed everything. He practically hurled himself up the arroyo wall. Reaching the top on his elbows and knees, he lurched up, took half a dozen running steps toward the road. The taillights of the SUV were mere pinpricks in the distance.

"I'll see you again, *thief*." His promise was as righteous as his fury. "I'll see you again. And when I do there's gonna be hell to pay."

7

So there you have it. Why I hotfooted it to the U.S.

I took an evening flight to Miami. On the first leg out of the U.K., I slept for hours. I dreamed of people screaming. After transferring planes in New York, the nightmare was with me still. I couldn't sleep, so sat staring out the window. Surreal cloud formations were a mild distraction. They piled all the way down the East Coast. Rink hadn't been exaggerating; storms were raging across Florida.

The air-conditioned terminal tricked me. I stepped out into rain, which I was used to, but the cloying humidity slapped my face like a hot rag.

Damp with the rain and wringing wet with sweat beneath my clothes, I walked toward Jared Rington's Porsche Boxster with a grimace of greeting for the big guy. Christ, I hadn't seen the brute in two years. Rink pressed a button and dropped the passenger-side window.

"What's with all the bags, Hunter?" he asked, nodding at the two I carried. "Figuring on staying a month?"

"As long as it takes."

"Fine by me."

I nodded at him. "Are you gonna invite me in or do I stand out here all night getting even wetter?"

"S'long as you don't get any stains on the upholstery," Rink said.

I checked out the Porsche, then looked down at my sodden clothing. "Maybe I'd best take a taxi," I said.

"The hell you will. Jump in. Toss your bags on the back shelf . . . if they'll fit. Otherwise you're gonna have to keep them on your knee. That's the problem with these beauties— no trunk space."

"Not much room for anything."

"I didn't buy a Porsche for its capacious luggage-handling qualities," Rink said.

"You got it to impress the young ladies, huh?" I clambered in, clutching one bag to my chest.

"Yup. But to be honest, I don't score as often as I used to in my old pickup truck."

Previously clean-shaven, he now sported what looked like a hairy caterpillar on his top lip. He caught me staring at it. He checked himself out in the rearview mirror. "What's wrong with my mustache?"

"Makes you look like a porn star," I said.

Rink grinned unabashedly. "Yeah, so I've been told. But then again," he puffed out his chest, "I've also got the *goods* of a porn star."

"Dream on, Casanova," I said. "Don't forget, I've seen you in the showers."

"Yeah," Rink agreed. "But you're forgettin' what battle stress does to a man. Sometimes adrenaline makes you shrink up like that."

"Never seemed to affect me," I told him as he was pulling away from the curb.

"Trouble is," Rink said, his tone losing its bantering edge, "*nothing* ever seemed to affect you the way it did us mere mortals. I sometimes used to wonder if you know what fear is."

"Oh, don't you worry," I said. "There were plenty of times I was scared to death."

"It didn't show."

"It was there, Rink. I just didn't *let* it show."

We joined a freeway headed west. "I made a coupla calls," Rink said as our journey took us toward Tampa. "Spoke to an old friend out in Little Rock. You don't know him.

Harvey Lucas. Ex-military. A good man. I worked alongside him during Desert Storm. Met him again by chance a few years back an' kept in touch since. He's done some diggin' around for me."

"So what's he come up with?"

"Not much. First day on the job."

"Anything's a help."

"He went to see this Louise woman."

"And?"

"She wasn't exactly friendly. Said she'd speak to nobody but you."

I nodded. Her reluctance made sense. "In her letter, she said that John had been acting strange, afraid of something. She could also be scared. I suppose she's not going to say too much to a stranger asking about John's whereabouts."

"Even after he mentioned your name, she wouldn't give Harvey diddlysquat," Rink said. "But he was able to set up a meeting with her. Tomorrow afternoon, three o'clock, after she gets off work. Another thing he found out: seems your brother liked to gamble."

Yeah? That was quite an understatement. "You think it's because of the gambling he's gone missing?"

"Could be. By all accounts he's left a large IOU with a local shark called Sigmund Petoskey. Petoskey's not the most forgiving of people. Could be a good starting-off point to see what he's got to say for himself."

"As good a point as any," I agreed.

"I remember Petoskey from years ago," Rink said. "A no-good punk with delusions of grandeur. Siggy likes to think of himself as some kinda new world Godfather type. He's gathered a gang of scum around him to do his head bashing when the punters are a little slow to pay up. Maybe John's simply had the good sense to get out with all his limbs intact."

"What's Petoskey into?"

"He's into all sorts. Got hisself a good cover as a businessperson. Real estate. Used-car dealerships. Those kinda things. But he makes most of his money from the gambling and corruption."

"Corruption?" I asked.

"Yup. Has a few names in local government by the balls. Certain cops won't touch him, either."

"What's he like?"

"A punk of the highest order," Rink said. "But I suppose with a gang behind him he's dangerous enough. To someone who's easily frightened, that is."

"Yeah, just like every other asshole we ever went up against," I noted.

Rink often seems to know what I'm thinking. "I've got the guns and stuff back at the condo," he said. "Petoskey won't give us squat unless we show him we mean business."

I nodded at his foresight. We both knew that when you went up against someone like Petoskey or Shank you had to show them that you weren't about to take any shit from them. Shank could be intimidated by a nasty promise, but in a land where every other blue-rinsed grandma toted a side-arm, you had to bring something even nastier to the negotiating table.

"Does Harvey know where Petoskey is?"

"I've got him on it. By the time we arrive in Arkansas, he'll be able to tell you where Petoskey squats down to take a dump . . . and at what time."

I said, "All I need to know is where he'll be this time tomorrow."

"Leave it with me. I'll give Harvey another call as soon as we get back to my place."

"Sure," I said.

Business sorted, Rink turned to me. A smile lit up his features. "It's good you're here, Hunter."

"Good to be here."

8

DUTY AND SOLDIERING GO HAND IN HAND. THE same could be said for family. I might have been a little remiss in supporting my loved ones since retiring from the forces.

Diane and I were history. She had made a new life with Simon. Nevertheless, there were others I could help if they needed it. I was ashamed that my niece and nephew were living in such squalor, that Jennifer had fallen so low that my skills for pressuring people were all I could offer them.

John is my brother. If you want specifics, he's actually my half brother. My father died and my mother remarried. Then John came along. Maybe it's because we have different fathers that we've turned out like oil and water. I was the war hero, John the stay-at-home ne'er-do-well. Of course, that doesn't mean much in some eyes. Funny how our parents always took his side.

Over his fifth beer, my stepfather had once said to me, "While you've been off gallivanting all over the world, John's been here. John's the one we've had to call for if we needed help. You've never been around. It's all right for you, Joe. You've had everything you ever wanted. What's that boy ever had?"

I hadn't had it in me to argue. I just walked away.

I found John at a bar, swilling down his paycheck alongside a couple of friends. I cornered him by the pool table. Grabbing him by the collar, I pushed him against a wall. His friends knew better than to step in.

"Where the hell's all the money I gave you, John?"

His eyes wouldn't meet mine. "I've got it back home."

"Don't lie to me, John. I've just seen Dad. He told me you've been round begging him for a loan." My jaw was aching from clenching my teeth. "He just gave me a load of grief about how I should help you out. Again."

John shook his head.

"Don't tell me you've gone and blown it?" I said.

Shame made his cheeks burn. "I got an inside tip," he said. "Five-to-one odds, what could I do?"

"Oh, for God's sake—"

I turned away from him.

John's fist thumped into my shoulder. Turning slowly, I saw my little brother setting himself up.

"Don't you dare," I warned him. "I don't care who you are, I'll punch your face in."

"Come on, then," he said. "Why don't you do it, huh? Every other tough guy around here wants to."

I almost did. But right then he was just too pathetic to waste my time on. Staring him down, I backed away. Lifting a finger, I aimed it at his face. "You're not worth it, John. I'm done with you. You got that?"

Pushing my way through the crowd of onlookers, I heard him call out, "I don't need you, Joe. You're done with me, are you? Well, to hell with you! You mean nothin' to me, either. You're not even my real brother. Just some sad *bastard* that I've been stuck with all my life."

Our eyes met over the shoulders of the drinkers that made a wall between us.

"I'm not your real brother?" I asked. "Fair enough. If that's what you want, John."

The light of anger went out of his eyes and he turned away. I turned away, too. Didn't look back.

They were angry words on both sides.

Despite them, John would always be my little brother.

We didn't get a chance to make amends.

The time had come to put things right again.

As a soldier, I hunted and killed men. That's what soldiers do. But with me the killing was up close and personal. It does something to you when you have to look into the eyes of those you kill. Violence breeds a sickness of the human spirit. Hatred consumes and gives birth to self-loathing. It doesn't matter that the deaths were sanctioned, just, or righteous. It's still death. Fourteen years spent tracking terrorists left me changed forever.

Maybe that's why I turned my back on my brother. If I'd stepped up to the mark then, maybe John wouldn't have run away.

I took my leave of the forces, determined that I'd settle down with Diane, lead a life of normalcy and peace.

I should've known I was pissing in the wind.

In some respects, John made me what I am. I dealt with his debts in the only way I knew how: I backed down his debtors. On the streets, that gave me a certain reputation. It wasn't long before my natural ability pushed my other, gentler attributes aside. Subtly, what began as a foray into private security consultancy changed into clients who demanded more. Occasionally I had to crack skulls and bloody noses. For fourteen years I'd met violence head-on with even more violence, and now it seemed that for all my good intentions, nothing had changed.

In another world I could've ended up as a hit man like those I'd waged war against, or as muscle for some lowlife gangster. Only because I had morals and—yes—compassion could I find any peace at all. Without my sense of decency, I'd be nothing more than a bigger thug amid all the little thugs.

I promised Jennifer I'd find my brother.

Nothing was going to stand in my way.

9

YESTERDAY MORNING, TUBAL CAIN'S RAGE HAD been epic. Little wonder. First, he'd lost his SUV, stranding him out on the highway like road kill left to dry in the increasing heat. Then, he'd realized that the unscrupulous bastard who had abandoned him had also stolen his second-favorite knife. Next, he'd discovered that his penny loafers were no good for walking any distance.

But as the saying goes, that was then and this is now. Almost twenty-four hours later, Cain was feeling rather pleased with himself.

For one, he was lying on a soft bed, wiggling his hot feet in the draft from a wall-mounted AC unit. Freshly showered and wearing clothes that weren't sticky with perspiration, he was a new man. Beside him on the bed was the quiet, still form of the Good Samaritan who'd brought him to this place.

She was dead, of course, not sleeping peacefully as her pose would suggest. Her hair was spread across the pillows like a sheaf of spilled corn, hiding her slack features. Deliberate posing so that her unnatural pallor wouldn't give the game away.

"Now, I'd appreciate it if you'd just lie there like a good girl," he said. "Like you're sleeping off the effects of a heavy party. It was a good party, believe me, and you certainly deserve a nap."

Cain prided himself on his expertise at covering his tracks. That was why he remained America's most prolific undetected serial murderer. Take George and Mabel, for instance: He'd rigged the explosion so that both of them would be so charred it would take a determined investigator to guess that they'd been murdered. Essentially, Mabel hadn't been too careful with the gas cooker when preparing their supper. Either the explosion or the subsequent fire would cover the fact that George was missing a couple of digits, while his wife had suffered numerous breaks to her limbs.

Here, though, it needn't be as dramatic as flames and carcass-ripping devastation. Subtlety was the order of the day. He'd cranked up the AC so that the growing stink wouldn't alert anyone too soon. And he'd tucked the comforter up to the woman's chin. That would help dissuade the blowflies from searching out the decaying matter as nurseries for their brood. By the time the proliferation of insect life made the room unbearable, he'd be many miles away.

The comforter served a threefold purpose. It absorbed the blood leaking from her body and would take a lot more before it showed. It also concealed the missing digits from her right hand. Ideally, Cain would've preferred to deliver her entire corpse to his repository in Jubal's Hollow; there were some nicely shaped bones under that alabaster skin of hers. For now, he had neither the time nor the inclination for further diversion. The fingers stripped from her hand would have to do. They were easily concealed in the pocket of his jacket, easily transported, and could be dropped off next time he visited his secret place.

It was like preparing for a school picnic. He'd wrapped the fingers in cellophane, packed like snack-sized hotdogs, and secreted them alongside the plastic bag holding George's thumbs. When he had time, he'd strip the flesh away and keep only the bones. He preferred them that way. Without the associated baggage of rotting meat. For now, he could content himself with fingering his souvenirs through their plastic casing without fear of getting her filth on his hands.

In his other pocket was a similar package. Fingers taken from the woman's boyfriend, who had kindly given Cain the fresh set of clothes and the keys to his VW Beetle. The boyfriend himself was in the shower, no more alive than the girlfriend was. Locked in the cubicle away from prying eyes, he would stay undiscovered for as long as the girl did.

Finally, Cain raised himself up. Bedsprings squealed in protest at the redistribution of weight. A creaking eulogy for the woman as she settled deeper into the mattress.

"I'd love to stay and chat a little longer," he said. The woman remained unresponsive beneath the bedsheets. "I'm not normally the type who just has his way with a girl, then makes off with hardly a thanks. It's just that I've got something that needs doing and time's a-wasting."

He sat on the edge of the bed amid further creaks and groans and pulled on a thick pair of hiking socks. He had some intense blisters on the balls of both feet, but the good-quality woolen socks alleviated some of the discomfort. Socks in place, he tucked the hems of his jeans into them before tugging on sturdy lace-up boots. Then he retrieved the lightweight anorak containing his souvenirs and pulled it over his checked shirt. A black baseball cap emblazoned with an American eagle completed the ensemble.

He paused to admire himself in the full-length mirror on the bathroom door. His fair hair and pale green eyes gave him a boyish air that he knew endeared him to the ladies. "Well, hello there." He smiled at his reflection. "Who is that ruggedly handsome guy?"

He'd entered this room the epitome of Joe College. He now looked like a seasoned hiker, exactly like thousands of others who passed along this highway day in and day out.

Before leaving the room, he wiped down all the surfaces he'd touched, as well as all those he couldn't remember touching. He used the cloth to wipe the door handle, then draped the cloth over it to prevent depositing fresh fingerprints when he finally left the room. "Pays to be extra careful," he told the woman.

Best that he didn't leave any incriminating friction ridges for a CSI person to find. That would really stir things up. He scanned the room for the minutiae he might have missed, but decided he'd been as thorough as ever. He wasn't concerned about hair or saliva, or even semen. His DNA wasn't on any *police* record. His fingerprints were another story. Twice in towns out east he had been caught with prostitutes in his car. Luckily, the cops had dirty minds; otherwise, they might have guessed his true motive for hunting the red-light districts, and he wouldn't have gotten off so lightly, with a fine and his prints taken—the old-fashioned way, thankfully, ink on cards.

A return to the bed allowed a straightening and tucking in of the comforter. A soft pat of his hand on the woman's head. "Now don't you worry. As long as I don't leave any prints, I'll remain anonymous. By the time the police get around to checking out a sample of DNA taken under warrant, I'll already be one of two things: famous or dead. Probably both. And by then it won't matter, will it?"

His old set of clothing was packed into the dead man's backpack, along with other articles that could come in handy. His utility belt for one. He slung the backpack over his shoulder, took one last look at the woman on the bed, winked at her, then slipped out of the room.

The early morning cool washed over him. Within hours this same place would be oven-hot, the air shimmering before his eyes. But now everything was calm, and he could see way off across the sand-blasted wastelands to an orange haze on the horizon. Not the dawning sun—it was on the wrong horizon. The light he could detect was artificial, half a billion streetlights tainting the skyline with their putrid glow. Toward those lights he must travel. For it was there he'd find fame.

Not to mention the thief who stole his knife.

The motel was your typical low-slung timber structure. A series of cabins set out in two parallel rows behind the booking office. The office was in darkness, as were the other cabins. Not too many patrons had stayed the night. Drawn up in the parking lot were only four vehicles, one of which was his recently acquired VW Beetle. True to his sense of destiny, the VW was an orangey yellow color. Just like the one driven by the man born Theodore Robert Cowell on November 24, 1946. Cowell would later adopt his stepfather's surname and be known as Theodore Bundy. Ted Bundy, the talented serial killer who was soon to be eclipsed by the exploits of one Tubal Cain.

A quick reconnoiter of the area satisfied him that no other guest was out of bed. He walked toward the VW, jangling the keys in his hand. The aged car was more stubborn wreck than it was vintage model. A little temperamental to start, if memory served. Hopefully the chugging of the engine wouldn't alert anyone nosy enough to see him depart. But then again, why should that matter? By the time the bodies were discovered, he'd have arrived in one of the cities and acquired alternative transport. The Beetle would be a burned-out shell in some vacant lot.

Opening the door of the car, he slung the backpack onto the backseat. Surprisingly, the car started on his first attempt, and he disengaged the emergency brake and drove off without a look back. He drove without hurry, but with purpose. From his shirt pocket, he teased out a slip of paper, on it a handwritten telephone number. Beneath it, he'd written the address of the hotel.

"Stupid, stupid thief." His laughter was as bitter as sucking on unripe lemons. "If you want to get into my kind of game, you have to learn the basic rules. First rule: Cover your tracks."

The amateur who'd hijacked him, taking his SUV and beloved Bowie knife, obviously hadn't thought of the consequences of wadding up the slip of paper and dropping it on the floor of his car. It had been a simple matter for Cain to ring the number and listen as a nasal girl had announced the name of the hotel in Santa Monica. The call didn't give him the thief's name, but that was academic. Cain knew where the thief planned to stay. A quick visit to the hotel itself would establish everything else he needed to know.

"Santa Monica, here I come," he said, laughing again. This time his laughter wasn't so bitter, the lemon rind sweetened with sugar. As he drove he shredded the slip of paper, depositing a tiny portion of it out the window every so often along the way.

A couple of hours would see him on the West Coast. Maybe he'd grab a little breakfast, see to the disposal of the VW, then go scout out the hotel. He'd locate the thief, then by tonight he'd be ready to move. He didn't care about regaining the SUV. It had served its purpose and would most likely have gone the way he was planning for the VW. But he did want his knife back.

Not to be sentimental about it, but the Bowie held a great number of satisfying memories. Some he liked to play back in his mind while holding the knife in his hand. He could soon buy or appropriate a replacement, but it wouldn't be the same. And besides, when he finally allowed the world to know his name, he wanted his arsenal right there beside him. The police should have the capacity to match the blade with each corpse it had been used on. He wanted the *genuine* knife to be kept as a museum piece documenting his infamy, not some second-rate, virgin chunk of metal.

Westward he drove. And despite appearances, the VW was a steady if plodding workhorse. He had only two complaints. First, the air-conditioning system was archaic, achieved by winding down the windows to promote a cross draft. Second, the facility for music was as outmoded as the AC unit.

He searched through the glove compartment, pulling out a couple of music cassettes. One of them, some inane hip-hop crap, he tossed over his shoulder onto the backseat. The second was more to his taste. Cain didn't recognize the band, but the bluesy guitar was to his liking. It wasn't as good as the swing music he preferred: playing air guitar wasn't as satisfying as imagining cutting away strips of flesh with a bandleader's baton.

The miles passed easily.

So did the gas in the tank.

Thirty miles short of his destination, he was forced to pull in to a gas station. Ten dollars' worth of gasoline would more than suffice. He would have paid his bill with the credit cards stolen from the dead couple back at the motel, but a credit trail would easily set the law on his path. It didn't irk him to have to use his own cash, not when it was so readily available to one who knew how to acquire it. The teller thanked him California-style and Cain smiled unashamedly. The girl—sun-bronzed and blond with a smattering of freckles on a cute nose—smiled back at him. Hey, it was good to be back on the West Coast.

Hungry, he purchased some prepacked sandwiches and a couple of Snicker bars plus a pint of chocolate milk. Skimmed milk, less than ninety-nine calories, he had a waistline to consider. He finished it before he was even out the door.

Outside the store, he stood for a while, watching traffic passing on the highway. Here the traffic flow was heavier than out in the desert. He watched vehicles sailing by like mirages through the shimmering heat, wondering what stories their occupants could tell. Where they were going, what they were doing. One thing he was certain of. None had a story to match his.

Beyond the gas station was a rest area. Picnic tables were set out on a patch of lawn so verdant it had to be fake. Bordering the grassy area, the land remained parched and gritty, the home of dust devils and windblown detritus. A family had set themselves up at one of the tables. Bottles of soda and food wrapped in tinfoil were laid out in front of them. Father was pointing out what the children should eat, while they ignored him and went straight for the potato chips. Mother sat on one of the benches, trying her hardest to coax some enjoyment out of a cigarette while squinting against blown dust and the high-pitched squalling of the kids.

Cain shook his head.

"Family bliss," he said to himself. God, but he was happy he'd left those trappings behind.

He surveyed the remainder of the rest area. There was a public restroom abutting the gas station. With the pint of chilled milk forging toward his bladder, he decided a visit was in order before setting off.

Someone else had the same idea. A heavy-built guy with uncontrollable hair raced toward the door. His moon face was contorting as though he'd been caught short many miles distant. He was the epitome of desperation.

When Cain entered the restroom, the man had already disappeared behind a cubicle door. Cain could hear him struggling with his belt, issuing soft, urgent noises. Then there was the clunk of the seat followed by the indescribable sound of the man's very essence dropping into a porcelain bowl.

"Now that's either extremely gross or mildly amusing," Cain said to himself. The man's disembodied sigh decided the issue for him. "Extremely amusing."

Smiling, he unzipped at a urinal and relieved his own body of a growing urgency. That done, he could concentrate on another, more pressing ache that required assuaging.

The sink hadn't seen a cleaner's administrations in many an hour. He used a hot air blower to dry himself.

Water flushed and the fat guy came out of the cubicle and bustled directly for the exit door. Cain caught his eye and the guy, looking momentarily abashed, turned fluidly toward the sink to wash his own hands. Cain nodded at him. "Things a little desperate there, buddy?"

Embarrassed, the man shrugged.

"Better out than in, eh?" Cain quipped.

"You betcha." The man grimaced. "Must have eaten some green meat. Didn't think I was gonna make it to the can."

"Lucky for you that you did. By the sound of things you'd have made quite a mess of yourself," Cain said. "Best to stay clean, though, don't you think?"

"Cleanliness is next to godliness," the man quoted, humiliated at having been caught out, "even when you're in a hurry."

The man made a brief run of his hands under the water, then turned toward the filthy-looking towel hanging on the wall. He paused. Looked to Cain for guidance.

"Seems a little pointless, doesn't it?" Cain said.

"You're telling me," said the fat guy. His bulk formed a line of its own behind Cain at the automated hand drier. Energized by his need to get about his journey, he hopped from foot to foot in anticipation of his turn at the hot air.

Cain took his time dry-washing his hands to a point where his skin began to stick together. A *tsk* of frustration from the man. Cain was pleased. Finally he stood aside, gestured the man forward.

"It's all yours."

"Gee, thanks," said the fat guy, not really meaning it.

"My pleasure," Cain said. Not meaning it, either.

It would be nice to kill the fat guy. But in the end, he decided not to. Too dangerous. What if someone walked in before he was finished concealing the gross body in one of the stalls? He could obviously kill them, too, but then he'd be right back to square one. Last thing he wanted was to end up in a loop where the only guarantee was that he'd finally run out of places to conceal the dead. He would allow the man to live, but there was something he could do that'd bring him a modicum of fulfillment.

It was more than a friendly gesture as he patted the fat guy's shoulder. Two solid slaps of his hand. The man flinched at the contact, blinked at him.

"See you, friend," Cain said. He moved toward the exit. Happy.

"Yeah, see you," the fat guy intoned. Then, stupidly, he muttered something under his breath.

Cain turned and stared back at him. His look was that of a prowling leopard eyeing a wounded buffalo.

"You say something, buddy?"

The fat guy blinked rapid-fire. His jowls hung slack, framed by long, wiry curls. "No, I didn't say a thing."

Cain stepped toward him, and a piece of grit crunched beneath his boot. The sound was more invasive than loud, an expression of Cain's aversion to the man before him. The fat guy reacted as though it was a gunshot. He reared back, lifting his chin in anticipation of avoiding a blow. Cain shook his head at the overreaction. He said, "That's funny. I'm sure I heard you call me an asshole."

Now the fat guy shook his head.

"Look, mister. I don't want any trouble, okay. I just want to dry my hands and get outta here. Wife and kids are waiting for me in the car. We're going down to see my wife's mother for a day or two is all. So I don't want any trouble with you. Gonna get enough of it off the mother-in-law if I'm more than a minute late."

Funny how people babbled when they were afraid.

"I was being polite to you," Cain said. His smile was mock whimsy. "Even looked after your health and well-being for you. Not many people would've bothered. Quite happily could've let you go and get back in your car with your wife and kids. Could've allowed you to spread all those nasty little germs to them. Take them on down to grandma's house, too, no doubt. But I didn't. I thought I'd be nice and remind you to wash your hands. No big deal?"

"No," the fat guy said. "No big deal."

"So why'd you have to call me an asshole?"

"I didn't—"

"Don't lie to me. Please?"

"I'm not lying. I didn't say a goddamn thing."

"Ingratitude. Lies. Now profanity?"

Sometimes even scared fat people got to a point when enough was enough. "Look, fella. I don't know what your problem is with me, but I'm outta here." He shoved by Cain, heading for the door. His exit was as desperate as his entrance.

From the open door, Cain watched him go. A hot breeze

lifted whorls of dust in his wake. The man kept glancing back, his hair waving Medusa-like. Cain waved at him. The man jumped in his station wagon, babbling loudly in distress, hands stabbing for the ignition. His prodigious wife and two equally fat children looked over at Cain. Red-haired, with pie-dish faces, they looked like orangutans in a zoo. He waved at them, too. Then the station wagon was headed for the highway with a little more haste than was sensible.

Too quickly, the show was over. While it lasted, the slight distraction had proved enjoyable. Would've been more satisfying if he'd sliced up the fat guy. But at least the look on the guy's face was a bonus.

"And I got another trophy."

In his palm was a strip of plaid cloth. A patch taken from the man's shirt when he'd patted him on the shoulder. Not just a friendly farewell, it was a well-rehearsed move. It was all part of a game he played. If he could get a slither of clothing and remain undetected he let the target live. Those who felt the tug at their clothes or the slice of the knife against their flesh he had to kill immediately.

"Fatty, you just don't realize it yet. Today is the luckiest day of your life."

10

RINK'S CONDOMINIUM WAS SET IN A SMALL COMmunity in Woodland near Temple Terrace, northeast of Tampa. Set on a limestone outcrop, it was elevated above the flat country all around. Across the way, I could see families in their backyards, reclining on deck chairs with a cool drink at hand, some splashing in private swimming pools. A different world to the one I knew back home. Rink had obviously been pulling in decent work to afford this kind of accommodation.

From the front of the house, I heard an engine growl, Rink announcing his return. Rising up from the chair, I wandered into the living room and met him coming in with his arms full of take-out food.

"Let's eat," he announced.

"You bet."

The food wasn't too fancy, but it was more satisfying than the artificial slop the flight crew offered on the plane. I chewed without really tasting anything other than the liberal quantity of Corona I washed it down with. After we ate, I collapsed in front of Rink's widescreen TV while he put on a fight DVD and passed me another beer.

Then we got around to business.

"Harvey called," Rink said. "He's gonna come to the meeting with Louise Blake. Then he wants a private meet with us after we're finished with her."

I took a sip from my beer and said, "Makes sense."

"He's got the location Petoskey does his night shift business from. Says he'll take us there if we need him."

Something was coming that I might not like. I nodded encouragement; might as well get it over with.

"Says he'll take us, but that's his involvement over with. Doesn't want a backlash from Petoskey if things turn sour."

"Fine by me," I said. "Things might turn sour."

It was Rink's turn to nod.

"Thought they might," he said.

"This nonsense about John leaving town because he owes money sounds like a cover story. I want the truth from Petoskey. If that means hitting him hard and fast, so be it."

"I'm with you, man."

"Never doubted you."

"Good."

"Shut up and drink your beer," I said.

And that was that. The planning would come later. When we arrived at Petoskey's front door. When we had a better idea of what we were up against. I hadn't been a secret agent; it wasn't for me to use guile and trickery to root out the bad guys. I was—along with Rink and a select few others—the weapon sent in when the planning was done with and all that was left was the ass kicking. Ass kicking I was good at. It got results.

Ergo, there'd be nothing fancy set up for when we paid Petoskey a visit. Either he'd be cooperative, or we'd make him wish he had been. End of story.

Rink indicated the TV with his beer can.

"I was figurin' on havin' a go at this extreme fighting stuff." On the screen, two buffed athletes were pounding the snot out of each other in an octagon-shaped cage. Unlike pro wrestling, this fighting was for real. The blows were aimed with intent, the strangles to a point where people passed out, the arm- and leglocks occasionally ending in fractures.

"I'm sure you'd do okay, so long as you didn't forget it was only a sport," I said.

"Man, it's all in the control," Rink said. "I know when to kill and when not to."

I shook my head. "What about when one of those monsters has you up against the cage and is pounding the life out of you? You telling me you won't gouge out an eye or rip off an ear with your teeth?"

Rink shrugged. "Biting's for the likes of Tyson, man. It was just an idea. Something to keep me fit."

"Go for it, then," I said. "If you're not too old."

"Too old?" Rink looked scandalized.

"Well, you *are* almost forty."

"I ain't too old. For God's sake, the damn heavyweight champ's in his midforties, and he's still showing these young lions what a real fighter is all about."

I had to agree. The champion was giving a man a foot taller and almost twenty years his junior some serious grief.

I'm a realist. I couldn't compete with the likes of those athletes. Not in their arena. But put them in mine, and I was positive that the man left standing wouldn't be the sportsman. My expertise lay in the battlefield, and they wouldn't stand a chance. You couldn't go to war, then tap out when an opponent was getting the better of you. Fail in my arena and you were dead.

The same was true for Rink. He'd had the same training as me and was equally dangerous in a fight. What Rink possessed that I didn't were black belts to prove his expertise. Even before he'd signed up as a Ranger, he'd been an interstate karate champion three years running.

The first time Rink and I worked together, it wasn't during a covert operation. We were off duty, but Rink had taught me a valuable lesson.

I had been aware of the big American, but only as the silent new recruit who only seemed animated when in action. We hadn't bonded yet, and I was as confused as anyone about why the strange-sounding Yank had been drafted onto our team.

Near to our U.K. base at Arrowsake was a small fishing town. The bar next to the harbor was a favorite of our unit when it came to downtime. Rink was standing by the bar. He was cradling a pint of brown ale but didn't seem to be enjoying it. I glanced across the barroom and saw why.

There were three of them, Special Air Service commandos who'd been brought in on a joint training operation. There'd been friction from the start. Even over the murmur of the crowd I heard one of them call Rink a "reject Nip."

I saw Rink set his glass down on the bar and turn to leave. The three SAS guys got up.

I didn't owe Rink anything, but for some reason I got up, too. There was a hush in the bar. The silence that preceded violence. Rink veered toward the side exit and the three SAS guys moved to follow him. No one tried to intervene. No one wanted to be pulled in as a witness.

The three men followed Rink into the backyard. Barrels were stacked against one wall, metal trash cans against the other. At the far end, a metal gate stood open and Rink walked toward it.

"Hey, slanteyes," one of the SAS guys shouted at Rink's back. "Where the hell do you think you're running off to?"

Rink didn't answer.

The three of them laughed and started after him. Rink closed the gate. He turned around.

I saw the three SAS guys falter in their stride.

Behind them, I closed the door of the pub, placed my hip against it.

One of them turned and looked at me.

"Got nothin' to do with you, pal," he said.

"Three to one," I pointed out. "I think it does."

I noticed Rink looking my way.

"I can handle it," he said.

"I'm just watching your back, buddy."

Rink nodded his thanks. Then he turned back to the SAS guys. "So who's first?"

"To hell with that!" one of them snapped.

The SAS guys weren't slouches. No Special Forces soldiers are. The one who'd spoken to me hung back while the other two moved in on Rink.

The first one to reach him caught Rink's front kick on his chin. He fell in a heap at the feet of his friend. The second one wouldn't be taken so easily. He feigned a punch but then turned and shot a sidekick at Rink's knee. Rink wobbled and I saw pain on his face. The man stepped in and drilled a punch into Rink's stomach. Rink folded at the waist as his hands sought the source of his pain. The SAS man stepped in, ready to finish it.

But Rink wasn't finished. He was play-acting. Even as the man threw his punch, Rink rammed his elbow upward and drove the point into the man's throat.

At the same time, the third one stooped and grabbed at an empty bottle lying on one of the trash cans.

I didn't stop to think.

I leaped after him.

The man spun, swiped at my head with the bottle. I was expecting that, so I was already ducking. My shoulder caught him in his chest and I continued to drive him backward, rushing him at speed across the yard. As we collided with the barrels, the bottle fell out of his hand and shattered on the floor. The SAS man struck at me, catching me on my left cheek. I gave him one right back and he staggered away from me.

He ended up in front of Rink. Rink grabbed him, spun him around, then head-butted him in the face. The man dropped to his knees, but he wasn't as unconscious as I'd have liked. I stepped in to put the boot in his ribs.

Rink lifted a hand.

"He's done," he said. "It's over with, okay?"

Looking down at the SAS man, I saw him blinking up at me with dazed eyes.

Rink was right then.

And he was now.

"Sorry, Rink. All those years of competition; of course

you could restrain your killer instinct. It's me who couldn't do it. I haven't had the etiquette ingrained in me the way you have."

"You know your problem, Hunter? You're too cool about it all. You get off on the violence."

"I thought you knew me better than that, Rink."

"Aw, lighten up, will ya? Here, drink some more beer." He underhanded me a bottle.

Despite what had just been said, my aptitude for hurting others has always been channeled, a skill forged for a strict purpose and with strict delivery in mind. The alcohol—or perhaps it was the jet lag—made me maudlin. "You remember our training, Rink? I don't know about you, but it was about the hardest thing I ever did."

"Sure was. An' that's counting the fifty-man challenge I had to complete to get my Kyokushin black belt."

Unlike that of regular soldiers, our training had been not only in weaponry and technology, but in the use of the body to achieve desired results. Back in 1940, Captain William Ewart Fairbairn had revolutionized the unarmed tactics of the British military. He was alleged to have had six hundred and sixty-six brutal encounters that he survived by using his knowledge of hand-to-hand combat. Basically, he was no slouch when it came to a fistfight, the ideal inspiration for headstrong guys like us.

Over the intervening years, other warriors had added to the roster of Fairbairn's skills, and through intense training, their legacies were passed down to us. In effect, you could say we were the direct descendants of those masters of empty-handed combat. I can't claim six hundred and sixty-six encounters, but I'm well into triple figures. My generally unmarked face was testament to my skills, as much as Rink's black belts were to his.

"See, it's not just about finishing your man," Rink said, with a nod toward the screen. "It's about doing it in style. Has to have entertainment value or the promoters won't be able to put asses on seats. What you do, Hunter, well, it just ain't pretty to watch."

"Aren't you afraid you'll lose your edge?" I asked. I was being serious.

Rink looked pensive for a moment. Then he hit me with his enigmatic look, all hooded eyes and downturned mouth.

"Hunter," he said slowly, "we ain't in the military no more. We don't have a license to kill. Hasn't that sunk in yet?"

It didn't take much ruminating over.

"Yeah," I finally said.

But it was a sore point.

11

ONLY EIGHT MILES FROM LOS ANGELES INTER-
national Airport and thirteen miles from downtown
L.A., Santa Monica was pretty much Tubal Cain's most favorite place on the western coast. He'd visited there many
times before but never grew tired of it. How could you be
bored with its striking contemporary style and architecture
or its shameless attempt at snaring a buck from the tourist
market?

Santa Monica had been a playground of chic Victorians.
Then in the early 1900s it blossomed again with movie-star
glamour. As early as the 1920s, stars such as Will Rogers,
Greta Garbo, and Marion Davies had built mansions there.
During the 1980s it boomed again after a multimillion-
dollar restoration transformed the city.

Many people thronged to take up residence there, but
many of them were transients with no roots to speak of. It
was the perfect hunting ground for one who preyed primar-
ily on strangers who wouldn't be missed.

Cain was hunting one of those transients now.

A certain thief of a certain knife dear to him.

Traversing Lincoln Boulevard in his Bundyesque VW, he
grinned at the characters he saw swarming the sidewalks.
Here were wannabe actors, wannabe directors, wannabe
rock stars. You name it, they were there. Then there were
the *others*. They were there to gawk in wonder at all the
other wannabes, to rub shoulders with the wannabe rich

and famous. To be sure, no one truly rich and famous would wander along those sidewalks for fear of being torn to pieces by starstruck souvenir hunters. Yet Cain could see a half dozen Michael Jackson look-alikes, a handful of Marilyn Monroes. Who would know if the star was real or not?

The world was twisted full tilt in this wondrous place. But that was what Cain loved so much. It was an escape from humdrum reality, a dimension to which one of his kind belonged. He knew that he didn't exist in the everyday world that most others belonged to. As a sociopath, he understood that what he was doing wasn't acceptable in ordinary society. But as a psychopath, he didn't care. Here in this modern-day Babel he could thrive and grow, easy in the knowledge that he was surrounded by a myriad of like minds.

Cain liked to speak to his dead victims. They tended not to butt in. For the same reason, he was equally happy conversing with himself. He could be as verbose as he wished. "Rule two, thief: The easiest place to hide is in full sight. Here, I'm a sardine in a massive shoal of sardines. I'm indiscernible from the thousands of others, and unlikely to be picked out when there are so many to choose from." Not that he particularly liked the sardine metaphor, but he had to admit that it served his purpose. He tended to think of himself more as a shark or a swordfish, lurking within the shoal, ready to spring forth from concealment to show his ripping teeth or flashing blade.

No doubt about it. The thief was most likely to be holed up in his hotel room.

"You're making it too easy for me, thief. You should be out here in the sunshine, mingling with everyone else in this crazy, topsy-turvy place. What chance would I have of finding you then?"

He parked the car in a massive lot filled almost to capacity. Nearby was the promenade that led to the pier, an easy stroll he relished after driving so far. Day or night, it made no difference; people would be on the pier fishing, watching the waves, entertaining themselves in the arcades or shopping for souvenirs, riding the carousels or roller coasters, laughing, yelling, screaming in delight.

Why bother locking the car or removing the keys from the ignition? If some thief should happen to steal his vehicle while he was gone, then all the better. It'd save him the job of disposing of it later. Wiping the steering wheel, console, and doors was both sensible and necessary. Wouldn't like to think that a cop discovered the car before the joyriders did.

He strolled on the promenade beneath the bluffs, sunlight reflecting from the windows of the houses built there back in Victorian times. Where the afternoon sun caressed his face beneath the peak of his cap, it was molten honey. A couple of girls Rollerbladed by, thong bikinis barely concealing their cute little assets. It was all for show, but so was his reaction. He smiled and nodded, adjusted his cap as if in amazement. Just like any other first-time visitor who was male and red-blooded would do. "Rule three, thief: it's an easy one to remember." To avoid funny looks, he kept his words to himself now. "When in Rome, do as the Romans do."

Good advice.

To Cain's delight, a woman rode by on a bike, towing a Jack Russell terrier on a skateboard. Screwball madness, insanity, and he loved it all.

He paused at a vendor to buy some food, then continued strolling to the pier, eating directly from the carton with his fingers. Man, but this really was the life!

The day and the sights were glorious. The sun was beginning its roll toward the Pacific Ocean, the sky and sea a holiday-brochure cerulean blue. The beach was packed with beautiful people glistening with the sheen of tanning oil. All that was missing was Pamela Anderson in a red swimsuit.

Cain felt good. Only one thing could make the day better. But that would blow his cover as a tourist. He dumped his greasy food tray in an overflowing trash can, felt for the scaling knife in his jacket pocket. A little bone harvesting was out of the question, but he had ample opportunity for a little game, he decided. With most people skimpily attired it might be a challenge, but that only made things more interesting. And as always, a challenge conquered produced more satisfaction.

His first target was apparent immediately, a statuesque woman in khaki shorts and a vest top. She was standing at the end of a line waiting to purchase ice cream. Cain didn't pause. He moved directly in, pretended to accidentally jostle the woman.

"Sorry, ma'am," he said. "I do apologize."

The woman, forty-something but looking every bit of ten years older under her makeup, gave him a frown. Not used to the concept of strangers copping a feel from the likes of her, she wasn't concerned by the unsolicited contact. She flung back her hair and turned back to the more pressing engagement of securing her place in the ice cream line. Cain walked away, clutching a belt loop from her shorts in his left hand.

"One–nil," he whispered.

He secreted the trophy in a pocket of his windbreaker, pushing it alongside the film-wrapped fingers and thumbs of his collection. Light of spirit, he climbed a series of plank steps to a ramp leading onto the pier. From this high vantage point, he spied the woman at the kiosk. She'd already forgotten him in her desire for raspberry whip delight. Standing behind her in the ice cream line was a man in taupe shirt and chinos. He didn't appear to be checking out the ice cream menu. He seemed more interested in Cain. Only a brief glance at first, but their eyes met and locked. Then the man looked away. Hmmm, interesting.

"Rule four, thief: Semper vigilo. Remain vigilant at all times."

On the pier, the pickings were even sweeter. The crowds were hemmed in, and accidental collisions were the order of the day. Within a minute, he had a button from an elderly gent's blazer and the tassel from a woman's parasol. Neither were what he considered too great a challenge, but they joined his collection just the same.

Cain wasn't finished yet.

"The catch of the day!"

She was stunning in a pale lilac swimsuit and matching sarong. Looked Hawaiian. A dark-eyed beauty with dusky skin and full red lips. Cutting her out of her bikini would make anyone a happy man.

She moved through the crowd with the fluid confidence that the masses would open a path before her. Sure, she was beautiful, but she had an innate disdain for the lesser mortals around her. Cain wouldn't hold that against her; she was a person after his own heart. He would have loved to teach her that there was at least one among the crowd who would not give way so easily. Trouble was, she was too prominent. More than one man gave her a lingering glance. Some women looked, too. But their stares were of the green-eyed variety.

The attention she commanded meant it wasn't a good idea to approach her. Someone would notice and remember. Guaranteed.

An older woman sitting on a deck chair was much more viable. He took two steps toward her and stopped. Something registered. A flash of taupe passing by. He blinked slowly. The color taupe wasn't something that would generally cause concern. Not unless you were as cautious as Tubal Cain.

He entered an arcade. Families fed coins into machines as though they were going out of fashion. A grandiose show of holiday overexuberance. Sweaty faces and the smell of popcorn. Cain absorbed and then discarded it all. He was in the Zone. He took five paces, then rounded on his heel. Walked back the way he'd come.

The man entering the arcade had no option but to continue inside. The flicker in his eyes, the almost imperceptible pause in his step, was the giveaway. Cain was more adept at this game. No one would guess that he was suspicious of the man.

Immediately outside, Cain turned toward the deck-chair woman. Spun on his heel again. Just in time to see the man in taupe shirt and chinos come out of the arcade. Pushing his hand through his dark hair, he scanned the crowd as though looking for someone else. It was good cover. Not convincing to Cain, though. Should have stuck to buying ice cream, Cain concluded.

No doubt about it, now: the man was following him. Only thing was, Cain couldn't quite guess his motive. Slowly, Cain turned around and began the walk along the pier.

He affected the look of one thrilled to be there, ogling the attractions like a country boy in the big city for the first time. But the storefronts and carousels held no real interest for him. They were cover for his own surveillance. In the reflective surfaces, he checked behind him. Taupe shirt was still there. Plus, another in a flamboyant yellow and blue striped number. He was being hunted down by at least two men.

"What have we got here, then? Muggers or cops?" Neither assumption boded well. "Time to go, I think."

Escape beckoned. The steps leading back to the promenade were in front of him. But a huge man blocked the way. He glowered like a bullmastiff as he whispered into his fist. Not muggers, then. Definitely police.

Feign indifference. Just walk on past him. Good plan, but the man stepped in front of him, held up a hand, and pushed it against Cain's chest. He was like a stuccoed wall, wide, pale as whitewash, and a little rough up close. Not too polite, either. Didn't even have the good grace to introduce himself. All he was capable of was a nod over Cain's shoulder. Ergo, his intention was to distract rather than contain. Taupe shirt or the other in candy stripes must be moving in on him.

Cain blinked up at the man. The innocent look. "Can I help you?" he asked.

"You can wait there a moment, sir." He did the over-the-shoulder nod thing again. The slight urgency told Cain that the man's friends weren't as close as they should have been.

"What's this about?" Cain asked as he pushed his hands into his pockets.

"Security," said the man. "We'd like a word with you."

"Security?" Cain's nervous laugh was real. But for a wholly different reason than he'd admit. "That's a relief, friend. For a moment there I thought you were about to rob me or something."

"We just want to ask you a couple of questions," said the man. "If you wouldn't mind waiting a minute or two?"

"Wait for what? What am I supposed to have done?"

"We've been having problems with pickpockets. Been watching you, and we'd just like to ask you to turn out your pockets." The man, large and impressive-looking, had a nervous cast to his eyes. Not been on the job long, Cain decided.

"I don't think you're at liberty to do that," Cain told him.

"If you'd just wait for my supervisor, he'll explain everything to you," said the security man. His hand was as big and hot as a Sunday roast on Cain's shoulder.

"Hey!" Cain shrugged him off. Amiable enough. A lack of aggression ensured that he didn't encourage a tighter hold.

Yes, the big guy was new to the job, obviously unsure of his level of authority here. His hand wavered in the air as though plucking at floating threads of lint.

Cain exhaled. *Rule five: If you're accosted, keep them thinking. While engaged in thought, the fools aren't acting. Gives you the opportunity to act first. Rule six: If you are going to act, do so immediately and without prejudice.*

"So where is your supervisor?" he demanded.

"Coming."

Cain glanced around, saw that the man in candy stripes was about twenty feet away, attempting to skirt a group of kids on an outing. He couldn't see the one in taupe. Good, that gave him a few seconds to spare.

"I can't wait here all day." Cain engaged the man by locking eyes with him. Simple but effective. It was all Cain required. His hand moved below their plane of vision. Motion that was barely a flicker. A quick jabbing action between the man's legs. Very little contact. Hardly noticeable. Then he was past the man and taking his first couple of steps down the stairs. The security man was motionless, looking down between his thighs at the lake of blood pooling between his feet.

Cain counted the steps, one, two, three, four; then the caterwauling began. A horror-movie scream as the truth became apparent. Cain's feet gave a backbeat to the howl, clattering down the remaining steps to the promenade. On the pier, heads were swiveling toward the commotion, but Cain simply ran. He needn't look back to witness the result of that one simple knife jab. A punctured femoral artery came with a guarantee; without immediate medical help, the security man would bleed to death in minutes. Confusion would erupt and allow him to escape. Also, attempting to staunch the flowing blood of their downed fellow meant the man's companions couldn't possibly pursue him, too.

Of course, Cain was also a firm believer in not trusting people to react the way you expected them to. A shout broke through the murmur of consternation rising behind him. He heard the slap of determined footsteps in pursuit down the stairs. He did glance back, a natural instinct that would not be denied. The man in taupe rushed after him. Cain swore and increased his speed.

As they had for the Hawaiian beauty, the crowds parted before him. Only the looks he received were anything but admiring. They were fearful. It was apparent to all that Cain was a fugitive. A dangerous fugitive, judging by the screaming overhead. There were no gung-ho heroes among the tourists, no one trying to snag his clothing or bring him down. But neither did they impede the man in taupe. Younger than Cain, and in reasonable shape, he was gaining fast. All the while, he shouted into a radio and—more worrying—clenched a revolver in his other hand.

Cain cut to the right, charged up some more steps and

onto the ramp arching over the highway, then raced head down for the anonymity offered by the stores a couple of blocks over. The man in taupe didn't stop, matching him step for step all the way.

At the shopping strip, Cain ducked down a service alley and into the twilit underbelly of Santa Monica that was immeasurably different from the beachfront. The sights, the sounds, the smells, everything was tainted with neglect. He grabbed at a wheeled Dumpster crammed with the ghosts of pizzas past, tugged it out to block his pursuer's path. Didn't stop running. He heard the man heaving the Dumpster aside and realized that barely ten paces separated them. Sprightly son of a bitch, that one, not your usual run-of-the-mill rent-a-cop.

Fortunately, Cain gained the corner of the buildings first. He spun to his left into deeper shadows and rushed headlong through a narrow alley, trusting to luck that he didn't smash headlong into an obstruction. Thankfully, he saw the turn and ducked left again.

Cain hoped that the security man would act with caution. He'd witnessed what Cain was capable of with his knife. Only a fool would relish the possibility of bleeding out in a deserted alleyway with only the smell of garbage for the final journey to the afterlife. Fearing ambush, he would slow at the corner. Cain sprinted on, gaining precious distance on his pursuer.

On a main shopping strip parallel to the beach, Cain slowed down. It was surprising how much anonymity a single block's dash had given him. All around him the vacationers' lunacy continued unabated. Not as much as a glance or a "How are you doing?" came his way.

A mini-mall enticed passersby with the promise of major discounts on all purchases. From within the entrance Cain watched the man in taupe rush by. Problem solved, almost.

Ducking through a service door, Cain took off his cap and jacket and dumped them in a waste bin. He freed his jeans from his socks. His shirt hung loose over his waistband, concealing the scaling knife tucked in the small of his back, as well as the large bulges his trophies now made in his jeans pockets.

Back out in the mall, he ambled in shopper mode. Shoplifting wasn't a skill he'd engaged in since his school days, but the appropriation of a pair of sunglasses was as dexterous as any swish he'd ever made with a blade. Suitably disguised, he backtracked toward the pier.

Back at the promenade by the beach again, he looked toward the pier. A swarm of buzzing hornets, the paramedics and police had arrived. The wounded security man was the sheeted-up load going into an ambulance. The man in candy stripes hung his head by the open doors. Two accounted for, one to go. Behind his newly acquired sunglasses, Cain squinted left and right. No more than ten yards away, the taupe security man walked toward him. Cain wasn't concerned; he stood looking out to sea, hands bunched around the trophies in his pockets. The man made the slow walk of dejection back toward the pier, totally oblivious that he was in stabbing range of the person he sought.

Cain turned away. He'd lost interest in this pointless game. Better he return to the VW to see if he still had the chore of getting rid of it.

Then the more pressing matter of finding the thief.

12

"SO THIS IS YOUR HOMETOWN, RINK? I HAVE TO TAKE back what I said about pickup trucks, huh?"

"Damn right!"

I don't mind admitting when I'm wrong. I thought I'd be flying into a sleepy town full of wooden shacks. Instead, I found a vibrant city to equal any in the midwestern U.S. I was knocked back by the sprawl of beautiful high-rise buildings, fine museums, and scenic parks along the banks of the Arkansas River.

Not that Rink was gloating. His smile was all pleasure while pointing out the major landmarks, reminding me that Little Rock was the capital of the Natural State, and not some piss-pot backwater as I'd thought.

"Pity we couldn't take the scenic route so I could see *even more* of your fine town."

We were in a rental car we'd picked up at Adams Field, otherwise known as Little Rock National Airport, following a four-hour flight from Tampa. The car was a regular sedan, nowhere near as flashy as Rink's Porsche, but clean and comfortable nonetheless. More trunk space, too. Rink drove. It was easier that way. This was his old stomping ground, and he could get us to our destination much quicker.

That had been the plan. Yet it seemed to me that Rink must've been a cabdriver in a past life, judging by the winding way we took through town.

"Yeah, Le Petit Roche sure has come a long way," Rink said as he pushed the sedan through a downtown convention and entertainment district. I think Rink himself was impressed. "I think you're forgettin' that this was Bill Clinton's first capital city, Hunter."

"I'm not forgetting, Rink. I didn't know. Full stop."

"Man, you're just too ignorant for your own good. Admit it, you weren't expecting anything like this, were you? We've even got the brand-new, one-of-a-kind William J. Clinton Presidential Center and Park right here in Little Rock," Rink said, indicating off to his right with a wave of his hand. "It's sure a sight to behold."

"Like Disney World?" I asked.

Rink frowned. I smiled unabashedly.

"We far from Louise's place?" I asked.

"Not too far. Another five minutes or so."

"You said that five minutes ago."

"I did. Now ain't that strange?"

"Harvey going to be there?"

"Said he'd meet us at a diner where we can speak to Louise on neutral ground. Doesn't want to be seen around her house in case anything comes back on him." Rink gave a shrug. "I don't know what he's gettin' all bowed up about. It's not as if Petoskey's the goddamn Godfather or nothin'."

"Like you said, though, he's got connections," I said. "I'm starting to worry that we're underestimating his outfit. City this big and important, he must be a key player if he's controlling the politicians."

Rink shook his head.

"Petoskey's a two-bit asshole playing at the big time, just like I told you. It's not as if he's got the governor in his pocket, just some minor politicians and low-ranking cops who're taking bribes for favors."

I grimaced, but nodded.

Rink shot me a look. "I'm telling you, man. There ain't nothin' to get riled up about. I know his type. Thirty years ago, he was frog-giggin' for meat to put in his momma's stew, now he's eatin' the best cuisine and drivin' around in flashy cars. He's poor white trash actin' like a big important hotshot. On the grand scale of things, he's nobody. An' he knows it."

"Maybe, but he seems to have put the scare into John. He must have some sort of weight behind him."

"From what you told me, John ain't too hard to scare. Ran away from this weasely Shank character. I take it your brother's not the bravest dude on the planet?"

My head shake was as much from memory as from disagreement.

"He wasn't running from Shank. Shank was Jennifer's problem, not John's. There were others involved."

"I know, he'd shacked up with this Blake woman, too," Rink said. "He was runnin' from his marriage."

"Among other things," I said.

Rink pulled the rental over to the side of the road. He sat looking at me.

"What haven't you told me, Hunter?"

"I didn't think this had anything to do with what happened before," I said, "but now I'm not so sure." I was pensive for a moment. Rink continued to give me the eye. "I told you me and John had a falling out, yeah?"

"Uh-huh. But you never told me why."

My face felt like clay, cold and clammy, as I rubbed my hands over my features. I was already tired, but more than that, thinking about John's predicament made me bone weary.

"Not long after I resigned from the job, he came to me with a problem," I said.

"Go on," Rink prompted.

"He'd got himself involved with some real heavy-duty shit. Stupid son of a bitch had been playing cards and writing IOUs he couldn't hope to cover. First went his car, then the house. But it wasn't enough. He had nothing left and had no one to turn to."

"So you did the honorable thing?"

"Yeah, I bailed them out. Jenny doesn't know it to this day. I gave John the cash to pay it off. But an addiction being what it is, John went and blew it on another *sure bet*. I called him on it—the money—and that's when we had the falling out. It was just a stupid argument."

"You didn't talk to him again?"

"No, Rink. I didn't even see him again."

Rink nodded. "That's when he run out?"

"He must have been planning it."

"Punk."

I shrugged. "After that, the only way I could think to help him and Jenny was to face down the guys he owed and make them back off. Wasn't easy. They weren't as easily intimidated as Shank was."

"They didn't back off?"

"No."

"You're slipping, Hunter."

"Seriously," I said. "Short of going to war with them, there wasn't much I could do. So instead, I arranged for John and Jenny to disappear for a while. It was all set, they were going to go off together, assume new identities, everything. Then John went and messed it all up. Unbeknownst to all of us, he'd been seeing this Louise Blake on the side. Before we knew it, they took off together. Just flew. Gone."

"Leaving poor Jenny and his kids behind to take the flack," Rink concluded.

"Yeah," I agreed. "I did everything I could for her. Helped her get back on her feet. I had space in my house, but she refused. Said she needed a place of her own. John didn't even get in touch and let her know where he was."

"And you want to help this peckerhead?"

"He's still my brother, Rink."

Rink raised an eyebrow, but then gave a soft nod.

"Plus, I'm doing this for his wife and kids."

"Okay. But I'm surprised she wants him back."

"Jenny doesn't want him back," I explained. "She's looking for some kind of closure. I think she wants me to find John so she can spit in his eye."

"I'm with her on that one."

"Me, too. Took a lot of work sorting out the problems he left. As I said, they were a major outfit with major connections. They put out a contract on him."

"Shit," Rink said.

"In the end they saw reason. I explained that John had double-crossed us all, that we were all equally aggrieved. So I made an agreement with them that they didn't go near Jenny or the kids. The alternative was that I'd call back up and wipe them out."

"They believed you were capable?"

"I think it was more fear of the unknown," I said. "They didn't know who I was or what I was prepared to do. But some of them had heard stuff. I believe in the end they decided it was more trouble than it was worth. You could say that going to war with me wasn't profitable."

"Did they call in the contract on John?"

"Who knows what they'd do if he ever showed up again."

"Which is why you think he's missing?"

"Nah." I shook my head. "There's more to it than that. John has other reasons. I guess the point I'm trying to make is this: He's a selfish son of a bitch. Doesn't give a shit for anyone but himself. But I don't think he'd be running from the likes of Petoskey if it's only about a couple of hundred dollars' gambling debt." I paused, summing up exactly what it was that I was trying to say. "Something big has happened. Something he's so frightened of that he's disappeared again and he doesn't want to go back. Louise Blake has been left high and dry, the same as he left Jenny. That means he's attempting to cut all ties, so he can disappear without a trace. You don't do that for any piddling gambling debt."

Rink agreed.

"Petoskey's an asshole," he reiterated. "But I see where you're coming from. What's he gonna do? Maybe order an ass whuppin', maybe a broken arm or something? He's not going to order John's death, is he?"

"Unless Petoskey's more dangerous than we're giving him credit for," I pointed out.

"Could be, but I stand on my first opinion. He's a small potato playing at the big time. The way I remember, he's too chickenshit to take someone out for real."

"You've been gone from here a long time. People change."

"Okay, I'll concede that. But it still leaves another option, doesn't it?"

"John's made an enemy of someone else? Someone who is prepared to kill him."

Rink leaned forward, turned on the engine, and pulled out into the traffic. He turned to me, said, "But you're still fixin' to start with Petoskey?"

"Yeah. We're going to do it loud and hard. We need to shake him up, Rink. Make him fear us. I'm going to make him tell us where John is. Hopefully, it'll end there," I said. "But I don't think so."

"No," Rink said. "Now that you've got me thinking, I don't figure so, either."

The city was behind us now and we were entering a grimier section of town.

"What are we doing here?" I asked.

"Just thought we'd take a detour and scope out the land. Harvey said Petoskey does business from an office downtown, also mentioned this place he visits when the dealings are a little more underhanded. Thought we'd just drive by and take a look. Thought it would be better to hit him there than downtown. Less chance of the cops arriving and saving his ass before we're through."

Up ahead was a building right out of a ghost story. Rink raised his chin to indicate the place.

"What do you think?"

"Is it haunted?" I joked.

"Only by hobos, I guess," Rink said.

The building was a huge redbrick affair, but little of the original color showed through the accumulated soot. Five stories high with a flat roof, rows of windows on each level. Not too many of the windows retained their original glass. Some were boarded over with molding plywood, while others bore remnants of glass like the shards of teeth in a crone's mouth. The uppermost windows had fared better; perhaps they'd been replaced more recently. Beyond the dull glass there appeared to be sheets of semiopaque plastic.

"What do you think the plastic's for?"

"Not the obvious," Rink said. "It's not there to catch blood. More than likely it's to dampen down any sounds from inside."

"Looks to me like there could be squatters on the lower floors."

"Uh-huh. Good cover. Who in their right mind's goin' to want to run a gauntlet of crackheads and thieves?"

"Only those who really have to," I said.

Rink spun the car around in an abandoned lot so we could take a second drive by Petoskey's hideout. Second time around it looked no better.

"Time to meet Harvey?" Rink asked.

"Yeah," I said. In the rearview mirror, the building took on the color of old blood. It seemed to exude the promise of unrestrained violence.

13

"MR. HUNTER?" LOUISE BLAKE LOOKED ME UP and down. "You're John's brother?"

"Yes."

"You look like him."

We shook hands.

"Please. Sit down. I've already taken the liberty of ordering coffee," I said.

She sat down and immediately reached for her mug. Quick gulp. Not so much a need for the caffeine as for something to occupy her trembling hands. She pushed the cup from her, almost empty. Fiddled with the handle. There was a faint knocking coming from the table as if the spirits were making contact at a séance.

You might say that she was a little nervous.

I'd never met her before, but I recalled John talking about the beauty he was working with. I'd suspected he was glorifying her through the bottom of his beer goggles, but seeing her now, I had to admit she was a good-looking woman. Even pinched with worry and nervously adjusting her clothing, she had the fine bones and full lips of a model. Not *Vogue* standard, but perhaps your mail-order catalog girl on the way to the big time.

Something else struck me. Louise Blake *was* a younger version of Jenny. One not changed by childbirth, and the ultimate betrayal of trust.

"I hope you don't mind meeting me here?" Louise said. She crossed her arms beneath her breasts to hug herself.

Most likely it was another attempt at concealing the shakes. "The thing is, I don't think it would be a good idea for you to show up at my house."

"This place is as good as any," I told her. I was nursing my cup of strong coffee, while Louise looked like she wanted more. She required reassurance that she was among friends. I made the introductions.

Harvey Lucas had arranged the meeting with seclusion in mind. Neutral turf, he called it. More like minimal space. We were squashed into a booth in a greasy spoon diner at the end of a strip mall. There weren't too many customers at this hour of the afternoon, and those who were there apparently understood the concept of privacy. The booths on either side of ours remained empty, which added to the ludicrous scene of the four of us packed together at a table designed for two. Rink and I sat on one side, while Louise and Harvey sat facing us. Pressed into the corner by the window by Harvey's imposing bulk, Louise looked like a cornered rodent menaced by a panther.

When you think of a private eye, you might picture a middle-aged white man in a houndstooth sports jacket and mustard slacks. Possibly wearing a fedora to cover his thinning hair. Harvey was anything but. He was six feet five, two hundred and twenty pounds of sleek muscle, with a bullet head. And his skin was blue-black to the point that it reflected the overhead lights.

Harvey Lucas looked like a professional boxer and dressed with the panache and flair of a movie star. I'd learned that he was an ex-army Ranger, the connection to Rink now obvious.

Harvey cut into the conversation in a rich baritone. "Been some strange-looking people hanging around Miss Blake's place these past coupla days. Thought it best we did our business out of sight."

"Petoskey's people?" I asked.

"Could be," Harvey said. "But if you ask me they look too

slick to be involved with Siggy. Got a few good photographs of them if you want to take a look."

"Yeah, we'll have a look when we're finished here," I said. Then I turned to Louise. "Do you know anything about who's watching your place?"

She shook her head and her reddish hair momentarily covered her features.

Harvey stepped in again. "Miss Blake was unaware of the surveillance of her home until I pointed it out to her."

"I knew something was going on," she offered in an attempt to save face. Apparently there was a tough side to Louise Blake. "I could feel it. As if there were eyes on me everywhere I went. But no, I didn't see anyone. Not that I'd know them anyway. I've never seen this Petoskey."

"What're your feelings, Harve?" Rink asked.

Harvey rolled his head on his broad shoulders, turned down the corners of his mouth. "Don't like it one bit, Rink."

Harvey had my complete agreement. To Louise, I said, "In your letter to Jennifer Telfer you said that you thought John was in some kind of trouble. Was it because of something specific he said?"

Louise shook her head. "He didn't say anything. That was the problem. What bothered me more was the way he was acting."

"What do you mean? You said he was frightened."

"Yeah, he was kind of jumpy. A car would pull up and he'd sneak to the window, peak out a corner of the blinds, that kind of thing. He couldn't sleep too well, either. Tossed and turned all the time, jumped at any noises from outside."

"Did you ask him what was wrong?"

"Of course I did. But he wouldn't tell me. Just said he had something on his mind."

"But you didn't push him about what it was?" I asked.

"No. I just thought it was to do with him starting a new job. Maybe it was too much for him to handle or something. You know, like the pressure was getting to him?"

"John started a new job?"

"So he said. Told me he was doing a bit of driving for a local firm, delivering to customers, that sort of thing. I didn't press him about who it was for. He looked a little embarrassed at first."

"Why'd he be embarrassed about a driving job?" I asked.

"Wouldn't you be embarrassed? To end up as a delivery boy's a bit of a comedown, don't you think?"

"Is that the way you saw it, Louise?"

Her gaze snapped onto me with power-drill intensity. "That's not at all the way I saw it! What do you think I am?"

"Sorry, I didn't mean it like that. I was just wondering if he'd got the notion in his mind that he'd let you down, and that was why he was acting so jumpy around you."

She exhaled noisily.

"Maybe he did have it in his mind, but he never mentioned it to me. Anyway, he wasn't jumpy around me; he was jumpy around everything else *but* me."

"You said he was acting like he was watching for someone?" I prompted.

Louise shook out her hair again.

"Not just like he was watching for someone," she said with a wave of a finger. "More like he was waiting for something to happen."

"Or something to arrive?" Rink asked.

"Yes." The momentary anger had gone from her eyes. "John said that if anything ever happened to him, you would know what to do, Mr. Hunter. So . . . I mean, do you?"

I swirled the coffee in my cup, pondering the patterns of froth as if it were a psychic's divining tool. I saw less in the coffee swirls than I already knew. Which wasn't much. Finally, I switched my gaze to her face. My exhalation told her everything. "I haven't seen or heard from John since he left England; I was hoping you'd be able to bring me up to speed on what he'd been up to since coming here."

Louise's shrug was noncommittal.

"We just got by. I took a job at a beauty salon. John went

from job to job. Nothing startling really. Parking valet. Stacking paint at a warehouse. Fast-food cook." She ticked off the jobs on the fingers of one hand. "Then, most recently, this driving job."

"But you don't know who for?"

"No."

"Was he delivering locally?"

She shrugged again. "Sometimes he'd be away for a few days, so I guess he got a few long-haul jobs. Don't know where he went, though. He'd phone from a motel or something, but he'd never say where he was. I didn't think to ask. I wasn't really that bothered."

"You weren't that bothered? Were you having problems with your relationship?"

Louise looked at me sharply. The power drill on overdrive. "Are you asking if he was seeing someone else?"

"Was he?"

"No."

"How could you tell?"

"Believe me, a woman knows these kinds of things."

I thought of Jenny; how she hadn't had a clue about her husband's infidelity. But then again, with the constant money worries, the fear that bad men would turn up and take it from their hides, Jenny probably wasn't capable of detecting the subtle signs that Louise was now hinting at. "If there wasn't another woman, was there anything else between you?"

Louise's lips trembled. I don't know if it was emotion or scorn. Then, to change the subject, she lifted a hand and waved over a waitress.

"Can I have another coffee?" she asked.

The waitress refilled her cup, offered more to the rest of us, but we all declined. Louise waited, a manicured fingernail tapping her cup, until the waitress returned to the serving counter. "As you know, John left his wife for me. Not exactly the ideal situation." She glanced around at the three of us, checking for any sign of disapproval. We were like the three wise monkeys. See, hear, and—definitely—say no evil. "Because of that, it wasn't really a good idea to keep in touch with anyone back home. We severed all ties. My family doesn't know where I am. John didn't tell his. There have been so many times that I wanted to pick up the telephone and speak to my mother, but I didn't."

"Was that your choice?" I asked.

"No. John always argued against it. Said it was best we remained anonymous for a little longer. Just another six months or so. He said it was to give everyone time to reconcile themselves with what we'd done. So that they'd forgive us." She laughed sadly at herself.

"Did you believe that?" I asked softly. "That John was concerned about what people back home thought about you?"

"I'm not a complete idiot," she said, and again a spark of anger flashed across her features. "We argued about it a lot. But that's not why he left. Believe it or not, we do love each other. It's not important what anyone thinks."

Her challenge was as direct as a laser-guided warhead. Aimed directly at me. After all, I was the only other constant here. I had come to America because of Jennifer's request as much as the letter Louise had sent. She wanted to know whose side I was on.

"You're right. It doesn't matter," I told her.

She nodded, pacified for now. "When we left England, I knew that he was hiding something. That he was running from more than his wife and children. He was in some sort of trouble and he *had* to run. That's the bottom line."

I sat back from the table, had to rotate my shoulders so that I could lean against the booth wall without nudging Rink into the gangway. I said, "It's not likely that the men who were after him have followed him here. The cost would exceed what he owed them."

Louise looked more than a little stunned at my words.

"I . . . I didn't know." Her eyes glazed over. "Are they . . . uh . . . bad men?"

"Yes. Loan sharks. The type who take body parts as payment."

She could've been slapped in the face and looked less surprised. "I had no idea. I thought the debt he'd gotten himself into was just the usual type that everyone ends up with." She shook her head, then met my eyes again. "Was it Jennifer's debt? He said he couldn't control her spending. He even cut up her credit cards, but it made no difference. In the end, they lost everything . . . and that's why he had to leave her."

I chose not to comment. But Rink, who had just heard the truth from me earlier, snorted in derision. Louise shifted her gaze between us. Challenging us to disagree with John's version of events.

"The men after him," I said, to steer the conversation away from John's lies, "are dangerous in their own right. But you needn't worry; they're not exactly an international outfit. They don't work outside the U.K."

"You know that for a fact?" Louise asked.

"Yes." To allay any fears about unlikely possibilities, I decided to elaborate on the truth. "I've already had a . . . well, call it a talk with them. They've backed off. They know the consequences of doing anything to John or any of his family."

"His family." Louise snorted.

"Present company included," I reassured her.

She looked at me again, and I gave her my most open-faced promise in return. She turned up her nose above a twisted mouth. She wasn't so pretty now. "You didn't even know who I was. How could you make the same agreement for me?"

"My demands weren't open to negotiation. They harm John or anyone close to him and they'd pay the consequences."

I saw fear creeping into Louise's face now. Not the worry that was evident before. Something new. Something scary that had just dawned on her regarding the man who'd traversed an ocean to help her.

"Who exactly are you, Mr. Hunter?" she asked.

"I'm John's brother," I told her.

"But, who . . . or what . . . ?"

I held up a hand to ward her off.

"Just leave it at that," I said. "All you need to understand is that I'm John's brother. And by association, you are family. I'm here to help you, okay?"

Louise picked up her coffee, drained it in one continuous gulp.

"After you leave," she asked, as she set down the empty mug, "will it be safe for me to stay here?"

I gave a quick glance toward Rink, who nodded. Harvey bowed his large neck and stared at the table. I shook my head slowly.

"Maybe it's time you phoned your mother," I said. "Ask her if it'd be okay to come home."

Tears welled in her eyes. Fear, it seemed, has many expressions.

"You think John is dead."

I didn't answer. It wasn't a question, anyway.

"Don't you?" she asked.

The air I sucked through my teeth wasn't the ideal reply. In hindsight, I wouldn't have done it. I'd have considered the action, and spared Louise my concern. Trouble was, I did fear the worst, and Louise was intuitive enough to know it. She leaned forward into her hands and wept. Around her, three big tough guys squirmed. I reached across and took her hands from her face.

"Sorry, Louise," I said. "I know that's not what you wanted to hear."

Louise sniffed. Shook her head. Sat up a little straighter, playing with her hair. Her way to regain composure. A smile forced into place didn't work; it was too redolent of misery.

"I don't know why I'm crying," she said. "It's not as if I haven't already thought of it. He's been gone for ages now. I mean, surely he'd have called me if he was still alive, right?"

In reality, she was asking why John would bother to pick up a phone when he'd never done the same with his wife. He'd cautioned her against phoning her own mother, for

Christ's sake. So just because he hadn't been in touch didn't mean he was dead.

"We can only hope that he's hiding someplace. Maybe he is. Maybe he's hiding out and won't call for fear of jeopardizing your safety." I gripped her hands with a little more pressure. "But you may have to accept the worst, Louise."

"I know," she said quietly. I gave her an extra squeeze.

"But," I said, expecting the sideways glance from Rink, "if it's possible, I'll find him. I will bring him back, one way or the other."

After that there wasn't much left to cover. Louise was done speaking and prepared herself to leave. Being the consummate gentleman, Harvey offered to give her a lift home, but she declined.

"I feel like a real shit," he announced after Louise was gone.

"No need to," Rink said.

"The more I look at this, the more I think I should be helping you guys more than I am," he said.

"We don't know what we're up against," I told him. "Don't know how it's going to turn out. So maybe it's best you leave things as they are."

He shook his head. "I've heard another whisper. I can't substantiate it, but some people are saying John disappeared owing Petoskey more than a bad debt."

"Like what?" I asked.

"No one is saying. But Petoskey is screaming murder. Making him speak to you might not be as easy as it sounds. He might very well resist. Big time."

"He's a punk," Rink put in.

"A dangerous punk," Harvey told him. "You might go in there and not walk out again. All I'm saying is it'd be better if you had an extra pair of eyes watching your backs."

"You live here, Harvey," I reminded him. "It's okay for me and Rink. We can shake up the local bad guys, but we don't have to hang around afterward. We don't have to live with the consequences of making any enemies here. You do."

"Appreciate that," he said. "But I still feel like a goddamn shitheel. It's like I'm running out on you guys."

"No need to," Rink said. "We ain't expecting you to put your head on the block for us."

"Anyway, you've done a lot for us already," I pointed out. "All we need from you now is the stuff we asked for. If Petoskey's as dangerous as you say, we'd better take it with us."

"It's in the car with the photographs I told you about," Harvey said.

The stuff we were referring to was a 12-gauge shotgun for Rink and a steel-bodied 9-mm Parabellum blowback semi-automatic SIG Sauer for me. Added to that I'd asked for a couple of military issue KA-BAR knives and an untraceable cell phone. To corner Siggy Petoskey, we'd be like ninja warriors assaulting the shogun's castle. A shogun, self-made or not, would have his private army of loyal retainers. However we looked at it, it was going to be a dangerous mission.

Then we got back to Louise Blake. Since she'd arrived, something had been bugging me. "There's something she isn't telling us," I said.

"Yeah," Rink agreed. "I was getting the same vibe."

Harvey simply raised his eyebrows, shrugged his wide shoulders.

"I'm not suggesting that she's involved in John's disappearance. But there's something that isn't gelling with me," I said. "She says that John was acting all jumpy and nervous, but she didn't press him for what he was concerned about. That strike either of you as normal behavior?"

"No way. We're talking about a woman here," Rink joked.

"She also said she didn't know who he was working for. I find that a little hard to believe," I said. "Even though my work was top secret, my wife still knew who the hell it was I was working for."

"I suppose he could've been doing subcontract work," Harvey offered.

"Or a little private enterprise," Rink said.

"Private *criminal* enterprise," Harvey added.

"If not Petoskey, who else could John have been working for?" I asked.

Harvey blew out in a harsh exclamation. "Take your pick, Hunter. Could be anyone."

"Yeah," I agreed. If John was involved in crime, he could be working for any one of half a million employers from anywhere in the States. "Louise said she didn't press him about his work, but twice she mentioned that John told her to contact me if anything happened to him. People don't give you those kind of instructions unless they're pretty sure something *is* going to happen to them."

"And," Rink added, "he's obviously been expecting something *real bad* . . . considering the business you're in, Hunter."

"Yeah," I said. "That's what worries me the most."

14 "DIFFERENT PLATES, SAME SUV."

Tubal Cain was in no doubt. The vehicle parked in the lot of the Pacific View Hotel was the one stolen from him yesterday. Even if it had been sprayed a different color, furry dice hung in the window, and whitewall tires added, he'd have known the vehicle for his own. It had a vibe that he could feel even from across the width of the parking lot. That vehicle had witnessed death, and the pall of violence hung over it like a miasma of poisonous fumes.

As nonchalant as a man with the right—which he certainly had, in his estimation—he ambled over to the 4x4. The locks were engaged. Not that they'd stop him from taking back what was rightfully his if he were of a mind to do so.

Nothing on the front seat but an empty water bottle and the remnants of a KFC meal, but on the dash was a disc removed from the CD player. *Swing When You're Winning,* the very disc he'd been playing prior to stopping for the stranded motorist. If he had required confirmation, there was his proof.

He wandered to the rear of the car. A cursory inspection of the license plate spoke volumes. The area around the locking nuts was clean, unlike the rest of the plate, which had a fine coating of dust. The clean areas proved that someone had turned the locking nuts very recently. It was obvious to someone with his expert eye that someone had removed the plates from another vehicle, then screwed them in place on this one.

"Guy's a freaking amateur," he reminded himself. But— and this was a caution he would heed—not to be underestimated.

Credit where it's due, then: changing the plates was on the way to being a good idea. The thief didn't know that Cain wouldn't be reporting the theft of the vehicle, so it was sensible to install a new identity.

Some constructive criticism was in order, though. It was good that the thief had tried to cover his tracks. It was just a pity that he hadn't taken the time to do so properly. Any cop worth his salt would notice the clean area around the locking nuts and know immediately that the plates had been switched. He shook his head in pure reproof. "I don't know if it's your lack of experience or whether you're just too lazy for your own good."

A slow walk took him around to the driver's side. Peering inside he saw no sign of his stolen Bowie knife. It meant one of two things: either the knife was concealed out of sight or the thief had it with him in his hotel room. Considering the third option wasn't pleasant: that the thief might have dumped the knife somewhere along the way.

Finished with the car, he made his way toward the front of the hotel. It was a three-story affair, built on land barely a stone's throw from Route 405. Prime location, except that larger hotels blocked the view of the ocean. The name of the hotel was a marketing lie. Probably wishful thinking. Either that or the name was thirty years out of date.

Inside, overhead fans spun indolent circles in lemon-scented air, the lobby as cool and clean as a spring morning. Cain's rubber-soled shoes made a soft squishing sound on the faux-marble tiles, barely disturbing the tranquility. On his right was a long reception desk behind which was a small office area. A young woman, a California cutie with straw-colored hair and rosy cheeks, was bent over a computer. Cain smiled at her, but she didn't as much as raise her head. Spreadsheets held more interest for her than a handsome man. Cain walked on past her toward the communal dining area.

The steward wasn't at his station. In fact, no one challenged him. The room was devoid of staff or any of the hotel's clientele. A glance at his wristwatch told Cain that it was too late for lunch and too early for dinner.

He stepped back into the lobby area, thinking about his best option. There were alternatives, but the sensible course of action would be to wait for the thief to show up at the SUV. From there he could take him out and regain what was rightfully his.

"Can I help you, sir?"

The blond woman had exited the office and now stood at the reception desk. She had a sheaf of papers in her hands and a smile on her face. Apparently a handsome man did override the attraction of a spreadsheet.

To miss an opportunity would be tantamount to a crime. Without pause Cain swung toward her, affecting his best humble-and-caring-guy face. "Yeah, uhm, I was wondering if someone could help me out. I didn't realize anyone was around when I first walked in."

Like many before her who'd come into contact with Tubal Cain, the receptionist was oblivious to his lies. The power of a smile and twinkling green eyes are never to be undervalued in a lunatic's arsenal. She waved the sheaf of papers in the general direction of her office. "Sorry about that, I had my nose buried in some work."

Cain waved off her apology. "It's nothing, really," he said. "I just pulled in and noticed that a car outside has its lights on. Just thought I'd come in and let you know. Wouldn't like anyone to find a dead battery. Bit of an inconvenience for them."

The woman swung sideways, pulling a large ledger toward her. "What kind of vehicle is it?"

"Mercedes SUV. Black and silver. Has Nevada plates."

The woman checked the register. Opportunities presented must be grasped with both hands. As calmly as possible, Cain leaned over the counter, watching as she traced down a list of names with a well-manicured fingernail. In the split second before she looked up, Cain turned his head aside and scanned a poster on the wall at the rear of the reception area as if it had held his interest throughout.

"I'll give the owner a call and let him know. I'm sure he'll be grateful for your help," she said.

"It's nothing," Cain reassured her, "but there's nothing worse than a dead battery. And it's so easily avoided, too. I'd only hope that if I were ever so careless, someone would do the same for me."

"Me, too," said the woman. "I remember one time I was at the mall and I left my lights on. Had to call a tow truck and everything. It was so embarrassing."

"And costly, I bet?"

"Oh, not too bad. It was more the inconvenience," the woman said. She covered the memory of her discomfiture with a hand over her mouth. To some the act would look coy, but to Cain it was reminiscent of a self-conscious halitosis sufferer.

"Pity I wasn't around that time," Cain said. "Could've saved you some trouble."

The woman's amused laughter was the tinkling of Christmas bells. Humble and caring guy strikes again. When she looked at him this time, it was with more interest. "Are you a guest here, sir?"

"No," Cain said. "I was just driving by and my phone rang. I don't have a hands-free kit, so I pulled over. Hope you don't mind me using one of your parking spots for a few minutes? I'd have been gone by now if I hadn't noticed the lights on the car I told you about."

"It's not a problem, sir. In fact, it's good of you to take the time to come in and tell me. Thousands of people wouldn't have even bothered."

"That's true," Cain said in agreement. But then again, he

always did suspect that he was unique. "Isn't it sad, though, that people have got to a point where they'll just walk on by without offering a hand?"

"It is." The woman nodded. "Not many people I meet are as nice as you."

Ooh, the *nice* word. Cain thought she was nice, too. Unfortunately, he had wholly different reasons for his opinion. His estimation was based purely upon the judgment of the ossuary-building artist within him. Clark Kent's X-ray vision was no less penetrating than his scrutiny. She had a pleasing bone structure behind the rosy cheeks. A little plump, perhaps, so that he couldn't easily define the fine skeletal lines he adored. He glanced from her face to her hands. They were slim and long fingered, the nails polished to a sheen. Now there were treasures he would cherish. Slowly he traced each digit in turn with his eyes.

She was aware of this examination. She stirred, ever so slightly uncomfortable under his gaze. Cain acted startled, offering her an abashed grin.

"Sorry. You caught me staring," he said. "It's just that . . . well, uh, you have such beautiful hands."

"My hands?" The woman didn't know how to answer, but she was flattered. Unconsciously she gripped the sheaf of papers tightly in one hand while she held out the other and studied it. Cain leaned toward her.

"I hope you don't think I'm giving you some sort of cheesy come-on," he said. "I'm simply speaking the truth. Your hands are lovely."

"Thanks," she said. "That's really sweet of you to say so."

The catch in her throat gave her an appealing huskiness. She coughed. Eyes darting toward the office as though checking for a disapproving supervisor. The unashamed impression she was portraying was frowned upon by the hotel management, either that or she genuinely was as naive as she appeared. She discretely slipped her hands below the counter. Her rosy cheeks had become twin candy apples.

"Sorry if I'm embarrassing you," Cain said. "I don't mean to."

"No, it's okay. I'm not embarrassed." Despite her words, her cheeks were growing even redder. She dropped her chin toward her chest, swayed in indecision, then laughed.

Cain laughed with her.

"Look," he said. "I have embarrassed you. I'm sorry. Please accept my apologies."

He put out a hand and the woman reached for it reflexively.

They shook hands.

"Apology accepted," said the woman, still laughing.

Cain was slow to release her hand. He allowed his fingers to trail along her palm, prolonging the sensation for as long as possible. One of his human frailties was a total lack of empathy, but what he lacked in compassion he more than made up for in sensory ability. He did not have the capacity to love a woman, but he did love to touch a woman.

He would lodge the sensation in some far recess of his mind, a memory to summon for later. If he couldn't have her hands, he could have the sensory recall of their touch whenever he desired. And that thought was enough to sustain him for now. The primary need on his agenda was his reckoning with the thief. Afterward, if everything went well—as it most definitely would—he could come back at his leisure and take her hands as genuine trophies.

Finally, he stepped back, gave a slight wave.

"Well, I'd best get going," he said. "I've taken up too much of your time as it is."

"Honestly, sir, it was no problem."

"See you," he said. "And once again, I'm sorry if I embarrassed you."

"Yeah, see you," the woman replied. She lifted her hand in reflex. Caught it in midwave. Then laughed and continued the gesture.

Cain gave her his most self-effacing grin. His wink was full of promise.

He walked back through the lobby. In the old Hollywood musicals, Gene Kelly or Fred Astaire would have made the walk a grand swagger, hands in pockets, whistling merrily before swooping around to catch her looking. Cain wasn't so flamboyant; at the exit he merely twisted at the shoulder. It was enough to confirm that, yes, she was still watching him. There was more than a little interest in her gaze. He waved again and she waved back, her face breaking into a wide smile. In true Astaire form he made a show of opening the door and pushing outside.

But as he walked away, his smile turned to a frown, then a scowl. Achieving his objective of flushing out the thief was one thing, but there was no way he could act on it now. The receptionist was a bit dim, but she still had enough of her wits about her to remember the man who had lured the client outside before he was brutally butchered.

Self-recrimination wasn't something he often indulged in, but even he could see that he'd made a mistake. *I shouldn't have flirted with her,* he thought. *I should've simply gone in, given her the story, then got the hell back out again. By flirting with the bitch, I've forced her to take a good look at my face. Stupid, Cain, stupid. If I take the thief now, she could give a good description of me to the police. And that just will not do.*

He'd put his identity at risk for the sake of a minute or two of banter with a pretty girl. Not good when you are the United States' current most prolific and undetected serial murderer.

Making matters worse, it wasn't even as if he needed to lure the thief outside. While the receptionist had checked the ledger, Cain had watched her fingers pointing out the room number of the owner of the SUV. Why bother ambushing him in the exposed parking lot when he could go on up, knock on his door, and call him by name?

Time for plan B.

Cain spun around, but all trace of Astaire was gone from his light tread. Once more, he headed directly for the entrance door. Quick inhalation for effect, then he bustled into the hotel with feigned urgency. The woman was midway between closing the ledger and reaching for a telephone. Thankfully, she never reached the receiver. Her startled expression was a mixture of delight and regret as Cain jogged to the counter and slapped down the palms of his hands.

"Hi," he said. "It's just me again."

The woman still wore the startled look. She visibly fought to regain her composure, achieving the fixed stare and open mouth of an inflatable sex toy. Not that Cain had any experience of *those* kinds of things.

"You haven't called the SUV owner yet, have you?" Cain asked in breathless fashion. As the woman shook her head, he went on, "Seems I might have been a little premature coming in about the lights. While I was inside, the owner must've come back out and turned them off."

"They're off now?" the woman echoed.

"Yeah, I guess there must be another exit. I didn't see anyone leave while I was in here."

"There are a number of exits. I suppose he could've used one of them." The ledger was still beside her, and she flipped it open with professional dexterity. She nodded confirmation. "Yeah, he's got a room at the back, so he could've used the rear stairwell. I guess from his room he could see his car and noticed that his lights were still on."

"That's probably it," Cain agreed.

"Okay," the woman said. Her face had regained its natural elasticity and a smile was beginning to bloom.

"Okay," Cain replied, giving her his version of a sheepish smile. "I feel a complete idiot now."

The woman crinkled her nose at him. "What for?"

"I must look like the dead battery vigilante or something." Cain laughed. "I just thought I'd come back in and let you know everything's fine now. Save you the trouble of phoning."

"It's not a problem," she said.

"Yeah, but the owner would've been wondering what the heck was going on."

"I'm sure he wouldn't have minded," she said. "In fact, I dare say he'd have told me he'd already been out and turned them off. That would've been that, I guess."

"Yeah, I suppose so."

"Anyway, thanks again for going to so much trouble."

"No problem. Just doing my bit."

"Dead battery vigilante." The woman smiled at him, crooking a finger in his direction. "Sounds like a super-hero."

"You got it," Cain said. A flippant gesture of his head and hands fisted on his hips made him more Boy Wonder than Man of Steel.

They both laughed as he walked away the second time. Before he reached the door, she called to him.

"Are you sticking around town for a while?"

Cain looked back at her, feigning disappointment. "No. Just passing through, I'm afraid. On my way to the East Coast. Have to be in Mississippi early next week for a sales convention."

Now it was the woman's turn to look dejected. "That's a shame."

"It is," Cain agreed. "But hey, who knows what's around the corner? I might be back this way in a month or so."

She gave him a lopsided smile.

"Well, if you're passing and you notice any lights on, give me a call, will you?"

Cain lifted his fingers as if they were a gun and feigned shooting her. "You got it, lady. If your battery is running down you can count on me."

Quickly he left the lobby to the sound of laughter.

"Dimwit could do with a couple of thousand volts up her ass," he assured himself.

Directly across the entry drive ran a walkway that led into the parking lot. From there he followed the side of the building, past bougainvillea shrubs arranged to add a little privacy to the rooms on the ground floor. At the rear of the hotel the grounds were laid out like an exclusive garden, verdant with golf-course-perfect lawns and bursting with color in the proliferation of flowering plants. The grounds contained a private swimming pool.

There were a couple of female guests sitting out in bathing suits, drinking from glasses smeared with lipstick. Cain sneaked a peek at them. Ordinarily he might have lingered and enjoyed the show. Sadly, neither of them was pretty enough to hold his interest. He paid them no attention, searching instead for the stairway the receptionist had mentioned. He saw it within seconds, a tiled staircase leading up to balconies on the two higher floors. Chancing a stiff neck, he craned upward, seeking door numbers. Then, happy with what he saw, he rapidly moved away, skirting the building and returning to the parking lot.

Time for plan C.

He took the scaling knife from his jacket pocket as he approached the SUV. Kneeling down by the rear tire, he thrust the blade into the rubber seal next to the wheel hub. Pulling the knife out again, he noted that the narrow slash was barely detectable, but the almost inaudible hiss of escaping air was encouraging.

"That'll hold you for a while," he whispered. A flat tire would royally piss off someone who couldn't even be bothered to rub a little dust on the license plate.

He dropped the knife back in his pocket and straightened out his clothes as he returned to his own vehicle. The vintage VW Beetle had gone the way of the dinosaurs. Not that he required the intervention of a planet-destroying meteor; he'd merely dumped it in a dry canal bed, then set it ablaze. It was quick work to replace it with an undistinguished light blue Oldsmobile.

On the rear bumper was a sticker some might think pathetic: I BRAKE FOR WILDLIFE. Though he tempted discovery by leaving such a distinct identifier on the car, he'd allowed it to stay in place. For one, it added to the disguise he'd adopted of a meek-mannered salesperson, plus it was a statement that actually resonated with him. Though he had no qualms whatsoever about butchering those of his own species, he had no desire to harm any other living creature. Faced with running down a rabbit or swerving into a line of children on a Sunday school outing, there would be only one choice in his mind. Sunday school would be missing a number of snot-nosed brats next week.

The temperature inside the Oldsmobile was a lot cooler than anticipated. When he'd driven the car here, the sun had made the heat inside almost intolerable. That's the drawback when appropriating an older-model car: no climate control. Plus the driver's window had a fault and he'd been unable to open it with the rotating arm. Oh how he suffered for his art!

When he'd driven into the parking lot, he'd left the car beneath a stand of palm dates to conceal it from the view of traffic on the interstate. His fortuitous choice had also brought him some welcome shade.

Settling in the driver's seat, he prepared for a long wait. To pass the time, he took one of the film-wrapped packages from his pocket and teased the contents within. Kind of gnarly now, but they'd polish up nice. He imagined that the fingers were those of the rosy-cheeked receptionist. Yes, he could be in for a long wait, but he was happy to do so with his mind thus engaged.

15

HARVEY HAD DONE A DECENT JOB OF MONITORING the movements of Sigmund Petoskey. True to Harvey's word, as soon as the third-generation immigrant finished his daytime business, he headed out to the derelict building Rink had shown me earlier. He left in an entourage of three vehicles that snaked their way from the opulent business center to the run-down building, driving in a fashion that said he wasn't concerned about police patrols pulling him over. In our rental car, Rink and I followed at a discrete distance.

When Petoskey ignored a red light, we pulled up; it wasn't necessary to keep a close tail when we knew where he was headed.

The lights were reflected in Rink's gaze.

"You up for this, Rink?" I asked.

He sniffed. "Ready."

"Things could get messy," I said. "But I can't think of a better way to shake Petoskey than raiding him in the place where he feels safest."

"You take guns into a man's house, things always get messy." He gave me a melancholy shake of his head.

"Been a while since you done any wet work?" I asked.

"Been a while, yeah. But it never leaves you, Hunter." Rink looked across at me, and for a moment didn't have to say more. Only those who have taken another man's life would know what we were imagining. He was right. It doesn't matter how hard you try to bury the memories, they never leave you.

The green light saved us further agony.

When we arrived at the old redbrick building, Petoskey's entourage had lined up in the lot to its right. As well as the original three, they'd been joined by a further two cars and a van.

A couple of bored guards stood to one side, nonchalant as they sucked at cigarettes. They weren't expecting trouble. They were there for appearance's sake.

These guards were of no immediate concern. We'd be going in via a different route and would not be seen by them. I was more apprehensive about the number of street people who wandered around the area. We were strangers, and they'd be suspicious of us. None of us knew—Harvey included—if the bums were belligerent to Petoskey or not. It'd ruin our chances of bearding King Siggy in his castle if any of them went running to him. I doubted anyone would do that out of loyalty, but the promise of a reward would be too much of a temptation for some.

Discretion *is* the better part of valor, and don't let anyone tell you otherwise. Rather than chance early discovery, we parked our vehicle the best part of half a mile from the building, donned shabby clothes we'd purchased from a thrift store, and then wandered in on foot. My SIG Sauer was tucked in the waistband of my trousers, my KA-BAR down my boot. Rink, however, had a shotgun to conceal. Without the luxury of a violin case, he carried his over-under 12-gauge in a large carry-on bag. To further disguise the gun, he raided a nearby Dumpster and pushed in a few old tin cans and a bundle of newspapers and magazines. On cursory inspection, his carry-on would pass for the sum of a bum's possessions.

The walk in took about ten minutes, but it was just what we needed to shake off the cobwebs of inactivity. Feeling keyed up, we took a position opposite Petoskey's building.

Behind a chain-link fence was another small building. It had also suffered over the years. The roof was gone, no windows remained, and the interior was the domain of rats. Even the graffiti were faded. No discerning street person would take up residence there.

We entered through a hole in the fence, negotiated a weed-choked courtyard, and entered the building through a doorless void. We had to then push our way through heaped rubbish to one of the abandoned offices from which we could watch and wait. The sunset was a raw wound on the horizon.

Without spoiling the decor, Rink emptied the junk from his bag. He checked the shotgun and seemed satisfied. He fed shells into it while peering out the window. Following his gaze, I saw that lights had come on behind the plastic sheeting on the upper floor. Though muted, shadows wove sinuous patterns on the sheeting as people moved through the rooms.

"I'd like to know what the hell's going on up there," I said.

"Don't hear nothing," Rink replied. "My guess is he's got a cook shop going."

It was a likelihood that Petoskey had some kind of lab going up there, producing crack cocaine or methamphetamine. On two counts, we were going to have to take care going in. If indeed it was a crack lab, inside there could be innocents who had been forced into this unwholesome line of work. Plus, the scum guarding the production line would be packing weapons. Scum with weapons plus innocent bystanders were never good mathematics.

"I don't know, Rink. Could be something else."

The location wasn't sitting right with me. Okay, we were in a run-down area of town, but normally crack labs weren't as public as this. People didn't turn up in limousines to conduct a quality control inspection, even if a few of the local cops had been paid to turn a blind eye.

Something I didn't doubt: whatever was going on, it was something illegal. We'd be in dangerous territory. "Looks like your standard one-two assault," I said to Rink.

He nodded slowly.

Where only two soldiers are involved in infiltrating an enemy stronghold, we always used a strategy termed a one-two maneuver. Like the name, there's nothing fancy about it. Advancing single file, the first—or point—man would engage and take out the enemy while the second would move on to the next position. Roles would then reverse, and so on, until the high ground was gained and no enemy was left behind to cause further trouble.

Of course, there are inherent problems with such tactics. It leaves way too much to chance and the ability of the individual soldier to neutralize the opposition. If things go wrong, the mission has to be aborted in rapid fashion. In the past, I've had worse experiences gaining exit than I have in the initial assault. Because of this, I prefer the less formal sobriquet of "smash and dash."

It remained our choice of approach on this occasion simply because it was all we had the numbers for. Maybe I should've allowed Harvey Lucas to join us. With three men, it lessens the chance that the enemy can outflank you. But not by much.

"Where do you suggest we start?" Rink asked. His expression was flat, but this was a front. Lights burned behind his eyes, and I knew that he was anxious.

I pointed out the opposite end of the building from where the guards patrolled. "See the fire escape? I'm guessing that there are doors at each floor. We'll go in through one of them, huh?"

Rink inclined his chin in agreement.

On its lowest floor the doors were most likely locked as tight as a miser's billfold. But the myriad broken windows would give us easy access.

It was a waiting game. The sun went down, and shadows

moved in like furtive burglars in the night. The lights behind the plastic grew brighter. Like zombies from some B movie, the street people drifted from their daytime hideaways, moving off in search of what they needed to feed their vices. More vehicles arrived. From our position, we couldn't make out how many people arrived, but from the excited yapping, someone had brought a couple of dogs with them.

"You hear what I'm hearing?" Rink asked.

"Yup. But you didn't expect this to be easy, did you?"

"*Easy* ain't a word in our vocabulary, Hunter."

Maybe the dogs were extra security Siggy employed after dark. I severely doubted that he was conducting doggy obedience classes. Rink and I shared a glance. Dogs, large or small, always made extreme stealth an issue.

We waited another half hour before leaving. Rink went first, shambling out through the gap in the fence. His pace was that of a man addled with drink and with no firm destination in mind. When he was out of sight around the side of the building, it was my turn to follow.

I followed the same route, joining Rink in the deep well of murk at the side of the building. There was an overpowering stench of vomit and urine. Welcome home, Hunter. It doesn't matter where my work takes me, it's always the same. I was only pleased that I couldn't see what I was standing in.

"Ready?" Rink whispered. He had the shotgun out of its bag, ready for action. I pulled out my SIG, held it at my side.

"Ready," I said.

Mounting the first set of stairs on a rusted fire escape, my mission to discover the whereabouts of my brother was finally under way. Whether or not John was inside the building, I wasn't sure. Petoskey was, and he knew something about John's disappearance. Taking Petoskey was the order of the day.

Gaining the first landing, I laid a hand on the door. The locking bar, like much of the remainder of the building, was an item lost in the past desecration of this place. The door swung open at the slightest tug. Rink immediately stepped past me, sweeping the darkness with his shotgun.

"Clear," he whispered, and I entered.

We stood still, acclimating ourselves to the ambient light leaking in from outside and listening to the natural sounds of the building. Far above, voices formed a discordant chorus. Someone was laughing. Then there were the dogs. No longer were they yapping, but snarling and barking maniacally.

"Dogfights," I whispered.

"Son of a bitch," Rink snarled. In the half-light, I saw his face grow hard. "I'm going to feed the punk his own balls."

"Yeah," I agreed. For one instant my mind shifted half a world away and I saw my own dogs, Hector and Paris. The thought of their being forced to fight to the death for the sick pleasure of the likes of Petoskey was enough to sicken even the stone-cold assassin in me.

Shake the anger loose, Hunter, I cautioned myself. It was bad enough that we were going in outnumbered. Never mind doing it in the wrong frame of mind. Go in in a rage and we'd be dead before we reached the next floor. I reached out in the dark to grab Rink's forearm.

"Go easy," I cautioned him.

"I'm cool," Rink replied. And I knew that he was.

"Okay. You take point."

"You want I go up or across?" Rink asked.

"Across," I said. In all likelihood, this stairwell was used exclusively by the dropouts who squatted here during the daylight hours. We had to go up by the route Petoskey would take, to ensure that we took out any possible reinforcements.

The corridor could have been a set from a horror movie. Cobwebs brushed our faces. Dust sifted from above and clung to my lips. From behind closed doors, the specters of this place tittered at our bravado. They beckoned to us; *come and join us in hell, there's plenty of room for two more.*

The far end of the corridor didn't come too soon for me.

Rink was waiting in a vestibule area. A door that had once held wire-reinforced glass but was now blocked by a tarpaulin hung on bent nails, barred our progress. The faint buzz of conversation filtered from beyond.

"What do you think?" Rink whispered.

Ever the smart one, I made a quick calculation. Held up three fingers to Rink. Not that he didn't trust me; Rink placed his face at the edge of the tarpaulin to confirm the estimate. We moved back down the corridor a safe distance.

"Two guys on the stairs. Looks like another one sitting down in a chair to the left of the door, but I could only see his feet."

"Armed?" I asked Rink.

"Nothing I could see." Rink shrugged. "Doesn't mean anything. They could still be packing."

Armed or not, it didn't mean a thing. I could chew my lips all day, but it wouldn't change our options. "We treat them like they're armed. Okay?"

"Yup," Rink said, hefting the shotgun so the barrel was skyward.

It's not what you want—and to be fair, it didn't lie straight with either of us—because it meant we were going in with what's known in our trade as extreme prejudice. In layman's terms: shoot to kill. These weren't international terrorists or even enemy soldiers, just half-assed gangland hoods. Killing them was extreme. Maybe too extreme under the circumstances. As Rink had reminded me last night, we didn't have a license to kill anymore.

"No, Rink, we can't. You happy with defense only?" I suggested.

Talk about weight coming off shoulders. I'd swear we both grew a head taller.

"Okay," I said. "We only shoot when necessary. Otherwise it's hand-to-hand."

"I'm happy with that," Rink said.

Rink again laid an eye to the edge of the tarpaulin. His raised thumb showed no change to the tableau.

Okay, we're rolling. Action!

Rink ripped aside the tarpaulin and stepped into the hallway beyond. I was a fraction of a beat behind him.

Confusion is the result of prolonged inactivity dramatically kick-started into life. The three men in the stairwell were caught catching flies, with their hands in the cookie jar, with their trousers down, whatever your choice of metaphor. The sudden intrusion of two armed men in their midst caused shocked silence. But that was only one frame of the action. Time jumped to fast-forward.

To my left a man erupted out of a wicker chair. He had a sawed-off across his lap and was snatching for it. It was an easy decision for me. I snapped my left hand sideways. Put a back fist strike to the bridge of his nose. The man went down into his seat like the world champion of competitive musical chairs. The fact that his hands didn't reach for his broken nose in reflex meant he was unconscious. The shotgun slipped out of his lap onto the floor and I swiped it away with the edge of my boot.

Giving them their due, the other two had more sense than to challenge Rink's shotgun. They stood like mute statues until he ordered them to come forward. The one-two was on; I immediately mounted the stairs. From below me, Rink said something. Knowing him, it would be funny, but no one was laughing. The silence was followed by the thump and scuffle of feet, and I guessed my suggestion of hand-to-hand was being followed.

The second landing was devoid of movement. I crept forward, stepping into dim light that leached from the floor above, bringing up my SIG to sweep the space before me. My darkness-adapted eyes sought the next flight of stairs. Below me, Rink mounted the stairs, and you'd assume that it was safe for me to go on. Bad move. You know what they say about assuming anything; it certainly made an ass out of me.

Maybe I'd grown a little rusty. I should have checked the corridor to my left before proceeding. As I committed

The stairwell echoed with the thump of feet. It could only be Petoskey's men looking for cover. There were four distinct voices as they called out to others in the building. Confusion was the reigning order. Someone was shouting that the police were here, while another shouted that Hendrickson's men were in the building. It didn't matter who the hell they thought they were up against; panic had turned their response deadly.

To buy a little respite, I unloaded a clip toward the head of the stairs, following my bullets with a headlong charge as I pushed another magazine in place.

Rink was still below me, snorting like a bull as he finished off the two who'd tried to take me from behind. Undoubtedly eager to finish the fight and come to my assistance. Time to wait for him wasn't a luxury I possessed. I sprinted upward to a point where there was a turn in the stairs. Suicidal I'm not, but that's what I'd have been committing if I'd poked my head around the corner for a look. Unfortunately, I had to get some kind of bead on the men waiting to ambush me. Choice made, I thrust my gun around the bend, firing three rapid shots. Just enough to force my ambushers to dive for cover. I spun into the cordite cloud searching for movement.

No one in sight, I sprang up the remaining stairs and into a recess on the left. I run regularly, occasionally go to the gym, yet I was still blowing hard. I blame it more on adrenaline dump than lack of condition.

The wall next to my shoulder was holed by one of my own bullets. I quickly pushed myself deeper into the recess, firing off two more rounds into the quiet corridor. There were doors lining the corridor on both sides, and any one of them could be concealing an enemy shooter.

"Rink! Are you about done down there or what? I could do with that shotgun up here."

Rink appeared on the stairs below me. Blood was seeping from a shallow nick below his left eye. Other than that, he appeared unhurt.

"One of the punks thought he'd do me with a set of brass

knuckles," Rink said. He dabbed away blood with the back of his wrist. "I soon knocked that silly notion out of his skull."

"Get yourself up here and give me some cover," I whispered to him. "Sounds like they're holed up in a room on my right."

Rink came up the stairs, feeding shells into his shotgun. There was blood on the stock. Thug with brass knuckles versus Rink wielding a shotgun like a club: no contest.

"I'm going to try and get by that door there. If it looks like it's about to open, give 'em hell."

"Leave it to me," Rink said. He moved to the head of the stairs where he could get a line on the door I'd indicated.

Cat-footed, I moved forward, my gun extended before me. The defenders behind the door had to know I was moving into the corridor, but there was nothing for it: I had to go forward. We had to stop them and stop them fast. I feared the arrival of reinforcements who'd be able to pen us in from below. Then there was the other consideration. That Petoskey was making a quick exit by another route. If he got away from us now, it'd probably be impossible to get a second chance at him.

Passing the door on the right, I nodded for Rink to follow, and he thumped up the corridor like Frankenstein's monster. True to form, the door exploded into splinters. Even the wall opposite was shredded, the bullets continuing into the rooms beyond.

As the first barrage ended, I swung in front of the shattered door, emptying my clip through the wood. Men yelled inside the room, one of them making a series of gasps. I'd hit one of them at least. That left—what?—three more?

Rink lifted a boot and smashed open the door. Immediately he blasted the interior of the room before swinging back out of sight. Two seconds of carnage were all I required to insert a full clip of ammo. Exchanging positions with choreographed precision, I opened up, firing off bullets as quickly as I could squeeze the trigger. Then I was in the room and had moved left as Rink let off another full load of pellets.

Armed confrontations do not resemble John Woo's battles of balletic gunplay; any somersaulting or leaping through space discharging bullets is reserved for the movies. Reality is not so pretty. I slammed my back to a wall, my gun out before me, and emptied it at every target that moved. I was shouting something that was unintelligible even to me. An animal shout of loathing, fear, and unrestrained rage.

It took all of a few seconds to deplete my gun of bullets, yet I felt as spent as the bullet casings littering the floor at my feet.

Rink hustled into the room, the stock of his shotgun to his shoulder as he sought targets. Smoke hung in the air. So did the unmistakable tang of blood. One man was huddled in a corner of the room, hands over his head as he sobbed in terror. Another was sprawled over a coffee table, a hole the size of a baby's fist in his shoulder. The man murmured, delirious in his agony.

That accounted for two of them, but I couldn't see where the other two were. As Rink covered the cowering man, I ejected my empty clip and inserted a fresh one. Rink moved over to the open window. Sounds of flight ricocheted from the fire escape beyond.

"Careful," I said. Both to Rink and as a warning to the man who cringed away from the business end of my SIG. Rink gave me a wry grin as he approached the window.

"Like rats down a drainpipe," he observed. "Two of them are running for it."

"Let them run," I said. The cowering man peeked up at me through tears and smeared snot. I nudged him with a boot. "Where's John Telfer?"

In those old Poe books, victims of terror often gave out a keening wail. I'd never heard one for real and couldn't imagine what one sounded like. Until now.

I nudged him harder. "I said, 'Where's Telfer?' I won't ask again."

He must have read something in my face. Maybe my hesitancy to kill in cold blood. Whatever it was, his demeanor suddenly changed. "Go to hell, asshole."

"So now you're the brave guy?" I put the muzzle of my gun to the center of his forehead. "You don't think I'll do it? Try me."

As suddenly, he was wailing again.

"Where's Telfer?" I asked.

"I don't know who you mean. Speak to Petoskey, man. Not us. For God's sake . . . don't kill me."

I took the gun from his skull. There was a scarlet ring where the hot metal had pressed into his flesh. "Second question, and the rules haven't changed. Where's Petoskey?"

He wanted to resist. Perhaps it was bravado, but more likely it was fear of his boss that held his tongue. Back went the gun.

"Where's Petoskey?"

Fear of a bullet in the skull now or *perhaps* one later from Petoskey if he survived; I could see the math going around in his head. It was a simple equation.

He nodded upward, eyes on the ceiling above.

"He's upstairs?" I asked.

The man nodded again.

"How many with him?"

"How the hell should I know?" the man spluttered.

"Guess," I said.

"Three, four . . . I don't know. Could be as many as a dozen for all I know!"

"Armed?"

"What do you think?"

It was a stupid question.

"Yes. It's the end of the line, buddy," I said. Then I slammed the butt of my gun against his temple, sprawling him sideways across the floor.

"Maybe you should plug him and be done with it," Rink said from behind me.

Was that really my friend speaking?

"Can't do it."

"I know it's not right, but it makes more sense. We don't want to be going up there, leaving one of them behind us. Not when he's armed."

"You're right. But I'm not a murderer."

Rink's gaze sought the man with the new open-vent shoulder.

"He'll survive. Anyway, that was different," I said. "He was trying to kill me. But I won't kill a man in cold blood."

Rink winked at me, his stern face softening. "Just checking, my old friend," he said. "Like I said last night, we don't have a license to kill no more."

"I hear you," I told him. And I meant it. But we still had a job to do, and it was my firm guess that others would die this night. My only hope was that it wouldn't be either of us.

16 THERE HE WAS.
The thief.

Purloiner of second-favorite knives and sports utility vehicles. He was just as Tubal Cain remembered him, though subtly altered, he had to admit. A handsome enough bloke as thieves go. Aged in his early thirties. He was dressed the way a million other guys were, in nondescript casual clothing with a ball cap down to his ears. The sum of his possessions in a knapsack slung from one shoulder. It was the same knapsack he'd carried when he carjacked Cain yesterday. Mirror-lensed sunglasses concealed his eyes.

In essence, the thief was very similar to Cain, Mr. Normal blending in with his surroundings. The thought had occurred already, but now, watching the man who'd signed his name in the hotel's register as David Ambrose, Cain came to a conclusion. "You're hiding your true identity as carefully as I am. Why is that?"

One thing was for sure, Ambrose wasn't hiding from Cain. He had no way of knowing that Cain would hunt him down. In his mind, Cain had been nothing but a hopeless freak he'd left out in the middle of nowhere.

"I'll tell you why. It means that you are afraid of someone else."

Cain leaned back in the driver's seat of the Oldsmobile, chewing his lower lip. Now this was an unexpected turn of events.

"Who are you running from, Mr. So-Called-Ambrose?"

he whispered as he watched Ambrose approach the SUV. "Who is it that frightens you more than Tubal Cain?"

Ambrose gave off a vibe. An electrostatic buzz of anticipation. Almost as if he were steeling himself for a sniper's bullet between the shoulder blades. It was the subconscious way he moved, trying his damndest to appear nonchalant, yet at the same time with a posture as taut as piano wire. He could pretend not to, but Cain knew that behind the mirrors of his shades, Ambrose glanced around, alert as a mouse in a rattlesnake's den. Turning, the sunlight and dappled shadows of palms played across his glasses. Cain thought of a beetle's eyes.

The insectlike gaze skimmed over the Oldsmobile, pausing for less than a heartbeat before passing on. There was a momentary pinching of the thief's lips as he scanned the car, but the strained expression was gone in the next instant. No, it was merely an unconscious reaction, not recognition. In the shadows of his parking spot, Cain felt protected from the amateur who'd made too many mistakes.

Approaching the SUV, Ambrose dug for keys in a trouser pocket. Unhitching the knapsack from his shoulder, he unlocked the driver's door and slung the bag onto the passenger seat. Another glance around gave Cain the impression of one of those hopeless spies that Napoleon Solo—and that guy with the Russian-sounding name that Cain could never recall, let alone pronounce—used to thwart every week in *The Man from U.N.C.L.E.*

Cain saw the headlights flick on. The engine coughed to life like a grizzly stirring from hibernation. The SUV barely rolled forward a couple of yards before braking violently. Ambrose had forgotten all about subtlety and blending in, if the way he stomped to the back of the vehicle was anything to go by.

"Gotcha," Cain said.

Ambrose crouched down by the flat tire, running his hands over it as though he could magically restore it by touch alone. Unfortunately, he was no sorcerer. Defeated, he stood up with his hands on his hips, and even heard from across the parking lot his language was choice.

It would be so simple to come up behind Ambrose while he was distracted. Push the point of his scaling knife into the juncture of his neck and clavicle. Dig down for the vital organs in one rapturous moment. End him right there and then. At his leisure, Cain could search the dead man's possessions and regain that which belonged to him.

"Yes, that's as it could be."

That *was* exactly as his plan had gone. By now it was hours later, his discussion with the dippy receptionist wouldn't be connected to an apparent mugging gone wrong. Cain could go merrily on his way, his sense of justice appeased.

"But, thief, that isn't how it's going to be."

The enigma of Ambrose's true identity, and what it was—who it was—he was hiding from, was enough to give pause to anyone with an inquiring mind. And don't let it be said that Tubal Cain was not a deep thinker. Yes, his needs might be basic, but he thought long on the ways of fulfilling those needs.

His curiosity was more than piqued. It was on turbodrive. He wanted to let this play out a little longer. "Who knows, thief," he decided, "it might make for an interesting conclusion."

17

EVENTS OVERTOOK OUR PLAN WAY TOO QUICKLY for my liking. Not that I was surprised; isn't that always the way plans go? That's always been the flaw with our tactics. Murphy's Law strikes again.

It was no longer a case of a one-two move, but a full head-long charge for the top.

The man I'd knocked unconscious didn't give me enough to make a considered judgment. There could be as few as three men with Petoskey or as many as a dozen. Think the worst, and anything else is a bonus.

It was a full balls-to-the-wall assault.

We headed for the upper floor with our guns blasting. The intent wasn't to shoot anyone per se, but to cause as much confusion as possible. Petoskey was a rat, and everyone knows what rats do on a sinking ship. I ruled out the fire escape at this corner of the building, guessing that Petoskey would head for the one we'd used to gain access.

"I'm going back across, cut off any escape route," I told Rink. "You okay with that?"

He racked the pump action. "As long as I've got ammo, I'll give 'em hell."

"When the shooting stops, I want you to come up and join me as quickly as you can."

"Damn, and here was me thinking it was time for a coffee break."

"After we're done I'll buy you coffee and doughnuts."

"Make 'em jelly doughnuts and you've got a deal."

"Sounds good to me."

Another volley of fire gained the attention of those on the populated side. I backtracked across the building.

Speed was an issue. Call me cautious, but I made my way through the building as though every nook hid an assassin. Better a minute late than thirty years too early at the pearly gates.

The remains of the door Rink had blasted were like an open mouth full of jagged teeth. The room beyond exuded the stench of battle like sour breath. Apart from the stink, the room was now empty. The unconscious man had obviously come to, and he wasn't as ill informed about our chances as he was making out. At least he'd had the sense to get the hell away from the shitstorm raging above. The man who had taken a bullet in the shoulder was gone, too. A smear of blood on the window ledge confirmed their escape route.

Happy that no one would come on me from behind, I ran along the corridor. Behind me, the boom of Rink's shotgun resonated as he unloaded it toward the upper floor.

I headed upward on the other staircase. Natural functions sometimes take a backseat when adrenaline shrieks through your veins; I took the full flight of stairs before I remembered to breathe. At the top I paused to exhale, sucked in air, then stepped out into a corridor much shorter than the one I'd passed through below.

A little over thirty feet away, the corridor had been blocked. What appeared to be a new metal door had been installed. It reverberated under the ring of urgent voices from beyond. A background accompaniment of baying dogs and shotgun blasts confirmed that I'd found Petoskey's hideout.

Cursory inspection of the metal door told me it was a nogo. There was no handle on this side, no keyhole. The soldier in me said it would be almost impregnable to anything short of heavy artillery. Abandoning the door, I stepped into the office on my left. There was the usual jumble of wrecked furniture and scattered documents.

I made my way to the wall and put an ear to it. I was quite

sure that all the action was at the far end, and the possibility of getting hot lead in my ear was pretty slim.

The wall was made of Sheetrock, and by the swollen roar of activity beyond it I could tell it wasn't as heavily fortified as the door. I crouched down and took the KA-BAR from my boot.

It took less than a minute to cut away a torso-sized portion of the wall. Beyond was a second layer of the same substance. Why the Americans called this brittle stuff Sheetrock always amused me. Using only the tip of my knife, I bored a small circle in the plaster and peered into Petoskey's hideout.

As if on cue, Rink stopped firing. Makes me wonder if the link we share exceeds mere intuition and laps at the shore of the preternatural. Then again, he may have been reloading his shotgun. Whatever, the lull in activity was just what I needed.

Through my peephole, I could see an open room that ran the breadth of the building. A group of men gathered by a second doorway at the far end had to be the hired guns. Their attention was on the stairwell below them. Two more men held pit bull terriers on leashes. The dogs were blood-soaked and torn in a number of places. Unconcerned by the madness of humans, they strained at their leashes to continue their own private war. That meant that the final three men standing by a jerry-built arena in the center of the floor were the highfliers. One of them had to be Sigmund Petoskey.

Okay, quick calculation and what did I have?

Ten men in total.

Two dogs.

It wasn't the most difficult summation.

The real question was: Could I handle them all?

Whether or not I was capable wasn't an issue. I was going to, and that was it.

18

WHEN I WAS A SMALL CHILD, I LIVED IN A HOME poor in money but rich in love. What my parents were unable to provide in fine food and modern conveniences, they made up for with hugs and kisses and quality time spent with their only child. I don't miss having little in the way of material belongings, but I do miss my dad.

After my dad died and my mother remarried, things changed. I still didn't possess the treasures children yearn for, but I did get a little brother. But then it was my brother who got more of the hugs and kisses. And I looked elsewhere for comfort.

My father instilled in me a love of books. Where other kids got stereo record players and portable TVs in their bedrooms, I had a collection of dog-eared novels passed down to me by my dad. Poe, Lovecraft, and R. E. Howard were my favorites. Next in line came the comic book superheroes that I grew into when a newspaper delivery route gave me the pocket money to spend on treats. Sometimes I wonder if the books taught me about the horrors of our world, while the superheroes taught me how to deal with them. Whatever, they did give me a fertile imagination.

Probably explained why I envisioned myself as the Incredible Hulk when I erupted through the wall. The Hulk had an extraordinary strength he used against his enemies, but I didn't have that luxury. I came out shooting in a spray of dust and plaster particles.

I didn't aim to hit anyone and fired above their heads.

Combined with my Hulk act, it was enough to startle every-one into immobility. Only the dogs responded with panic, circling and ensnaring their handlers with their leashes as they spun.

"No one move or the next bullet will kill you," I shouted. In reality, if all of them had turned on me at once, I wouldn't have stood a chance. The thing was, without exception, ev-eryone thought I was shouting directly at him. No one wants to be a dead hero.

"Guns on the floor," I shouted as I took a half-dozen paces into the room. The three men nearest me weren't armed. They thrust their hands toward the ceiling.

The dog handlers were too busy trying to untangle them-selves to pay me immediate attention. Stuck between me and Rink, who approached the opposite door at a gallop, the five guards at the far end quickly dropped their weapons and kicked them away.

"Inside the room, boys," I heard Rink shout. His voice jostled them like bowling pins.

My unorthodox entrance, not to mention the demand-ing muzzle of my SIG, commanded compliance. The three men by the fighting arena moved quickly toward the plastic-shrouded wall, their hands seeking heaven.

A shadow in the doorway morphed into Rink. It was good to see the big guy again. He shot me a wink as he ushered the five goons before him.

"Get your butts in the ring and sit on your hands," Rink told them. They crowded into the center of the fighting area. Space was at a premium as they jostled to be farthest away from the 12-gauge. Rink turned to the two dog handlers. "You, too."

One of the handlers, a skinny youth with a huge nose cov-ered in acne, twisted his face at Rink. He was uglier than his mutt. At least the dog had an excuse; it had already gone a couple of rounds.

"Got a problem with your hearing?" Rink demanded.

"The dogs will fight," he said.

"Then it's your job to stop them, Zit Boy," Rink said. "Now get the hell in there. One of you at either end."

The big-nosed youth entered the ring first, pulling his struggling dog to him. When he was as settled as he could be, the second dog handler entered. Rink pushed the gate to, flipped a catch in place. No one moved in the arena. The tough guys huddled together. Dogs' teeth and a 12-gauge shotgun made the proverbial rock and hard place.

Harvey's surveillance shots of Sigmund Petoskey came in handy. He looked like a typical wealthy businessman. Shirt, tie, suit, and shiny shoes. Well groomed and manicured. He looked out of place in this setting. Even if I'd never viewed a photo of him, I'd have picked him out by the contempt that radiated from him.

"Hi, Siggy!" I said. "Like to bring your ass over here?"

Petoskey's eyebrows rose and he lifted a finger to his chest.

"Yeah," I confirmed. "I want a word with you."

Pointing my SIG at his chest, I indicated the bulge in his breast pocket where ordinary businessmen would carry a notebook.

"Lose the piece."

Petoskey pulled a Berretta out of the shoulder rig. Two fingers; like he'd done it before. He placed the gun on the floor at his feet, kicked it away from him.

"Okay. Get over here."

He stood his ground.

"You are making one hell of a mistake, you goddamn ass-hole," he directed at me. With his Eastern European name, you'd half expect him to have the stilted accent of a villain from a James Bond movie. You would be wrong. Just as Rink is a contradiction of his ancestry, so is Sigmund Petoskey. He spoke with the cultured tones of an Ivy Leaguer with top honors.

Admittedly, his first words weren't anything you'd expect from one of such a background. Then again, you only have to recall Rink's summing up of Siggy's childhood to imagine where the gutter language came from.

"No," I told him. "You're the one making the mistake."

"Who the hell are you, coming here and shooting up my place? My personal friend the mayor will have something to say about this!"

"I don't give a damn what the mayor says," I told him.

"He'll have your job for this," Petoskey said. He rounded on Rink. "And yours."

"Like I said," I told him, "you're the one making the mistake. We aren't police officers, Siggy. For all I care, your friend the mayor can kiss my ass."

For a second time Petoskey's eyebrows sought the top of his head.

"Not the police?"

"Not the police," I echoed.

"Then you're with Hendrickson. I should have known . . ." His words faltered at the shake of my head.

"I don't know Hendrickson from Jimmy Hendrix," I told him.

"So who the blazes are you?"

"Someone who needs answers. And I want them quickly."

Petoskey looked at his feet, gave a slow shake of his two-hundred-dollar haircut. Something dawned on him and he slowly raised his face to look at me. A scowl broke across his features. "This is about John Telfer, isn't it?"

John was indeed why I was there, but I'd expected to have to draw the information from him like rusty nails from a knotty plank.

"Where is he?" I demanded. "If you've hurt him I'll—"

Petoskey sneered. "You think I have him?"

"Maybe not here, but I believe you know where he is."

"Look," he said, stepping toward me in defiance, "I already told your friends I don't know where he is. The son of a bitch took off owing me a substantial sum of money. Do you think if I knew where he was, I *wouldn't* have brought him back by now? Jesus Christ, how many times have I got to tell you people the same damn thing?"

I didn't answer.

This wasn't a put-on. Petoskey's words rang true. He really didn't know where my brother was. So it was pointless questioning him any further regarding John's whereabouts. Time for a change of tack.

"You've already spoken to my friends?" I asked.

"Twice!" he said. Full of impotent fury, he held out his hands. An expansive gesture, taking in the entire room. "And now this?"

"Okay, Siggy. Just cool it," I told him.

"I'll do no such thing." He lifted a stubby finger toward me. "You come in here shooting and making demands. Now you want me to act reasonably toward you?"

"Unless you want me to start shooting again, you will," Rink drawled from across the room. For emphasis, he aimed the shotgun directly at the group of men in the dog-fighting pit.

Petoskey wore righteous anger like a dead man's suit. He folded his arms across his chest. Challenged Rink with a sneer. Then he turned it on me. It faltered when I shoved my SIG into the dimple on his chin.

"Tell me," I said. "Who are these *friends* that you're talking about?"

"You should know," Petoskey said.

"Indulge me," I said.

"Your friends from the government. Who else?"

It was a war to keep my features flat, but this was a surprise, and it probably showed. Petoskey misread me. Maybe it was the way I allowed my gun to drop from his chin.

"See. I knew it," he announced. His two friends nodded along with him. One of them opened his mouth to say something. I shot him a warning look. The man clammed up immediately.

To Petoskey I said, "You're saying that *CIA agents* have spoken to you about John Telfer?"

"Aren't you listening to me? Twice they've been at my office. Twice they've demanded to know the location of John Telfer. I wish I'd never seen Telfer's goddamn face!"

"These agents actually said they were CIA?" I asked.

"They didn't need to. I can smell a spook a mile off."

"So you're only guessing?" I said, with not a little hope.

Petoskey shook his head. "They didn't exactly introduce themselves, if that's what you mean. One of them flashed a badge the first time they came around; they didn't bother the second time. Pretty much the way you haven't now, eh?"

Again I didn't answer. CIA agents, by virtue of their secretive trade, aren't in the habit of flashing badges or announcing their identities. Petoskey had to be confused, must have misread the acronym on the badge. It would be easily done, I suppose, though I doubted that the Child Support Agency would go to such lengths to trace an absent father.

Judging my silence to be guilt, he said, "You can go back and tell your bosses that they're barking up the wrong tree. For the third time, *I do not know where John Telfer is*. Have you got that?"

We had lost a major advantage, and unless we started shooting again, it was an unsalvageable situation.

On the same wavelength, Rink moved toward me. His shotgun still menaced the men in the arena. No one moved. It wasn't so much the fear of being shot as that they thought we were CIA. Worse than going up against the police, they weren't prepared to risk the ire of the government. They wouldn't make a move. Apparently, neither would we. Not now that we'd been uncloaked as government agents.

Petoskey was wearing a smug look on his face.

"Quite a mess, eh?" he crowed.

Yeah, it was a mess, but not for the reason he thought. We backed toward the demolition job I'd done on the wall.

"Oh, for pity's sake. Use the door, will you?" Petoskey said.

"We'll leave as we came," I said as we continued to back out.

"Do me a favor," Petoskey called as we stepped through the hole into the abandoned office. "When you do find Telfer, tell him I want my ten grand. Plus thirty percent interest.

And you can tell him not to show his face around any of my places again. He's not welcome. Tell him he can post the money to me."

If he'd let it lie at that, I don't know where the hunt would've taken us next. As it was, like many self-righteous punks, he loved the sound of his own voice too much. "And tell him my car had better have a full tank of gas when he drops it off."

I stepped back into the opening. What a difference a couple of seconds had made. Tough guys all, the goons in the ring were already fighting their way past one of the dogs in an effort to get out. To win face with their boss, and without exception, they offered to chase us down. Petoskey and the other two suits had moved toward them, and Siggy wasn't a happy puppy.

My SIG rapped a sharp command, shattering the light fixture above their heads.

Did you ever play the children's game called Statues? You stand with your back to an advancing group, you turn around sharply, and the group has to become petrified in place, as though under a gorgon's stare. Anyone who moves is out of the game. Well, that's what it felt like then.

My gun was now a useless threat, but I aimed it anyway.

"Telfer took one of your cars?" I demanded.

"Yes," Petoskey snapped. "If you'd taken the time to read your friends' reports you would already know that."

"Must've missed it," I said. "What car are we talking about?"

"Read the damn report," Petoskey said.

I took three steps, my anger level rising with each one. Grabbing Petoskey by his lapels, I jammed the SIG under his chin with my other hand.

Petoskey's eyes went wide. That a government agent would actually have the balls to shoot him with all these witnesses standing around was now a definite possibility. Maybe I should have shot him. Undoubtedly, the world would've been a better place with one less scumbag in it.

"Just tell me what damn car you're talking about or I swear to God I'll kill you," I said.

"Pontiac," Petoskey snapped. "It's a goddamn Pontiac. Okay?"

"Write down the license number," I ordered.

"I haven't got a pen," Petoskey said.

"Find one." I pushed him away from me. Petoskey's face was scarlet. He actually stepped back toward me.

"Here," one of the other suits said quickly, pulling an expensive-looking gold-plated pen from a jacket pocket. Petoskey snatched it out of his hand, then glanced around looking for paper. Again the suit came to the rescue, tearing a page from an equally expensive pocket diary. Petoskey quickly scribbled down a number, then thrust it at me.

"Satisfied?" he asked.

I snatched the paper out of his hand.

"Thank you," I said.

"You're welcome," Petoskey said. Not that I believed him. My spite was reflected by his bilious glare. We were rival wolves meeting on a forest trail. We edged backward, neither wanting to be seen to be giving ground, but each recognizing the prudence of doing so.

Rink was at my shoulder. He made a cautious noise in the back of his throat, Rinkese for "We've outstayed our welcome, Hunter." How could I possibly disagree? It was definitely time to leave if the clamor of reinforcements charging up the far staircase was anything to go by.

We played it cool as we stepped through the hole in the wall. Then we ran like hell.

19

MR. SO-CALLED-AMBROSE WASN'T A NAME THAT came easily to the lips, so Cain decided he'd refer to him simply as *thief.* It was all he was, and he didn't deserve to be called anything else. Thief, thief, thief.

Names always fascinated Cain. To be named is the achievement of recognition, and he wasn't about to give Ambrose the honor. He was nothing in Cain's estimation. Just a bum. Below contempt. Nothing but a sneaking thief.

The thief was back in his room now. Probably wondering what to do about the flat tire. There was a spare bolted to the rear of the vehicle, but the thief appeared to be the type of man too easily defeated when it came to mechanical contrivance. He was both inept with a lug wrench and too damn lazy to use it. The latter was probably the overriding factor. Why go to the trouble of changing a defective tire when he could go steal himself another car?

Evening was fully upon the hotel now. Way out over the ocean the stars were pale glimmers on a velvet backdrop. Here, the light cast through tinted lenses onto the hotel facade was mint green and coral pink. A cornucopia of shadows jittered and danced as a faint breeze stirred the foliage.

Cain watched as the rosy-cheeked receptionist finished her shift, wandered out into the parking lot, and drove off in an imported Ford Ka. He was tempted to follow her, to act out the fantasy that had been playing through his mind these past hours. In the end, he let her go. Weighed against the risk of losing sight of the thief, it wasn't worth it. Other opportunities would arise to invite the girl back to his special place.

Cain opened the car door and stepped out onto asphalt. The air still held the heat of the day. He shrugged out of his jacket, pulled off his tie, and unbuttoned his collar. Jacket and tie went in the trunk of the car.

He wandered around the side of the building to the garden area, savoring the scent of jasmine only slightly tainted by exhaust fumes from the highway. The pool rippled under fluorescent lighting, a vibrant blue that was now unsullied by the bobbing forms of overfed children and grandmothers floating on inflatable beds.

He sauntered over to the foot of the stairs.

Act furtively and you're done for—another pearl of wisdom from his killer's rule book. Cain mounted the stairs as if he had the right to be there. He took two steps at a time, almost bounding up to the first landing. He slowed slightly as he climbed to the next floor, tilting his face down. The thief could be on his way down, and he didn't want to be recognized before he could engineer a proper reunion.

At the top of the stairs he turned slowly to the left, surveying the scene. Then, happy that no one was approaching, he walked along the terrace toward the door of the thief's room. His rubber-soled shoes squeaked on the terra-cotta tiles. He stooped down and pulled them off.

The thief's room was at the corner of the building, and the terrace terminated just to the left of the door. If the thief happened to come out now, Cain would have nowhere to hide. Immediate action wouldn't be as satisfying as the drawn-out torment he had in mind, but there would be nothing else he could do.

At the door, he bent down and placed his shoes on the floor. Minuscule drifts of sand abutted the wall next to the door, blown there on the wind, or maybe the remnants of someone walking on the beach and carrying proof of their labor back with them.

"This rule is the one that takes priority above all others,

thief," he whispered. "Be mindful of Locard's principle." That precept of forensic science held that a person left behind a small part of himself wherever he went, be it hair, saliva, semen, skin cells, clothing fibers, or soil or plant matter transported on the soles of shoes or in the folds of clothing. The list was endless. And included fingerprints.

From a trouser pocket, Cain pulled out a roll of plastic bags and some rubber bands. Cocking an ear toward the door so its opening wouldn't surprise him, he stooped down and pulled a plastic bag over each foot, stuffed the cuffs of his trousers inside, then sealed them with the rubber bands. That done, he repeated the process with his hands.

The bags were spacious and flopped at the ends of his fingertips like translucent flippers. He looked ludicrous but didn't care. The last thing the thief would think of when folds of flesh were being stripped from his body was Cain's diabolical fashion sense.

Lastly, he pulled a cloth bag from his pocket. He'd prepared eyeholes earlier, burning them into the white cloth with the cigarette lighter from the Oldsmobile. The mask made him think of the KKK. Not that he was a racist. He wasn't. Regardless of race, creed, or color, he hated everyone with equal passion.

Low and away from the balcony's edge, he slipped the bag over his head before standing up and facing the door. The eyeholes took away a little of his peripheral vision, but that was okay. He had a single intent and would be going forward from now on.

Readiness for the long-anticipated reunion required only one more thing. He reached under the tail of his shirt and pulled free the scaling knife. He held it up before his eyes, admiring the rainbow effect along its cutting edge. Sharp, so very, very sharp.

Now he was ready.

He knocked on the door.

20

MORE THAN ONE THING WAS TROUBLING ME ABOUT the whole setup. Louise Blake continued to nag at me like a bug burrowing its way through my cerebral cortex. There was much that woman knew but wasn't telling me. Her reticence, I believed, was linked to the below-the-belt strike that Sigmund Petoskey had dealt us. The CIA could be involved, and that had jarred me to the core.

"I have to make a couple of calls," I said. Harvey Lucas extended his hospitality in the manner of a southern gent, and I was going to take him up on it. The telephone was on a desk across the room.

Harvey watched with an expression that was hard to define. I caught myself in midstride. To gather our wits after such a crushing blow, we'd returned to his office—a rented unit in an industrial complex on the other side of town. Harvey seemed pleased to see us, as if we deemed him a worthwhile ally after all. However, once I'd mentioned the CIA, he didn't appear to be anywhere near as enthusiastic. Pausing with my hand over the handset, I waited for him to object. Harvey inclined his chin.

"Sure you don't mind?" I asked.

"Go ahead." He rolled his neck, then turned to his computer screen and studied it with way too much intensity.

"When you finish up, I got a call to make, too," Rink said. He was standing behind Harvey, and I saw him reach out and grip his friend's shoulder. Rink's never patronizing; his gesture was more one of reassurance. "Can you look me up the number for the Arkansas Humane Society, Harve? Gotta drop 'em a tip concerning illegal dog fighting on their turf."

Harvey nodded, then bent to the task.

"If you'd prefer I didn't use your phone, I'll go find a public phone," I said.

Harvey returned his gaze to mine.

"Go ahead and use it, Hunter. If the CIA is involved, you can bet your ass they're already aware of my involvement." He rocked back in his seat, resigned. Nerves made him more effusive than usual. "Makes no difference if you conduct your business from here or anywhere else, they'll have you hooked up in less time than it takes you to dial the number. If you've got anything to say that you don't want them to hear, I suggest you forget about phone calls altogether."

"Yeah," I agreed. But I wasn't concerned. Truth is, it didn't matter what the CIA overheard, considering that it was one of their controllers I was about to call.

A number I hadn't used in over four years leaped straight from my memory to my fingertips. From the handset, I heard the beeping of a long-distance connection as it bounced via service providers and satellites throughout the world. A phone finally rang in a nondescript office in Langley, Virginia.

The call was picked up by an electronic answering machine, which gave me options and asked me to key in a twelve-digit number. Again from long-term memory I typed in the sequence. The line went dead for a split second. In that unfathomably short space of time recording devices kicked in. It didn't matter. Then came a purr as the connection was made. The phone was picked up after only three beeps.

"This better be good," grunted a man's voice.

"That'll depend on your perspective," I grunted right back.

"My perspective is always from the bottom of a deep dark place, you should know that by now."

My laughter was humorless. "You should get out more. Get a little sunshine on your face. You spend too much time in your little cubbyhole."

"Tell me about it," the man said. Over the line came a minuscule shift in the white noise as buttons were flicked. "You can speak now, Hunter. Line's secure."

"I've got a favor to ask," I told him.

"So much for the pleasantries, huh? Straight down to business. Even after all this time."

"No time for pleasantries, I'm afraid. It could be that we're sitting on opposite sides of the fence on this one."

I heard the creak of leather: Walter Hayes Conrad IV shifting uneasily in his chair. By that subtle shift of his body, I knew I'd struck an uneasy chord with him.

"Opposite sides of the fence? I thought you were no longer in the game, Hunter?"

"I'm not in your game."

"So you're still retired?"

"Retired, yeah, but not out to pasture yet."

"I take it this is a private job we're talking about, then?"

"It was private until I heard some of your boys might be involved."

"Oh?" Walter shifted again, and I could visualize him reaching for the on switch for the recorder.

"Just give me a minute before you make our conversation public," I said.

"Like I said, Hunter, the line's secure."

"Yeah, so let's keep it that way for now?"

"You know I can't promise you that, Hunter. If this concerns one of our operations, I can't let it go off the record."

I sniffed. "All I'm asking is that you confirm if the CIA is involved."

"That'll depend."

"I appreciate that. I'm not asking for specifics. A simple yes or no will do."

"Then the answer's no."

"Is that what you term plausible denial?"

"Nah, there's nothing plausible about it."

"You're right there," I said. "Considering I haven't even told you what job I'm involved in."

"There's no need. I haven't heard your name mentioned, Hunter."

"Well, there's a surprise," I said.

"We did wonder what you were doing on our home soil," Walter said. Walter doesn't offer information for nothing.

"So you knew I was in the country?"

"Of course. What kind of intelligence community doesn't track foreign agents flying in?"

"I'm not a foreign agent, Walt. I'm retired. Remember?"

"Same difference."

It wasn't overly surprising that my presence in the USA had rung warning bells. Neither would it surprise me if Walter had already made calls to my old commanders at Arrowsake to check that I wasn't back on the payroll of the British government. Or—worse case scenario—that I was on *someone else's* payroll.

"You needn't worry, Walter. I haven't turned to the dark side."

Walter laughed as if he were choking on a bitter pill.

"So what's the deal? I know you hooked up with Jared Rington. Believe me, Hunter, we dropped it there. Not interested."

"Rink's with me now," I said. "He says hi."

"I'm sure he does," Walter said scornfully. All part of the act.

"I find it hard to believe that you aren't wondering what I'm up to," I said.

"To be honest, we ain't the least bit interested. Far as we're concerned you're here visiting your old buddy. We're prepared to leave it at that. So long as nothing else comes to our attention."

"Appreciate it, Walt. But now that I have come to your attention, how are you going to play it?"

Walter sucked air through his teeth. Not the nicest sound in your ear. "Depends on the job you're about to describe."

"The one you've already told me you're not involved in?"

"One and the same."

"Figures," I said, paraphrasing Rink. "I take it that what you're not telling me is that you've no one in Little Rock, Arkansas."

"I don't doubt we've got agents there, Hunter, but not on anything you're involved in."

"You're sure about that?"

"How can you doubt me? I don't have anyone on your case. Okay?"

"Okay, that's good enough for me." I paused, considering my next words. It was a gamble mentioning anything about the job I was involved in, but it was probably too late for that now. By calling Walter, I'd guaranteed that the CIA would indeed be watching me from now on. "What about my brother, John Telfer?"

Up in his office at Langley, Walter Hayes Conrad IV went silent.

"I take it by your silence that his name means something to you?"

Walter breathed into the mouthpiece. Was that remorse?

"It does, Hunter, but not for the reason you're thinking."

"I'm thinking you've got guys on him."

"Nope. It's not that at all."

Judging by the ache between my eyebrows, my face was fertile ground begging for a frown. I was afraid to ask. "What is it then?"

"I take it you haven't looked at the TV lately?"

"No time for TV."

"Make time. If you're interested in John Telfer, you'd better get yourself acquainted with CNN. Telfer's currently their number one news slot."

I turned from the phone. "You got a TV, Harve?"

"Got one at home. Why?"

"What about your computer? Can you get CNN?"

"The news channel? Sure."

"Do me a favor and log on, will you?"

Harvey's eyebrows danced toward his shaved head. Rink was watching me expectantly. A shrug was all I offered before turning my attention back to Walter. "I'm just about to take a look now."

"Might explain a thing or two."

"So what's the deal?" I asked him.

"Take a look and make up your own mind."

"Fair enough," I said. "But you're telling me this isn't anything to do with you?"

"No matter how many ways I tell you no, you're still going to have reservations, Hunter."

"Old habits die hard," I told him.

"You doubt my honesty, but that's okay, I don't bear any grudges. If I were in your shoes, I'd be the same. For the record, I'll say it again. Then it's up to you . . ." His breath came slow and steady. The pause was not for his benefit. Bad news was coming. "The CIA is not on your case. We're not on your brother's case. But then again, I can't speak for the rest of the civilized world. Or the FBI, in particular."

"The FBI?"

"Just watch the news. You'll see what I mean."

"Okay, Walt. I appreciate your help."

"No problem," he said. "Good speaking to you again, Hunter."

"Likewise." I paused, considering. Then, "Walt, seeing as you've been so open with me, there's something I have to tell you."

"Go on."

"I was involved in a job an hour or so ago. Guy I was up against said he'd been visited by some of your boys asking about John."

"Wasn't us."

"I appreciate that. But I think you might want to look into who's going round posing as government agents. Might cause a stink for you if something goes wrong."

"I get it now. That's why you wanted to check in with me?"

"Yeah. Just in case I have to defend myself."

"They're not mine, Hunter. So . . . *stay safe.*"

Stay safe. This from a sub-division director of black ops.

In other words, Walter had just given official sanction to retaliate with lethal force if that situation should arise. What's known in the trade as an executive decision.

"Thanks, Walt."

Walter isn't big on pleasantries. I was left holding a handset issuing the soft purr of a dead line.

Something popped up on Harvey's computer screen. I set the phone back in its cradle. All I could think of to say was "Shit."

With equal lack of verbosity, Rink cursed loudly. After a beat, Harvey joined in.

On the screen of Harvey's computer were headlines I could barely comprehend.

FBI CLOSES IN ON MASS KILLER
THE HARVESTMAN FINALLY NAMED

Beneath the headlines was a photograph of my little brother.

21

CAIN KNOCKED AGAIN.
    Louder this time.

Again there was no answer. Frowning beneath his im-promptu hood, he stepped to the side of the door. By press-ing close to the glass, he could make out any movement from within. Or in this case, lack of movement.

No one home? How unbelievable is that?

Letting out a sigh, he pulled the hood free and stuffed it into his trouser pocket. His palms were sweating inside the plastic bags, but he didn't take them off yet.

"Where the hell are you?" he wondered aloud. There was a possibility that the thief had given him the slip, but he didn't give it much credence. He'd been parked in a position where he could watch the major exits from the hotel, and unless the thief had come down the back stairs and scaled the nine-foot perimeter fence, he was still here.

What are the chances of that happening? Slim to zero.

There was a chance he'd gone down to the restaurant for an evening meal, but again it was highly unlikely. From the furtive way the thief acted when he was in the parking lot, he was hiding from someone. He wouldn't eat in plain sight in the restaurant, not when he could order food to be deliv-ered to his room.

That left two or three possibilities. The thief was asleep and hadn't heard him knock. Or he was in the bathroom, and had again missed the knock. Or he'd slipped out while

Cain had made his way around the back of the hotel and was even now in the parking lot looking for another vehicle to appropriate. Maybe an Oldsmobile.

Vacillation danced a quickstep through his mind. He could run back out to check on the state of play, or he could gain admittance to the hotel suite and check out his other theories. In the end, he chose the latter.

As quietly as possible, he tested the door handle. The door didn't open. Not a problem. He inserted the tip of his scaling knife between door lock and frame and twisted. The lock snicked open with barely any pressure.

The door swung open to reveal a short vestibule with two closed doors on one side. At the far end a door was open, and he could see part of a combined sitting room/bedroom apartment. Next to a recliner was a pair of running shoes, and a denim jacket was slung over the arm of a chair. Looked like the thief hadn't packed to leave.

Inside the vestibule, Cain listened. He could discern neither running water nor snoring. He took another step, the plastic bags making a faint sucking noise on the tiled floor. Watching the open room at the end, he pushed the front door closed, then turned to the first door to his right. Slowly he pushed down on the handle, allowing the door to swing open.

He sneaked a look into the room. It was a tiny kitchen. A couple of buzzing flies bashed themselves against a window in an effort to escape the stifling heat. There were a few dirty dishes piled in the sink and a ring-stained coffee cup on the drain board. He reached out and touched a kettle. Through his plastic shrouding, he could feel that the kettle still bore the heat of being boiled. Proof of recent or current occupancy, Cain decided.

Leaving the kitchen, he moved along the vestibule. He held his breath, anticipation building. If his assumption proved true, the next door would open into a bathroom, the most likely place to find the thief. Cain smiled to himself, imagining opening the door and finding the thief sitting on the toilet with his trousers around his ankles, a shocked look on his face. How ignoble!

He pressed an ear to the door, listening for the telltale sounds of an industrious man at work. Nothing. No soft grunts, no delicate splashes, no sighs of relief or rustle of newspaper. Neither was there the sound of a shower or faucet trickling, but that didn't mean the thief wasn't prone in a tub and taking a moment of silent reflection.

By habit, Cain always bolted the door to his bathroom, even when he knew he was alone. But the door swung open as easily as had the kitchen door. Cain stepped into the cooler confines of the bathroom, a delicate breath of lavender invading his senses. The lid on the toilet was up. The bath was empty. Unfortunately, the shower curtain was pulled to one side, so there was no chance of a Hitchcock moment.

He fought down the impulse to swear. That is for the uncultured killer; he of the chainsaw or machete and lampshades made from human hide. Turning back to the vestibule, he walked with the stealth of a ninja assassin. His blade led the way, lifted like that of a matador poised for the coup de grâce.

The open room remained constant. He attempted to tune himself to the still air, to feel the subtle drafts and eddies of the atmosphere around him. Feeling for restrained hints that human life stirred in the space out of his sight but not beyond the reach of his other senses.

At the threshold, he once more tugged the hood from his pocket and pulled it over his head. The shock of a hooded man stepping into the room would have the desired effect and halt the thief in his tracks. All he required was a second or so of addled wits in order to take charge. He drew a deep breath and stepped into the room.

"Damn it!"

The room was sterile.

Sighing now, Cain looked back over his shoulder.

"Perhaps I should've checked the parking lot first." He sighed. There was nothing he could do about that now. Might as well search the room. The thief could have left his precious Bowie knife behind in his need to move on.

Cain checked the layout of the room. The recliner was off to his right, but all that remained there were the denim jacket and the running shoes. On a coffee table there was a yachting magazine with photos of an exclusive club over at Marina del Rey.

Cain moved over to a bed and chest of drawers that took up the far wall. The bed was unmade. A pair of boxer shorts lay crumpled on the floor at its foot. Cain walked over and kicked the boxers until he could read the label inside. They confirmed the thief's nationality. Definitely an Englishman. The label read St Michael, the brand name of Marks & Spencer, the source of many a conservative Englishman's underwear.

He next tried the drawers in the chest. T-shirts were pushed into the top drawer along with more underwear and wadded socks. The next drawer down held a pair of folded sweatpants but nothing else. The final drawer held nothing belonging to the thief, just a stack of well-fingered brochures and menus from local businesses. As well as the obligatory welcome message from the hotel manager that no one ever reads.

Cain made a noise in the back of his throat. Scorn given timbre. He cast his eyes around the room. A TV rested on a table next to the recliner, but there was nothing of the thief's sitting on top of it. He turned instead to the built-in wardrobes that made up the wall next to the entrance door.

He stared at the double doors. If the thief had fled the apartment, then he would surely have taken his clothing with him. If the cupboard contained his coat and other belongings, then it was apparent that he'd be returning sometime soon.

Cain approached the wardrobe with a new idea in mind.

It was the ideal hiding place. Concealed inside it, he could wait for the thief to return and then spring out when he was least expecting it. Smiling at his wisdom, he pulled open the doors.

"Ah," he said.

The thief's coat was still there. But something else assured Cain that the thief hadn't fled as he'd first feared.

The barrel of the gun pointed directly at his face.

22

"YOU OKAY, HUNTER?"

No. I was numb.

The face on the screen was unquestionably my brother's. His hair was shorter than I remembered, and there were a couple of new lines at the corners of his eyes. But it was definitely John.

"This can't be right," I said.

Reading the accompanying story wasn't helping. I couldn't concentrate for glancing at the photograph to remind me that I wasn't reading an unconnected piece of hack journalism. My heart drummed in my chest like a volley of cannon fire. Even the adrenaline rush of battle didn't affect me in this way.

"I don't believe it," I said for what must have been the umpteenth time. "There must be some kind of mistake."

Rink wasn't so certain. He didn't know John the way I did. Okay, John was a self-centered, lying, cheating thief who'd run out on his wife and kids. But there was one thing I was certain of: my brother wasn't a depraved psychopathic killer collecting the bones of his victims as trophies. Rink was taking things at face value. He tapped the screen to prove his point. "You can't argue with the forensics, Hunter."

I shook my head like there was a wasp in my ear.

"No, I can't accept it. Something's wrong here."

"How do you explain it, then?"

"I don't know, but I'm sure as hell going to try."

Reading the news release once again didn't calm my

racing heart. The FBI had been searching for the perpetrator of a number of brutal murders that spanned the country from coast to coast. The deaths had reputedly occurred over a three-year period. The FBI was unwilling to divulge the quantity dead at this man's hands, but would confirm that the killer's signature was the removal of skeletal parts. The killer had finally been named as John Telfer, a British subject living in the Little Rock area.

"It's all a load of bull," I told the screen. Rink threw up his hands.

Fair enough, John had been in the country during the three-year period and had, by Louise Blake's admission, been employed as a delivery driver some of that time. This gave him the opportunity to have visited the places listed. But according to Louise, John had gone missing less than a month ago. Surely if he'd been involved in these random killings, he'd have left town much sooner than he had.

Experience indicates that a serial killer starts slowly, the time span between his kills narrowing with each attack as he craves more and more depraved satisfaction, until he reaches a point where he can no longer restrain the urge to kill. I suppose, with that in mind, John could have been doing the killings, and it was only now that he'd spiraled out of control and gone off on a final rampage.

Not that I was about to admit that for a second.

I read about a man and woman found murdered in a motel at the fringes of the Mojave Desert, how they'd both had fingers removed as trophies by the maniac the press had dubbed the Harvestman.

A witness related how the murdered couple had been seen picking up a stranded motorist the previous morning. The police examination of a vehicle found abandoned a short distance from where the motorist had been picked up showed it was registered to one Sigmund Petoskey of Little Rock, Arkansas. Mr. Petoskey had only this evening informed police that a former employee, John Telfer, had stolen the vehicle.

Tests of fingerprints inside the car confirmed that the driver had indeed been John Telfer.

Police and FBI agents were now searching for the location of a yellow Volkswagen Beetle stolen by the killer after murdering the young couple found dead at the motel. There was no corroborating forensic evidence at the murder scene to tie Telfer to the motel, but due to the balance of probabilities, the FBI felt that naming him as the chief suspect was justifiable under the circumstances.

"Justifiable under the circumstances?"

"It's a logical assumption when you think about it," Rink argued. "John breaks down, he's picked up by these motorists, then they go to a motel together. John then kills the couple, steals their car, and goes on his way, headed God knows where."

I wasn't having any of it. "No way. They say here that the car contained John's fingerprints. Why wouldn't he wipe down the car the way he's supposedly done at the motel?"

Rink shrugged.

"Maybe he didn't think about wiping down the car before he was picked up," Harvey offered.

"According to the FBI, they've been searching for this Harvestman character for the past three years. Never once have they found any evidence of fingerprints before. Isn't it a stretch to think he'd forget to wipe down a vehicle he was driving if he was on a killing spree?"

"Maybe," Rink offered. "You know how these crazies are. They get to a point where they don't give a damn anymore. They believe they're indestructible, that the police can't catch them. They start taking chances, dropping the feds the odd clue. Makes it all the more exciting for them."

"So why be so meticulous at the motel? If you want to drop the feds a clue, why not leave your prints at the scene of the crime?" I sat back, crossed my arms over my chest.

"That'd probably be too blatant," Harvey offered.

"And leaving a car full of evidence isn't?" I asked.

"Not if you never suspect that the car and the killings are going to be connected," Harvey said.

"Yeah," said Rink. "It was only by chance that John was seen getting picked up by the couple. Maybe he didn't think the abandoned car would be tied to what happened at the motel."

Okay, it was a fair assumption. Not one that I shared. John was no killer. I'd have staked my right hand on it, if the wager weren't inappropriate under the circumstances. I rubbed my hands over my face, groaning with a mixture of frustration and fatigue.

"What time is it?" I finally asked.

"Late," Harvey replied.

"Does that mean it'll be morning in England?"

Both Rink and Harvey glanced at each other and made faces. Rink finally turned to me and said, "It'll be *early* morning. Who are you thinking of calling? Jennifer?"

"I'll have to ring her at some point. But that's not who I was thinking about."

"Who then?" Rink asked.

"Raymond Molloy," I said.

"Detective Inspector Molloy?" Rink asked. "The cop you did that job for? What do you want to call him for?"

"I need to check up on any similar murders back home. See if there's a pattern. To show if John's involved or not."

"What if he won't speak to you? It's not as if you're still on the government payroll, Hunter."

"He'll speak to me. He owes me a favor."

DI Molloy did indeed owe me a favor. I'd sorted a little problem for him concerning a pimp who'd tried to extort money from him after Molloy dallied too often with some of the pimp's girls. It wasn't a problem his own resources could handle without his indiscretion becoming public knowledge. It took only one visit to the pimp for him to see sense—and to hand over the incriminating evidence of Molloy getting very creative and athletic on a waterbed.

That didn't mean Molloy was pleased to hear from me. I'd

saved his professional reputation, but I'd also made it very clear that rough treatment of a woman—paid or not—might just make me forget about helping him next time. He answered my queries curtly. Little more than yes, no, and kiss my ass.

"Thanks for nothing," I said as I placed the phone back in its cradle.

"Well?" Rink asked.

"As ever, Mr. Molloy was his charming self."

"But did he give you what you wanted to know?"

"Yeah," I said. "There are no cold investigations into murder victims subject to postmortem mutilation. Rules out the chance that John was killing before he came here."

Rink hiked his shoulders. "Doesn't mean that he's innocent. Just that he didn't start killing until he arrived in the U.S."

I shook my head as I got up and paced the length of Harvey's office.

"You don't go from being totally inexperienced to hacking up bodies and taking skeletal remains as trophies. You build up to something like that. There's nothing in John's background that hints that he was even violent. Christ, he was a number one asshole toward the end, but that was because of the problems he was having. In all that time, though, he never lifted his hand to anyone. Not Jennifer, not his kids. He wouldn't even stick up for himself when Shank threatened him. Does that sound like someone who's capable of murdering people?"

"Most murderers are nothing but low-down cowards," Rink reminded me. "It doesn't take a brave man to take a woman hostage at knifepoint."

"I agree," I said. "But it takes some balls to take out a man and a woman at the same time."

"Unless he took out the man first," Harvey said. He peered up at me from his swivel chair. "Sneaked up behind him and slit his throat or whatever. Then he could have done the woman."

Rink said, "Regardless if John's their man or not, the

FBI is searching for him. Kind of complicates matters a bit, don't it?"

"Yes and no," I countered. "They've more resources than we have. They might be able to find him for us. When he's cleared of their suspicions, it could be as simple as going and picking him up."

"You think they're just gonna let you walk in and take him home?"

"If he's innocent, yes."

"And if he's not? If he does turn out to be this punk Harvestman?"

"Then they're welcome to him," I said. The words felt cold in my mouth.

"You think Jennifer's going to be happy with that?"

"Jennifer isn't going to be happy whatever the outcome," I told him.

"And what about you, Hunter? What if you don't take him home? How will you feel?"

"How d'you think I'll feel?" I pondered for a moment. "What about my family? How d'you think they'll feel when I have to tell them my brother's locked up in an American prison?"

"Won't be good."

"No, Rink, it won't."

Harvey swung his chair side to side. The machinations of thought whirred away behind his furrowed brow. In the end, he looked up at the two of us and said, "Neither of you boys thought about it yet?"

"Thought about what?" Rink asked.

"The obvious," Harvey said.

"Obviously we haven't or we'd have mentioned it already."

Christ, it was like working with Abbott and Costello.

"Thought about what?" I asked.

"When you spoke with Petoskey earlier, why didn't he mention that the FBI had been in contact with him? That they'd already talked to him about his car? That John was a suspect in the biggest hunt since the Unabomber?"

"Son of a bitch was lying to us," Rink said. "Unless he got mixed up when he said the CIA had been on his back."

"Bit of a difference between the Feebies and the Spooks," Harvey said.

"It doesn't make any sense," Rink said.

"No, it doesn't," I said. "And John as a serial killer doesn't make any sense, either."

"I'm beginning to think that nothin' about this case makes sense," Rink said.

"Me, too," I admitted. "Petoskey knows more than he's saying, that's for sure."

"What about Louise Blake?" Harvey offered. "Should we talk to her again?"

"Yes," I said. "Let's see her first thing in the morning."

"We'll have to be careful, Hunter," Rink cautioned. "With the heat on John over this Harvestman thing, you can bet your ass that the FBI is staking out her home."

I nodded.

"Harvey, you said someone was watching Louise's place. You think they were feds?"

Harvey shook his large head. "No. They've been watching her since before Telfer became a suspect in these killings."

"Any ideas?"

"All I can say is they're not from around here. They look Mexican or Puerto Rican, could even be Cuban," he said. "I spotted two of them, but there could be more; looked like backing singers for the Kings of Mambo. Slick-dressed muthas."

Whatever involvement these two had, it wasn't good.

"We have to find these guys," I said.

"Shouldn't be too difficult," Rink said. "Ain't too many homeboys hanging around Louise's hood."

"Unless," Harvey reminded us, "the FBI are already there and they've beat a hasty retreat."

Rink sniffed. "You want to have a run over and see if we can round them up now?"

I glanced around, looking for a clock. Other than that it was *late,* I hadn't a clue what time it was. Finally I said, "We'll wait for morning. I don't know about you boys, but I need a couple hours' sleep. Jet lag's got to me, I think."

Rink shook his head sadly.

"Jet lag, my ass. Admit it—old age is finally catching up with you."

I gave him a weary smile. "No, I just think it'd be better if we speak to them at a more civilized time."

"And," Rink asked, "in a more civilized manner this time?"

Only thing is, there's no such thing as dealing with scum in a civilized manner.

23

"SON OF A BITCH."

Cain sighed as the gun barrel pressed to his hooded forehead. Even cultured killers let a little profanity slip now and again.

"You've got that right," said the thief as he stepped out of the wardrobe. Pressure from the gun made Cain step backward. "Now drop the knife or I'll shoot you where you stand."

Cain dropped the knife. It landed with a faint thud on the carpet.

"Kick it away," the thief ordered.

Cain glanced at his bagged feet.

"I might cut myself."

"I don't give a rat's ass if you cut yourself. Kick it away *now.*"

Cain used the edge of his foot to prod the knife away.

"Satisfied?"

The thief grunted.

"Sit on the bed."

Argument was pointless. He sat down.

"Sit on your hands," the thief said.

"What for? You have a gun. You think I'm crazy enough to come at you?"

"Humor me."

Cain sighed expansively. Could things get any worse? Of course they could, the thief could shoot him. He was no killer, but a nervous finger could slip. Cain pushed his hands beneath his thighs.

"If you take your hands out I'll shoot you."

"Fair enough."

"You think I won't?"

Cain shrugged. "I have to give you credit. You got the drop on me."

"Good. It's best you remember that. Now . . . tell me. Who the hell are you?"

"You could call me a concerned member of the public."

"Bull."

"Honestly. I'm simply a member of the public attempting to right a wrong."

"So you say. Who the hell do you think you are? Dressed up like friggin' Batman?"

Cain tilted his head. "You don't like my costume?" he asked.

"You look like a reject from a beekeepers' convention. What's the deal? Your employers can't afford to buy you a ski mask or decent gloves?"

Cain frowned. *My employers? Now what's that about?*

The thief continued. "Who's with you?"

"No one."

"Bullshit! You assholes always hunt in packs. You're like a bunch of damn hyenas."

"I'm telling you," Cain said slowly. "I'm alone, so you needn't worry. You can stop waving that gun around if you like. I won't move. I only want what is rightfully mine. Then I'll walk out of here and leave you alone."

The thief made a sound of scorn deep in his chest.

"Do you think I'm an idiot?"

"No, like I said, I've a healthy respect for you. You got the drop on me. In fact"—Cain laughed in good humor—"you ambushed me exactly the same way I was planning for you."

The thief sniffed. There was a hint of self-conceit in his eyes. He was proud of his accomplishment and equally pleased at its acknowledgment. Conceit and vanity, both weaknesses Cain could exploit.

"You're too good for the likes of me. I should've known better than trying to sneak in here."

"Don't patronize me," the thief warned.

"I'm patronizing no one. Just showing my appreciation of your skills."

"Just cut the crap, will you? Tell me why you're really here?"

"To regain something that belongs to me. I told you."

"Something that belongs to Hendrickson, you mean?"

Hendrickson? Who the hell is Hendrickson?

"I've no idea who you're referring to," Cain told him. "I think you're confusing me with someone else."

"I'm not confusing you with anything but a piece of lying crap."

"Oh, but you are," Cain said. "And if you would only let me take off my hood, you'll see."

The thief paused. Considering. Then he shook his head.

"No, I don't want you to move."

"Then *you* take off my hood. It'll explain everything."

The thief considered a moment longer, then he pointed his gun at Cain's head as he snatched the hood away. His look was testament to the confusion Cain's face produced.

"You're that weirdo from the desert?"

"Got it in one."

"What the hell are you doing here?"

"I've told you."

"You're trying to regain something belonging to you. Yeah, you already said. But that's—" The thief shook his head. "You want your SUV back. Is that it? You can have it and you're welcome to it. Has a flat tire anyway."

"I'm not bothered about the car," Cain said. "It's something personal to me that I want."

"If you're after revenge, you can forget it. I'm the one holding the gun, remember?"

"Not revenge, either," Cain said.

"What the hell is it, then?" The thief's face was a picture of concentration. If only for a second or so. "Oh, I get it. You want your knife back."

Cain smiled.

"Well, you're wasting your time. I threw it away. All this has been for nothing."

Cain shook his head. "I don't believe that."

"Believe what you want."

"Why'd you throw away a perfectly good Bowie knife?"

The thief shrugged. He'd be useless in a game of poker; deceit was painted across his features as plain as a billboard advertising Honest John's Quality Used Cars. "What good was it to me? I've got a gun. Why would I need a knife?"

"If that's the case, why did you take it?"

"Because I wanted to," the thief said. "And anyway, I don't need to explain myself to you. You're the one who needs to start giving *me* answers."

"There's nothing more to say. You stole my knife, I followed you, and I want it back. End of story."

"Can't help you."

Cain shrugged. "You could at least tell me where you left it, so I can go and find it."

"Who says you're going to walk out of here alive?"

"Oh, come on," Cain said. "We both know you're not going to shoot me. If you were any kind of killer you'd have left me for dead out in the Mojave."

"I did leave you for dead," the thief said with no conviction. "I didn't think a soft ass like you would survive more than a few hours."

Cain laughed. "Next to a major highway?"

"I made a mistake."

"You made more than one," Cain told him. "Haven't you wondered how I found you so easily?"

The spark in his eye told Cain he was intrigued. Maybe more than intrigued, perhaps a little concerned.

Cain sat back on the bed, resting his shoulders against the wall. The inconspicuous movement had a twofold purpose:

one, he was attempting to disarm the thief by appearing relaxed; the other, he was subtly relieving the pressure from his hands. "It's obvious you're on the run from someone. This Hendrickson guy you mentioned—you're afraid of him, right?"

As ebullient as a piece of driftwood, the thief sniffed.

Cain went on, "When you're trying to lose yourself, there're a number of things you don't do. For one, you don't use any credit cards or ATMs."

"I know that."

"I believe you do," Cain said. "Next, you don't use an alias that's anything like your real name. For instance, if you're called David Johnston, you don't go calling yourself John Davidson. It's too easily spotted."

"Yeah, I know that, too," the thief snapped.

"Third, you never write anything down that'll give away your hiding place." Cain paused, waiting for the truth to dawn on the thief. "Or if you do, you make sure it's destroyed."

The thief nodded. "I wrote down the telephone number for this shithole."

"Uh-huh."

"But how did you find it? I threw the damn thing out the car window."

"The wind must have blown it back in." Cain's shoulders lifted. "Hey, don't be so disappointed. We all make mistakes. I made a mistake by underestimating you, didn't I?"

"Yeah, you did," the thief reminded him. "But don't think I'm gonna underestimate *you*. I know what you're trying to do. Trying to get me to think of you as someone with my best interests at heart. I can smell the bullshit from here, so you may as well give up now."

Cain shifted marginally. He wasn't at a loss, the way the thief was. He'd just slipped one hand out of its plastic bag. His palm was slick with perspiration and he gripped the bed sheets beneath him to dry it off.

"I'm only trying to help," he said.

"Right," the thief snapped. "Why would you want to help me?"

"Because I want to." Cain shook his head. "Another lesson for you, my friend. Never turn down help; it may save your skin."

"Two things. First, I'm not your friend. Second, I don't need any lessons from you."

"You're partly right," Cain agreed. "You don't need any lessons from me. You're the one with the gun. I'm the one made the mistake. But you might want to reconsider the friend part."

"Yeah, right. What the hell do you take me for?"

"Someone in need of help," Cain said.

"I don't need or want your help."

"Shame," Cain said, "because from where I'm sitting it looks like you need all the help you can get."

"There you go again. Patronizing."

"Take it as you will. I only want to help."

"I don't need your help."

"I beg to differ."

"You'd be better off begging for your life."

"Nah," Cain said. "Why bother? We've already established that you aren't going to kill me."

The thief lifted his gun, pointing it directly at Cain's face. "Maybe not in cold blood. But who knows what I'll do in self-defense?"

Cain smiled up at him. "Like I've already said, though, I'm not going to make a move on you. So you won't get the opportunity to test your theory."

The tableau held for the best part of a lifetime. At least a lifetime counted in seconds. Finally the gun barrel wavered and dropped away from Cain's face.

"So what have we got then? Stalemate?" the thief asked.

"More like an impasse," Cain offered.

"Same thing, isn't it?"

"Depends on your perspective," Cain said. "A stalemate's when two enemies are at a deadlock. If we look at our situation as one of companions with a shared problem, then we can look to resolve it together."

"Only problem I can think of is how to get rid of you," the thief said.

"You can't very well call the police, can you?" Cain asked. "Fair enough, you could say I was an intruder, but what happens when I explain I followed you here because you hijacked my car? Two wrongs don't make a right, my friend."

The thief pondered a moment.

"I could tie you up and leave you here, though. Then I could make an anonymous call to the cops."

"They're still going to ask questions. They'll identify you in no time. I take it your fingerprints are all over this room? Not to mention the SUV—which, I'll remind you, is not going anywhere soon. And before you consider wiping everything down, may I remind you about the front desk downstairs? Are you positive you didn't leave your fingerprints there when you signed in?"

The thief sniffed again. "You're assuming the police are after me. I'm not on the run from the cops."

"You will be if I tell them you kidnapped me."

The thief watched him and Cain smiled.

"Impasse," Cain said.

"No," the thief replied. "Stalemate."

"Look," Cain said, "we could go on like this all evening. We've both wronged each other. I'll admit that. If you're prepared to let bygones be bygones, so am I."

"I can't trust you," the thief said.

"But can I trust you?"

Now it was the thief's turn to smile. Honest John's Quality Used Cars had a new head salesclerk.

Cain closed his eyes. "If I tell you something, then you're going to have to trust me. I don't want the police involved any more than you do."

The thief shook his head. "I don't want to know anything about you."

Cain opened his eyes slowly. "You did earlier."

"That was then. That was when I thought you were one of Hendrickson's men."

"And you believe now that I'm not? Well, that's a start."

"Something's bothering me, though," the thief said. "You're not here on some stupid quest to recover a stolen knife. What's the real reason?"

"I was telling you the truth," Cain said. "I do want my knife back."

"What the hell for?"

"Sentimental value," Cain explained.

"You follow me hundreds of miles, sneak into my room like some psycho from a cheap horror movie, just to get a knife back?"

"Yes."

"That's it?"

"Well," Cain said, "if you want the full truth, I did intend to make you pay for putting me to the trouble."

Glancing down at the discarded scaling knife, the thief laughed, shaking his head in disbelief.

"But now you want to help me?"

"Yes," Cain said. "Believe it or not, I like you. You're a man after my own heart."

"You like me? You're so full of crap I can't believe it," the thief said.

"Of course, if I'm going to help you, there are conditions attached."

"I give you back your knives so you can stick them in me first chance you get?"

"Exactly," Cain agreed with his most disarming grin. "And one other thing. If I keep your secret, you do the same for me."

"You don't know my secret."

"But that's part of the bargain. It's the only way we can work together. You tell me why you're on the run, and I'll do the same. Call it leverage against one another. We have to work together to keep both our secrets. That way we can't afford to betray each other."

"No, I'm not having any part of it," the thief said. "This is all just a trick so that you can escape. You'll drop me in it first chance you get."

"Not if I tell you my secret first," Cain offered.

"So what's the big secret you're hiding?" he demanded.

"We have to make a deal first," Cain said.

"Uh-uh, not until I know what the hell you're talking about," the thief said.

"Okay. But first, you have to show a little faith. Put the gun down."

"No."

"At least point it at the floor, then. I don't want it going off by accident."

"Don't worry, there's nothing you could tell me that'll surprise me that much."

"Want to bet?" Cain asked.

The thief shrugged another time, but there was something in Cain's face that made him lower the gun.

"Come on, then," he said. "Tell me."

"Okay," Cain said. "Drumroll please."

"Just get on with it."

"Fine, but it is a little dramatic. You could at least allow me my big moment."

And then the thief made *the* mistake. He sighed, glanced up at the ceiling as if in search of spiritual guidance. It was the moment Cain had been waiting for. He erupted from the bed in a blur of motion. He grabbed the thief's gun hand before he could bring it back up. Then Cain's other hand was at the thief's throat as he snaked a leg around the back of his ankles. In the next instant Cain was standing over him as he sprawled on the floor. And now pointing the gun at his chest.

"My big secret," Cain said with a look of triumph, "is that I'm a killer, and unlike you, I'm prepared to prove it."

24

ONCE, I WAS PURSUED THROUGH A RAINSTORM THAT did little to dampen the fires raging through Grozny. Rebel Chechen soldiers were nipping at my heels. It was unfortunate; I wasn't their enemy. Trouble was that I was in the wrong place at the wrong time, on a mission to take out a rogue Russian *Spetsnaz*—special forces—soldier who was just a little too fond of prepubescent girls. To infiltrate his position, I'd gone disguised in Russian uniform, and now the Chechens were after my blood. Ironic, you might say. I was there to kill their worst kind of enemy, yet here I was being hunted like a rabid dog.

I had no intention of returning fire, so I chose to run. They were persistent. To elude my pursuers, I lay up beneath the corpse of a steer. The poor thing had avoided slaughter to feed the invading Russian troops by haphazardly wandering into a pasture sown with land mines. The steer's folly was my salvation. Even so, it was about the most miserable twenty-eight hours of my life. The stench was bad enough, but the crawling infestation of maggots made it almost unendurable. Believe me; I came close to surrender.

Yes, I've slept in some pretty grim places in my time. But even a steer's belly can be comfortable when compared to an office chair.

I slept fitfully, waking at dawn with a stiff neck and the feeling of an intense hangover.

Harvey had invited us back to his split-level ranch out

beyond the suburbs, but we'd declined, wanting an early start and knowing that the tranquility of a remote farmhouse and a soft bed wasn't conducive to an early rise. Struggling out of the chair, I cracked my lower back and blinked around the small office. Rink was gone. Probably a good thing. I wasn't a pretty sight. I rubbed my eyes with both hands and yawned.

I pushed into the washroom, yawning again. Rink was standing by one of the two small sinks, his upper torso bared. The tattoo on his left shoulder was stark even against his tawny flesh. I have an identical tattoo on my shoulder, a testament to our time in the joint Special Forces unit we'd both been part of for all those years. It was a tattoo sported by only a handful of living men, and not one we ever wore when we were active in the field.

Midstroke with his razor Rink paused, glancing at me in the mirror. "Boy, you look like shit this morning."

"Gee, thanks," I said. "I feel like shit, too, if it's any consolation."

"There's a spare razor if you want to use it."

I ambled over to the sink and picked up the disposable razor. "Courtesy of Harvey?"

"Yup," Rink said, taking another stroke at his chin. "Keeps a stock of them for shaving his head."

I grimaced at the blade, checking for short bristles caught between the twin blades. "He hasn't used it already?"

Rink laughed. Didn't answer. I shrugged, ran the blade under the tap. Rink tossed me a can of shaving foam. I nodded my thanks at him, then stopped.

"Problem?" Rink asked with a twinkle in his eye.

"You've shaved off your mustache?"

"Can't hide anything from you, can I?"

I grunted. "That's what makes me a damn good detective."

Rink slapped me on my shoulder as he brushed past, heading back to the office. I washed and shaved, dried off. When I returned to the office, Rink was on the telephone to Harvey.

"Harvey's over at Louise Blake's place. He wants us over there," Rink said. "He just watched a couple of guys go inside. Didn't look like they were selling home insurance."

"How slick did they look?"

"Like eels in a bucket of sump oil."

25

JOHN TELFER SAT ON HIS HOTEL RECLINER AND stared at a blank canvas no more than a couple of centimeters past the end of his nose. Light from the overhead bulb filtered through the cloth, and if he stared closely enough he could make out the minute nuances of texture and pattern in the cotton weave. It was all he'd had to visually focus on for the best part of five hours. His other senses hadn't been given many stimuli, either, not since the man had forced the bag over his head and tied his hands behind his back with an electric cord torn from a desk lamp.

He sat mute, listening for any telltale sign that his time was up, that the maniac was approaching, knife or gun ready to take his life. But all he heard was the occasional shifting of body weight on the bed across from him. Not for the first time he wondered if his captor had fallen asleep.

He heard a soft grunt. Was it the sound a man makes as he slips into dreamland? Or more likely, the sound of one coming to a decision? Fearing he was about to find out, he straightened and craned his neck to try to shift the hood enough that he could see beneath it.

"Sit still," the man commanded from across the room.

"What are you doing?" Telfer asked. His own voice was strained and distant.

"Thinking," answered the maniac. "Now please be quiet and allow me to do so."

Telfer nodded beneath the bag. *Show that I'm not a threat,* he thought. But he couldn't help asking, "What're you gonna do with me?"

The man snorted in derision. "What do you think?"

Telfer's shoulders slumped. He felt like asking, Why didn't he just get on with it then? But that would be suicidal. He didn't want to die, and every second of life he could hold on to, he'd do so with all his might. He kept quiet.

The minutes passed and Telfer went back to scrutinizing the inside of the cloth bag. He stared at the blurry cloth, lost in some still, Zenlike place. After a while, he began to rock back and forth.

"Will you please be quiet?"

"Unh?" Telfer asked.

"You're humming again," said the man. "That same godawful tune that has no melody."

"I didn't realize," Telfer said. Beneath his hood, he blinked slowly. He had no comprehension of having been humming a tune.

"It's getting right on my nerves. Maybe I should just cut out your voice box so you can't do it anymore?"

Telfer shook his head. "I won't do it anymore. I'm sorry."

"Good. Now if you'll just give me a little peace and quiet, I can come to some sort of decision."

"Are you going to kill me?"

"Probably. Only thing is, I haven't decided how yet."

"Thanks for being so honest."

He heard the man get up from the bed and walk over. Telfer's whole frame tightened in response. He made a short wailing sound, before something made him stop. He didn't want to die, but if he had to, he didn't intend shrieking like a lost soul. In defiance, he lifted his chin, exposing his throat for a quick slash. Then he blinked at the sudden intrusion of light as the hood was snatched away. The man wasn't holding a knife, but Telfer's own gun was pointed at him.

"I've asked and asked for you to be quiet," said the man, "but you just can't seem to keep your mouth shut. So I've decided. What I want you to do is to keep right on talking. Okay?"

Telfer squinted up at him. "What do you want me to say?"

"I want you to tell me who you are and how you wound up here. And I want the truth. No lies. Believe me, if you lie to me, I will know. And I will hurt you. Understand?"

"Yeah, I understand."

"Good. Now go ahead. But don't go raising your voice. We don't want anyone eavesdropping on our conversation, do we?"

Telfer glanced at the wall behind him. Like most hotel walls, these were about as porous as a sponge. He couldn't be sure if anyone was in residence next door, and he couldn't take the chance that their conversation would be overheard. A bit of a strange notion, considering that a psycho was holding him at gunpoint. He looked back at the man and saw a faint smile playing about his lips. He seemed amused, as though he knew that Telfer could not shout for help.

"My name isn't Ambrose," he began.

"I know that. So what is it? Your real name?"

"John."

"Mmm."

"Honestly. My name's John Telfer."

The man nodded as though he was confirming something he already knew.

"I'm from England."

"We've already established that." Again the nod of the head, the amused smile.

"I came here on a work permit," Telfer said.

"That has since run out?"

It was Telfer's turn to nod. "I haven't been able to get a full visa yet."

The man nodded. "You and a couple million others."

"So," Telfer said, "I've had to move on. If I stayed put, I'd have been deported back home."

The man watched him steadily for more than half a dozen heartbeats. Then he moved closer, pushing the gun down in the waistband of his trousers. He took out the curved knife and held it below Telfer's nose. Telfer edged back from it, the cords in his neck tightening.

"I told you not to lie." The man placed the blade so that it lay flat on Telfer's cheek, the point millimeters from his right eye. "That also includes half-truths. Now I don't doubt that you have no visa, but that's not the reason you're running. I want the full truth. Take this as your last warning." He turned the blade on its edge and sliced through the flesh. Not a deep cut, just enough to part the outer dermis. Still, blood flowed warm down Telfer's face to pool at the corner of his mouth.

"Jesus," Telfer hissed.

"Hurts like a bugger, doesn't it?" said the madman. "But you know that's just the start, Johnny boy. No more lies?"

"No more lies," Telfer echoed.

The man retreated a couple of steps, wiped the tip of the knife on Telfer's knee. He placed the knife back in his trouser pocket. Then the gun was back in his hand and pointed at Telfer's face.

"I've done something wrong," Telfer began.

The man nodded, sitting on a corner of the coffee table.

"I'm on the run."

"Also already established. Get on with it."

Telfer twisted his mouth into a knot. He didn't want the knife coming out again. "I stole something."

"Yes," said the man.

"I'm not a thief," Telfer began.

"Oh? What about my car? My knife?"

Telfer shook his head. "Okay. But I'm not *normally* a thief."

"You're not? You do a good impression of one."

"Until four weeks ago, I never stole a thing in my life." Telfer stopped. He knew he was lying to himself. There was the small matter of the money his brother Joe had given him to clear off a debt. Money he'd immediately lost on another hopeless bet. In one sense that did make him a thief. Then there was the matter of Jennifer and the kids. He'd stolen their hearts. Broken them into little pieces and snatched a random handful that could never be returned.

"What are you crying for?"

"Uh?"

"You're crying," the man pointed out. "Was this theft so dreadful that it brings you to tears?"

Telfer sniffed. "No. Not the theft."

"Oh. I see. There's more to it than that? Go on. Tell me."

"I have a wife and kids."

The man nodded slowly. A shadow passed behind his features. "Haven't we all?"

"I wronged them," Telfer went on. "I wanted to make things right for them again."

"Which is why you stole this thing?" The man bent down and pulled Telfer's backpack from beneath the coffee table. Telfer jolted as if he'd sat on an exposed electrical wire. He watched, eyes intense, as the man fished in his backpack and pulled out an oblong package wrapped in black tape. He placed it on the coffee table next to him, then he upended the bag and thick wads of cash thudded onto the carpet.

Telfer had no words. He simply sat looking at the taped package. The money was of no immediate interest, though there had to be upward of $600,000. Likewise, the man gave the money no attention. He nudged the package with the muzzle of the gun. He said, "I've got a feeling I know what this is."

26

LOUISE BLAKE'S HOUSE WAS MODEST WHEN COM-
pared to some in her neighborhood, but a palace
compared to the flat John left his wife and kids in back
home in England. It was a single-story clapboard cape, with
a porch and adjoining garage. The lawn and shrubs were
well tended. A ginger tomcat cleaned himself on the front
stoop.

The scene was one of suburban tranquillity.

But that was about to be shattered.

Rink parked the rental a block away and we rushed toward
the house. Dawn in Arkansas can be cool at this time of
year, but that wasn't why we wore coats. Rink's Mossberg
was slung from a harness beneath his armpit. I had my SIG
holstered in a shoulder rig.

Harvey was waiting for us, standing in the shadows of a
shed on the next-door property. He gave a low whistle and
we angled toward him.

"What kept you guys?" he hissed. "I thought I was gonna
have to start the party without you."

"What's the deal?" I asked. "They still inside?"

"Yup. Two of them." He nodded up the road. "Another
guy in a Chevrolet parked a block over."

"Same guys as before?"

"Yeah."

"Any movement?" Rink asked. Our view of Louise's
house was partially blocked by a hedge. But we could see

her kitchen windows. They reflected the early sunrise. Our vantage point didn't offer a view of the front, but as we had arrived, I'd noticed that the blinds were drawn.

"Haven't seen anything since they went in. Heard raised voices just before you got here, but it's been quiet since." Harvey held my gaze. There were the beginnings of a cold sweat on his brow. "We going in or what?"

"We're going in," I told him.

"Good," he said. He pulled a Glock from within his leather coat, racked the slide. "They've touched her, I'm gonna rain some hurt on these assholes."

"We don't know what we're going into," I cautioned him. "Could get nasty."

"Believe me, Hunter. If they've hurt her, you can bet your ass things *is* gettin' nasty."

"Just so long as you know things're gonna get hot in there."

He winked at me. "Don't you worry. I'm up for it."

"Okay." That was the prep done. Now all that was left was the hard part.

We fanned out. No preamble, just instinct sending us on our merry way. Harvey headed for Louise's backyard, Rink and me to the front door. Best tactic? In fast and noisy, shoot anything that wasn't wearing lip gloss.

The ginger cat was wise enough to flee.

From within, I heard something crash to the floor. Before the sound stopped echoing, I rammed straight through the screen and unlocked door and into a scene straight out of *Goodfellas*.

It was one of those snapshot moments where everything is so vividly imprinted on the optic nerves that you don't have to physically look to see even the minutest of details.

It was like this:

Louise Blake on her knees, flowery skirt gathered up around her thighs. Streaked mascara. Smear of blood on her lips.

First Latin male holding her bunched hair and her two hands in one of his. Stretching her up. Exposing her ribs.

Second Latin male lifting a rolled telephone directory for another whack at her side.

These guys weren't CIA or FBI. Even if they were, they still deserved to die.

I fired.

The report of the SIG set the world back in motion.

The man with the impromptu torture device took my 9-mm slug high in his shoulder. The directory spun from his hand, pages fluttering. He staggered away, crashing up against a dresser. Stacked dishes slid and exploded onto the floor.

My next step was followed by another shot. We all have imperfections; this bullet missed him, drilling a hole in the plaster behind him.

Rink burst into the room all spit and venom. His shotgun remained silent. The second man had the sense to place Louise in the way of Rink's attack. Shielded by her body the man backpedaled. From his hip he snatched a semiautomatic handgun. The gun flashed metallic blue as it passed through a beam of sunlight pushing through a gap in the curtains.

I leaped and rolled, putting a chair between us. It wasn't any protection from a high-velocity round, but that wasn't my purpose. I threw myself into the room to draw the man's attention to me. Away from Louise.

Sure enough, he shot at me. I kissed the carpet and tatters of upholstery sifted down on me. Then I was up and moving. So was Rink. The man was caught in a pincer move and there was only one way out. He spun Louise into Rink's arms. His gun came up. And for one second I feared he would put a bullet in her spine. My response was to fire.

Lucky son of a bitch jerked aside at the exact same moment and my round nicked only a small portion of his ear—instead of a large chunk of skull. The slippery bastard

lurched away from me, and now Louise and Rink were between us. Encumbered with Louise, he couldn't bring the
Mossberg to bear on the man.

The man took three running steps and dove headlong at
the nearest window. Drapes tangled him, glass wedged in his
deep blue suit, but then he was crashing out into sunshine.
I charged across the room and leaned through the window
after him. The man vaulted through the topiary hedge we'd
so recently stood behind. That suit of his was going to be a
mess.

As he charged through the neighboring yard toward the
street, a pale blue Chevrolet squealed along the asphalt
toward him. I got a bead on him. I squeezed. His suit was
going to get messier.

A bullet cracked the window frame next to my head.
Splinters of wood jabbed into my cheek. Automatically I
flinched, the action transposed to my trigger finger, and my
bullet went wide.

Only one person could have fired on me. The guy I'd already winged. *Move, Hunter, or die,* my mind screamed at
me. I dropped and spun onto my haunches. My gun began to
rise, but I was again caught in a snapshot moment.

The injured man was coming toward me. His mouth was
wide with a silent curse. The muzzle of his handgun was a
yawning black hole about to suck the life out of me. John's
face flashed through my vision. Eyes sad.

There was a single crack.

Despite myself, I jerked against the pain.

Above me the man swayed. His angry face lengthened
in surprise, eyelids shuddering. I saw a deep red blossom
on the breast of his silk shirt. His knees folded and he fell
toward me. He was limp as I shoved him aside. Beyond him,
Harvey Lucas was like an angel with a Glock in his fist.

"Welcome to the dance," I said to him.

Harvey stepped forward and, gripping the shoulder of the
man, pulled him over onto his back. Air escaped from the

man's lips. A grunt. A spark remained in his eyes. He made a futile attempt at lifting his gun. Futile because Harvey's size twelves ground his wrist into the floor.

"You like hurting girls?" Harvey asked him.

Then he placed a single round in the man's open mouth.

It was a classic hit. One in the heart, one in the head. It's the only way to make sure your enemy is dead.

Harvey stretched a hand out to me. I took it and he hauled me up.

"Thanks, Harvey," I said. "I owe you."

"Was nothin'." His eyes were a reflection of my own. As a Ranger, he'd known action. But not up close. Eye to eye. Harvey was now one of the exclusive club that Rink and I held lifetime membership in.

27

THERE WAS NO TIME FOR CLEANUP.

We had to move fast.

Priority was getting Louise away from any backlash from the turmoil at her house. Harvey was up to the task. He took Louise one way with instructions to meet us in an hour. Rink and I streaked away from the house and the rising wail of approaching sirens.

Away from the cordon of police vehicles, I asked Rink to pull up at a telephone booth.

The call was enough to ensure that police action would be in our favor. Walter has that effect. It's the weight a sub-division director of the CIA wields.

We met at the same diner as last time. Louise was dressed as before. Still good-looking. Still worn around the edges. But she was different now. She held herself tentatively, like every muscle in her body ached. Fear haunted her eyes.

She was hurting from the beating she'd taken. Scared half to death by what she'd witnessed. I sympathized with her, but that wasn't why we were there. The men who'd tortured her did so for a reason. She knew more than she was admitting to.

She'd already swallowed a cup of black coffee and was asking for more when we walked in. Harvey, playing chaperone, was sitting opposite her in the same booth. He looked as sharp as Samuel L. Jackson did in the remake of *Shaft*.

In contrast, I felt, and probably looked, like someone who'd slept in his clothes and tended to his ablutions in a tiny bowl in a cramped bathroom. Though washed and shaved, my body felt gritty and as rumpled as my shirt. The splinters of wood in my cheek itched like hell.

I sat down in no mood for wasting time.

"So what've you got to tell us, Louise?" I asked.

Louise shook her head, reaching for her coffee. I put my hand over her cup and she snapped her face to mine. There was fear there, but not a little anger. Good. It was the ideal mix.

"You haven't come up with anything that'd help us find John?" I asked.

"No," she said. "I haven't exactly had the time, considering I was held captive all morning."

"Have you seen the news?"

From the tight grimace on her face, I could tell that she had.

"Have you spoken to the FBI yet?"

"Yes. They were at my place half the night. Another reason I didn't get around to looking for *clues*."

"So what did you tell them?"

"Just what I told you."

"Which is just about nothing," I said. Sarcasm was heavy in my voice, but I was in no frame of mind to worry about hurting her feelings. In my estimation, she wasn't the sensitive type anyway.

"I don't know anything."

"Bullshit!" I said a little too loudly. The waitress behind the serving counter shot me a concerned look. I raised an apologetic hand. The waitress nodded and went on about her business. She knew when to keep her nose out of other people's affairs.

"The men who were in your house," I said. "What did you tell them?"

"Nothing," she said. Her voice was strident. She pawed at the tail of her blouse, hitching it up. Her ribs were red and swollen from repeated whacks from the Yellow Pages. "Why do you think they were hitting me?"

Okay, then. She did have a point.

She didn't tell them anything. But it didn't mean there was nothing to tell.

Her hands were icy cold when I took them in mine.

"Now, Louise. We're going to start over again. This time you tell me what you know. Okay? You asked me here to help find John. I've traveled thousands of miles. The least you can do is tell me the goddamn truth."

Louise prized her hands free, then looked down at the table. I thought I detected a tear at the corner of one eye, but I could have been mistaken. She pushed her hair off her face, maybe surreptitiously wiping away the tear. When she looked up at me, it was with clear, defiant eyes.

"John's no killer," she said.

"I know that," I told her. "But he has been up to something illegal. And you know exactly what it is."

She shook her head, a lock of hair breaking loose and floating across her features. "If I say anything, he could go to prison."

I snorted. "If you say *nothing* he'll be going to prison for a damn sight longer."

"If he doesn't go to the gas chamber, that is," Rink added for emphasis.

"He didn't kill anyone," Louise said. She was adamant. Her fingernails dug at the tabletop. "He was with me when some of the murders took place. I can swear to that!"

"You have to prove it, though," I pointed out. "Your solemn word isn't worth shit, Louise. Can you also give him an alibi for the other times of death?"

"That's the problem," she said. She glanced over at the waitress, checking that she wasn't listening. She leaned toward me and whispered, "If I say where he really was, he'll get put in prison anyway."

I looked at Harvey, then at Rink, for support. Both sat with frowns on their faces. It was helpful having such sage counsel at hand. When I spoke, I'd lost the hard edge to my voice. "Tell me what he's been up to, Louise. If I'm going to help John, I need to know."

She chewed at the corner of her lower lip. Any other time it would have looked as sexy as hell. Not now, though. She simply looked like a woman terrified of the consequences of her next words. "The delivery job," she said.

"Oh," I said.

She shook her mane of hair. "It's not what you think."

"Not *drugs*?" I asked.

Louise looked like I'd just thrown salt in her face. "No. Not drugs. Do you think I'd stand by him if he *ever* went near that crap?"

I placed my hands flat on the table, leaned forward to stare in her face. "Depends on how much you love him."

Louise snorted and gave me the dead eye.

"Okay. Sorry. I don't doubt that you love him."

"It wasn't drugs," she stated.

"Okay," I said, relieved. "So what was he doing?"

Louise picked up her coffee in defiance, drained it, placed the cup back down. A stall while she ordered the words in her mind. "He was couriering."

"Couriering what?"

"It wasn't so much what as who he was doing it for." She glanced around again. "Like I said, if the police find out, he'll be in deep shit."

"Let's worry about finding John first," I said. "We can worry about the police later."

Louise dropped her head in acquiescence.

"He stole something. Something big."

I blinked. "Something big?"

"That's all I know. He wouldn't say what it was."

I pushed my hands through my hair, back down over my face, then leaned my elbows on the table. "You've got to be kidding me," I finally said. Though I knew she wasn't. John had got very good at hiding secrets toward the end.

"Honestly. He wouldn't say, so I didn't ask. Whatever it was, he said he could sell it, to make life better for everyone," she said. As if that made things all right.

I swore under my breath. I knew exactly where this was

taking us now. Who the fake CIA agents probably were. "Who was he working for?"

"Sigmund Petoskey," she said.

"Uh-huh," I said. "But who was he collecting from?"

"I don't know for sure. A gangster from up north. Henry-something-or-other."

"Hendrickson?"

"Yes. That's it."

"The men who were beating you this morning," I said. "They work for Hendrickson, huh?"

"They're the ones that John's running from," she agreed. She turned her face to the table, began playing with her empty cup.

"Have they been pressuring you for John's whereabouts?" I asked. "Before this morning, I mean."

Without answering, she leaned back, lifted up her blouse. I saw a toned abdomen. She pulled down the waistband of her skirt and there were three definite cigarette burns peeking above her panty line. "I'd show you more," she said, "only I don't know you as well as my gynecologist."

I bit down on my lip. One thing I was sure about: there was going to be a reckoning with the two who'd escaped us this morning.

"Why didn't you say something, Louise? We could've stopped them from hurting you again."

Her downcast eyelids trembled. "I was trying to protect John."

I looked at Harvey. "Any word on the street about the two who got away from us?"

"Nothing, Hunter," he replied. "You ask me, they heard the news and took off to the Mojave to try an' pick up John's trail. Which I suggest is probably your best play, too."

"I've been thinking the same thing," Rink told me.

Yeah. Me, too. But there were still a few loose ends I wanted to clear up first. When we'd raided Petoskey's building, I thought he'd been too ready to talk. Made me wonder if he'd been hiding something else about John. His anger at my brother had never been about a gambling debt. It had all been about this *something big* Louise mentioned. "Louise, what involvement did John have with Petoskey?"

She pulled her hair into a rope with her hands. "Petoskey was paying him decent money to drive up-country. I don't know where he was going, but he was gone about three days each time. He'd come back with his van loaded with packing crates and he'd drop them off at a warehouse Petoskey owns. That was his only part in it."

"What happened to the packing crates after they were dropped off?"

"I don't know, John didn't tell me."

"And you've no idea what was inside them?"

"No."

Rink asked, "Any word about what Petoskey is up to, Harvey?"

"Nope," Harvey said. "Petoskey's probably only playing the middle man. Likely, whatever's in the crates is getting shipped out of the country."

"Where to?" I asked.

"Beats me, man," Harvey said.

I had my suspicions but let them lie for now.

"What do you think?" Rink asked me. "Petoskey, Russian Mob? The Mambo Kings, Cuban? You think there's some kind of communist connection? You know where I'm going with this?"

"Could be. But it's not our concern just now. I'm more interested in finding John before anyone else gets to him."

Rink exhaled. "You want me to wait before I call this in?"

"Yeah, Rink. The last thing I want is more involvement from the government. It's bad enough we had to call in a cleanup crew for this morning. As far as Walter's concerned, we offed a hit man. That's all."

Walter had come through for us on this one. However, just the sniff of foreign involvement would mean the entire weight of the Central Intelligence Agency coming down on us like an avalanche. At best our movements would be severely hindered, at worst we'd be locked in a small dark place for fear we'd jeopardize their mission. Our suspicions had to remain just that.

"Don't worry, Rink. If things do turn out as we suspect, Petoskey will be made to pay when this is over with," I told him.

Louise watched us with dawning horror. Panic was building in her and I gave her a look to stop her from raising her voice. But she did blurt it out. Maybe it was more of a frantic whisper. "Are you saying those men at my house could be *terrorists*?"

"No, I'm not saying that," I told her.

"They could've killed me."

"Of course," I said. It was pointless lying. If the beating didn't finally get what they wanted from her, who knows what they would have done next? Louise's face fell. She wrapped her arms around her body as if to stop her aching ribs from exploding. She rocked in place.

I felt shitty. After all she'd been through, I wasn't coming across as the sympathetic type. Sure, she'd been lying . . . at first. But what woman wouldn't do that to protect her man? It was probably the ideal time to give her a little hope again.

"Now that they've got a lead on John, I guarantee you won't see them again," I said.

"But what if they don't find John? Won't they come back?"

"They won't," I promised. Not if I stopped them first.

Louise was growing despondent again, speeding up her back-and-forth movement. She snatched the rope of hair into the corner of her mouth and began gnawing on it.

"At least we've got a starting point," I said. "We'll leave for Los Angeles this afternoon, try and pick up John's trail from there."

"Why Los Angeles?" she asked, coming to a sudden halt. I wondered if I'd touched on something she knew. But she didn't say anything, only waited for me.

"It's obvious that John was headed west. His car was found abandoned only a few hours from Los Angeles; I'm betting that's where he is now."

"Some big-time players out on the West Coast," Rink agreed. "You think John's out there looking for a buyer?"

"Yeah," I said.

If John wasn't the killer of those people at the motel, something had suddenly become very obvious to me. The real killer and John had crossed paths. Maybe John was already dead, buried somewhere out in the Mojave Desert. In all likelihood, the killer now had what John had stolen, which probably meant he'd be looking for a buyer for it. That meant the killer was probably in the L.A. area trying to hook up with one of these big-time players. Whatever this *something big* turned out to be, it was a curse; he was welcome to the damned thing. But if he had killed John, he'd just made himself a major enemy.

28

"KEN BIANCHI AND ANGELO BUONO," CAIN whispered to himself.

As serial killers go, their names aren't easily recalled. Not like Bundy or Gacy. Not until their singular epithet is apparent: the Hillside Strangler. Now that's a name that's familiar to every American citizen over the age of puberty.

Cousins Bianchi and Buono terrorized the western states in the 1970s, raping and killing in unison. The law only caught up with them after Bianchi's lust became too great and, without the aid of his partner, he'd botched the abduction of two women.

It isn't often that killers work together. As far as Cain was concerned, Bianchi and Buono were the only true serial killers to do so. Which was why he'd been toying with the notion that the world was overdue for another terrible twosome.

The thought hadn't appealed for long. For a number of reasons. John Telfer didn't have the gall to pull the trigger when he'd had the opportunity. He was no killer. He was a thief who deserved only to be punished. But mainly, why the hell should John *freaking* Telfer share any of his glory?

No, any thought of a fledgling partnership was out the window. Telfer had to die. Perhaps he'd even be Cain's magnum opus, his announcement to the world. The death that would make him famous.

However, there was still a task or two to be completed before Cain allowed himself the satisfaction of flaying the hide from Telfer's thieving hands. First off, there was the subject of what he'd discovered in Telfer's backpack.

The denouement had come as a surprise to him.

"I've got a feeling I know what this is," Cain said.

Telfer sighed. "They're plates."

"Litho plates? For printing counterfeit money."

Telfer sighed again.

Cain slowly bent down and picked up one of the wads. As Telfer eyed him expectantly, he peeled one of the bills loose and held it up to the light above his head. The watermark was there.

"Not bad," Cain said. "Though if you look closely, there's a little merging of the whorls along the edge. It wouldn't pass the scrutiny of a Treasury agent." He was lost momentarily as he studied the note, turning it over in his hand. The gun was no longer pointed at Telfer, and for a split second the opportunity was there for Telfer to leap at him. Even with his hands bound, he might have wrenched the gun free and turned the tables on his captor. But the moment passed. "This paper stock. How did you get it?"

"I don't know," Telfer said. "I had nothing to do with the printing of the money. I was just a courier."

Cain nodded to himself. "Apparently the paper's the hardest thing to come by. It's all produced up at a mill in Massachusetts. Under guard of the U.S. Treasury Department, no less. It's some sort of high-grade cotton and linen mix, extremely hard to duplicate. And see these little blue and red lines? They're rayon fibers mixed in to make the paper even more difficult to fake. Most counterfeit bills don't have these. Oh, wait, I see it now." He held the note very close to his face. "The security marks aren't actually in the weave of the paper. They've been added at the printing stage. Still, it's a very good copy."

Telfer looked at him as though he was mad—which in effect he probably was.

Cain laughed to himself. "I have a keen eye for detail, that's all."

"You sound like you know what you're talking about."

Cain waved down the flattery.

"I just know these kind of things." He laughed in a self-conscious manner totally out of character. "I suppose you could say I'm well read. A mine of useless information, huh?"

"Or you do work for the people who are after me," Telfer said. He made it sound as though he was joking, but the idea had obviously invaded his thoughts.

Cain twisted his mouth. "No. I work alone."

By the look in his eyes, Telfer believed him. But it didn't make his predicament any less dangerous.

Cain dropped the bill on the coffee table, reached for the litho plates. "These can't be originals?"

"I don't suppose they are," Telfer replied. "But they're still worth decent money to the right person."

Cain gave him a shallow smile. "Are you attempting to bribe me, Mr. Telfer?"

"If it's going to save my life, yes."

Cain's smile turned into a full grin. "At last! We're being fully truthful now. That's more like it." He pulled the tape free from the stack of four litho plates and held one of them up. "They're not real plates. They've been etched from a copy after a hundred-dollar bill was scanned into a computer. That's why there's no clarity on the scrollwork. Still, like you say, they'll be worth good money to the right buyer."

Telfer grinned along with him. "So what do you say we make a deal? My life for the plates?"

"Nah," Cain said, dropping the litho on the table. "It's not as simple as that. Why would I let you go when I can kill you and then take the plates for myself?"

Telfer inclined his chin. "You seem to know a lot about the process of making counterfeit notes. Do you also know who's in the printing game? Who'd be prepared to buy the litho plates from you?"

Nodding his head, Cain said, "Well, I have to admit . . . you've got me there."

"I've already set up a deal. I'm supposed to meet the buyer tomorrow."

Cain snorted.

"It's the truth. Why would I lie to you?"

"Who are you meeting with?"

Telfer shook his head. "Christ, man. Give me a little credit, will you? I'm trying to save my life here. You can't expect me to tell you who I intend selling the plates to."

"I could cut the name out of your throat," Cain pointed out.

"Yes, you could. But it wouldn't do you any good. My buyer won't deal with anyone but me. He's too afraid that the FBI is onto him to deal with anyone he doesn't know. If I don't show at the meet, he won't show."

"Touché."

"So that means that you need to keep me alive, or the deal will be off."

"How much money are we talking about here?"

Telfer exhaled. Indicating the pile of money, he said, "About two hundred grand for that." He paused. "Maybe half a million for the plates."

Cain raised an eyebrow. "Seven hundred thousand?"

"Three fifty apiece."

Cain shook his head. "Seven hundred for me. You get to stay alive."

The corners of Telfer's mouth turned down.

"That's the deal," Cain told him. "All or nothing."

"Okay," Telfer said after a beat. For the first time in hours, he appeared to have relaxed into the seat. "You've got yourself a deal."

Cain smiled as well, restacked the litho plates. "Yes," he said. But his voice held all the promise of a serpent.

It had been a long night. And he'd done a lot of thinking.

He wasn't a greedy man. If he wanted something, he just took it as his own. Appropriated the chattels of his victims as if they were the spoils of war. He'd never found it difficult to finance his lifestyle before, but he had to admit that the thought of a cool seven hundred thousand bucks rang sweet even to his ears. Especially when enunciated slowly.

Seven. Hundred. Thousand. Dollars.

Undeniably, the subject of the money was a distraction. He'd pondered taking what was already available and making do, but the thought that the bogus money could spell his downfall made him hold back. Why risk blowing his cover by passing a fake note at a goddamn McDonald's when he could have as much of the real thing as he'd ever require?

Not only that, but the thought of playing Telfer like a pawn appealed to his sense of the grandiose. He'd allow Telfer to touch the money, hold it in his hands, let him sniff the stench of riches beyond his dreams, before finally snatching it away from him. That would be just punishment for the trouble he'd caused.

Then, of course, it would be a pleasant trip out into the desert for the final reckoning.

Yes, the subject of the money was a distraction. But so was what he'd just witnessed on the motel's TV set. He wasn't one for watching television. Never had been. The only reason he'd switched it on was to mask their conversation from guests in the adjacent rooms.

He wasn't averse to seeing his handiwork on the screen. But there was a major difference this time. He had a good mind to telephone the freaking FBI and put them right about a thing or two. Particularly regarding Telfer's part in the slaying of the two drifters he'd appropriated the VW from. Why the hell should Telfer get any of the glory from that?

"Don't you be getting any big ideas," he said. "We both know who killed those two, and before long *everyone* will know the truth. How anyone could even think you were responsible is beyond belief."

He turned from the TV to observe the trussed form lying on the recliner. Telfer hadn't the faintest idea what he was referring to. He was asleep, fatigue finally overcoming his fear and discomfort. Cain raised an eyebrow. He listened to Telfer's breathing patterns. Not feigning, then? Definitely asleep.

Cain made a noise deep in his throat, the call of a quizzical owl. He leaned forward and switched off the TV. Then he walked over to the recliner, lifted his foot, and nudged Telfer awake. It was Telfer's turn to make owl noises, this one startled and ready to take flight.

"Chill out," Cain told him. "I'm not going to harm you."

Stiffly, Telfer squirmed up to a sitting position. It wasn't an easy task with both hands and feet bound. "What's going on?"

"Almost time to go," Cain told him.

Telfer sucked in a couple of breaths, exhaled long and loud. Then he rocked forward so that he was on the edge of the recliner. He nodded at his bonds. "You planning on carrying me outta here?"

"No," Cain said, "I'm going to allow you to walk. But remember that I'll be holding a gun. Shout or try to run and I'll kill you. I don't care how many people are around, I'll do it. The truth—as they say—will out."

Telfer gave him an odd look. He had no idea what Cain was referring to. Cain smiled to himself. Let him wonder. Let him fear.

Cain indicated Telfer's feet. "I'll cut you loose in a moment. Your hands'll stay tied until it's time to leave."

"Okay."

"If you want to use the bathroom I'll let you."

"That's good of you," Telfer grunted.

"That's okay. Don't want you thinking I'm a total bastard."

"The thought never crossed my mind," Telfer said. He watched Cain. The ghost of a smile played across Cain's lips.

"What've you got in your fridge? Anything cold to drink?" Cain asked.

"Nothing. Unless you like milk."

Cain made a face. Then, hopefully, "Chocolate milk?"

"Cow's milk."

Again the face.

"There's always tap water," Telfer offered.

"I'll pass," Cain said.

"You know, I think I do need to go to the toilet."

Cain tsk-tsked. "Better only be a number one. I refuse to wipe your ass for you."

"You could always loosen my hands," Telfer suggested with a smile.

"Your hands stay tied till I'm good and ready."

Telfer shrugged. "Do you want to unzip me?"

"Forget about it," Cain said deep in his throat. "You can go just before we leave."

Telfer gave him a wink and a jerk of his head.

"What are you so goddamn happy about?" Cain demanded.

"It's good to be alive," Telfer said.

"Yeah," Cain said. "Just keep that thought in mind and we'll do just fine." He glanced at his wristwatch. "Okay, time to cut these ropes. And no Bruce Lee stuff. You try to kick me and I'll shoot your feet off."

If Telfer could have raised his palms, he would have. "I thought we'd made a deal. I'm not going to try to escape. I've promised you I'll do the deal for the litho plates. You've promised that you'll let me live. I'm happy with that."

"I'll only be happy when you're out of my frigging hair," Cain grunted.

"You could always let me go now," Telfer offered.

Cain snorted. There was something disarming about John Telfer that appealed to him. Something that made him smile. Maybe killing him was a little extreme? No, it was just. An eye for an eye. Telfer had stolen his Bowie knife and thrown it away. It was fitting that a knife be used to punish him in turn.

Cain made Telfer push both feet out. Then, in a swift draw that would have shamed a gunslinger, Cain brought out the scaling knife and swiped it down in a shallow arc. The cord from the Venetian blinds that he'd used to tie Telfer's ankles gave with a twang and Telfer's legs sprang apart. Before Telfer could control his wayward feet, the knife was back in Cain's waistband.

Cain gave him a tight smile. The quick-draw display was for more than the purpose of loosening his prisoner's legs; it was a show of his skill with a blade. Something for Telfer to dwell on while they traveled together.

"So how're we gonna do this?" Telfer asked.

"We're going to go out to my car. I'll have the gun. Simple as that."

"Do I get to put my shoes back on?"

"Obviously," Cain said.

"What about my backpack?"

"I'll carry it."

"My spare clothes?"

"Leave them," Cain said. Again he smiled, but this time there was a cold edge to it. "If you wish, you can always come back for them afterward."

Telfer sat back, lips pursed. "Do you want to pass me my shoes or can I fetch them myself?"

"Here," Cain said, slinging his shoes to him. Telfer squeezed his feet in without the benefit of untying the laces. "Ready?"

Telfer smiled in affirmation.

Cain came forward. He held the gun in his left hand, and again drew the scaling knife with his right. This time the motion was languid. He pressed the gun to Telfer's forehead. "Easy now," he warned.

Telfer didn't move except to raise his bound wrists. Cain snicked apart the electrical cord. Telfer dropped his hands but continued to work his wrists in small circles, attempting to get the blood flowing again. Cain backed away.

"Now," Cain said. "We do this nice and easy. We go out of the room and down the back stairs. You'll lead the way.

When you get to the ground floor, go to the right, go around to the parking lot. When we get there, I'll tell you where my car is. Okay?"

"Got it," Telfer confirmed.

"And remember: try to alert anyone . . ."

"And you shoot me."

"Got it," Cain mimicked.

Telfer rocked his weight back in the recliner, using the motion to bring himself to his feet. As he came up, his right hand remained behind him, hidden momentarily from Cain's view.

Cain was ready for Telfer to make a break for freedom, but not at that instant. Not while Cain still held the weapons. He was totally unprepared for Telfer whipping his arm toward him, the blade of his very own Bowie knife slicing the air before him.

"Whoa!" Cain yelped, taking a step back. Out of reaction his response wasn't to bring up his gun, it was to grab his scaling knife. If Telfer wanted to, he could have sprung in close and gutted him in one motion. But despite Cain's dazed senses, Telfer never followed through. Instead, with a smile on his face, he twirled the knife over and presented the handle to Cain.

"What the hell?" Cain demanded.

Telfer said, "This the knife you were so concerned about?"

Cain gaped at Telfer for a long moment. Telfer returned his stare, watching him steadily. Finally, Cain gave his head a little shake, seemed to come out of his daydream. "So you didn't toss it away? You had it all along?"

"Down the back of the recliner," Telfer said. "A trick I learned back home. You never knew when you'd get a visitor with less than your best interests at heart. Not that I ever needed to pull a knife before, but I was always prepared. Just in case."

"You could've killed me. You could've escaped." Cain appeared to be mildly impressed. "Why didn't you?"

"I'm not a killer," Telfer said.

Cain stared at him.

Telfer sniffed. "Just call it an act of faith, okay?"

Cain's eyebrows shot heavenward.

"I've given you back your knife." Telfer paused. "All I ask is that you stay true to your word."

Cain bobbed his head in answer. Slowly he reinserted the scaling knife in his waistband, then tentatively reached for the hilt of the Bowie.

Taking it, he withdrew it slowly from Telfer's grasp. "I've done you an injustice, after all. Perhaps you're more dangerous than I thought. Maybe I should kill you now and get it over with, huh?"

In answer, Telfer raised his shoulders. "If that's the way it's gonna be, there's nothing I can do about it. Not now that I've given you back your knife."

His head tilted to one side, Cain beamed a smile. "You know something? For a thief, I think I'm beginning to like you, John. Maybe I will let you live after all."

"Just maybe?"

Cain tapped the flat of the Bowie on John's chest. "Let's not attempt to fool each other. We're both the same in many respects. One thing is obvious; we can both lie. If I told you that I promised not to kill you, would you believe me? Perhaps it's best I simply say 'maybe.' At least then you can't be sure. Does that not give you a modicum of hope?"

Telfer shook his head in bemusement. "When you put it that way, I suppose it does. Can I ask you one thing before we leave?"

Cain raised his chin.

"Can't we do this in a civilized manner? Without the threat of a gun constantly pointed at me?"

Cain agreed. "As an act of faith?"

"Precisely."

"Lead on, then, John. You know the way."

Telfer turned toward the vestibule. Cain slipped the gun

into his trouser pocket and followed on behind. The Bowie he held like a baby cradled in his arms.

"Where are we going, anyway?" Cain asked.

"Marina del Rey," Telfer said over his shoulder.

Cain glanced down at the magazine spread out on the coffee table. All the beautiful yachts. He laughed. "I should have known."

29

WE WALKED OUT OF LAX INTO BRILLIANT SUN-
shine tinged with smog.

"Welcome to Los Angeles," Rink said.

I stifled the urge to cough.

Rink laughed to himself. "You get used to it. Just try not to breathe for the next week or so and you'll be fine."

We hailed a cab and followed Route 405 north. Off to our left was the vastness of the Pacific Ocean. We only got snatches of the blue expanse, but I was constantly aware of it. Something about the sky over the sea, like it hovered over a magnificent precipice. Signposts over the highway indicated Marina del Rey, Venice Beach, Santa Monica, all off toward the sea. All places I'd have loved to visit given the opportunity.

To our east, Hollywood and Beverly Hills beckoned, but we continued north past the Getty Center until we hit the 101, then joined the flow of traffic heading east. We passed Universal Studios, and like most, I craned my neck hoping to see someone famous. Then we were fast approaching Pasadena, where Rink had set us up a place to stay.

We had to speak to a house manager, something like a low-rent concierge, who had an apartment on the lower floor of the apartment block where we were going to stay. He gave Rink a key card and directed us to our apartment, gesturing with the ham sandwich he held in his hand.

When we found our apartment, it turned out to be bigger than I'd expected. We both chose a bedroom, then convened in the lounge area. It was clean and roomy, and the air-conditioning was a blessing after the sweltering drive. Still, neither of us wanted to remain cooped up there for long.

"Want to hit the shower, then go out and get a bite to eat?" Rink offered.

"Sounds like a plan," I admitted. "But I think the shower can wait. My stomach thinks my throat's cut."

"What do you want?" Rink asked. "Silver service or burger an' fries?"

"Burger and fries all the way, big guy," I said.

"I know just the place," Rink said.

He took me to a diner with the unlikely sobriquet of Spicy Johnny's—I couldn't stop myself laughing, the name conjured up the kind of ad you see emblazoned across those coin-operated machines in men's restrooms. I have to admit, though, Spicy Johnny flipped a mean burger, and his Caesar salad topped off with breaded onion rings was to die for. A side plate of Cajun-spiced potato wedges and a huge banana shake finished me off.

Back in our rooms, we fell asleep almost instantly. Even my worry about John was shoved to one side by the more urgent need for quality rest. I slept for the best part of two hours, waking when the sun was at its zenith and its most intense.

My body was dripping with perspiration and I could put off my shower no longer. Coming out of the stall feeling almost human again, I could hear Rink moving around in his own room. Vacating the bathroom, I went into the living room. I popped a bottle of mineral water I found in the fridge and sat back on a comfy chair in front of the TV. The news was on, so I watched.

When Rink was finished getting ready, he joined me. We'd already discussed local contacts, and Rink was going to set us up with an LAPD officer named Cheryl Barker to see what they knew. Before that could be done, there were still a few things left over from Little Rock that I wanted to lay to rest.

"I feel a bit of a heel leaving Harvey to pick up the pieces we left behind."

"Harve'll be fine," Rink assured me. "If we hadn't allowed him to do something for us, it'd have hurt his feelings. He's a sensitive guy, you know."

I laughed. To look at him, Harvey was unstoppable, as if you would blunt an ax trying to mark his shiny dome. But Rink was right; I'd seen Harvey's vulnerability when he had to take a step back from the assault on Sigmund Petoskey. It wasn't easy for him to sit on his haunches while the rest of us went into the thick of it.

Then there was the other side.

The cool way he'd shot the hit man in the mouth.

"He'll get Louise Blake to a safe place," Rink went on. "Don't worry about that."

"As long as nothing happens to them before he gets the opportunity," I said.

"What's goin' to happen? You ask me, the homeboys who were puttin' the heat on Louise are in L.A. now. I don't think Harve's got anythin' to worry about."

"You think the FBI is going to let Louise go? She's a direct link to John; they'll be watching in case he tries to make contact."

"Harvey's good. He'll get her out safely. Whether the FBI likes it or not."

I took Rink's word for it. He knew Harvey and had told me prior to meeting him that he was a good soldier. Now I'd witnessed his skills firsthand, and I had no doubt that Rink knew what he was talking about.

"So what do you make of what Petoskey told us?" I asked.

Rink shrugged, made a clucking noise with his tongue. "All bullshit."

"In particular what he said about CIA agents?"

"Bullshit. He knew full well who those other guys were. He was just spinning us a line because he thought we were federal agents."

"You remember the name someone shouted when we were in the building?"

"Yeah. Hendrickson's men are here," he said. "They were shouting like we were from a rival gang."

"Yes. A *rival* gang. I think Hendrickson sent them to mess with Petoskey. I get the feeling Petoskey and Hendrickson aren't on good terms anymore. Shit, we went in there and blasted the hell out of some of his guys, shot up his building, probably ruined his evening. But he hasn't made one word of complaint to the police. If he believed that we were government agents, don't you think there'd have been a massive lawsuit lodged by now?"

"Unless he knew we weren't with the CIA and was only playing out a scenario for the benefit of his guests."

"Nah, too slim." I mulled it around my head a little longer. "Could be he thought we were sent by Hendrickson, and he mentioned the CIA to put a scare into us. You know, like a subtle threat?"

"Unless these Latinos *are* government agents?"

"They're not CIA. Walter confirmed that."

"He could've been lying."

"No, Rink. He wouldn't've given me approval to shoot to kill if they were any of his men."

"So why all the bull from Petoskey about the CIA?"

Back to square one.

"We can only wait and see," I said.

30

THE SUN WAS WARM ON CAIN'S FACE. ABOVE HIM, a yellow-and-white-striped awning dotted with dried insects flapped on a lazy breeze. He was quite at home sitting outside a café overlooking the boardwalk in an exclusive part of Marina del Rey. He could see himself living in a place just like this. Then again, seven hundred grand wouldn't buy him a toolshed here.

Beyond a six-foot wall was a yacht valued at more than five million bucks. In keeping with the area, even the concrete wasn't tacky. For its entire length, there was a bright mural lovingly painted in azure, emerald, and stark, brilliant white. Beyond it, he could hear the lapping of the water, the groan of boats as they moved against the pilings of the dock. Gulls wheeled above the masts that heaved like a forest in a gentle breeze.

Against his better judgment, Cain had allowed Telfer to enter the private harbor alone. Before agreeing, he'd first made sure that the only exit—apart from the open sea—was through the wrought-iron gate thirty yards to his right. It was of course the only way the deal could be struck. Telfer had argued that his buyer would panic if he saw a stranger tailing him onto the boat. In that case his likely assumption would be that Telfer had set him up, and he would do one of two things: refuse to negotiate or, worse, have Telfer and Cain sunk to the bottom of the sea at the next high tide.

Cain had to agree. Though he wasn't happy about relinquishing either the bag of goodies or Telfer, had he walked aboard the yacht with a gun trained on Telfer, he could say good-bye to the promised riches and to the reckoning he still planned for him.

A waitress brought Cain an espresso in a cup hardly bigger than a thimble. He drank it in one gulp and ordered a second. The woman gave him an odd look that he greeted with a sour expression of his own. She went off to fetch another.

"Make it a double," Cain called after her, as though ordering whiskey at a Wild West saloon.

When she returned, she placed the cup—more like a teacup this time—on his table, then hurried off before he could tie up any more of her precious time. Service, it appeared, was not customary for those who came to ogle the rich dudes' yachts.

Fifteen minutes passed without any activity. Cain was sure that Telfer hadn't slipped away undetected, unless he'd snorkeled his way to freedom beneath the waves.

Still, he was beginning to grow uncomfortable.

Fifteen minutes wasn't a long time for someone to make a deal for seven hundred thousand, but it was fifteen minutes too long for Cain. Scenarios were beginning to play out in his mind, and he knew he couldn't wait another five minutes. His inner pessimist was working overtime.

What if Telfer had done the deal, but then appealed to his business partners to help him escape? What if they'd already called the cops, telling them that a self-confessed killer was sitting outside, sipping bitter coffee at the harbor side? What if, even now, plainclothes detectives were creeping up on him, disguised as rich men in Armani suits?

He surreptitiously scanned the boardwalk. Could there be police posing as tourists who, like him, feigned interest in the elegant yachts? *Are they moving on me now?* he wondered.

It was enough to make him squirm. Cain didn't like squirming. He liked to make others squirm.

"Enough is enough," he told himself.

Telfer had too much to lose if the police became involved. Okay, his life would be back in his own hands, and likely he would get the money, but chances were that the police would be onto him and his business associates as thick as stink on a mangy goat.

Knowing the way a thief's mind worked, Cain believed that Telfer would do the deal, then return to him with the hope of escaping and relieving him of the money when a healthier opportunity presented itself. If the tables were turned, that's exactly what he'd do. So he could do nothing but bide his time and take charge again when Telfer returned with the money.

He might as well enjoy the sunshine and his coffee.

Then he saw the two men.

They were both dark, with wavy hair and thin mustaches. Both wore silk suits and tooled leather loafers without socks. They were alike in so many ways that they could be brothers. The only thing that differentiated them was that the slightly taller of the two wore a gauze dressing on one ear. The bandage stuck out like a blind cobbler's thumb.

Something else; they carried guns. Not out in the open, but pushed down the backs of their trousers. He could see the telltale bulge in their lower backs as they sauntered past. He couldn't make out what they were saying; not only were they conversing in hushed tones, but they were speaking in Spanish or Portuguese. Cain could speak five languages, but—unfortunately—none of them of Mediterranean descent.

Ordinarily the men's presence wouldn't have alarmed him. It wouldn't be unknown for armed security to prowl the harbor side. But there was something about these men that rang his inner alarm. Their furtive approach to the gate was untoward, as was the way they glanced up at the rigging of the yacht Telfer had boarded and nodded to each other in affirmation. Then there was the way they sauntered along while unconsciously glancing over their shoulders every couple of steps. They were so obviously trying to remain inconspicuous that their presence screamed at high volume.

Cain couldn't sit on his thumbs any longer. He rattled a handful of coins onto the table and stood up, gulping down the remains of his espresso. After he'd stretched and rolled his neck, he fell into step behind the two men. Unlike them, he stayed close to the entrances of the cafés and boutiques lining the harbor, using his cover as a browsing tourist to mask his interest. Without alerting them, he got to within five yards of them.

They still conversed in whispers, but one word stood out. He heard it mentioned twice. A name. Telfer. And he knew that the men Telfer was running from had finally caught up with him.

Oh, such a dilemma. But oh, what a challenge. Cain smiled to himself, slipped his hands into his pockets, and caressed his keepsakes. Pretty soon, he decided, more bones would be joining his collection. Happy with the thought, he watched as the two men approached the pier gate that Telfer had passed through to get to the boat. One guy hailed the security guard sitting in a booth on the other side. The guard walked over, looking ridiculous in pale blue shirt, knee-length Bermuda shorts, and deck shoes, with a peaked cap perched jauntily above his sun-weathered face.

One of the men flashed something at the guard. Just a brief glimpse, but Cain got the impression of a badge in a leather wallet. The guard looked impressed, and not a little excited. He nodded vigorously as he bent to unlatch the gate. All that was missing was a tug of the forelock.

Cain's smile grew sour. Anyone worth their salt could get hold of fake credentials; the guard needed a good kick in the ass for not paying more attention to the man's ID. Likely he was a frustrated wannabe cop who couldn't help but worship those who carried the badge for real. His fawning was almost sickening.

The two Latinos were admitted to the inner compound. One of them rewarded the guard with a pat on the shoulder and the guard looked like he was ready to salute. He was still standing with a hand on the open gate, watching the two men walk along the pier toward the boats, when Cain stepped up behind him.

"Excuse me," Cain said, and the guard turned to him.

"Yes, sir, how may I help you?"

"I'm Special Agent Kennedy. FBI. First off, you can keep your voice down," Cain said. He used a tone like he was about to reward the man with a message of great importance. Hooked, the guard looked at him expectantly. Cain leaned in close and whispered, "This is a matter of extreme sensitivity."

Cain steered the guard back toward his booth. "Can we speak inside?"

Caught up in the mystery of the moment, the guard allowed himself to be propelled toward the booth. He even opened the door and allowed Cain to press inside the booth with him. The enclosed space had the locker-room smell of sweat.

The guard was pressed up against the single chair, almost buckling at the knees. He didn't object. He accepted this invasion of his personal space as simply one aspect of the clandestine encounter.

Cain asked, "The two men who just entered, what did they say to you?"

"They said they were with the government," the guard answered quickly. "Agents Ramos and Esquerra. They wanted to know the location of Mr. Carson's boat. Why do you ask, sir?"

"Because I'm a real government agent and those two aren't," Cain said. He tipped a nod toward Carson's boat.

"You mean their badges were fake? Damn."

"As fake as Pamela Anderson's breasts," Cain told him.

The guard appeared stunned at Cain's choice of words. "I didn't know," he finally said, as though in apology. Cain couldn't decide if he meant the men's badges or Pammy's main assets, but he let the notion pass without smiling. He said, "They're a pair of international drug traffickers, and I'm about to bust them wide open."

"You are? All alone? Don't you have backup or some-thing?"

Cain shook his head in mock disappointment. "Me and my partner got separated. I don't even have my goddamn walkie-talkie with me to get in touch with him. These guys are real good. We've been after them for months. When I spotted them, I had no option but to follow them."

The guard was nodding along with each new nugget Cain fed him. "You want me to telephone for help?"

"I'd appreciate it if you would," Cain said.

"No problem," said the guard, turning to sit down. As he picked up the receiver and brought it to his ear, Cain was happy that the guard was sufficiently distracted. Plus, sitting in the chair, he was out of sight of any passersby. Pretending to spy out the window at the receding men, Cain leaned over him. He pulled out his scaling knife.

"Who should I call?" the guard asked. "The FBI?"

"No, 911 will do," Cain told him. "Maybe you'd best call for an ambulance."

The guard didn't detect the change in tone. In fact, he didn't detect anything more than the pressure of Cain's hand on his shoulder. He glanced up and back, and as he did so, Cain drew the knife across his exposed throat. Reflexively the guard dropped the telephone receiver, reached toward his throat, but already he'd lost control of his extremities and his palms flopped uselessly against his upper chest. Blood spurted from his severed arteries. Cain held him, placing steady pressure on the guard's shoulders to keep him from rising out of the chair. The guard's feet kicked and skidded in the blood pooling beneath them.

It didn't take long.

He was dead before the two Latinos made it to Carson's yacht.

"Totally inept," Cain told the unhearing guard. "No wonder your application to the LAPD was denied."

With no time for keepsakes, he paused only to pull down a screen that closed off any view into the interior of the booth.

He felt around in the guard's pocket and found a bunch of keys, which he used to lock the door behind him.

The two bogus agents were poised at the base of a gangway that led to Carson's yacht. There was a third man on the boat itself, and he had a radio pressed to his ear. As Cain began walking toward them, he saw the third man nod, and the two Latinos began the ascent of the ramp.

"What's going on here, then?" Cain wondered aloud. Telfer had said that the man he'd stolen the litho plates from employed the men following him. The guy on the boat, Mr. Carson, was a rival of their employer. So how come the two Latinos were given unchallenged access to the boat?

Only one conclusion: double-cross. Couldn't be anything else. Telfer had been set up. And by association, so had Cain. And that made him angry. He began to walk faster, his shoes squeaking on the boardwalk. He slipped his hand into the small of his back, came out holding the gun. With his other hand, he drew the Bowie.

Only twenty yards away he heard raised voices, and he began to hurry.

Ten yards from the yacht he heard harsh laughter, then, "You think I'm about to go to war with Hendrickson over you, you goddamn asshole?"

Then Telfer's voice: "You bastard, Carson. I trusted you."

"Shame," said Carson. "Let that be a lesson for you. Money talks and shit walks, my friend."

"You—"

"Quiet!" someone barked. One of the Latino men. "You're coming with us, Telfer. Dead or alive, I don't really give a shit."

Then Cain was at the bottom of the gangway. Without pause, he went up it in two bounds. Stepping onto the deck, he saw the man with the radio. Minder, Cain decided. Probably one of a number of guards on the boat. Cain's arrival caused the man to turn. Before the surprise could even register in his face, Cain was chest to chest with him. The man grunted, looked down, and saw the handle of the Bowie knife jutting from beneath his breastbone.

"Quietly does it," Cain hushed him as he tugged down on the handle. By the law governing leverage, the blade's tip sawed upward. Eight inches of honed steel easily found the lower chambers of the man's heart. He was dead before he could make a further sound. Cain lowered the man to the deck, then tugged loose the blade, wiped it clean on the man's trousers, and turned toward the cabin door.

The yacht was huge, and the living area was about as plush as any five-star hotel Cain had ever seen. Wide sliding doors led to an elegantly furnished sitting area. It was all cut glass and sumptuous leather. Even chandeliers. A massive plasma screen satellite TV dominated the forward wall. Then there were the six men.

John Telfer was sitting in a chair across a glass table from an older man in an open-neck shirt and tan slacks. His hair and the tufts that poked from his chest were white, standing out against his deep tan. That'll be Carson, then, Cain decided.

On the table was Telfer's backpack, open to show the spurious treasure within, and a briefcase that was shut tight. Inside it, Cain guessed, was the seven hundred grand. The two Latinos were there, their backs to Cain. He noted that they hadn't yet drawn their guns, but the two other men in the room had. These were minders, like the man Cain had just stabbed. Hard-faced men who crowded Telfer yet wore cautious expressions in front of the Latinos.

Cain detected movement on the deck above him. He glanced up, ready to lift the gun, and saw a young bikini-clad woman move hurriedly away.

One of two things was about to happen. The bitch would have the good sense to get the hell off the boat, or she was going to set up a racket to alert her sugar daddy in the cabin. Cain couldn't take the chance it would be the second option. He had to act now, while he still had surprise on his side.

And with the decision came action. He only had six bullets and he had to make them count. The minders first.

Cain stepped up to the doorway. One of the sliding partitions was open, so he stepped inside. He was only ten feet away from the first minder when he lifted the gun and fired. The man's head erupted in cherry-red fragments.

Then chaos ensued.

Chaos was fine with Cain. He loved chaos.

Telfer's face came up, registering shock, and not a little relief in a mad sort of way. The Latinos were spinning, both going for their guns, the second minder already rounding on Cain. Only Carson had the good sense to throw himself to the floor and attempt to escape beneath a nearby counter.

Cain snorted, and shot the second minder. He hit the man in the right arm, the bullet passing through it into the flesh of his thick chest. The man went down, though Cain knew immediately he wasn't dead. Didn't matter, he'd dropped his gun, and he saw that Telfer had the presence of mind to snatch it up.

The two Latinos were next. Cain shot the one with the bandaged ear, hitting him in the thigh as the man leaped away. The bullet spun him, and the man went to the floor at the feet of his friend. The second Latino was already bringing up his gun to fire, and Cain realized it was time to move. But instead of bolting for cover, he leaped farther into the room, shouting, "Move your ass, Telfer!"

The second Latino fired. Not at him, as Cain had hoped, but at Telfer. The bullet struck the back of Telfer's chair. Directly where his head had been an instant earlier. Telfer was already bent double over the glass table, reaching for the briefcase. As the Latino tried to draw another bead on Telfer, Cain shot him. Twice, once in the gut, then higher up at the jawline. The man went over backward, trailing a ribbon of blood that was stark against the chandeliers' twinkling lights.

Cain turned on Telfer. "Get a freakin' move on!"

Telfer snatched the briefcase to his chest, rising up at last. Cain stepped toward him. The gun trained on him. "Give me the gun."

Telfer shook his head. Lifted his own gun and pointed it at Cain.

"We haven't got time for this now," Cain warned him.

"No," Telfer said. "We haven't."

They both eyed each other over the ends of their guns.

"Let's get the hell out of here and worry about the rest later," Cain offered.

Before Telfer could accept or decline the invitation, a door burst open at the front of the cabin and another man skidded through. He had a compact Uzi submachine gun in his hands. He made a quick scan of the living area. To give him his due, the chaotic scene didn't appear to faze him much. He lifted the Uzi and let loose an arching stream of bullets as he thudded over to cover Carson. In the same instant the injured Latino rolled over, grabbing at the gun he'd dropped on the floor. Two targets, one bullet, more coming his way. Cain decided the best course of action was to get out as quickly as possible.

As bullets churned the decor behind him, he flung himself through a side window, crashing through glass to sprawl on the deck. Shouts came from inside the cabin, then Telfer was sprawling on the deck beside him, the briefcase clattering away from him. Telfer's shirt was bloody and he groaned as he rolled to his knees. Cain grabbed him, checking his hands.

"What the hell're you doing?" Telfer demanded.

"Where's your gun?" Cain snapped.

"I dropped it," Telfer said.

"Jesus Christ," Cain said. He slapped Telfer's shoulder. "Get the briefcase. We're out of here."

Telfer went on hands and knees, grabbing at the Samsonite case. He came back to Cain, the case against his chest. "That better be *real* money," Cain said.

"Course it is. I'm not a friggin' idiot."

Cain nodded, indicated the front of the boat. "That way. Now."

They both lurched up as the fourth minder appeared at the window they'd recently crashed through. He gave an angry shout, twisted so he could bring the Uzi into play. As he did, Cain sprang toward him with his Bowie knife. The knife connected before the man could depress the trigger, severing his thumb. The man screamed and the gun flopped sideways, bullets splintering the wooden deck next to Telfer. Cain chopped again, this time deep into the man's wrist and the man withdrew his seriously wounded arm from further harm.

Telfer was up and running. Cain glanced at him, then down at the deck. He paused in his flight to retrieve the severed thumb, popping it into his pocket alongside his other mementos.

The bodyguard was back at the window again, but only to scream in abstract terror while he attempted to replace his drooping hand in its rightful place. Cain grinned at him, then charged after Telfer.

He caught up with Telfer at the helm of the yacht. Telfer was wide-eyed as he looked down at the seemingly bottomless gulf below them. The water had a turquoise sheen from the thin layer of diesel oil on its surface.

"Jump," Cain told him.

"No," Telfer said, the briefcase clutched tightly to him.

"Jump, Telfer."

"No way. I can't swim."

"Jesus Christ on a freakin' bike! You can't swim?"

Again Telfer shook his head.

"I don't believe it," Cain said. He grabbed at Telfer and propelled him toward the rail. "Get the hell over the side. If you think I've gone to all this trouble to let you drown . . ."

Telfer resisted, though he knew it was his only chance of survival. Even as he dithered, he could hear the slap of running feet from inside the cabin.

"One of them spics is still alive," Cain snapped at him. "So are two of the guards and Carson. Any second now, they're going to be out here and we'll be dead. You got that?"

Telfer nodded but still held back from jumping.

"Oh, Holy Christ!" Cain said as he grabbed him and flung him bodily over the railing. Telfer hit the water like a stone and sank immediately. Cain lifted a leg to the railing, just as the minder he'd shot in the arm rounded the deck. Blood had made a patchwork of his chest but he was still in the game. He had the Uzi and was already searching for a target.

Cain lifted his gun and fired.

Not at the man, but at the scuba-diving tanks he saw stacked neatly along one wall of the cabin. It was a desperate shot, one he hadn't time to calculate, but even as he plunged headfirst into the sea he felt the concussion of the explosion send shock waves through the water around him. Cain hit the water and swam deeper, his ears thrumming with the concussive blast, until his clawing hand found Telfer's shirt. Telfer twisted and tugged, in the throes of panic.

Cain cursed, letting loose a stream of bubbles. He couldn't get a grip on Telfer because he was also holding on to his Bowie. All the trouble he'd gone to in order to regain his knife and now this? He let the blade drop from his hand, watched it sink with a wistful look on his face until it was lost in the murk. Then he angrily grabbed hold of Telfer's clothing and kicked upward.

They broke the churning surface, Cain behind Telfer with an arm looped around his neck. Telfer gagged, spat, and sucked in great lungfuls of air as he cradled the briefcase to his chest like a baby. Cain guessed his death grip on the case had nothing to do with what was inside, but rather that the sealed case was a handy flotation device.

Twenty feet away, the yacht was on fire. When the tanks had gone up, they'd taken the minder with them, not to mention a good portion of the deck and cabin. Cain spied a bikini-clad figure leaping from the boat into the water. Another figure hobbled down the steps onto the pier, a white patch on the side of his head. Even from here, Cain could tell it was the remaining Latino.

Of the remaining minder and Carson, there was no sign. Perhaps the Latino had turned his gun on them before making his escape. But Carson appeared, staggered to the railing, and fired a handgun at the limping Latino trying to escape. His aim was useless, and the Latino made it to the shelter of a second boat. The Latino proved a better shot, firing back at Carson three times in quick succession. Carson folded, somersaulted over the rail, and sprawled facefirst on the boardwalk. Didn't look like he'd be getting up again.

Cain paid them no further heed. He kicked with his feet, trawling Telfer and his precious cargo backward. They'd just made it to the ladder of a yacht about a hundred feet away when the air turned inferno hot around them. Cain held Telfer down, following him beneath the water as Carson's yacht erupted in a churning fireball that scattered steaming chunks of metal and wood across the harbor.

31

"YOU'VE GOTTA BE YANKIN' MY GODDAMN CHAIN."

Rink was standing with his knuckles on the hood of Cheryl Barker's squad car. His bowed head emphasizing the breadth of his shoulders, equally emphasizing his dismay.

I wasn't feeling much better. I was thinking much the same thing as he was.

We'd both caught the TV news earlier.

A man with a hangdog expression related the disaster that had struck an exclusive yachting club only minutes earlier. The camera cut from the studio to an on-scene reporter who was standing amid crowds of stunned onlookers as a huge pall of black smoke breached the heavens behind them. I'd grimaced at the screen. The world was full of doom and gloom. Even, I'd decided, in exclusive rich men's playgrounds like Marina del Rey.

Uninterested, I'd switched channels. Then we'd driven out here to meet with Cheryl Barker.

We were parked on the ridge of a shale embankment at the head of a valley in which we could glimpse the roofs of houses amid lush greenery. Palms and peppertrees dominated. Birds called and flapped in the skies above us.

Cheryl had chosen this place for an impromptu meeting simply because it was a halfway point for us all. I could hear the disjointed chatter and squeals of children and guessed it was playtime at some park hidden in the trees. It was a surreal moment, us talking about death and destruction while dozens of kids laughed and whooped with delight below us.

Barker, an attractive woman with light freckles and short but unruly red hair, shook her head. "I ain't the one yankin' chains, Jared. It's just come over the air. The fireball in Marina del Rey is down to your good buddy John Telfer."

Rink glanced my way, and I lifted my shoulders in a noncommittal way. Since the nonsense I'd read on Harvey's computer, not to mention the subsequent newscasts I'd caught on TV and our rental car radio, it didn't surprise me that this latest atrocity was being laid at John's door. It seemed that John had superseded Osama bin Laden as the most notorious felon in the western hemisphere.

Barker was almost as tall as Rink but she was much leaner, and that made her appear diminutive next to my friend's bulk. She stood with her thumbs hooked in her belt like some Wild West gunslinger. Annie Oakley in the flesh.

Rink turned from bracing himself on the hood of the LAPD mobile. He looked Barker up and down. He took in the officer's pristine uniform.

"You ain't made detective yet?"

"Nope," Barker said.

"Someone has to see sense soon," Rink offered.

"Tell the truth, I'm in no great hurry. I'm as happy swanning around in a squad car as steering a desk. If I get the promotion, all well and good. If not, well, I'm as happy busting the balls of gangbangers and writing misdemeanor tickets for little old ladies driving the wrong way up the freeway." Barker glanced down, brushed an imaginary piece of lint off her black shirt. "Anyways, I'm partial to the uniform. Can't see why there's such a big deal about getting into civilian duds."

Rink gave Barker a tight-lipped grin. "Plus you get to drive a cool car, huh?"

"Yep, beats the hell outta the pool cars the detectives limp around in. More power under the hood, for one thing."

"You'll need it when you're chasing all those rogue grandmothers in golf carts." The small talk out of the way, Rink asked, "You putting much credence in it?"

"What? The fireball? No doubt about it, Jared. Eyewitness testimony places your boy at the scene."

"They sure it was John Telfer?" I asked, stepping into their circle.

Barker turned and squinted at me.

"Joe Hunter," I said, introducing myself. I stuck out a hand and Barker accepted it, shaking it languidly. "John is my brother."

Barker frowned and glanced at Rink, who said, "It's cool, Cheryl."

Rink's word was enough for Barker.

"Your boy's been on every network and newspaper in the country. Witness swears that Telfer was the one who brought hell to that boat."

I still wasn't convinced and it obviously showed in my face.

"Before the boat went supernova, the witness managed to get off it unscathed. She says that John Telfer must've brought a bomb on board with him. He was carrying some kinda backpack when he arrived." Barker sucked air through her teeth. "Mind you, we ain't giving the bomb part much weight. More than likely, something on the boat went bang. Apparently there were a lot of guns going off prior to the explosion."

"It's not like John," I said, thinking aloud.

Barker lifted her knobby shoulders. "Just telling you what's been said."

"Was there any mention of why John was on this boat in the first place?"

"Nothing the witness will admit to."

"Who is the witness?"

Barker said, "A hottie Rhet Carson picked up over on Catalina Island. You know how these old rich guys are. They like a touch of eye candy draped over the rails of their yachts when they pull into dock. Gives them, whaddaya call it, self-esteem?"

"Are you saying your eyewitness is a hooker?"

"Hookers have eyes the same as anyone," Barker replied. "She says that Telfer wasn't the only one to come on board. Two guys in sharp suits turned up. Then some other guy. She seems to think that the last guy on board was with Telfer. The shooting started just after he got there."

Rink and I looked at each other.

"Did she give a description of any of the three that turned up after John? The two guys in suits, for instance?"

"Let me see." Barker pulled a notebook from her shirt pocket and thumbed through to a page marked with an elastic band. I doubted she needed the prompt. "Yeah, here we are. An APB was put out for them. Both guys are in their thirties, medium build, dark haired. Kinda swarthy-looking. Dressed in designer suits by all accounts."

"The Mambo Kings." I nodded to Rink.

Barker lifted the corner of a lip at my remark. "You know these two?"

"Not personally," I said. "But I intend to."

Barker looked off across the valley. "Whatever your intentions, you can scratch one of them from your 'to-do' list. Got another dispatch not ten minutes ago saying one of them was among the dead found in the burned-out wreckage. The other could be at the bottom of the harbor for all we know. They're sending divers down as we speak."

"What about the third man? The one she thought was with John?"

Again Barker scanned her notebook. She made an exasperated noise as she puffed out her cheeks. "White guy. Late thirties to early forties. Cold eyes. That's about it."

"Nothing about his clothing? His hair coloring?"

"Nope. The witness said she only got a quick glance at him. Something about the way he looked at her was enough to send her scuttling for cover, she said." It was apparent Barker didn't like what she was reading. "Not to mention the fact he'd just gutted one of Carson's bodyguards with a knife."

It was my turn to puff out my cheeks. I looked at Rink and saw him staring back. Turning back to Barker, I asked, "Did the witness say anything else about him or John? Did they make it off the boat before it blew?"

"She says they jumped in the harbor just before the boat went up. She didn't see them after that. Chances of them surviving that kind of explosion would be pretty slim."

"John can't swim," I said, a feeling of dread gnawing at my insides. Burned or drowned, neither would be pretty. I had the fleeting impression of John's bloated face peering up at me from some infinitely deep place. Shaking off the disturbing vision wasn't easy, but I had to remain optimistic. I wasn't prepared to admit defeat just yet. Neither was I ready to give up looking for him until the police divers dragged his corpse from the murky water.

"He could've made it out," Rink offered. "Boats are generally moored closely together. Its likely he made it to another one and climbed out of the water."

"I hope so," I said.

"Funny thing is," Barker said, "this other guy, the one who was with Telfer, apparently he did something extremely odd while he was on the yacht."

"Apart from gutting someone with a knife?" I asked.

"Yeah. One of Carson's bodyguards survived the explosion. He was pretty mangled up and not making much sense. He was off his head with pain and blood loss, but he kept on saying, 'He stole my thumb.'"

I glanced sharply at Barker, who gave me a wry smile in return. "Apart from burns over much of his body, his wrist was cut open and he was missing a thumb. Of course, his injuries could've been caused by flying shrapnel from the explosion. Thing is, he was adamant that this mystery man picked his thumb up off the deck."

"Jumpin' Jesus," Rink said, and I could only agree with him.

My theory about John crossing paths with this Harvest-man was beginning to take greater shape. Only thing I couldn't fathom was what that meeting meant to them. What was John doing going there with a murderer? Were they acting as allies, on some mad spree where they were working together? Or was John being compelled to work with this beast? I could only hope it was the latter. For everyone's sake.

I didn't realize I'd fallen silent, caught up in my own thoughts, until Rink nudged me. "You hear that, Hunter?"

"Uh? Hear what?"

"Rhet Carson? The guy who owned the yacht?"

I squinted at Rink in miscomprehension.

"I knew we'd lost you there," Rink said.

"Sorry," I said. "I was just thinking."

"Yeah," Rink said. "I could hear the cogs turning from here."

I shook myself into the here and now. "So what did I miss?"

"Rhet Carson's a major player. Head man of one of the outfits out here."

"What? Like the Mafia?"

Barker gave a little laugh. "The Mafia doesn't hold much sway any longer. Not if you're looking for the old-time God-father type. But you could say he was a key player in the local underworld. Nowadays your most successful mobsters shun the old-style Cosa Nostra methods. Carson's a top-flight business executive. Runs his business from a downtown commercial center, even advertises on the cable networks."

"His business being?" I asked.

"Banking," Barker said. "But more specifically, money-lending."

I said, "You telling me he was money laundering? What better front than to use your own bank?"

Barker snapped her fingers. "You've got it, my friend. There have been a number of high-profile investigations into his business, lots of supposition, but nothing that would stick. There was the rumor that he was laundering counterfeit dollars for some outfit from the East Coast, but the case never really got off the ground. He's laid low for the last coupla years, kept his nose clean, spent more time on his boat. I'm thinking Carson was maybe about to get back in the business again."

I'd had my suspicions since our last talk with Louise Blake. What the *something big* was that she'd referred to.

Forged money has never been a big problem in the U.S., obtaining decent paper being just about impossible. But I also knew that it was a ploy of some terrorist groups to flood countries with fake currency. Kind of destabilized the value of the dollar, bringing down the almighty American Dream. What they couldn't achieve with bombs, they made up for in Mickey Mouse money. Petoskey and Hendrickson would have been making top dollar, selling to the enemies of the USA.

And Rhet Carson had wanted in on the action.

To Cheryl Barker, I said, "But without the drawback of being the middleman this time?"

"It's a fair assumption," Barker said.

"This outfit he was working with, do you know who runs it?" I asked.

"Not personally," Barker said. "I suppose I can find out."

"I might be able to give you a couple of names."

"You already have your suspicions?"

"Yeah. A couple. Could be a guy called Sigmund Petoskey. He has his base in Little Rock, Arkansas."

Barker shook her head at that. "Nah. The mob I'm talking about was rumored to be up in Virginia, maybe Georgia, I can't recall."

"How about Hendrickson?" I asked.

"Like I said, I don't know the names personally. Hendrickson? Sounds familiar. I'll find out."

Rink gave Barker his cell phone number.

Barker, looking every bit the cowgirl, tipped the brim of an imaginary Stetson our way. "I'd best be on my way.

Dallied a little too long. Dispatcher's probably wondering if I've got myself shot dead and is already planning a search party."

I shook hands with Barker, wondering if we'd ever cross paths again. Probably not. Then Barker and Rink hugged as if they'd been intimate once. I didn't ask. Barker then turned to her car and slid behind the wheel. She gave us both an exaggerated wink. "I'll be in touch."

We watched her drive off, her vehicle almost concealed by the plume of road dust churned up by her wheels. After she was gone, we stood kicking our heels.

"So what's the plan of action?" Rink finally asked.

"Marina del Rey's about as good a place as any to start," I suggested.

32

JOHN TELFER WAS LEAKING BLOOD. ORDINARILY that would have been good. But not under these circumstances. Not when the bleeding got in the way of Cain's plans. Not when it could alert a nosy observer to Telfer's plight. Anyone with an ounce of brains would immediately tie a bleeding man to the recent events occurring at the not-too-distant harbor.

"We have to do something about your wound," Cain said.

Lying flat on the bottom of the dinghy, Telfer grimaced up at him. Cain sat at the rear, guiding the outboard motor with one hand. With his other, he held the now-empty pistol aimed in Telfer's direction. The waves were choppy, causing the rubber boat to lurch as it breasted each successive wave.

"Feeling nauseous?" Cain asked.

"What do you care?" Telfer grunted.

"I care. Isn't that enough?"

Telfer twisted his face. "The only thing you care about is getting your hands on the money."

"Not true. I also care about your well-being."

"Yeah. Right."

Cain shrugged. "Think what you will," he said. He made another scan of the horizon. Off over his right shoulder, distant Catalina Island was wreathed in sea haze. He could see the ferry to the mainland chugging toward the harbor, and there were other boats on the water. There were a couple of yachts, a speedboat, and half a dozen chartered boats hauling groups of men off to favorite fishing sites. Thankfully, none of the boats appeared to be coast guard or LAPD. Equally thankfully, none of them was near enough for anyone to see Telfer lying in the bottom of the dinghy.

"Were you shot?" Cain asked.

Telfer ran a hand up his chest. He was tentative, expecting the worst. Finally, he shook his head. "I think it was more of a ricochet. Luckily whatever hit me didn't go all the way in, just scored along my flesh. Hurts like a bugger, though."

Cain nodded solemnly. Inwardly he was relieved. He didn't want Telfer dying on him before he was ready. Still, he didn't want Telfer to know that. The last thing he needed was for Telfer to start kicking up a commotion out here on the water. If Cain had to kill him, it could attract unwanted attention. And he didn't relish attempting to outrun the coast guard in this paltry boat.

"As soon as we make land I'll take a look at it for you," Cain offered. "I know it's only a couple of hours since, but it shouldn't be bleeding now."

Telfer rolled his shoulders. "It'll be okay. I think I just opened the wound crawling into the boat."

"Maybe so, but it won't harm you if I take a look."

Telfer sighed. "Why're you bothering?"

"Bothering? Because it's important to me."

Telfer shook his head. "You don't give a shit about me. I know you've got no intention of upholding our bargain."

"You can think what you like. Just ask yourself one thing. If I intended killing you, why would I bother saving you when I could as easily have left you on that yacht back there?"

"That's easy. You needed me to carry the money."

"So what about when you were in the water? I could've let you drown. It'd have been easier for me to take the briefcase than to haul your sorry ass to safety."

Telfer thought about that one. In the end, he had no reply. Instead he asked, "So what exactly do you intend doing with me?"

"First things first, eh? First, we get to dry land. We clean you up. Then I'll decide what happens from there."

"What about this?" Telfer reached behind him and touched the briefcase he was using as a somewhat uncomfortable pillow.

Cain gave him a smile. "I'll unburden you of that. You're injured. It would be unfair of me to expect you to lug it around with you."

"I've still got one good arm. It'll be no problem, really."

Cain laughed. "I like your sense of humor, John."

"I'm not joking."

"Regardless. You're still a funny man."

Telfer smiled at the thought. Even under the circumstances, he felt strangely pleased with himself. "You should see me when I'm happy. I'm the life and soul of the party."

Cain shook his head, as though at the amusing antics of a toddler. He adjusted the outboard so that they began angling toward land. Here there was a stretch of golden shore, where beach houses on stilts crowned the low horizon. Beyond them loomed mist-shrouded tower blocks where the urban sprawl of South L.A. crept past Redondo Beach toward Long Beach. He selected one of the beach houses at random and headed for a wooden jetty that nosed out into the waves.

Beyond the jetty was a summerhouse; a playground for the not so rich judging by the way the paint flaked from the window frames. There was only one car, a battered Dodge sitting under the porch that abutted the southern side of the house, and no speedboat at the mooring point. The house had a semidilapidated edge, as though it were used infrequently, and maintained even less. There were no kiddies' swings or toys strewn along the edge of the beach, and no sign of a family in residence at the stone-built barbecue, which contained only ashes and a lingering scent of burgers gone by. If anyone were home, it would be barely more than one—two at the most.

He deftly steered the dinghy up to the pilings, a lasso

action snaring the boat to a stanchion. He used the threat of the gun to motivate Telfer. "Bring the briefcase," he ordered. "I'll take it off you when we get inside."

"What if there're people home?" Telfer asked.

"Then we impose on their generosity to get you fixed up."

"That's all?"

"What else?"

Coming to a painful crouch on the jetty, Telfer studied the empty windows. "You won't hurt them, will you?"

Cain looked pained. "I thought you were beginning to understand me by now."

"I am," Telfer said. Then to himself, "That's the trouble."

"I heard that," Cain said in singsong fashion.

"You were meant to."

Cain's features went from night to day in an instant. "I suppose it all comes down to whether or not they're willing to be of assistance. I don't care for selfish people. What about you, John?"

"I don't suppose they have much choice when you're pushing a gun under their noses."

Cain shrugged.

"What if there are children?" Telfer continued.

"I haven't killed a child lately," Cain said.

Telfer didn't reply, concentrating on shuffling by his nemesis to conceal his disgust. Cain allowed him to take the lead. He glanced down at the empty gun, considered its convenience as a tool, and decided that as long as no one suspected it was empty, it was still worth the effort to lug it along with him.

Telfer shuffled the length of the jetty, the briefcase stuffed beneath one armpit. Behind him, Cain grinned to himself. Telfer reminded him of a shambling mummy as he clawed at a railing to help him up the steps to the house. Beyond them the summerhouse presented a skull-like visage, dark empty eye sockets for windows and a grinning jaw of picket-rail teeth. It was an image that appealed to Cain but only added to Telfer's apparent foreboding. He turned and gave Cain an imploring look.

"On you go, John. You've got nothing to worry about."

Telfer shook his head. He set his shoulders, unresigned to the prospect of further violence. Cain nudged him in the small of his back but he resisted the push.

"You don't have to kill anyone."

"No," Cain agreed. "I don't have to."

Telfer still refused to move.

Cain said, "But I might just start here and now if you don't move your ass."

A propane blaze of anger flushed Telfer's face. Slowly he turned and faced his captor. Cain glared back. The tableau held for half a dozen heartbeats. "You know," Telfer said, "the more you threaten someone, the less those threats mean."

Cain grunted, but this time in humor. "You should know by now that I don't make threats idly, John."

"I'm fully aware of what you're capable of. All I'm saying is that maybe you should take care who you direct those threats at. Sooner or later you're going to have to do something about it."

"Now who's making threats?"

"No. Not a threat. Call it friendly advice."

Cain winked. "Okay, John, I get you. Now do me the honor of getting yourself inside on your own two feet before I have to plug you and drag you in by your ears."

"Another threat?"

Cain shrugged. "Call me Mr. Predictable."

Telfer loped on ahead, and Cain glanced down and saw a pattern of dark splotches on the wood planks. Telfer was bleeding worse than he'd thought. Probably the reason for the bravado. A last-ditch attempt at showing he had a backbone after all. Following the trail, Cain lifted his gaze once more to Telfer's shuffling form. Maybe patching him up was a waste of effort; maybe he should just end it now. Dead, he'd no longer be the hindrance he was proving. And he'd be more manageable stuffed in the trunk of the Dodge than up front riding shotgun. But that would mean changing the plans he'd fantasized over these past hours. Killed here with little fuss or later at the designated place with all the pomp and ceremony the occasion demanded? It wasn't too difficult a choice. He followed on behind, his mind made up.

Although the house looked uncared for, the tiny yard was a different story. Bougainvillea in terra-cotta troughs made a pleasant border for the final approach to the front door. He curled his lip. Kind of spoiled the overall ambience. So, too, did the tinkle of piano music coming from beyond the screen door.

Exhaling at the homeliness of it all, Cain hurried so that he came to the door just as Telfer raised a hand to rap on the door frame. He was about to halt Telfer when the crunch of feet on gravel achieved that for him. Synchronized, they turned and greeted the man rounding the side of the house. Then they both glanced down at the Rottweiler that strained at the leash in his grasp. Telfer's mouth held the ghost of a smirk as he looked at his captor.

"Help you gentlemen?" the man asked from ten feet away. He appeared to be about sixty years old, sunburned and paunchy. An early retiree on a short break. Cain would bet his right testicle that this man prefers to take his holidays in a mobile home. The massive dog continued to tug at the leash, tongue lolling in anticipation of a couple of tasty morsels.

In another sleight of hand, Cain spirited the gun into his waistband and his hand clapped down tight on Telfer's shoulder to halt any telltale movement. "Hopefully you can, brother," Cain said, stepping past Telfer. "My friend here is injured. I'd appreciate it if you'd call 911 for us."

"Need an ambulance?" the man asked, craning to see past Cain as though attempting to ascertain the severity of Telfer's injuries. Subtly, Cain shifted onto his other foot. The blood on Telfer's shirt was like a flashing light to the man.

Eyes wide he lurched forward, aided by the pull of the heavy dog. "My God," he spluttered. "You're bleeding!"

Cain held up a hand. "Don't worry, brother. It looks worse than it is. But we'd appreciate your help nonetheless."

"Yes, yes," the man said, coming forward at a trot. The dog bounced along at his side, no longer tugging at its leash. Cain gave the dog a nanosecond of perusal. He feigned alarm. Stepped away. The man saw the movement, gave a shake of his head. "Oh, don't be worried about Popeye none. He looks scary, but really he's a big old softie. More likely he'll lick you to death than bite you."

"Phew. That's a relief," Cain said. For Telfer's benefit he raised an eyebrow, gave a lopsided smile. Telfer gave a short cough, but already Cain was dropping to a knee as if to greet the dog.

As the dog brushed past, Cain swiped his hand under its muzzle. An innocent enough looking pat of its broad chest. It took only two further paces before it collapsed. It didn't even offer a startled yelp before it died. Stunned, the man stared down at his dog. Eyes pools of bewilderment, he looked back at Cain who was rising from his crouch.

"Don't like dogs," Cain said.

The man's gaze traveled the length of Cain's arm, fixed on the ultimate point. The scaling knife was almost devoid of blood, so quick and easy was its entry and exit.

"They're competition," Cain said. "For your bones."

"Oh," the man said, his knees buckling at the same time.

33

THE LAST TIME I WAS ON A MOTOR LAUNCH IT WAS at night and I was being deposited on a deserted beach in the Indian Ocean. I was part of an eight-man team sent to extradite suspected terrorists who'd been holed up there since a predawn attack on a village full of women and children.

On that occasion I didn't take too much notice of my surroundings. It was an in and out, a smash and grab mission that left no time for sightseeing.

Now, standing on the prow of the launch, I took the time to feel the spray of the ocean on my face, to smell the tang of brine in my nostrils and feel the wind in my hair. The Bailey motorboat was riding high on the ocean, lifting majestically with each swell, dipping down with each trough. I stood with my legs braced against the motion, but neglected to reach for the handrail.

"If you close your eyes and hold out your hands it feels like you're flying," Rink said from behind me.

I snickered at the image. "Start singing like Celine Dion and I'll throw you overboard," I promised him.

Rink grunted, moving up next to me. He leaned forward and rested his meaty forearms on the guardrail. "What makes you think they've headed south?"

"Just a feeling," I said.

"A feeling? What? Like a sixth sense or something?" Rink wasn't kidding. Like most soldiers, he knows there's a force out there that isn't tangible in the proper sense. Many a soldier's life has been saved by an enhanced sense that borders on the supernatural. Something that warned him about the concealed tripwire or sniper lying in ambush. Some argue that it's simply a product of supercharged adrenaline and a keenly trained eye, but I believe there's more to it than that. It's more than the creeping-flesh sensation that unseen eyes are watching you. But the feeling I was referring to had nothing to do with that or any other power. It had simply to do with deduction.

"No, a feeling that if I was in their shoes I'd've headed south, too."

"If they survived."

"There's no doubt about it, Rink. Whoever this guy is that John's with, he knows his stuff. Only someone with training goes onto a yacht full of armed men and ends up blowing it and everyone aboard to shit."

"Unless he's got the other important ingredients: he's as crazy as a bag of weasels, has more balls than sense, and he's the luckiest goddamn son of a bitch on the planet." Rink raised his shaggy brows, inviting disagreement.

I shrugged, moving to join him at the guardrail. Below us, the bow wave split like blistering phosphorus against the deep aqua of the ocean. "Maybe he has both," I said. "The training and the other ingredients. He had a get-out plan. You can bet your life on it."

"So it stands to reason," Rink acquiesced, "that he heads out to sea to avoid the cordon of blue lights converging on the harbor."

"Coast guard has their base to the north. It's what I'd've done," I told him, and Rink nodded in agreement.

"So who is this guy? You think it really is this Harvestman the media's screaming about?"

"Has to be," I said. "It'd explain why John's fingerprints turned up in connection with the killings of that couple at the motel. Somehow, John's got himself into something way beyond his ability to get out of. Only thing I can't fathom yet is what part he's playing in all this. I can't believe he'd be a willing participant to murder."

Rink said, "Maybe you don't know John the way you think you do."

"You keep saying that. Maybe you're right, Rink, but until I'm proved wrong, I prefer to give him the benefit of the doubt."

"Fair enough," Rink said. "But what if he has turned, Hunter? What if your brother has acquired a taste for blood? What if he's a goddamn willing participant?"

I didn't answer for a moment, my gaze fixed on the horizon. Like the point where the sky and ocean met, my reason blurred into a haze of nothingness. Finally, I turned to Rink and saw that he was studying me with an intensity common to him. I blinked slowly, breaking the connection. "If that's the case, it puts a whole new slant on my purpose for finding him."

Rink nodded sagely, lifted a hand, and placed it on my shoulder. "Let's hope it doesn't have to come to that, huh?"

A shout from behind us broke my melancholy and I turned to squint back at the skipper who was at the wheel of the boat.

He was pointing with excitement toward the shore. A little more than five hundred yards away I saw what he indicated. To me, it was nothing more than one more boat tied to a short pier.

Together, Rink and I made our way back to the skipper's cabin. He was grinning. "The dinghy over there," he said with an exaggerated nod of his head. "It's from the *Morning Star*."

"The *Morning Star* being one of the yachts moored in the harbor?" I asked.

The skipper snapped his fingers, then pointed a gnarled digit at me. "Got it in one."

"How can you be sure?" Rink asked.

The skipper's eyebrows did a little jig. "I've been around

them boats all my working life. I know what skiffs belong to what and to whom. Not only that, but if you look at the painting on the outboard, you can see that it's a five-pointed star coming up over the sea, not the sun, as you'd expect."

I squinted across the waves. I could barely see the outboard motor, never mind the motif on it. I looked back at the skipper, and he grinned again.

"I'll trust your better eyesight," I told him. "But couldn't there be a rational reason why a dinghy from the *Morning Star* would turn up here?"

"None that I can guess at," the skipper said.

"No, I suppose not." I looked back at the dinghy. "Can you bring your boat in close to the same berth?"

"Tide's a bit low for my girl. I'll get in as close as I can, but you might have to wade to shore."

"Okay," I said, turning to Rink. "You ready for this?"

Rink patted the bulge under his armpit. "Ready, willing, and able."

Returning my attention to the skipper, I indicated the beach house a short way up from the jetty. "Do you know whose place that is?"

He shook his head. "I'm good with boats, haven't a clue about houses."

I shrugged. "Okay. Can you get the emergency services on your radio?"

"Yeah. Of course."

"Yeah," I agreed. "Once you've put us ashore, shout for help. Tell the cops to get to this location as fast as they can."

The skipper was no naive old fool; he knew we'd chartered his boat for the strict purpose of hunting someone fleeing the scene of devastation up at Marina del Rey. What he didn't know was exactly who we were chasing. Or why.

"You expecting trouble, son?" he asked.

"Maybe of the worst kind," I told him.

"So why don't you wait till the cops get here before you go ashore?" he asked. For the first time, there was a hint of something less than his ordinary ebullience.

"We could have some kind of hostage crisis. I can't wait for the cops to get here before any innocents are harmed." The first was for the old man; my next was directed at Rink. "If the men we're after have already been and gone, I've got a horrible feeling that there'll be some cleaning up to be done. Best we leave that to the authorities this time."

Rink nodded in understanding, while it was the skipper's turn to squint at the rapidly approaching shoreline. He didn't ask for an explanation and I offered him none. He guided the prow of the Bailey toward the jetty, and as he'd predicted we were more than fifteen feet short of the boardwalk when we felt the judder of sand beneath us. The skipper threw the boat into reverse, edging back until we were in clear water. From the front of the boat, I gave him a thumbs-up and the skipper nodded at me.

"You want me to wait for you?" he called from the cabin.

I shook my head over the sound of the idling engine. Whatever the outcome, I didn't believe I'd be boarding a boat again anytime soon. "Maybe it's best you pull back from the shoreline. Could be bullets flying around before long."

"I appreciate the warning, son, but you don't have to worry about me. Completed two tours in Vietnam, so the prospect of flying bullets means nothing to me."

"Fair enough, but I don't want your death on my conscience."

The skipper grunted, but then he winked, dipped the peak of his cap. "It's your mission, son. Keep safe. An' tell your big buddy to do likewise."

"Will do," I said, glancing Rink's way. He was standing at the prow, scanning the beach for movement. His shoulders twitched, adrenaline searching for release. As I walked toward him, I placed my hand under my armpit and felt the reassuring bulge of the latest SIG Sauer supplied only an hour earlier by Cheryl Barker. It was the older Swiss P230 model, with no manual safety button, so the weapon could be brought into action very rapidly. Brought back memories from my Point Shooting days.

We went over the side of the boat together, splashing waist deep in the foam. Sand immediately invaded my shoes, and my trousers clung to my skin. I forgot my discomfort as we pushed toward the dinghy.

"Blood," Rink observed even as we approached. It was smeared over the edge nearest the dock as though something limp and lifeless had been dragged onto the walkway. I pressed up to the boat. More frothy blood was pooled in the bottom. Rink and I shared a look. All this blood wasn't a good sign that we'd find John alive, but it meant my hunch was correct after all. There couldn't possibly be a more likely explanation for this boat to be here than that it had carried escapees from the carnage at Marina del Rey.

Pulling my SIG out of its holster, I chambered a round. I heard a similar *kachunk!* as Rink followed suit with his Mossberg. We followed the dock on to the beach. Rink fanned off to my left. Before us was a wooden house with a well-tended yard. A dust-streaked Dodge was parked alongside the house. There was no further room in the lot for another vehicle so I guessed that John—if he was still alive—was inside the house. Not good in one sense, it added to my apprehension of a possible hostage situation escalating beyond my power to control.

Rink was twenty yards away now, moving toward the house. I sucked in a deep breath and moved onto a gravel path that led to the door of the house.

I saw spatters of blood on the doorstep. Hearing the sputter and roar of an engine, I saw that the skipper was heeding my warning. I wondered if he'd already called for backup, and then searched the sky for a helicopter.

Nothing.

Just a single speedboat hurtling along about a quarter of a mile to the north. Even from here, I could tell it was a private boat, so I gave it no further thought. Even if the skipper had immediately called the authorities, they were still many minutes away. Which meant I had no time to waste: if John was inside, especially accompanied by the Harvestman, I had to take decisive action before any innocents were injured.

Given the opportunity, I'd have scoped the place and gained a better understanding of what it was we faced. Rink and I would've devised a plan of approach. But like always, Murphy's Law took precedence here. I could only hope that the chaos rule held us in its favor as it had done innumerable times in the past.

With this in mind, I'd no recourse other than charge the screen door, lift a foot, and crash through, hurtling into whatever hell storm would follow.

Which is exactly what I did.

34 Snapshot.

On first perusal, it was a nice home.

Reminded me of my grandparents' bungalow.

On deeper reflection, the memory of their home told me everything I was afraid of.

There was a cancer at this house's core.

To maximize the sunshine, all these beach houses had been built so that their fronts were to the ocean. Therefore, through the door I shattered was a vestibule leading directly to an open-plan living area on one side and a bedroom on the other. Toward the back of the house would be a kitchen and perhaps a utility area, but these were of no interest to me.

Kick-start the world.

I moved.

My entire attention was skewed to the left as I swung into the living area. I say living area; I could already see the corpse of some hulking dog lying alongside its ceiling-staring master. The man was indisputably dead judging by the mess of his throat and the cataract-glaze of his eyes. His mouth hung open in shock, and pink spume clung to his contorted lips. Another thing I took in during that nanosecond of horror; his left hand was missing, shorn off at the wrist. The Harvestman was living up to his name.

Apart from the corpses, the room was as ordinary as any home supported by a modest income. There was the obligatory TV, settee and chairs, trinket-type ornaments, and photographs in frames. The thing that stood out was the large piano that took up most of one side of the room. Then there were the three people standing around it.

Perhaps standing around it isn't the most apt way to describe the scene.

One figure, an elderly woman, was being helped off the piano stool by the tug of a man's arm around her throat. As she stood in an awkward spasm, her fingers clawed at the piano keys and a deep-throated note vied for dominance over an equally harsh one. The man pulling her backward stared at me over the woman's shoulder, his lips split in a feral snarl.

My SIG came up. Ordinarily I'd have fired, but the man placed the muzzle of a gun to the side of the woman's face and I stayed my hand. My gaze flicked to the nearer side of the piano. Immediately I saw my brother.

At the time, I can't honestly say if I was pleased to see him. I think, deep down in my soul, I'd secretly hoped that John was dead, that the possibility that he'd become a monster had been removed.

John turned his face to mine, and shock struck his dull expression. Then a bit of hope flared. That look was all I needed to confirm that John wasn't a consenting player in this game. Immediately my attention skipped back to the man holding the woman.

"Drop the gun," I shouted.

The man's snarl broadened ever wider and I saw ice behind his pale green eyes. Using the woman as a shield, he pressed the gun under her jaw.

"I think it's you who'd better drop the gun," he said.

My SIG didn't waver. I took a step closer. Finger pressure increased on the trigger. Calmer, I said, "Drop the gun."

In answer, he thumbed back the hammer on his own gun. "Think you can drop me before I kill this old bitch?"

"Yes." I stared at him along the barrel of my gun.

He shook his head. "I don't think you're as confident as you're making out. If you could do it, you would've done so by now."

"You've got another five seconds to comply," I told him.

The man laughed. His captor whimpered in terror. Her arthritic knees threatened to dump her on her backside, and only the dragging arm around her throat held her up. She was no lightweight, but the man didn't seem to be struggling to control her. The arm looped around her throat bulged with lean strength.

"One," I counted.

"Aw, cut the dramatics, will you," he taunted. As he did, he shuffled sideways, putting himself in a corner of the room. It wasn't an attempt to find an exit, but to ensure he couldn't be triangulated. His back to the corner of the room, he took away any opportunity for Rink to get a bead on him. I glanced to my left and saw Rink standing outside the open window, his shotgun trained on the man. My friend gave a subtle shake of his head. No line of fire.

"You're cornered," I told the man. "Let the woman go and you'll live. Harm her and we'll shoot you like a mad dog."

"No. What you are going to do is put down your weapons. I leave with the woman." He glanced over at a briefcase I only now noticed on the lid of the piano. "And that."

"No deal. You're going to let the woman go first."

"Uh-uh. Maybe I'll just shoot her face off and take my chances, huh?"

He pressed the barrel of his gun into her left eye socket, eliciting a shriek from the woman. Again my finger tightened but didn't follow through.

Think of damp ashes, that was the color of John's face as he turned to me. He supported his weight against the piano, body racked with pain. Weak and hurting. "He means it, Hunter. He'll do it."

My gaze jumped between him and the gunman. A smile flickered at the corner of the gunman's mouth, a tensing of his eyes. Did he recognize my name? How could he, I told myself, it's not as if I'm James Bond. To John I said, "Get over here behind me, John."

The gunman grunted. "You two know each other?"

Neither of us answered, but the silence was palpable.

"Wait a minute. Hunter?" The man searched my face. Lines crinkled at the corners of his eyes as though something amusing had struck him. "Not Joe Hunter?"

Unbidden, my face pinched. My teeth ached as my jaw tightened. Some secret I turned out to be. Maybe I should have worked under a code name after all.

"Well for the love of all that's holy! Who'd have thought they'd have put *you* on my trail?"

Again I didn't answer, and the man turned his attention to John.

"Wait a minute . . . I see it now. The family resemblance. You're so full of surprises, John. You didn't tell me you were related to such a notorious assassin as Joe Hunter . . ." He squinted across at Rink, who remained statue solid at the open window. "And don't tell me . . . not Jared Rington as well?"

John's face puckered. It can't ever have occurred to him before just who—or what—his big brother really was. He was aware that my work involved hunting terrorists, but I don't think he appreciated what that actually entailed. To him, I was just a soldier killing other soldiers. Now he was probably wondering, *Aren't assassins the bad guys?*

I don't appreciate the term *assassin,* but I suppose, at the end of the day, it all comes down to your perspective. Rink and I were either saints or sinners. At that moment, I saw myself as the saint; the man with the gun shoved in an elderly woman's eye socket assured me of that.

"Let her go," I commanded.

The man wasn't interested. My identity seemed to please him in a way I found troubling. His next words went some length to explain his apparent pleasure. "I guess I should be honored. Does that mean I've finally won the notoriety I deserve? Huh? I suppose that means you know who I am now?"

"I don't give a shit who you are, or what insane reason you have for murdering innocent people. All I'm interested in is you dropping your gun before I put a bullet in your head." To assure him of my intentions, I took another half step toward him.

In return, he giggled. Said, "If I'm going to die, I'm taking her with me. Maybe one or two of you, as well."

I drew back again. Inwardly I cursed myself. I'd just made the mistake of showing him that I wasn't in charge of the situation. One up for the *real* bad guy. He moved the barrel of his gun so it was under the woman's ear now. Once more the woman murmured in fear. Her eyes rolled my way, beseeching. I had to do something.

"John," I snapped. "Get yourself over here."

He staggered over, one arm tight against his chest where his sodden shirt clung to him. I moved a step to my right, giving him clearance to gain the doorway. At my shoulder, John came to a stumbling halt. Something bothered me about the abruptness.

Without thought, I pivoted on my right foot, smacking against the near wall, eyes still on the gunman to my right, but my peripheral vision searching out what had stopped John. I saw the gunman's eyes widen in surprise, saw him flinch, and I knew that there was new danger in the house. Danger to us both. I was caught between two equally vicious enemies, and it was a split second's decision on my response. Even as I swung to my left, I gave a silent prayer that Rink would cover the killer I couldn't keep my eyes on. My gun swept the air, and I fired without pause.

Even as he was stepping into the living room, my first bullet caught Hendrickson's hit man in his right shoulder, spinning from his fingers the gun he'd pointed at John's head. I'd seen this man before—testament to that was the wound on his ear. Even if I'd never had the privilege, I would've recognized him for what he was: a stone-cold killer. Something else: he was an apt stalker in his own right, and he'd used Rink and me to lead him to John. The memory of the speedboat racing toward us after we'd disembarked from the skipper's launch came to mind.

Injured, the Latino dropped low. He grunted, but he was already reaching left-handed for a second weapon concealed in an ankle holster. My gun boomed again, but even as I fired, I snatched the barrel up so that the bullet swished above his head to splinter the door lintel. I'd missed him, but it was a good job I did. It meant I also missed John, who'd chosen that moment to stagger into my line of fire.

Things were rapidly turning to shit.

I ran around John, expecting the killer at my back to put a bullet in my spine.

I cleared John just as the hit man came up from his crouch. His gun fired. Instinctively I'd already twisted, but a searing coldness snapped alongside my ribs. Wind whooshed out of me, but I couldn't allow the thought of the hit to stop me.

Before he could fire again, I struck his gun hand with the barrel of my SIG, knocking his aim wide. His bullet lifted keys from the piano with a tympani of discord. Moving swiftly, as though it were a rapier, I swept my gun under his forearm and snaked my arm up his back.

In close and dirty, we went to town. I ground him against the wall, both our guns momentarily scraping and rasping against wallpaper. His gun went off, further marking the wall. With his free hand, he grabbed at my testicles. I stabbed my fingers into his eyes, tore at his damaged ear, and he forgot all about squeezing my balls. Instead, he punched me in the mouth. The tricky bastard. *Right back at you,* I thought, as I smashed his nose into a new position on his face.

He was slippery, even shot in three different places—he had a wounded thigh that I was only now vaguely aware of, plus the two I'd given him. His nose was broken and he was bleeding, but the adrenaline-charged flood of endorphins gave him the strength of desperation.

He fought back, tried to head-butt me, but instead found the point of my elbow as I rammed it into his cheekbone. His eyes rolled upward. Before he could recover from the ringing concussion, I pulled his head down, straight into the path of my up-rising knee.

It was like a mallet pounding a watermelon, and the tendons in the backs of both knees failed him.

As he dropped, my gun followed him, and even as he sprawled out, I put two bullets into the rear of his skull.

"That's for Louise Blake," I hissed through my teeth. Then I shot him again between the shoulder blades. Touching my ribs where I could feel the first sting of contact, I added, "And that one's for me."

Captain Fairbairn once wrote that the average armed fight is over in seconds, it is literally a matter of *the quick and the dead*. I had acted instinctively, relying on speed and the extension of the gun in my hand. Now the hit man was dead. Once again my mentor's ghost spoke volumes. But it wasn't over.

No other guns had barked during the few seconds it took to dispatch Hendrickson's man. The threat of Rink blasting him had likely stayed the Harvestman's hand. Allowing the Latino to lie in his own blood, I shifted again, reaching down and clawing John from the floor even as I swung my gun to find its next target.

Coming up with John clutched beneath one arm, I eyed the man who still grasped the elderly woman as a shield. But he wasn't pressing the gun to her head so forcefully.

"I couldn't have done a better job myself," he said.

"I'm not interested in what you think," I snapped back at him.

"I remain impressed nonetheless. If my hands weren't so full I'd applaud you," he said. "I'm leaving now. I'm taking the woman as insurance. If you stay put, I promise you she'll be released unharmed. If you follow me she will die."

The deal wasn't an option. I knew the only way the woman would be returned to us would be without significant portions of her anatomy. I slowly shook my head. Prodding the dead assassin at my feet I said, "You know what I can do. You've seen it with your own eyes."

"I don't doubt that you're good. But are you really prepared to put this dear old lady at risk?" His smile was that of the Antichrist. "Even if you shoot me now, are you certain that the trauma of a bullet in my skull won't make me jerk this trigger? Are you willing to take that chance?"

Reluctant to give him an edge, I said, "We'll just have to see."

Again the old woman mewled, and a torturous pain shot through me at having to subject her to such terror. Unfortunately, I had no recourse. To allow the Harvestman to take her was out of the question. If she didn't die now, she would certainly die later. And it wouldn't be at the mercy of a quick and painless bullet through her brain.

On the grand scale of things, if this woman were to die, then it would be best if the murderer died along with her. It would be a supreme waste of life, but her sacrifice could mean the difference between life and gruesome death for many others if the psychopath was allowed to live.

Surprisingly, John came to my rescue.

Cradled in my armpit, I felt him shift. Then he clawed at my shirtfront, as if drawing himself upright.

"Let me go with him," John said. His voice was as brittle as month-old crackers.

I shook my head.

"You have to let me go, Joe," he said. "Cain, let the woman go and I'll be your hostage."

The Harvestman's brow furrowed.

"John?" I said, grabbing at his collar, but my brother pulled himself loose. He took a faltering step toward the murderer, hands wrapped around his torso in an effort to subdue the pain he felt.

"Let the woman go, Cain. Take me instead."

The murderer looked beyond John, staring at me. I didn't move. I hated this guy but had to concede that this arrangement was a way out for him. Complex emotions were churning behind his cool facade.

Taking another step, John said, "We have unfinished business, Cain. We both know that. If you let the woman go, I'll see it to the end. I'll sacrifice myself for her."

"What do you say, Cain?" I asked. "Do we have a deal, or do we start shooting?"

Cain gave me a serpent's grin. "Bring the briefcase, John."

Cain removed the gun from the woman and waved me aside with it. "Back off, Hunter. Go over there next to the window with your friend."

Rink gave me a subtle shake of his head, not for a second taking his aim from Cain. His features were set in bronze. "I think we can take the frog-giggin' son of a bitch," he hissed.

"No, Rink. Stand down," I said. Without lowering my own gun, I crabbed over to the window, blocking Rink's line of fire.

"What you doin'?" Rink whispered harshly. "I can take the punk."

"Just let it go, Rink," I whispered back. "For now."

Behind me, Rink's curses were blasphemous, whatever Good Book you follow.

"Hunter?" he pleaded, but I was already refocused on Cain. John had grasped the briefcase to his chest and was nearing him. As he blocked my view of Cain, the woman was unceremoniously shoved to the ground, then Cain had John by the shoulder and was spinning him around. Without pause, Cain used him as a shield as he moved away. At the door, Cain issued a final warning. "Don't try to follow us too soon. If you do, John dies in more agony than you could ever imagine."

I stayed put. Rink was as itchy as a flea-bitten dog, and without taking my eyes off Cain I whispered, "Just wait."

From behind me I heard the answering response, indicating that Rink understood. "I'm waitin'."

Cain didn't hear the whispered exchange. He was as nutty as squirrel shit, but he was no fool. He paused in his tracks. "I guess this won't be the last time I lay eyes on you?"

"Count on it," I told him.

"Don't worry, I will," Cain said. "I look forward to it. It'll look good to have such a formidable trophy as Joe Hunter on my résumé."

Cain held my gaze a moment longer; then, in an act I should have expected from one of such a depraved mind, he waved good-bye. It wasn't his hand he used. It was the bloodless souvenir taken from the old woman's husband.

Then Cain and John were gone.

Before I could move, the old woman wailed and began scurrying across the floor on her hands and knees to the still form of her husband. She folded over the top of him and her sobs were pitiful.

Grief is a savage torment, especially when so raw as this. It can leave a person insensible to what is happening around them, and totally unaware of consoling hands. My soft words were probably gobbledygook to her.

While she wailed, I gave her the quick once-over. Her injuries were minimal, a little bruising on the throat, a bumped elbow. Searching for any broken bones, I traced the folds of her blouse with my fingertips. Bodily she was intact, but there was a narrow rent in the fabric. I studied the slashed cloth, noting that a patch about the size of two fingers was missing, stripped away, wondering how in hell that had happened.

I shook off the thought as Rink charged into the living room. "They've taken the old lady's car."

I nodded at him.

"So what're we doin' standin' around? Let's go after the son of a bitch," Rink said.

"There's no rush," I told him.

Rink inclined his head. "What's goin' on?"

"Like I said, we only have to wait."

Rink wasn't aware that John was laying down a trail for us.

"When John was holding on to me," I explained, "he took my cell phone out of my shirt pocket."

"I can't see him gettin' the opportunity to call in his location," Rink said.

"Doesn't need to," I said.

"No. Of course. We can have the phone signal triangulated. It'll lead us straight to him."

"I trust you have someone in telecommunications that can do it for us?" I asked.

"I might know a woman who does."

"Cheryl Barker? It's okay, Rink, I've just had another thought."

The sirens came.

It was only minutes before Rink and I were kneeling with our hands behind our heads as we were frisked for concealed weapons.

"Get me Walter Conrad," I told a stern special agent from the FBI's Hostage Rescue Team. "He's a sub-division director with the CIA."

On reflection, I was in no position to make demands, but if anyone had the ability to trace the phone John was carrying it was Walter.

To my surprise, he said, "Don't worry, Mr. Hunter. Your boss is already on his way."

35

YOUR BOSS IS ALREADY ON HIS WAY.

It's not often that Walter Hayes Conrad IV gets into the field these days. As a handler of undercover agents, most of them up to their elbows in wet work, he has to maintain a degree of anonymity and distance himself from the dirty deeds used by his government in the name of national security. On this occasion, however, it was necessary for him to fly out to this place marginally north of Long Beach. Everyone's orders were to contain what was rapidly escalating into a massive embarrassment for both him and the security community at large.

He walked into the bedroom where I'd been confined for the last twenty minutes. All that was missing was a fanfare blast of trumpets to announce his arrival.

Walter greeted me with a tight-lipped smile, an unlit cigar clamped between his fingers. Without preamble, he dismissed the two Hostage Rescue Team troopers who'd been my uneasy jailers. Funnily enough, the FBI agents immediately deferred to his authority.

"Walter," I acknowledged with a nod. I stood up from the bed, smoothing out the rumpled comforter with a tug.

Walter's cigar went from one hand to the other. Gripping it as though it were a lifeline, he offered his other damp palm. I shook hands with him, regarding him solemnly. He didn't say anything.

"You must have hotfooted it out here, Walter," I said, "seeing as it's less than half an hour since the call went in."

Walter bunched his prodigious cheeks in what was supposed to be a smile. "Got my very own Lear."

"You're telling me," I said. But he didn't get the joke. When he didn't respond, I added, "Even a jet couldn't have got you all the way across country in that time."

"It's a very fast jet," Walter said, and now the smile was genuine. "Nah, I've been in L.A. since early this morning."

"Can I ask the reason why?"

"Of course not," he said.

It was a game. His game; one that Walter loved to play.

I offered my deduction, to see what lies he came up with.

"When we talked on the phone I piqued your interest. Got you thinking, huh?"

"Pure speculation."

"So tell me, Walter, who is the Harvestman?"

"What makes you think I know that?"

"Don't play with me, Walter. You haven't flown all the way across the country for nothing. You're here because you know who he is. You're on a containment mission."

Walter jammed the unlit cigar between his teeth. "I gave up smoking eight months ago," he said. "Still carry a cigar around for moments just like this."

"So it's not for celebrations?"

"No, I'm talking about a reminder of how much I've fucked up in the past." For the first time I honestly believed him. "There's a lot of truth in that concept, Hunter. That your past always catches up with you in the end."

"Yeah," I agreed. His words echoed my own feelings precisely. He sat down on the bed I'd recently vacated, fists on his ample thighs.

"The Harvestman knew me," I told him. "He also knew Rink. Makes me think he has to be a member of the security community."

Walter nodded but didn't volunteer anything.

"Is he one of yours, Walter?"

Walter shook his head. "Not CIA."

"Secret Service?"

He wagged a fat finger, pleased with his top student.

"So how is it you're involved?" I asked. "Last I heard the CIA and Secret Service were separate entities."

"Like you said, Hunter. Your call got me thinking, made me tie a few loose strings together. It's a joint agency decision that I step in as SAC."

"Special agent in charge? You pulled rank?"

"Of course." He smiled.

"Figures," I said. "So what happened? What makes a bodyguard turn into a killer?"

"Is there a difference, Hunter? Isn't the purpose of a bodyguard to kill or be killed? We're talking brass tacks here, none of that ethical bullshit you see in the movies."

"There's a huge difference, Walter," I reminded him. "Bodyguards protect the sanctity of life; they don't take trophies to display on their dining room wall."

"Not in the classic sense," he demurred. "But they take trophies nonetheless. You just gotta speak to any long-serving agent and they wear their trophies on their sleeves. Metaphorically speaking."

I shook off his comment and sat down on the bed next to him.

"So are you going to tell me?" I pressed.

"Situation's kind of delicate, Hunter," Walter said. He shifted uncomfortably and the bed creaked in protest.

"Everything you touch is delicate. What's so different this time?"

"Do you realize the extent of the scandal if it gets out that a former Secret Service agent's responsible for murdering upward of twenty people?" He turned his large head to me, and I could see the pain behind his slick brow. "Christ, Hunter, it'll be ten times worse than all the screaming over the Iraq campaign. It'll lend weight to the naysayers who're preaching that our government is allowing the murder of innocents in order to justify the invasion. Hell, if they find out the Harvestman has had free rein for over four years, do you think for one moment they'll believe it wasn't with the blessing of the government? Next thing you know, the crazies will be swearing that he's still on our payroll and has been taking out people who knew the truth behind JFK's assassination."

"Are you telling me that you've been aware of him for four years? That nothing's been done to catch the crazy son of a bitch? Makes *me* wonder if he's still on the payroll."

"He's only recently come to our notice," Walter said. "FBI have been investigating a number of random killings spread the length and breadth of the country. It hasn't been an easy task, simply because most of the bodies have never been found. People were reported missing, presumed dead. Others, well, you know the headlines, they've turned up missing body parts. Other than the MO nothing could tie the murders together."

"What? No forensics? I find that a little hard to believe." Frustration made me get up and stomp the length of the bedroom. I leaned on a dressing table that wouldn't have looked anachronistic in the 1970s. Hands on the cabinet, I stared at my reflection in the mirror. It wasn't a face I recognized. Or liked. "This is all bullshit, Walter!"

Walter eyed me with not a little annoyance. "It's the truth, Hunter."

I turned around so I could hold his gaze. "Walter, you wouldn't know the truth if it sneaked up and bit you on the ass."

"I'm telling you the truth."

Returning to the bed, I again sat down next to him. "So what alerted you to the Harvestman's identity? I mean, considering that you haven't found any forensics? Did he start sending you taunting letters challenging you to catch him?"

Walter made a noise in his throat. "There's no need for sarcasm. And anyway, I didn't say there were no forensics. You said that," he said.

This time I didn't bite.

"The thing is, the forensics have only just recently come to *our* notice," Walter went on. "The FBI didn't have access to the USSS DNA records. We did. We only became aware of the Harvestman's identity following the murders of the couple at the motel out in the desert."

"You mean the murders that my brother's been blamed for?"

"Exactly."

"Yeah, but you know it wasn't John," I said.

"I know. But it served our purpose to put that story out."

"Served your damn purpose? Walter, you know I love you, but sometimes you're a complete asshole!" I was challenging him to disagree with me. In reply, he could only shrug.

"Comes with the job," he said.

Yes, I suppose it did. "So you tipped the media about John? What for? To draw out the real killer? You thought his ego would get the better of him and he'd show himself in order to take back the glory? Or was it a ploy to conceal the Harvestman's true identity?"

"A bit of both, I suppose," Walter said.

"Christ, Walter! Even when you're being truthful I can't get a straight answer out of you."

"Okay, I'll explain. That way you'll have everything I have." With a grunt he rose and walked away from me, fumbling the cigar to his lips. "Are you familiar with the book of Genesis?"

"I've read it, don't necessarily believe it," I answered.

"It's not necessary that you believe it, only that you have some idea of its content."

"I remember there are a lot of people with odd names begetting one another. Everything else I know I learned from Charlton Heston movies."

Walter shook off my sarcasm. "You've heard the story of Cain and Abel?"

"Yes."

"It's nothing new for some demented bastard to take on the name of Cain," Walter said. "In fact, the psyche of a murderer is often referred to as the Cain Complex. Murderers often look up to the great grandpappy of all murderers as to some sort of godhead in his own right. They think they're carrying out his work on earth and all that bullshit."

"And your sicko is no exception?" I asked.

"No, no, no. Not *the* Cain."

"Who then?"

"I'll come to that in a minute. First a little background on our man," Walter said. "His name is Martin Maxwell."

"Doesn't ring any bells."

"It won't. He didn't use that name when he was on active duty. Called himself Dean Crow. Thought it sounded tougher than Marty Maxwell. More befitting a U.S. Secret Service agent."

"Sounds like a complete peckerhead," I offered. "But I must admit I do recall something about him. Some low-level scandal involving a presidential candidate's wife, wasn't it?"

"He was relieved of duty after he was found supposedly looting the good lady's wardrobe for what he called in an interview 'a token of his skill.'"

"He's a damn panty sniffer?" I asked.

Walter shook his head. "Nothing so gross. He cut a patch from one of her blouses is all."

I recalled the missing piece of cloth from the old woman's blouse after she'd been held hostage next door. I was about to say this when Walter added, "I say supposedly. The truth is the good lady was wearing her blouse at the time. Marty said he took the token to show her how vulnerable she was, how much she relied on him at all times."

"Crazy," I said.

"Yeah. Supremely crazy."

"So how'd he get through the net? Surely the psych tests should've singled him out before he achieved agent status?"

"Some psychos are good at covering their true identities. Up to that point Marty Maxwell was well respected and had seniority. It was a surprise to find that one of their most able men was crazy as a fox."

I grunted. "And all that happened was that he was discharged from service? Why didn't anyone keep an eye on him? Surely the signs were there, that he was capable of spiraling out of control?"

"Secret Service kept an eye on him as best they could. Only thing was—crazy or not—he was no fool. He knew that he'd be under surveillance for the foreseeable future. He wasn't prepared to let that happen."

"He went underground?"

"More than that. He faked his death. Supposedly, in an act of shame, he killed himself. And the other members of his family. Wife and two kids."

"Oh, God . . ."

"Shot them dead in their beds, turned the gun on himself, stuck it under his chin, and blasted off his head. He'd set up an incendiary device to burn the lot of them. Left only charred corpses in the burned-out ruin of their home." Walter hung his head in shame, but I guessed it wasn't in memory of Maxwell's wife and children. "Their identity wasn't in dispute. That was an end to it. They messed up."

"You're telling me. Obviously the DNA wasn't matched or they'd have known before now that he was still on the loose."

"I don't fully understand the science. They were happy it was Marty Maxwell. Considering he'd blown away half his head, they had no teeth for a dental comparison. His fingerprints had been burned off down to the bone. With the odds-on favorite that it was him, where would you have put your money?"

"Considering the training he'd had, what he'd have known, I'd have looked at the possibility that there was more to his death than met the eye. Who was the fourth body? If not Marty Maxwell? His father? A brother?"

"According to Marty's file he was a single child. Both parents died years before. Mother died following complications during childbirth, father from congenital heart disease. Let's not forget that until then, he hadn't committed any crimes. It was put down as a murder-suicide. They believed Maxwell was dead and that was that. Case closed."

"But obviously he did have a brother?" I asked.

"Turns out he had a half brother called Robert Swan. Daddy Maxwell had been a naughty boy on his stag night, got an old sweetheart of his pregnant. It was Daddy Maxwell's best-kept secret. We only found this out afterward. The brother's mother noticed he was missing when her money stopped coming in. She's a lush, lives alone in a tenement up in the Bronx; seems like the son was sending her money whenever he could. A good boy. Looked after his ma, like any good boy should."

"But Maxwell found out about his brother? I thought you said it was a secret."

Walter grimaced. "Daddy Maxwell must've come clean in the end. Maybe he confessed his transgression on his deathbed. His wife was already on the other side; I guess he could've been seeking absolution. From what we've been able to put together, Maxwell sought out his half brother, but still kept his identity secret from everyone else. Makes you wonder if he had the brother in mind for this very purpose all along, doesn't it?"

I thought about Walter's story; wondered what level of insanity it took to not only murder your family but plan it for God knows how long before doing it.

"If Maxwell had had the foresight to kill his brother's mother, we would probably be sitting here right now wondering how the hell a dead man had risen from the grave," Walter said.

I asked, "So what has the Cain reference got to do with it? Other than that the psycho likes assumed names?"

"His half brother was a musician," Walter said as if that would explain everything to me. I looked at him blankly. "Genesis. Like you said, everyone begetting one another."

"I'm still not with you."

Walter raised a stubby finger again. Sermon part two. "Well, if you've read your Bible you'll know that there was an old blind guy named Lamech."

"I must have missed that bit."

"Lamech had two sons. Jubal and Tubal."

"Yeah," I agreed. "I remember now. Jubal and Tubal Cain."

"Jubal was the inventor of music," Walter began.

"Tubal was the forger of knives and swords," I completed. "I see the connection now. If the brother, a musician, is synonymous with Jubal, that makes the Harvestman Tubal Cain."

"Took a load of FBI profilers to come up with that one."

"Hence Maxwell's love of knives?"

"Yup."

"And the bones?"

"Some of these profilers have got it in mind that he's set himself some kind of mission, that he's taking the bones from his victims for some express purpose."

"What?" I asked. "Other than that he's demented?"

"Believe it or not, they believe he's feeling remorse for the killing of his brother, that somehow he's attempting to make amends."

"Why his brother? Why not his wife and kids?"

Walter gave a body shrug. "It's just a theory."

"It'd make sense, I suppose. If he has this notion that they're Jubal and Tubal Cain reborn, it'd only be right that he'd attempt to make amends. You think the killings are symbolic? Y'know, Bible-related?"

"Nothing in the Good Book that extols the virtues of offering up body parts," Walter said.

I was puzzled. "So what do you think he's doing?"

"Don't know. Could be making soup stock for all I know."

"John said that they had an arrangement, that he would see it through to the end. That he'd sacrifice himself for the old woman. You don't think he was *literally* talking about sacrifice?"

"Hmm," Walter said. "Sacrifice *is* something that appears in the Old Testament. Maybe it's something that would appeal to Maxwell."

Until now I'd been relaxed enough about going after John.

But with this new understanding of Tubal Cain's intentions, I was off the bed in an instant.

"We can't stand around here any longer," I said. "Where's Rink?"

"Cooling his heels next door," Walter said. As I started for the door, he said, "Hold it, Hunter."

"You aren't in a position to stop me, Walter."

"I don't intend stopping you. That's not why I was brought in. I want to give you my blessing. And to ask you a favor."

I stirred restlessly. "A favor?"

"A favor. When you kill the son of a bitch, you don't breathe his name to anyone. Ever."

I scowled at him. Then nodded slowly.

"Help me, Walter. Give me the resources I need to find the bastard, and I promise you that Marty Maxwell—or Tubal Cain, or whatever the hell his name is—will be buried without a trace."

"I knew I could count on you."

36

Back on the road again.

I knew then, even as we sped away in a commandeered government SUV, that the outcome was bound to be bloodshed. The only thing that gave me heart was that I wouldn't be the only man doing the bleeding. By the grim set of Rink's features, he knew it, too. Cain had made two implacable enemies in us, and I could almost pity the fool. Almost.

Rink drove. I held the Global Positioning Satellite receiver supplied by Walter. On the display screen a red cursor blipped on a map of the Los Angeles area. Periodically the cursor shifted on the map, meaning not only that Cain was still on the move but that he hadn't yet realized that John was in possession of the cell phone.

It could only be a matter of time before Cain discovered John's duplicity, or the makeshift tracking device became obsolete when John was buried in a Dumpster or sunk to the bottom of a river.

Going for us was the fact that Cain was using diversionary tactics to shake off pursuit. Guessing that he might be followed by more conventional methods, he was taking surface streets and alleyways to navigate the sprawling city. Though he had more than an hour's lead on us, we'd been able to gain back much of that time by following a direct route. Another thing that very quickly became obvious—even though he often backtracked or ran parallel to his intended target—

Cain was making for Interstate 10, the main eastward route out of Los Angeles.

Initially picking up the 405, we hurtled north past Redondo Beach toward LAX, struck eastward on the 105, then again headed north on the 110, hoping to cut Cain off where the two major routes converged near the downtown L.A. Convention Center. It was apparent that it wouldn't be as easy as that when Cain jinked northeastward, skirting the center of the city on its northern border, while we continued east again toward Interstate 5 and became snarled in traffic.

I watched the cursor skip across the map, pick up Interstate 10, and continue past the Rose Bowl as Rink cursed and pressed on the horn, attempting to force our way through the traffic.

After twenty minutes of very little forward progress, the traffic began to open out ahead of us, and Rink pressed the throttle with disregard for the speed limit. Slaloming in and out of lanes, he gained open road and booted the SUV.

Picking up Interstate 5, we made the short trip northward before meeting Interstate 10 again and swinging in pursuit of our quarry, now more than thirty minutes ahead of us.

"We can still make it," I told Rink. "The prick's certain he's in the clear. He doesn't seem to be traveling much over sixty." I glanced over at the odometer. Rink was pushing the SUV to 120 miles an hour. "If you can keep this up, we'll catch him in no time."

"Darn tootin' I can keep it up. If all these goddamn Sunday drivers would get the hell outta my way." To add weight to his promise, Rink laid his hand on the horn, causing vehicles ahead to swerve out of our way.

It was an exhilarating ride. If it weren't for the fear of arriving too late to save John, I'd have whooped and howled like a kid on a roller coaster. Instead I stayed grimly silent, my gaze on the GPS screen. I didn't have to be so observant. Cain was already out of the urban sprawl and headed toward the vast American southwest.

Even at breakneck speed, it was almost an hour before we caught sight of the Dodge hijacked from the house at Long Beach. We were tempted to continue at top speed, attempt to catch and then force the Dodge off the road. Though I didn't want to believe that John was dead, now, at least, we could stop the Harvestman's reign. Of course, stopping him here would bring further complications.

Conclusion? It would be more prudent to follow at a safe distance and act when there was no likelihood of an innocent passerby being caught up in the gunfire.

Cain wasn't a fool. He was a crazy, murderous bastard, but he was also shrewd. Along with that, he'd been trained as a government agent, and it was a given that he was an expert driver, versed in all manner of countersurveillance measures and reactive driving. We fell into line, allowing more than a quarter of a mile, and at least four vehicles, to separate us. Though that was a meaningless exercise.

"He knows we're here," Rink said.

I looked across at him. There he was again, reading my thoughts.

"He knows we're here and he's taunting us," Rink embellished.

I nodded. "Probably."

"Back at the house, it was almost like he was challenging you to find him. Makes me think that's why he spent so long in the city; to let you catch up."

When I thought about it, I realized Rink was right. "Yeah, he was taking a big chance driving through the center of L.A. when there could've been an APB out for him. He could've easily switched vehicles, too. Looks like he wants us to follow him."

"You want me to get up a little closer? Put a little pressure on the squirmy little punk?"

"No. Just hang back where we are. Let's see where he wants to take us."

"My guess is it's going to be somewhere remote. He's

looking for a showdown. Doesn't want anyone else getting in the way."

"If it's a showdown he wants, it's what he's gonna get."

Rink and I exchanged glances.

"He's certainly made this personal, ain't he?" Rink asked.

"He made it personal when he took John prisoner," I pointed out.

"Maybe so," Rink said. "But I'm referring to him and you. When he found out who you were, I could see it in his face— it was almost as if he was excited. As if he'd found a worthy adversary, y'know? You think he's lookin' to die, Hunter? Some of these sickos like to go out in a blaze of glory. Think he's lookin' for you to kill him?"

"Whether he is or he isn't, that's what's going to happen," I promised.

"Yeah," Rink grumbled. "But be wary, man. If he has a death wish, he intends to take you with him. If he's looking to bolster his reputation, who better to have on his dead list than you?" Rink looked across at me again. "Apart from me, of course."

Even in that moment, Rink could find humor. It made me smile. "Of course."

"No, man, I'm serious. The psycho's looking to make himself famous."

I shook my head. "You really think anyone will ever know the truth about him?"

"Not if it's left to Walter."

"The provision he put on us—allowing us to bring the Harvestman down—was that his name never got mentioned again. How likely is it that my name hits the news if the maniac manages to take me out?"

"Not very, I suppose. But then again, what about your folks back home? Don't you think they're gonna want answers, that they won't make a scene if anything happens to you?"

"Diane knows what my line of work is. She'll receive a

call from Walter's office. She'll be told to keep quiet. She wants a quiet life, she'll comply."

Rink grunted. "An' here was me thinkin' you really understood your ex-wife."

I squinted across at him and he looked at me as though I was a complete idiot. "Hunter, man. You're not in that game anymore. How many times do I have to remind you? There's your mom and dad. Jennifer. An' you really think for one goddamn minute that Diane ain't gonna scream to the rafters if anything happens to you? You think she'll give a shit what line Walter tries to feed her about the Harvestman's identity being an embarrassment to the U.S. government?"

I exhaled. He was right again. Of course Diane would want—no, demand—answers. Suggesting otherwise was doing her an injustice. I nodded.

"Not only that," Rink went on. "But don't you think I won't raise the subject? I don't owe Walter a goddamn thing. I never made any promises to hide the identity of his little black sheep."

"No, Rink. I made the promise for both of us. By coming along, you bought into this."

Rink's face twisted, but he was giving in.

We drove for another hour and a quarter and silence reigned over the many miles.

"Look familiar?" Rink suddenly asked.

I glanced toward a rest stop across the highway to our left. There was a diner and rest area, beyond them a cul-de-sac of single-story cabins. I shook my head.

"That's where the couple was murdered. The man and woman who picked John up in their car."

"You mean the couple who picked up Martin Maxwell or Tubal Cain or whatever it is he calls himself? It's obvious now, isn't it, what really happened?"

"You're saying that somehow the Harvestman ended up with John's car—the one he stole from Petoskey—and it was him, not John, who the witnesses saw being picked up?"

"Yeah. Exactly."

"So how do you explain John and the Harvestman tying up together again? I mean . . . it's a bit of a stretch, ain't it?"

"Not unless something happened between John and Cain. Something that ensured Cain would hunt him down."

Rink gave an expansive shrug. "Who knows? They coulda been acting together long before any of this happened."

"No. I don't believe that. Chance threw them together. I think John became an unwilling puppet. The evidence is all there. Remember that it was John who saved the old woman, that it was John who gave us the tools to hunt Cain down. It was his decision to take my cell phone. Do you really believe he'd have done that if he was working with Cain?"

"No, I don't. An' I don't think he'd offer himself up as a sacrifice, either. I'm only playing advocate here. I don't suppose we'll ever know the true story."

"Only way we're gonna find that out is to save John," I said. "If I have my way, Cain won't be around to do any explaining."

Out here on the fringes of the Mojave Desert, there was a surreal cast to the early evening sky. Behind us, hovering above the Pacific Ocean, the sun's final gasp made the sky a mother-of-pearl banner. Alongside the road, Joshua trees cast elongated shadows like accusing fingers, pointing the way to the showdown ahead.

Four vehicles ahead, Cain flicked on his lights, ensuring that we could follow him as the night began to descend over the desert.

While he drove, Rink drank mineral water courtesy of the government. He offered me some. Pity that the bottle didn't contain something a little stronger. Nonetheless, I accepted it and chugged down a grateful mouthful.

Really, I should've been thirstier than I was, I should've felt the need for food. Neither of us had eaten anything since early that morning. However, the continued release of adrenaline ensured that nothing would pass my lips that required my stomach to hold on to it. Anything more solid than the spring water, I suspected, would end up projected out the window in a couple of miles.

As night came, Rink pushed the SUV on. One of the cars between us turned up a side road and Rink filled the gap it left.

For two more hours Cain led us on a merry dance. Then, as if concerned that we might miss him turning off the main route, he used his turn signal, slowed down dramatically, and crawled to an intersection.

Two of the cars ahead of us overtook him before he reached the turnoff. As Cain swept to the right, the remaining car continued on to the east, and I saw Cain hit the brakes a couple of times, ensuring that we didn't lose him.

"Considerate son of a bitch," Rink muttered.

Then Cain was on the overpass, crossing the interstate, heading northward. On the bridge he slowed to a crawl, watched as we swung onto the off ramp. Then he gave the Dodge gas and peeled away.

"I guess we're getting close now, and he wants time to prepare," I said.

The GPS tracker had been obsolete for some hours now. Throughout it had traveled cradled in my palms, for no other reason than it stopped me fiddling with my gun. Luck, or maybe foresight, caused me to check the screen. The cursor indicating the latest triangulated location of the cell phone had finally stopped moving. I didn't even bother to frown. Cain had discovered our deception. Maybe he'd found John was carrying the device as soon as they'd left the house at Long Beach; maybe it was much later. Whatever. When he'd slowed down, it wasn't to taunt us, it was to throw away the phone.

It was clear that he wanted us nearby. More clear was his need to buy a little time before we arrived at the meeting ground.

"Put your foot down, Rink."

"I can still see his lights," Rink said. "I won't lose him."

"He won't let you lose him," I said. "He'll make sure we know exactly where he is. But he'll be prepared for our arrival, and I don't want to allow him that advantage."

37 "YOU DON'T LOOK SO GOOD."

Cain studied his passenger.

His words, he decided, were an understatement.

John was spread across the backseat of the Dodge like yesterday's fast-food wrappers; cold, soiled, and greasy. Blood from his wound caked his clothing all down his side. His hands were also reddish-brown and he had smears on his forehead. Perspiration oozed from him like water from a half-dead boiler.

"I said that you don't look so good, John," Cain said, watching John's eyelids flutter in the rearview mirror.

"Turn off the light, willya?" John mumbled incoherently.

"I need to check that you're okay," Cain said, but he reached up and flicked off the interior lights.

"Why? You're gonna kill me," John said, his voice coming out like marbles over a tin sheet. "Or have you forgotten?"

"You keep saying that. I might have a change of mind."

"Yeah, right." John forced himself to sit upright.

"Lay back down."

"I'm fine."

"The road gets kinda rough up ahead. It would be better if you were lying down. Less chance you'll open up your wound again."

"My wound's fine."

Cain gave a humorless laugh. "Suit yourself."

"Better than suiting you," John said with little conviction.

Cain drummed his fingers on the steering wheel. "You know, I'm not sure this old heap will get us where we're going. Not in any shape, at least."

"Won't matter," John told him. "You won't need it for the return trip. You'll be getting a lift in the coroner's car."

"Ha!"

"I mean it. You mess with my brother, you're buying your own body bag."

"Keep thinking that way, John. Optimism will keep you alive."

"I'm not gonna get outta this alive. I know that. I've known it all along. My only hope is that I see you die first."

"If anyone ends up dead, it'll be your high and mighty brother. Chances are I'll have to do Jared Rington, too."

"You actually believe that?"

"Are you saying that confidence in my abilities is a bad thing? Shame on you, trying to tarnish my self-esteem."

"Nothing I say would make you think badly of yourself. You're a fuckin' psychopath."

"Sticks and stones, John. Sticks and stones."

"Stop being so damn patronizing. Why don't you come clean and tell the truth? You've intended killing me all along, haven't you? I can't believe you saved me from drowning so that you could murder me. That's so twisted, nobody would believe it."

"The truth is, you're here now. Makes no difference whether you believe me or not."

John snapped, "You're gonna get your head handed to you on a plate. My brother isn't like me; Joe *will* kill you."

"Nah, I don't see things turning out that way."

John gave a disgusted cough, squirmed down in the seat. Either his strength was failing him or he'd decided that it was pointless talking. Not that it made a difference; if Cain wanted to talk, he would talk. "Now, then, where is the big bold Joe Hunter?"

Cain squinted into the mirror, adjusting it. Some distance

back he could see the headlights of the pursuing SUV. In response, he turned off the Dodge's lights. "Don't want to make things too easy, now, do we?"

"I thought you wanted him to follow you?"

"I do, just not too closely."

"You might as well give up. Joe isn't gonna be reading you your rights. He's gonna put a bullet right between your eyes."

"Then I'll just have to make certain he doesn't see me, won't I?"

Cain grinned into the darkness.

The road had become a dirt trail, with ruts on either side and sagebrush along its center where the desert sand gathered. The moon hanging low over the horizon offered a little light, so Cain could make out the road ahead. Not that he needed to concentrate; he knew this trail as well as he knew his own dark heart's desires. Despite his misgivings about the worthiness of the Dodge, he pushed it to greater speed, smiling at each jounce and the wince of pain it elicited from his passenger.

"I bet you wish you hadn't pulled that stunt with the cell phone," he said. John didn't answer. "Right now you're thinking that—not only have you signed your own death warrant—but your brother's as well. Deep down, some errant grain of honor is festering like a malignant cancer, eating away at your insides. You're thinking, I should've paid my dues and spared the others. Now I've put my brother in terrible danger."

"No," John said. "I'm thinking you're so full of crap I can't stand the stench any longer. I'm outta here, you maniac!"

Then John grabbed the door handle and thrust the door open. The rush of wind banged it back against him.

Cain would never admit to panic, but realizing John's insane plan, he let slip a shout of denial. He immediately stomped on the brakes. John's body was thrown forward, and his forehead slammed the back of Cain's neck. The shock of the collision knocked Cain's hands off the steering wheel, and momentarily he had to fight both the movement of the vehicle and the wave of agony washing over him. In those few seconds, John threw his weight against the partly open door and fell away into billowing dust.

"Son of a bitch!" Cain screamed, stomping on the brake pedal a second time. The Dodge fishtailed, sending up plumes of dirt, ending up crossways in the road. He threw open the door and lurched out, eyes scanning the road for John. Not on the road. He began running. In the distance were the telltale lights of Hunter's car.

Forty or so paces along the road he found John sprawled at the base of a gnarly cactus. Momentarily he feared that John was dead, but then he saw the fire in the man's eyes as he squirmed around to face him.

"You stupid, stupid idiot," Cain snarled.

"Screw you," John grunted.

Cain stepped forward as John attempted to rise up against him. Cain's foot pushed him down again, pressing savagely against the wound in his chest. John screamed. Cain pressed harder. And the screaming stopped as John passed out at last.

Cain grabbed him, thrust his arms around John's chest in a bear hug, and began backpedaling. Dragging the groaning man, Cain looked up. Hunter's lights were some distance away, but looming nearer. "I should just leave you here to die, you goddamn ass. Leave you in the road so your freakin' brother rides right over you."

It was a hollow threat because he still had a plan for John Telfer.

38 THE ENIGMA THAT WAS TUBAL CAIN KEPT NAGGING at me. How does a psycho like Martin Maxwell bluff his way through the rigorous selection processes employed by the Secret Service? How does he manage to conceal his true self—a depraved stalker and murderer—and pass himself off as normal?

Not only that, but to his wife and kids, had he been the epitome of the family dad? What had gone through their minds when they'd finally seen his true face?

What had his long-lost brother imagined when they'd first met? That they'd pick up on their missing past, that they'd shoot pool together, share a couple of beers, become bosom buddies? I bet he never imagined that he'd end up a scorched corpse in a house he'd never known, the ghosts of Cain's wife and children keeping him company.

"You're doing it again," Rink said.

I looked over at Rink, who was doing a good job of looking at me without taking his full attention from the trail.

"Doing what?"

"Wearing that face."

"What face?"

"The face that says you ain't worried about what's to come. The one you always wore on missions."

"I'm worried, Rink."

"Don't look like it."

Then he changed the subject.

"Heads up, Hunter. The lights have just gone out."

I peered into the darkness ahead. I couldn't see the Dodge's taillights, either. They'd long taunted us, and their sudden disappearance brought an uncomfortable feeling. Like a hole had opened up and the devil had escaped us by fleeing back to hell.

"You think he's stopped? Maybe fixin' to escape?" Rink glanced my way again, back to the road.

"No. He's running blind. He wants to get ahead of us so he can set up an ambush."

"Time we played catch-up, then," Rink said. The SUV surged ahead, bouncing over the higher ruts, blasting directly through others so that gravel and small rocks banged and clattered in the wheel wells.

Now the chase was truly on.

Again I checked my SIG. Full clip. Two spares in my waistband. Then I reached down and felt the hilt of my military issue KA-BAR where it was tucked in my boot. Somehow I suspected that the knife would be my weapon of choice when I finally came eye to eye with the murderous bastard.

Stars twinkled in the vault above us. Out here, in the middle of this empty space, the sky was endless, the starlight sharply defined. Shadows were stark, and the sand and gravel had a faintly luminous quality. Rocketing across the night landscape, the beauty of the desert was lost on me. I didn't give any of it a second's notice. How could I think of beauty when I was chasing something as loathsome as Tubal Cain?

I was inclined to lean out the window to check the night sky for another reason: as we'd used the technology Walter had given to us, I had no doubt we were being tailed as diligently as we tailed Cain. They wouldn't be coming in cars; they'd have command of helicopters, possibly even an AWACS aircraft high in the heavens to plot our course. In the end, I didn't bother looking. Helicopters would be piloted without running lights, and a high-altitude spy plane would be impossible to spot.

"When we find him we do him quickly," I said to Rink.

"My intention all along."

"Walter's goons will be coming," I added.

"They won't try and stop us."

"I know. They'll be coming to mop up, to make sure everything's clean. I don't want John falling into their hands." I looked pointedly at Rink, and he jerked his chin in response. "They'll make John disappear. They might even make us disappear."

"They'll goddamn try, frog-giggin' punks."

I returned my attention to the road ahead. The brush country was giving way to a higher elevation. On the skyline ahead, I could detect a deepening of the shadows, as if a colossal wall had been erected astride the desert.

"You any idea where we are?" I asked Rink.

"Nope."

I looked for the GPS, switched it on, and studied the faintly glowing map on the LED screen. Tightly knit lines showed that the terrain was more mountainous ahead. The road wasn't marked on the map, but that came as no surprise. I placed the GPS down at my feet. "Keep on going. Looks like we're heading for those hills."

Rink obliged. But we'd traveled no more than a quarter of a mile before I slapped my hands on the dashboard and commanded him to stop. I craned around so I didn't lose sight of what was at the side of the road. Rink brought the SUV to a halt even as I was opening the door to get out.

I jogged back the way we'd come, slowed down, and came to a halt twenty yards from what I'd noticed protruding from a clump of brush.

I listened.

Nothing moved in the sandscape. All I could hear was the throaty hum of the SUV behind me and the rushing blood in my veins. Still, I remained motionless, using my peripheral vision to probe the shadows. What is often missed when viewed directly can be picked up in the peripheral, the slightest movement amplified tenfold. It's a prey animal thing, a throwback to the days when man was hunted by carnivorous beasts.

Finally satisfied that this wasn't part of Cain's ambush, I stepped forward. A quick inspection showed that the dirt and gravel at the side of the road had been disturbed. More concerning, I saw a damp patch of blood where a body had been dragged across the earth. I guessed that John had made some effort at escape, only to be captured and forced back into the Dodge. Cain had John, yes, but he hadn't noticed the briefcase that was hung up in the bushes farther along the trail.

I trotted over and snatched the Samsonite case from the brush. I was in no doubt that it was the one I'd seen John clinging to at the beach house. Chance could have dumped a briefcase way out here in the desert, but not one glistening with sticky blood. I didn't spare the time to check its contents, noting only that it was heavy before I stuffed it under my arm and headed back to the SUV.

When I was back in the car, Rink set off again after Cain. He asked, "You thinking what I'm thinking?"

"Money," I said. I opened the case on my lap. Bundle upon bundle of bills filled the case. Rink gave a low whistle.

"Counterfeit?"

I checked.

"No. The real thing."

"So that's what this is all about," Rink said.

I shook my head. "I don't think so, Rink. It was never about the money. Cain wants blood. That's all it's ever been about."

"Bones," Rink corrected.

"But I do think this is what it's all been about for John."

"Goddamn greedy fool."

I shook my head. "Believe it or not, I don't think he did this out of greed. I think he sees it as a way to put things right."

"Yeah," Rink said with no conviction. I shrugged. I knew John better than that. I believed that he'd changed. The old John wouldn't have jeopardized his safety for the old woman; he wouldn't have risked lifting the cell phone from my pocket for fear that Cain saw him. To me, John had turned a corner in his life, where more than his next bet meant something to him.

Even what we'd just come across back there on the trail now made sense to me. He hadn't attempted to escape at all; he'd jumped from the Dodge so he could leave the cash for me to find. The money wasn't for him; it was for Louise, it was for Jenny, it was for his children. Stuffing the case beneath my seat, I put the money to the back of my mind. I could see to it later.

39

"HOW DO YOU LIKE THE PLACE?"

Oblivious to Cain, John slumped against the wooden support-beam, smearing it with blood as he forced himself upright. His head lolled on his shoulders and he mumbled something incoherent.

"You could act a little more enthusiastic than that," Cain said. "I've gone to a lot of trouble to get the place just right for *my* brother. Put a lot of time and effort into the decor. Don't you think the ambience is just right?"

John staggered. Cain clutched him under an arm, mindless of the way his fingers dug into flesh. "Watch that first step; it can be a real bitch."

Then, with a shove, he pressed John forward. Watched as his captive tumbled down the short flight of steps into darkness. Only semiconscious, John made little noise. He fell as if constructed from rags that made only soft contact with the steps. A grunt was all that marked his resting place.

"That'll teach you to pay attention," Cain said. He wasn't happy that John had lost the case of money, but neither was he unnecessarily concerned. Either Joe Hunter would fetch the money for him, or he could backtrack and collect it when all this was over. Concern was unnecessary, but a little necessary cruelty would remind John Telfer what it meant to cross Tubal Cain. Taking one last glance behind him, Cain followed John into the darkness.

Fifteen feet down, the steps leveled out on a floor made

of bedrock. Last time Cain had been here he had swept the desert sand away, but already he could feel windblown dust beneath his feet; it was the main downside to his hideaway that he had to continually maintain it by brushing and sweeping to keep the desert at bay.

He prodded John with a foot, moving him aside as he reached out in the dark and clutched for the padlock that held the metal door shut. Holding the lock in one hand, he traced the fingers of the other up the near wall, found a narrow niche he'd dug into the sandstone, and pulled out the concealed key. The key opened the lock with little resistance. Cain pushed and the door swung inward on well-maintained hinges.

The smell buffeted him.

He smiled.

Even in his semiunconscious state, John gagged at the stench.

"What the fu . . . ?" John groaned.

Cain didn't comment; he bent down and grabbed John's shirt, hauling him to his feet and pushing him into the room before him, urging him into the charnel stink. John gave some resistance, refusing to breathe, steeling his shoulders as he attempted to ward off the sickening stench of rotted meat.

"Get inside," Cain said, almost a whisper.

"No," John gasped.

"Yes." Cain pushed him into the cloying darkness.

Cain entered the room with a breezy exuberance. He fairly skipped over to the nearest lamp, scratched around until he found the butane lighter beside it, then set flame to wick, casting writhing shadows around the room. That done, he emptied his pockets of the bones he'd garnered during his latest trip. They made quite a mound. Then, hands on hips, he surveyed the space before him.

"Now what do you think, John? Do you think Jubal would be pleased?"

On the floor, John was curled into a fetal ball. One arm covered his face, but Cain could see the whites of his eyes reflected in the lamplight, searching the room with a mix of fascination and revulsion. His pupils were like pinpricks in yellowed snow. Yes, Cain decided, John was very impressed.

40

"REMIND ME NOT TO INVEST IN A HOLIDAY HOME out here," Rink said. "Could be a bitch lettin' it out during the winter season."

"It'd be a bitch in any season," I told him.

The Mojave Desert occupies more than 22,000 square miles, bordering California and portions of Arizona, Utah, and Nevada. Where we were at that given moment I couldn't even begin to guess. I was only pleased that we had a vehicle. If we'd had to walk out of there in the daytime, I didn't think much of our chances for survival.

Not that it was a desert in the true sense of the word. It wasn't made up of mile after mile of dunes like I'd experienced in the Sahara. But one look at the blasted landscape told me it was every bit as arid.

We were climbing higher into the foothills. All around us the night sky was torn along the horizon by weird shapes that I knew were Joshua trees. In my imagination, they appeared to be misshapen giants waving us on to our doom. The road was now all but gone, and what Rink followed was the faint trail Cain's Dodge had left upon the earth.

During the day, this area was hot, and through the middle hours of the night the temperature could drop uncomfortably low, but we were driving during those hours when the heat stored during the daylight hours still radiated from the rocks and gravel. Still, even with the heat on in the SUV, I felt the first hint of the cold. I shivered, found myself tightening in reflex.

"You okay, Hunter?" Rink asked.

I mumbled assent.

"Everything's gonna go fine, you just mark my words."

"I'm okay, Rink," I reassured him. "Just felt like someone walked over my grave."

Rink fell silent. Maybe my words were too prophetic for his liking. He concentrated on guiding the SUV up an incline toward a pass into the foothills marked by two gargantuan crags. Nearing the summit, he turned to me. "It's Cain who's gonna die."

I exhaled. "I hope it's all over tonight."

I looked at him. He coughed deep in his throat, a low grumble. "Cain's number's up. That part'll be finished. But what about the rest?"

"What rest?" I asked, but already the question was rhetorical. He was referring to John, to Louise Blake, Petoskey and Hendrickson, Walter, the Secret Service. All the victims and the families of the Harvestman. Maybe Cain would die tonight, but how long would the repercussions last? There were other deaths—Cain's victims aside—involved along the way. In particular, the hit man killed at Louise's house, the other I'd killed back at the beach house. How were those going to be resolved?

"We're gonna have us a three-ring circus out here," Rink said.

I stared straight ahead. The two gigantic pillars of rock dominated the skyline. Against the purple sky, they looked like monoliths, stones to mark the tombs of twin giants. And we had to pass between them.

Driving between the huge crags, I knew we'd just gone beyond the point of no return. Clichéd, yes, but true. Once more, I checked my weapons. They were still prepared, just as they'd been minutes earlier. Momentarily I wondered if they would be enough.

Beyond the rock gates was a flat expanse of sandstone. It sloped gently toward the horizon, shelf built upon shelf of petrified sand. Millions of years ago, this area had been the

bed of a prehistoric ocean, teeming with weird and aston-
ishing life forms. But now, hundreds of feet above present
sea level, the huge rock was devoid of life. Only dust devils
moved here, tiny zephyrs plucking and whirling particles of
grit across the unresponsive land.

"Looks like we just touched down on Mars," Rink
breathed.

It was apparent by the way the table of rock disappeared
into the night that we were on a massive shelf of land, and
I cautioned Rink, urged him to slow down. Just something
about the color of the night beyond the scope of our vision
gave me pause, as though we were standing at the edge of
the world and an unwary step would pitch us over the edge.

Rink pulled the SUV to a halt. We leaned forward, craning our necks to look down on the mist-shrouded valley
below us. We shared a look. If Rink hadn't stopped when he
did, we would've dropped two hundred feet to our deaths.

"Which way now, Daniel Boone?" Rink asked.

"Any way but forward," I said and we both laughed.

Careful not to slip us over the rim of the cliff, Rink edged
the SUV to the left, then drove with the caution of someone
suddenly struck blind. Here the rock became rutted with
deep crevasses, and Rink drove back inland, did a complete
U-turn, then swung back the way we'd come. Out of the night
loomed queer shapes. Only as we drew alongside them did I
realize that we were traveling amid the husks of burned-out
vehicles. Predominantly they were camper vans and Winne-
bagos, the occasional minivan. Cain, it seemed, had a major
gripe with the drivers of those vehicles. Then we found the
Dodge abandoned. Both front doors stood open and the interior light was a yellow glow against the night sky.

Nothing stirred inside the car. Cain could've been
stretched out across the backseat, waiting for us to blunder
over and poke our heads inside so that he could shoot us. Or
he could've been hunkered down behind the car. I dismissed
both ideas.

What fun would that be?

He hadn't brought us all the way out here just so he could hit us with potshots while we were out in the open. Cain had planned a more interesting game than that.

But we still had to check.

We got out of the SUV fifty feet shy of the Dodge. Cautiously we moved to the Dodge and checked it out. While I trained my barrel on the interior of the car, Rink moved in closer and checked the rear seat.

"Clear?" I asked.

Rink nodded me in closer.

"Check it out, Hunter."

I did. And I could do nothing but groan. The backseat was covered with blood. Not pools of the stuff, but enough streaks and smears to indicate that John didn't have much time left on this earth.

While I continued to stare at the mess in the car, Rink quickly checked the trunk of the Dodge, finding it locked. Cain wasn't about to slip out from inside it while our backs were turned. Rink came to stand beside me and nodded to where patches of scuffed rock marked someone's passing. So did the periodic droplets of blood that glistened darkly against the paler surface.

We were off again. Fanning out so that a dozen paces separated us, we edged forward. Then no more than a hundred yards from the parked car, we reached the brink of the cliff. Out of the confines of the SUV, we could approach nearer to the cliff than before, so the void below us no longer appeared so empty. The cliff fell more than two hundred feet to a sloping embankment of shale and sand before leveling out into a natural amphitheater that extended farther than I could see. It was a great bowl shape, alkaline white, with gathering mist hanging over it like a multitude of specters. The sun-bleached basin reminded me of only one thing: the scooped-out, hollow interior of a human skull. I hissed. If Cain could call any place home, this would be it.

Outlined on the escarpment's rim, we made easy targets for anyone positioned below. We stepped back.

"Over there." Rink motioned. "Looks like a way down. Has to be the way they went."

I saw the fissure in the earth and nodded. Moving toward it, I peered over the edge. A casual glance probably wouldn't have revealed the fabricated steps leading down the cliffside, but they were what I'd been looking for. Cain had been here many times in the past; the steps were testimony to that.

"I'll take point," I told Rink. Then I set off. The steps weren't as sheer as they first appeared, and surprisingly, you wouldn't have had to be mountain-goat nimble to climb down. However, burdened with John, I did wonder how Cain managed to make his way down without tripping and carrying them both to their deaths. It gave me a healthy new respect for what the man was capable of.

I reminded myself that he was a trained Secret Service agent, that he was probably whalebone-tough beneath the unassuming exterior. Now I had to credit him with above-average strength and determination. He wouldn't be easy to take out in a chest-to-chest fight.

Rink didn't need guidance on how to handle our descent. He waited until I'd hit the bottom before he set off.

While he descended, I covered him. When he reached bottom, I stalked forward. Rink followed, scanning left and right, periodically behind. We traversed the slope of the bone-white hollow in that fashion until we found level footing. The ground was no longer as treacherous as it had been on the descent, but the mist rose up before us, obscuring our view. That was bad enough, but it also played tricks on our ears. As I stepped out on the sand, I could've sworn I heard the tinkle of music. I paused, turned back to Rink.

"You hear that?"

Rink's eyebrows knitted. "That a radio playing?" he whispered.

I shrugged, stepped forward. Between patches of mist, I thought I saw something move. In response, my hand swung toward it, fingertip caressing the trigger of my SIG. Again the tinkle of music. Then the mist writhed and the shape I'd glimpsed was gone.

"What the hell was that?" Rink hissed at me. Which confirmed I wasn't hallucinating.

"Don't know," I replied.

"Freakin' ghost," Rink muttered under his breath.

Music tinkled from in front of me. Like the dissonant chimes of a musically challenged orchestra. Once more I snatched a glimpse of the conductor waving his baton. And inured to horror as I'd become, even I cringed back from what stood before me.

"Crap," I breathed.

Rink had been right; the monstrosity before me was indeed best described as a ghost.

41

CAIN WHISTLED WHILE HE WORKED. HE KEPT HARMONY with every wince of agony from John, exhaled loudly in time with every grunt of pain, laughed when John ground his body against the rock wall in an effort to pull away from his slicing administrations.

"The pain will go away soon," Cain reassured John. "Once I'm through the dermis, as far down as the bone, I'll be beyond the nerve endings."

John howled.

Cain stepped in closer, eyes like lasers, guiding the scaling knife with a surgeon's precision. In such deep concentration, the tip of his tongue poked from beneath the slash of his lips, writhing like a fat worm as he plied his tool. Beyond flesh was bone, and that would require effort. His whistling stopped, and now he moaned more often than John did.

John was beyond agony now, beyond the point of human endurance. Cain sighed. His work wasn't the same, didn't hold the same satisfaction, if his subject wasn't around to appreciate it. Shaking his head, he stepped away. Then, hands on hips, he surveyed his work of art.

Not bad, I suppose, he told himself. Though it still lacked a certain flamboyant statement to finish it off. If this was to be the magnum opus of both Jubal and Tubal Cain, he required a truly magnificent centerpiece to finalize it.

He slipped the scaling knife into his waistband, retrieved the empty gun from where he'd laid it on the floor, and headed out into the night.

42 I'VE OFTEN WONDERED IF THERE'S ANYONE MORE superstitious than a soldier. You'd think that with such a reliance on fact, science, and technology, the basis of modern warfare, there'd be no room for a belief in the supernatural. But there is the firm belief in many a soldier's mind that paranormal skills are often within the warrior's arsenal. I am a believer in a sixth sense, the heightened ability to detect the unseen watcher, the sniper on the rooftop or the tiger hidden in the long grass. It's so widely believed that it has even been given a term: *Rapid Intuitive Experience,* the soldier's very own ESP.

I accept that the proof of such a thing is subjective, but it has saved my life enough times that I give it full credence. But up until now, despite my fanciful notions during the assault on Petoskey's building, I hadn't given the existence of ghosts much credibility. How could I? The number of men I've killed, I would go insane if I dwelled on the number who must haunt me.

Still, belief in ghosts or not, for more than a heartbeat I genuinely accepted that the thing in front of me was a vengeful spirit risen from its grave to exact retribution. I stepped back, eyes wide, mouth hanging open. And if the blade it held in its clawed fist had been animated, I doubt that I could've stopped it scything my head from my shoulders.

"Holy Christ!" I heard the words, but was unsure whether it was me or Rink that said them. Maybe we both did.

Point Shooting is based entirely on the natural posture,

the natural reaction to lifting the gun and firing wherever danger presents itself. When confronted by this diabolical creature, my reactions failed me. The SIG hung useless by my side.

Then Rink was beside me. He laid a hand on my shoulder. "Hunter . . . we gotta keep moving, man. Can't let this damn thing throw us."

"It's a little hard not to," I croaked.

The miasma of fear gripped me, and it was an effort to shake free of it. When I did, it was through the exhalation of pent-up fear.

"What the hell is it?" Rink asked.

I looked again at the specter in the mist. A human skull grinned back at me. But I could see now that there was no life behind the recessed sockets, no drool dripping from its widely splayed teeth. It was a simulacrum, given the illusion of life by Cain's artistic dementia. The skull was mounted on a pole pushed into the sand. A tattered blanket was draped over a crossbar to give the semblance of a body. Hands and forearms—withered skin and tendons holding together the bones—were bound to other poles concealed within the blanket. I shuddered.

"It's a warning," I finally managed. "Or a gatekeeper. I think we've found him, Rink."

"You're not kidding."

We both heard the music again; a sonorous piping this time. I stepped closer to the skeletal form. The music was coming from its bones. Tiny drill holes along the radius and ulna of the forearms made for a maniac's idea of a flute. When the wind picked up, it disturbed the blanket and produced a racket like a wind chime.

"Son of a bitch's crazy as a bag of weasels," Rink offered.

As we walked on, I couldn't help peering back at the ghostly form. *Who do those bones belong to?* I wondered. Is there a family someplace that to this day hopes that their loved one will turn up one bright morning and announce that he's fine, that he only needed to get away for a while

DEAD MEN'S DUST 281

but now he's back? I promised myself that I would see to that return, that I would take this person home again. The day wouldn't be bright, and neither would he be fine, but he would be going home.

As would the next twelve skeletons we came across as we walked.

It was an unholy baker's dozen.

All were posed in similar styles to the first, strung up on poles, bodies formed of blankets. But some were in reclining postures, others placed to give the impression of flight, two of them strung together as though engaged in a slow waltz. Cain was indeed crazy, as dangerous as a pit of venomous reptiles, and every bit as sly.

Across the amphitheater we went, and with every step my dread grew. I wondered if we were already too late. If John were already strung up in an insane effigy to Cain's dementia.

The tiny bones strewn in the sand gave me an even greater loathing for Cain than before. Many were the remains of tiny animals and birds fallen out of the sky, but here and there, I saw the phalanges of human fingers protruding from their graves as though clawing their way to an afterlife denied them. Rink looked equally disturbed. I didn't know what face I wore, but I was sure that if my friend studied me now, he'd see that I, too, could fear.

The wind was picking up. The mist—not true mist, but particles of the alkaline desert borne on the wind—billowed around us. It invaded my mouth and nostrils, caused me to squint. I had the horrifying notion that the desert was actually formed of particles of bone, and I gagged and spat in reflex. It was an absurd notion, but it was there. I pulled my shirt up over my face as protection against inhaling dead men's dust.

"Hunter."

I heard Rink's whisper. He was thirty feet to my left, crouching down, gun trained on something I couldn't see. I stopped, took up a crouch of my own. Rink indicated something beyond him that I couldn't discriminate from the shifting veil of sand. Duckwalking, I made my way over.

"There" was all Rink said. I could make out a hulking formation of rocks jutting out of the desert like the ruins of a mythical castle. Like the sand, the rocks were chalk white and glowed with phosphorescence against the night sky. If this amphitheater had once been the floor of an ocean, then the rocks were millions of years old, ancient testimony to volcanic activity that had shattered the sea floor in a cataclysmic upheaval. Directly ahead of us, two more spectral forms marked a fissure in the rocks. Truly, they were gate-keepers this time.

This had to be the final place. Cain's place.

43

ALONE, EITHER MAN WAS A FORMIDABLE ENEMY. Together, Cain had no hope of defeating them. Not when he was armed only with his scaling knife while both of them had semiautomatic handguns. The only chance he had was to separate them; use their loyalty for each other against them. It was a weakness Cain immediately saw. Though they were fearless warriors, neither wanted to die or to lose his friend. Cain, on the other hand, had no such qualms. He was prepared to die to achieve his aims.

Both Joe Hunter and Jared Rington transcended the level of even the most hard-boiled soldier. Their training . . . no, their indoctrination . . . had seen to that. Maybe they were beyond the normal psychological and physiological responses to the death of a friend guaranteed to halt even the sturdiest warrior in his tracks. Perhaps, like Cain himself, they had reached that ultracognizant level where they could elevate themselves above the ken of mortal man, to float on the seas of chaos where the "natural" order of being meant that nothing was as it seemed. This was the realm in which Cain existed; what if these two had achieved the same level of consciousness? What if, after all these years, he had found worthy protagonists, contenders for his title of Prince of Chaos?

He chuckled to himself. Careful that the sound didn't betray his hiding place.

Not a chance.

44

STANDING AT THE THRESHOLD TO CAIN'S DOMAIN, I balked at entering without a full reconnaissance of the area. Yet at the same time I knew that time was of the utmost importance. John was in terrible danger, possibly with only seconds to live, and I was dithering at the entrance to his torture chamber. Still, that unnatural talent for spotting the viper in the grass was screaming at me and I had to heed it.

I had to choose between my own and John's well-being, and at the end of the day I was left with very few choices. If I waited, he'd be dead. If I charged in, he could still end up dead. I had to act.

I stepped forward.

Rink was behind me. I knew that Cain couldn't come on me from that direction. Rink, on the other hand, had me as a buffer if Cain chose to come at us from the rocks. I went slowly, gun out, eyes and ears scanning for any sign of life. Periodically I looked up.

The rocks towered over me. They were sheer enough that I didn't believe Cain could scale them, but more than one soldier had lost his life by ignoring what was lurking above his field of vision. In Vietnam, many a jarhead was taken by surprise by a noose dropped around his throat, or even by the constriction of an assassin's legs dropping from an overhanging bough. The martial art named Viet Vo Dao is based upon that very premise.

I know I was crediting Cain with more tools than he perhaps possessed, but at that moment, before meeting him in combat, I had to credit him with everything possible. In my line of work, to underestimate an individual is to invite death.

The twin sentinels watched my progress. They were larger than those skeletons we'd already passed. More formidable to the eye, with their bison skulls and hulking forms of tattered rags and strips of leather. They looked like something out of a Tolkien novel; chimeralike demons guarding the door to the lower realms.

Beyond them, I came upon a well-beaten path that led to the center of the rock formation. The fissure in the rocks was natural, but here and there I detected evidence that Cain had helped widen the doorway by means of hammer and chisel. Also, he'd marked his progress with weird symbols and pictograms straight out of a Hieronymus Bosch painting. In retrospect, I believe the paintings on the rock surface were a history of his killings, but at the time, I couldn't give his demented story much more notice.

Rink was disciplined enough that he didn't immediately follow me into the passage. I was aware of him somewhere behind me. I could hear his breathing as he crouched at the entrance to the passageway, the strange acoustics amplifying his trepidation. But no words passed between us now. Talking would identify our position. We had to rely on stealth to get us through this thing unscathed. I walked on, mindful of not stepping on a loose pebble or piece of wind-blown brush that would alert Cain. Sweat moistened my brow, tickled between my shoulder blades. My vision was constricted to a narrow focus and my blood rushed in my ears. Not the ideal conditions for hunting. But they were a response to the adrenaline racing through me and there was nothing I could do about it.

The passage widened out, opening into a cul-de-sac hemmed in on three sides by the towering rock formation. There was only one way in; the ideal location for a trap. Quickly I scanned the rocks above me, my gun at the point of my vision. Nothing stirred; there was nothing to indicate that an ambush would come from above. I stepped into the cul-de-sac, circling on my heels to cover all directions as best I could. Twenty feet in, I found the hole in the ground. Steps leading down into darkness. Breath caught in my throat.

I couldn't make out anything beyond the first few steps. The night had fully descended, and though my eyes had adjusted to the darkness, the steps descended into a space I can only describe as being devoid of *anything*. It was beyond night, beyond black.

I couldn't bring myself to step into the hole. I even looked back for moral support from Rink. If he could have seen me then, he would have seen the face of terror. I couldn't allow that; I quickly stepped forward, tracing the first step with the toe of my boot. Then, before my desperate boldness fled, I descended the stairs as rapidly as I could.

When I reached the bottom, I could make out the faint outlines of a door before me. The reflection of a flame leaked out from beneath the door. Beyond the door a lamp burned. That knowledge gave me the courage to reach out and tug on the door handle. I did so sharply, then stepped into the room it revealed, my gun searching for targets.

The smell hit me first.

I gagged. That was bad enough.

Then my eyes began to make sense of what I was looking at, and for the first time in my life, I retreated with a cry of alarm.

45

OH, WHAT AN IDIOT. YOU'RE BARING YOUR NECK TO the headsman's block. You deserve to die with ignominy, you stumbling, sightless fool! To think I credited you with respect when you're as blind as all the rest. Die, cretin. Die, Jared Rington.

Rink was there, no more than an arm's length from him. The big lummox's nerves were strung taut, shredded, fraying under the pressure. His head swung from side to side. He didn't know which way to look. Because of that, he didn't look anywhere. He saw everything, but in doing so, he saw nothing. His mind was so full of stimuli that it was unable to process what was right before his eyes.

And that was all Cain required. He would use Rink's blindness to his advantage. He timed the rhythm of Rink's movements, watched and discerned the momentary gap where the eyes swung a fraction of an instant before the barrel of the gun followed. Into that fraction of space, Cain would insert himself. Before Rink could make any sense of his appearance, it would already be too late.

A-one and a-two and a-... now.

From within the shroud of blankets that was the body of the bison-skulled monstrosity to Rink's left, Cain erupted. He made as little sound as possible, and didn't so much leap out as jut forward from his waist, arm streaking down at the juncture of Rink's neck and shoulder. It was a guaranteed instant kill. The point of his blade jabbing down to puncture the heart from above. Rington would die instantly, drop like a slaughtered steer. No shout of warning to Joe Hunter.

Except Rink wasn't as blind as he looked.

He detected the shifting shadows and he jerked away. The blade still slid into flesh, but instead of finding that pinpoint where the blade could be forced down into the heart, it found resistance in the form of his sturdy clavicle. The metal scoured bone, but it was deflected away from the vitals and into the pectoral muscle.

"Sumbitch!" Rink grunted, his gun coming around. He fired in an arc, not waiting for the target to present itself before jerking on the trigger. Three times he fired. Two bullets cut chips from the rocks, one snatched at the blanket swathing Cain's form. Then Cain's knee thumped against his forearm, halting the gun, and the knife once more cut a swathe through the night. Rink staggered back, blood from his sliced forehead invading his vision.

Move, move, move. A mantra for both men.

Even as Cain extricated himself from his hiding place, Rink was firing again. Blind, but with determination. One bullet scoured Cain's left thigh, another plucked hair from his head. But then Cain was out of the line of fire and he cut again at Rink.

Sliced to the bone, Rink kicked back. His foot caught Cain in the gut, propelled him backward. Cain was too canny a fighter to be caught so easily. Instead of floundering for balance, Cain allowed his momentum to take him over in a roll that brought him back immediately to his feet. And in that instant he was already coming back at Rink. Rink was big, powerful beneath his clothing, trained to deal with dangerous foes, but unprepared for one as determined as Tubal Cain, Father of Cutting Instruments. The Harvestman.

Rink shot again. But the bullet passed through space that Cain had occupied a second before. He was already two paces to the left. As Rink swung toward him, he arced his blade under the barrel of the gun. The pinching of Rink's eyes showed Cain he'd cut him. Then Cain gained the space below Rink's armpit, squirmed under and behind the big man, and looped his free arm around his throat. He jerked backward, sliced at the throat.

Rink grabbed at his knife, but Cain heard the telltale groan of someone in pain. Cain released him, kicked him away. Rink staggered and his head banged off the rock wall. Pivoting, he fell flat on his face. Blood mingled with the chalk-white sand.

Finally, Cain gave voice.

But all he had to say was "Ha!"

He stepped forward. Rink didn't get up. Cain smiled. Leaned down and plucked the gun out of Rink's grasp.

Distantly, he caught the sound of someone calling his name.

He turned quickly, heading into the narrow passage.

46

I SHOULD'VE EXPECTED SOMETHING LIKE THIS. Cain's history should have prepared me. The photographs of his victims viewed on Harvey's computer. The skeletons posed out there in the desert. The grotesque art daubed on the rocks outside. But nothing primed me for the chamber I now stood in.

The chamber wasn't huge. But Cain had used the space economically.

There wasn't a surface more than the width of my hand on walls or ceiling that wasn't decorated with human skulls, scapulas, or pelvic bones. Femur, humorus, radius, and ulna bones formed strange mosaics. Spinal columns had been arranged as borders to separate one insane montage from another. Interspersed between the human remains were countless bones gleaned from road-killed wildlife. And equally disturbing in their own way, myriad patches of cloth snagged from unsuspecting bodies were woven between the bones. Human rib cages dominated the far end of the room like shields on coats of arms. And there, as the living embodiment of Cain's insanity, was his centerpiece.

"Oh, my God. John?"

My voice came out as a wheeze and my arms reached out. My feet wouldn't follow them.

"John?" I asked again.

He was displayed like all the other of Cain's exhibits, attached to the walls of the cave by chains fixed to iron spikes hammered through the stone, his chest against the bedrock.

Cords were looped around his throat, woven around his skull, and fixed to a hook in the ceiling. His head was forced back on his spine so that he peered upward. His arms were outstretched, the skin peeled from his back stretched taut beneath them like demonic wings. I could see what Cain was attempting to portray. He intended that John be seen as a supplicant, beseeching a higher spirit in the heavens above him. A fallen angel begging for God's grace?

Walter said that FBI profilers had concluded that Cain might be attempting to make amends for slaughtering his own family. Perhaps John was representative of the demon that was Martin Maxwell, and in reality, it was he who begged grace from God. Maybe we'd never know the true meaning, and everything was simply the product of his depraved mind.

It wasn't just the pose that shocked me. In itself it was terrible. The way in which Cain had stripped the flesh from John's back, exposing the musculature, went way beyond awful. Yet that wasn't the worst. What made me shrink inside was that John still shivered with life.

Caught in a snapshot moment again, eternity was measured by the thrum of one heartbeat.

Then I was moving forward with no sense of volition.

One moment I was standing at the threshold, the next I was cradling John's head between my palms. My SIG was lying in the dust at my feet, forgotten in my urgency to help my brother. All that was in my head, my heart, my soul, was to give John a modicum of comfort. He wasn't conscious; not in the real sense of the word. He stirred. I didn't want to look at his wounds, but inexorably my eyes drifted down. My eyes screwed tight, blocking the image, but I knew I'd see it for a long time to come.

"Oh, my God," I moaned again. Beyond reason, the prayer was for my own mortal soul. I gently caressed John's head, and this time he responded.

He shrieked.

He pulled away from me, shrieked again.

"John. It's all right. It's me. It's Joe. Your *brother*."

John squirmed away from my touch.

"John. John." I couldn't find words to comfort him. To let him know that he was going to be okay. I was there for him. I wouldn't allow the beast to harm him further. I would save him. Find him medical care. I would do all those things. But I was useless. I averted my face and allowed my frustration to escape me in a ragged howl of fury and loathing. All the while, I hung on to John so that—if nothing else—he would know I was there.

I pressed my face to his shoulder, held him. I was talking to him, though I can't recall my words. They were nothing more than low, gentle platitudes that issued between wrenching sobs.

Finally, I reached across and tested the iron nails that had been hammered into the wall. The nails were slick with John's blood and I couldn't get a grip on them. I couldn't undo the chains without the key. So instead I started pulling free the cords that bound his head. Only distantly was I aware that the cords were the dried tendons and ligaments stripped from previous victims. I managed to pull them free, and John's head lolled on his shoulder.

The resilience of human nature is outstanding, the terrific injuries bodies can endure before life finally flees. That John was not only alive but in charge of his faculties was truly remarkable.

"Joe?" he croaked.

"Yes, John." I almost burst out crying again. "It's Joe. I'm here to help you."

And just as I said it, I heard the gunfire.

I spun from John, stooping for my SIG and lifting it toward the door. The gunfire was from somewhere outside. *Rink,* I thought. Killing Cain. Or being killed. I took three hurried steps before catching myself. I turned back to John.

"Everything'll be okay, John," I promised. "I'll be back."

"No," John moaned. "Don't leave me."

I shook with indecision but my training took over. "I'll be back. I promise."

And I started for the steps leading out. I had to defend this place. If Cain had taken Rink out, then he only had to keep me penned inside with no recourse but to watch my brother perish. If there was any way possible that he'd survive his horrific injuries, John required immediate medical help.

Even as I reached the steps, I heard gunfire again. A second of nothing, then one last shot. Then silence. I quickened my pace up the steps. I took them in three bounds, then I was out. Searching for targets, finding none. Immediately I set off in the direction of the narrow cleft between the rocks.

I shouted one word: "Cain!"

The cleft was a dark slash between the towering boulders, but I thought I could see movement there. Instinctively I pulled the trigger. And as reactively, someone shot back. I felt the wind of its passing as the bullet punched through the air next to my head. In midstep I dropped and rolled, came back to one knee firing again. A return shot tugged loose cloth at my elbow. I didn't let it stop me, kept on firing. Six shots in rapid succession, directly into the narrow passageway where I just had to get at least one killing shot into Cain's body mass. I heard him curse and knew that I'd hit him.

I dropped to my belly, fired the remaining two rounds in my gun, snatched backward at my waistband for a fresh clip even as I ejected the spent one.

It was a practiced movement I could achieve in less than two seconds, but it's surprising how much ground a determined man can cover in less than two seconds. Even as I pushed the clip into my SIG, Cain came charging at me out of the gloom.

Point.

Shoot.

The bullet caught him. It struck his left arm. But he didn't recoil; he fired back. Kept on coming.

Bullets punched the earth in front of me, spraying me with salty dust. I felt fire sear my left calf. I grunted. Fired again. And this time Cain doubled over. Though it didn't stop him. He launched himself at me.

Prone, I was at his mercy.

I had to move.

I twisted sideways, barely avoiding the elbow that Cain thrust at my skull. Then I twisted back toward him, firing at point-blank range. Only Cain had also twisted away and my bullet missed him. He slashed at my gun hand, and the stiffened edge of his hand struck the nerves on my forearm. The SIG fell from my lifeless fingers. Cain's gun swung toward me. I kicked at his chest and his aim went wide. Then we'd thrown our bodies together, and even as I thrust at his throat with my left hand, Cain jabbed his knee into my groin. I head-butted him in the face, reached for his gun, and wrenched it from him. He chopped at my wrist and I allowed the gun to drop so that I could return the blow.

We rolled across the sand, and there was no reason behind the strikes we aimed at each other, only that they were vicious and aimed at vulnerable points. Delivered with evil intent. Neither had the advantage. We were both wounded. Both of us were insane with hatred. Both of us wanted only to kill. At any second one of us would get what we wanted. Then the earth gave way beneath us and we were falling into space.

Somewhere deep inside I knew that our battle had taken us to the lip of the stairs leading to Cain's lair. We caromed against the steps, each taking the bone-jangling force as we somersaulted downward. Hitting the bottom we were forced apart, scattered on the floor.

I pulled myself to my knees, my teeth bared as I spat blood from my mouth. Cain was in a similar pose. There was a wound along his scalp that made his pale hair stick straight up. Another wound above his right hip leaked blood. His eyes were pinched; pinpricks of fury.

"I'm gonna rip your fucking head off," I promised him as I pushed up from my crouch.

"Come on." Cain beckoned. But even as I stepped forward, he spun on his heel and charged into the chamber. I half expected him to throw the door shut, and I primed myself to throw my shoulder against it. But Cain did nothing of the sort. He took half a dozen running steps into the chamber, then turned to face me. Almost languidly, he drew a knife from his waistband, held it up before his eyes, grinned at me. "Come on. If you think you're up to the challenge."

I stooped, drew my KA-BAR. Nodded. Stepped into the chamber.

"Ding, ding. Round two." Cain looked like he was enjoying himself.

I pointed the KA-BAR at him, a matador taunting a bull.

"Sanctimonious shithead," I called him.

Cain's lips pinched. "I can see where John gets his colorful language."

I swung my head. "Let's leave John out of this. It's between you and me, Cain."

He jerked forward. I feinted at his gut, and we both skipped back out of range. Cain prowled to my right. I turned with him. He hopped to the left. Ten feet separated us. Beyond him, John hung on the wall, an unwilling witness to our duel. I spared him only a glance. Cain also glanced John's way.

"You see this, John? The great liberator has arrived. You really think he can help you? That it makes one iota of difference to your fate?"

"Leave him out of this," I snapped. "Me and you, Cain. If you've got what it takes."

Cain smiled as if he were hiding a great secret. "Oh, I've got what it takes. Believe me. But what about you? Up in Washington I heard your name whispered. Like you're some sort of silent killing machine that even presidents are afraid of. Me, I think it was all hyperbole. I don't think you're anywhere near as good as they say you are. Me, on the other hand, well, just look around. I reckon the proof's in the pudding. Just take a look at what I did to our mutual buddy John Telfer."

John made a noise, a hiss of anguish. I lunged forward, cutting at Cain's torso in a bottom-to-top oblique slash. Cain skipped away laughing. My knife edge had missed by a mile. But that was okay. I'd only cut to get Cain to move, allowing me to leap through the space he'd left and position myself before John. Realizing his mistake, Cain shook his head. Made a tut-tut noise.

Now it was my turn to be the facetious one. I wiggled the fingers of my left hand at him, beckoning him to me. "Come on, Cain."

Cain did come on. He dropped low, thrusting at my abdomen. As I shifted to block his knife, he twisted to one side. He slashed in an S, bringing the blade perilously close to my throat, a centimeter shy of my carotid artery. Only I was also ducking and my return stab forced him back on his heels. I followed him, jabbing at his throat, at his groin, back to the throat. Cain shouted in forced humor. Slashed back at me. I struck at his knife blade with my KA-BAR and sparks danced.

I thrust my left foot into his gut. Cain absorbed most of the kick—but not all. He went into a wall, scattering bones across the floor. Immediately he spun, struck at me. It was all I could do to save my throat, at the expense of a deep cut across the back of my left hand. I flinched, and Cain saw that as a weakness. He came at me again. To show him I was no weakling, I jabbed my blade into his thigh. I'd have preferred to rip out his femoral artery, but the meat was as good a reminder of my potency as anything was. Cain didn't like it. He jumped back, slapping his free hand over the wound.

He stood there, breathing deeply through his nose as he slowly lifted the blood-smeared hand before us.

I nodded at him. There you go, you son of a bitch. I repositioned myself so that I guarded John from his blade. Inclined my head, inviting him in.

Cain postured. He did an adjustment with his feet reminiscent of a young Cassius Clay—a show of bravado to indicate that the wound wouldn't slow him down any. I smiled knowingly. Bravado was the tool of a frightened man.

"What's wrong, Cain? Not so sure of yourself anymore? It's one thing cutting up helpless people. What's it like to have your victim turn on you?"

"Fun."

"I bet." I took a slow step forward. "Bet it isn't as much fun as when you murdered your wife and kids."

Cain stiffened slightly.

"Or when you killed your brother, huh?"

"Leave *my* brother out of this," Cain said.

I gained another half step on him. "What was it like, Cain? Murdering those that loved you? Was it a thrill? Some sort of sick fantasy come to life?"

Cain growled. My taunting was having the desired effect. For one, my words were angering him. An angry man doesn't reason. And when reason goes, so does training. And my speaking was forcing him to consider the actual words. Even if his response was only to swear, his brain was engaged as he deliberated his answer. While he was measuring those words, he wasn't capable of planning his next attack. It was a lesson I learned many years ago. Ask a question of your enemy. As he answers, hit him.

"Did you watch them burn, Cain?"

"Yes," he replied. "Watched them burn like torches."

"Bit of a waste, though. Bet you wish you'd brought them here, eh? What a waste of good bones."

Cain paused. I could see that there was regret behind the scowl. He opened his mouth. I didn't wait for his response. I leaped at him.

It should have ended then. My knife should have found his throat. He should have fallen to his knees gripping his wound, attempting to halt the flow. But as I'd always been cautioned, should-haves and could-haves have nothing to do with the reality of blood and snot combat.

Even as I stabbed at Cain's throat, he was already lifting a hand. Instead of the soft tissue of his throat, I found a sinewy forearm. All right, I wounded him sorely. If he didn't staunch the blood loss, then he would ultimately weaken and die. But he was still in the fight. And unfortunately, my KA-BAR was wedged in muscle and bone. And Cain's blade was still free.

47 YOU'VE UNDOUBTEDLY HEARD THAT OLD STORY about how at the moment of death your entire life flashes before your eyes. It's not true. Well, not for me it wasn't. I guess my life had been way too eventful for that. Not many people get the luxury of playing out a billion reminders before sinking into oblivion, not when death comes in an instant. Instead of the whole panoply of incidents from an event-filled thirty-nine years, only two things flashed through my mind. First, the face of my ex-wife, Diane. It wasn't a genuine image, but one my mind conjured of future events. She was standing at my grave, but she wasn't grieving. She wore a face of disgust, even anger. As if she'd always known that this was how it was going to end.

Second—and equally poignant—an image from only minutes before. John beseeching me, "Don't leave me."

On reflection, those two images whorled through my mind in less than a heartbeat, so I suppose the important facets of my life could've been played out within seconds. But I didn't have the luxury of seconds. If I was to live at all, I had to act now.

I loosed the hilt of my KA-BAR. It was pointless attempting to wrench it free. While I tried, Cain could have cut enough of my hide to fashion himself a new pair of boots. Instead, I stabbed my fingers at his eyes. It didn't stop his knife from parting flesh and grating on bone, but it was enough to deflect it from my heart. It also forced us apart. It was a slow release, and I swear that I could feel every cold

inch of steel as it sucked free of my chest. Cain went backward, eyes screwed tight as he tried to fight the response of
tears invading his senses. I went to one knee, clutching at
my chest.

Cain backed to the wall again, his shoulders brushing
more bones on the floor. He scrubbed at his eyes, cursing
me in short guttural snatches of sound. I remained kneeling,
almost overwhelmed by the agony. His knife hadn't killed
me, but at that moment I wasn't sure that the pain wouldn't
finish the task for him.

Ignoring the agony, I rose up to see where he was, and already Cain was coming for me. He was half blinded, but he
didn't need eyes to know I was at his mercy. He was armed.
I wasn't. I was severely wounded. It would be a matter of
seconds to finish the job.

But would-be is a phrase that sits alongside should-haves
and could-haves in combat. And the difference between Cain
and me was that only I understood that at that moment. He
hadn't seen Rink step into the doorway behind him. Rink
was bleeding from his belly. He had a gash across his chin,
another across his arm. His face was plastered with gore
from another wound across his forehead. But life seethed in
his furnace-hot gaze.

Cain faltered. Something in my face must have alerted
him. He stumbled to a halt. Swung around to face Rink.

"Drop the knife," Rink roared as he lifted a gun and aimed
it at Cain's face.

Cain laughed. "You found my gun? I wondered where I
dropped it."

"Drop the knife, Cain," Rink said again. He stepped
closer, the gun trained between Cain's eyes.

"Sorry. Can't do it."

"Drop it now or I blow your goddamn head off."

"I'm surprised you're still alive," Cain said, as if he genuinely cared. "I really thought that I'd opened you up back
there." Cain sucked air through his teeth, noting that Rink's
throat was fully intact. "I didn't realize that you got your

arm in the way. I only cut your chin, eh? Suppose that'll teach me for rushing the job."

"Don't try messing with me," Rink warned. He looked unsteady on his feet. Loss of blood and what looked like a knock on the head were making him weak. "I know what you're trying to do. Do you think you can get me with that pigsticker before I blow a hole in you?"

Cain glanced my way. I could see a smile begin across his face. "You know something, Rington, I believe I could."

I knew it. Cain knew. Even Rink knew it. The gun was empty.

"Shoot him, Rink," I shouted.

Rink pulled the trigger.

A click as the hammer fell on an empty chamber.

But it was enough. Cain almost swaggered as he advanced on Rink. As he did so, I was already moving. I snatched at the clutter on the floor, came up with the first thing my grasping fingers found, and with all my might I forced the broken end of a human rib into the soft flesh in the hollow of his throat.

The result was instantaneous. Cain shuddered, his knees gave way. He stumbled toward Rink, who was already coming at him. I snatched at his left arm even as Rink grappled with his right, pulling the knife from Cain's listless grasp. Cain twisted toward me. His eyes were wide, as though caught in an epiphany of insight. His mouth was wide, too, but nothing issued forth but a gurgle. My own face was flat, emotionless, as I plucked my KA-BAR from his flesh.

We could have done it then. A frenzy of stabbing and slashing. Doling out as much torment as Cain had subjected his victims to. But neither of us succumbed to our base instincts. We did something immeasurably crueler. We allowed Cain to suffer the ignominy of a slow and painful death. If he hadn't reveled in displaying the trophies taken from his victims, I would have been left weaponless. No doubt about it . . . he'd have won the day.

Instead, he had to suffer his last few minutes of life in the knowledge that he'd messed up.

He collapsed to his knees. He searched our faces. We both grinned at him. Miraculously he found a laugh. But it was lost on us. He was simply pathetic. And he knew it.

He sobbed. Lifted a beseeching hand to me. I shook my head. He lifted faltering fingers to the half-inch stub of bone protruding from his throat.

His eyes said it all.

"You reap what you sow," I told him.

Cain laughed a final time at the irony of it.

48

JUST AS I SUSPECTED, WALTER ARRIVED LIKE A CE-
lebrity at a Hollywood bash. There's no show without
Punch. He entered the chamber only after the storm troopers had given him the all clear. Medics were in the throes
of strapping John to a gurney—belly down, of course—
hooking up IV bags and inserting all manner of hypodermic
contraptions into his failing system.

Sitting in the dust, clutching at a dressing on my chest, I
watched it all with a strange sense of distraction.

Medics fussed over Rink, but I gave them as little notice as
I did those working to save John. I was only concerned with
Walter. I wasn't worried that any of us would end up buried
under the dirt as I once contemplated. Walter was seeing this
through the right way. Showing his gratitude. Otherwise, the
armed strike force wouldn't have given ground to the medical team; they'd have simply shot us where we sat.

"What kept you?" I asked.

Walter came to stand beside me. He even gave me a fa-
therly pat on the shoulder. But his eyes were on Cain. We
had left him where he'd come to rest, slouched on his knees,
hands folded in his lap, head tilted forward on his chest.
Apart from the blood dripping on his breast, he looked like
a supplicant at prayer.

"I didn't want to step on your toes," Walter said. "This
was your gig, Hunter."

I spat phlegm and dust and God knows what else on the
floor.

"You could've come sooner. You were monitoring us all along. Why didn't you send in your team before now?"

"And would you have thanked me if I had?"

"No," I answered truthfully. "I suppose not."

"Then all's well that ends well."

I gripped the dressing a paramedic had placed on my chest wound. Thought about how close Cain had come to finishing me. All's well that ends well? "Yeah."

Walter walked away from me then. It wasn't that he didn't care for my well-being, only that Cain held a more immediate fascination for him. He went and stood over Cain, stared down at him for a long time.

"He's dead."

"As disco," I said.

"You know," Walter said, "there's many a profiler up at Quantico would've given their eyeteeth to speak to him before he died."

"My heart bleeds for them," I muttered. In hindsight, considering how close Cain's knife had come to finishing me, they weren't the most appropriate words. Even Walter glanced at me to see if I was serious. I slowly blinked.

Returning his attention to Cain, Walter went on, "Don't know how he managed to elude us all this time."

"Maybe you didn't look hard enough."

Walter nodded. Then, totally out of character for a man who'd ordered plenty of wet work but never gotten his own hands dirty, he gripped Cain's hair and pulled back his head. A shadow crossed Walter's face. He looked to the medics.

"See to this man," he ordered.

I jerked. Walter stepped in front of me, pressing me down as Cain was loaded onto a gurney. "Don't worry, Hunter. I'm going to bury him."

"He *is* dead?" My words were more question than fact.

"We don't bury the living," he pointed out.

That wasn't necessarily true, but I wasn't of a mind to argue. Walter never talked straight.

As Cain was rushed away, Walter and I watched him go. Walter sighed, and I should have guessed what was coming. "We were looking in the wrong place."

I squinted at him.

"It's not him."

"What?"

"It's not him," Walter repeated.

I experienced a moment's panic. "What do you mean *it's not him*? It's definitely Cain." To emphasize the point, I threw out a hand, inviting Walter to take in the sheer horror of his surroundings. Walter lifted a palm, a calming gesture, but I struggled up from the floor to stand beside him. My nose was inches from his. "Can't you see what the son of a bitch did here?"

"Easy now, son," Walter said. "It's Cain all right. No doubt about it."

"So what the hell are you talking about?"

"It's not Martin Maxwell."

"What?" I stared into Walter's face. Searching for the lie. Not that it helped. I didn't know Martin Maxwell from Mickey Mouse. Only thing I was sure of was that I'd stopped the Harvestman.

"It's the brother," Walter explained.

"The brother? You mean . . . ?"

"Uh-huh. Robert Swan. The musician."

I got it then.

"You need a name to give to the press, Walter?" I said. "And you want Swan to take the blame for this. To protect the good name of the Secret Service."

"Yes."

Thing is, at the end of the day, it didn't much matter to me. Whoever Tubal Cain ended up being, it didn't matter in the large scale of things. He was a demented killer regardless. One that I'd put down like a rabid dog. And for that I was thankful. If Walter needed to spin the world a line of bullshit, then so be it.

I grunted, looked Walter dead in the eye. He stood there expressionless. Then I nodded. "The musician? If you say so, Walter."

Walter winked. "I say so."

I turned my back on him and clutching my chest I limped toward the exit door. The bullet graze on my calf hurt worse than the chest wound. It was still night out, but the sky was ablaze with searchlights from the helicopters coming and going. As I reached the stairs, Rink joined me. He placed a hand on my shoulder. I couldn't determine whether it was to support his weight or mine. It didn't matter. As always, we'd support each other.

"You going to be all right, Rink?"

"Fine and dandy," he said, yet involuntarily his hand went to the dressings on his face and chin. "He got me good, Hunter. Slashed my gut, but luckily for me he only got the muscle. He came close to getting my throat, too. If I hadn't been knocked cold when I banged my head, the son of a bitch might have really finished me off."

"It was a close one," I said. The cut on his chin wasn't life-threatening, but if it had been an inch lower, my friend wouldn't be beside me now. Most likely I wouldn't have been alive, either.

"Too close," Rink said.

With no sense of volition, I'd made it up the stairs and found myself standing ankle deep in the white sand. The cul-de-sac wasn't large enough to accommodate all the choppers and personnel brought in by Walter, but there were a fair number of men and women in jumpsuits and body armor. They stood around with their weapons cocked, as though Cain were still a threat.

Leaning on each other, Rink and I made our way to the cleft in the rocks. It was awkward walking through the gap shoulder to shoulder, but we made it.

Outside was as Rink had earlier described it—a three-ring circus. Helicopters dominated the sky. Hummers and SUVs prowled along the lip of the escarpment in the distance. Undoubtedly FBI and Secret Service, but this was now Walter's gig, and he was calling all the shots. Everyone else had to make do with prowling on the periphery. The only thing that concerned me was the presence of the air ambulance Walter had had the foresight to call in. And even as I confirmed its presence, paramedics rushed past us with John strapped to the gurney.

"Think he'll make it?" Rink asked.

I remembered the awful wounds on his back and couldn't see how.

"It's amazing what the doctors can do these days," Rink said, his words sounding hollow. Even *he* doubted them.

"He'll pull through," I said softly. "He has to. Otherwise all of this will have been for nothing."

"Not for nothing, my friend." Rink slipped an arm around my shoulders and pulled me into an embrace. "We've just stopped a monster. Me an' you, Hunter. Just like the old days."

49

IN THE DAYS THAT FOLLOWED, WALTER ATTEMPTED to explain the thinking behind it all. In his take on the Harvestman, Martin Maxwell hadn't gone off the rails. All right, he'd messed up his life when he'd gone playing with the governor's wife's lingerie, but that, it turned out, was his only transgression. Other than a sleazy penchant for women's underwear, he wasn't the fiend he was suspected of being.

Some would even argue that Maxwell was a decent enough fellow. After all, he'd sought out his less privileged brother. Taken him into the fold of his home. Given him the kind of life he'd been missing. But it appears that the man who would become Cain wasn't one for gratitude. His was a soul festering with jealousy, and with dark fantasies and desires he couldn't achieve as a no-name musician in a nation of musicians whose talents far outshone his. So Cain instead coveted something that could never be his. He stole the skills of his brother. Maybe Martin gave the knowledge willingly. He had to have taken the brother under his wing, for Cain's skill with weapons, particularly the knife, didn't come without many hours of practice. Or his understanding of tracking and surveillance. Or—and this was the most troubling aspect of Walter's take on Cain—how he could have known my name. But that was easy enough for Walter to explain: he simply left me out of the equation. As far as anyone would ever know, it was federal agents who'd taken Cain out.

In the end, I didn't bother thinking about it. Let Walter play his games. It was what he did, after all. What better way to cover up the depraved actions of a government employee than to deny that he was one? Plausible denial. That was what Walter thrived on. If he wanted the world to believe that Martin Maxwell wasn't their man, then so be it. He could feed them the bullshit about Robert Swan, but I knew the truth.

I had other, more important things on my mind.

John for one.

He was currently recuperating in a military hospital beyond the prying eyes of the media. As far as anyone was concerned, Cain had left no living victims. I was happy enough with the arrangement. It got Hendrickson's men off his back. Walter promised me that on his recovery John would be placed in the witness protection program. In effect, he would disappear. New name, new identity, the works. The only time he'd be drawn back into the limelight would be if charges were brought against Hendrickson and Sigmund Petoskey for their part in the counterfeiting ring. Then John would be returned to obscurity.

It meant never going home for him. But given that he'd been gone so long, that his time with Louise Blake was now behind him as well, maybe it was for the best that John start over.

My next concern was for Rink. My best friend. Who'd given so much for me. Who had suffered as much as I had. We went off to the hospital together to be patched up. My chest wound turned out to be superficial, as did the wounds to Rink's chin and arm, but the slash to the gut meant he had to undergo observation for a few days.

After Rink was cleared from any signs of complications, Walter extended his hospitality to the use of his Lear. A few hours later we were back in Florida. We spent two days at Rink's condominium in Tampa. The rain had passed and we spent those forty-eight hours reclining in the sun and drinking. Of course, it wasn't all partying. There was a lot of healing to do.

Plus, we still had work to do. A certain briefcase liberated from a boat at Marina del Rey required our attention. Not to mention the seven hundred grand that was inside it. I'd no qualms about putting the money to good use; John had paid in blood and agony for this reward. As far as anyone was concerned, the cash had burned along with Rhet Carson's yacht. The problem being, blood money never brings happiness. It was handed over to Walter as evidence that would help bring down John's enemies.

As a sweetener for my time in the U.S., Walter transferred a sizable sum of money into a fund set up for Jennifer and the kids. This was cash from his department's budget, so did not reek of agony and blood. It was clean. So was my conscience.

I spoke to Harvey Lucas. He told me he was looking after Louise Blake. Something in his tone made me smile. He was looking after her? I bet he was.

Job done, Rink was as affable as ever. The scars would forever be a reminder of how close to death he'd come, but he wasn't overly upset. The scars on his face gave his rugged good looks even more appeal to the ladies. Or so Rink said. There were tears in our eyes when we said good-bye at the airport.

My final concern. And the most pressing. Going home. Wherever that turned out to be.

Epilogue

JUBAL'S HOLLOW.

A sun-blasted landscape in the middle of nowhere. The G-men had come and gone. An army of anthropologists, medical examiners, and crime scene investigators had picked the barrens clean. The remnants of Cain's depravity had been listed, labeled, sealed, and shipped off in packing crates to a secret location. And with them, the media hubbub had died down. The Harvestman story was old news now, other atrocities in the world taking center stage. The camera vans and anchors in starched suits and starched hair departed for more immediate bad news stories.

Now there was nothing but scrub, sand, and more sand.

As it should be.

But there were visitors. Hundreds of them. People came to stare and shake their heads. Twisted souvenir hunters came away with nothing but fragile bones from birds or lizards, but to the casual observer true remnants of the Harvestman's ossuary. A number of entrepreneurial tour operators made a killing from the fascination of the ghoulish tourists who sought out more than the glitz of L.A. The Harvestman was big business. Big money. He was, after all, the most despicable of all murderers this side of the new millennium. He had achieved the notoriety and fame he'd desired.

However, under constant armed supervision, the patient known only as John Doe must have found it difficult to curse through his ruined throat. For though the Harvestman was the name on the lips of every person with a penchant for dark history, Maxwell meant nothing. To the world, Robert Swan, a mediocre guitar player with hopeless dreams of the big time, had at last achieved his fifteen minutes of fame.

Acknowledgments

A VERY BIG THANK-YOU FROM THE BOTTOM OF MY HEART to all those people who have helped me along the way. To Denise, who is everything to me. To all my family, particularly my father, Jacky, and brother, Jim, who have helped me immensely in writing this book. To Luigi and to Alison, I owe you a massive debt of gratitude for having faith in me and championing me all the way. To David Highfill and Sue Fletcher, editors extraordinaire, for all your brilliant work and guidance. To Lee Child for your kind support. To Jeanette Slinger for making everyone take notice. And to everyone else in the background on both sides of the Atlantic for all your hard work.

If you enjoyed
DEAD MEN'S DUST,
don't miss
JUDGMENT AND WRATH,
the next Joe Hunter thriller
from Matt Hilton

Available in hardcover August 2010 from

WILLIAM MORROW
An Imprint of HarperCollins*Publishers*

NOT NORMALLY ONE FOR MOVING IN THE KIND OF CIRCLES the people of Baker Island enjoyed, I would be forgiven for missing *just another rich man* as he took an evening stroll along the dockside. But as one who had spent fourteen years hunting terrorists, and the last four dealing with criminals ranging from moneylenders to a bone collecting maniac, I recognized a stone killer when I saw one.

An island this wealthy, it was probable that a large portion of the populace was ex-cops, ex-military—and everything in between—employed as executive protectors to those that called Baker Island their home. But there was something about the sinuous way this man moved that told me he wasn't the type who celebrated the sanctity of life. For one, he was too watchful of his surroundings. Even switched-on security men don't act that way when they aren't covering their mark.

The cigar was a prop. Too exaggerated, the way he put it to his mouth, then removed it with a grand, sweeping gesture. And all the while the other hand didn't move from his pocket. It fiddled with something, and I could tell his hand extended much lower than the confines of his pocket. He was packing.

He flicked the cigar away, watching it with a strange air of fascination as it pin-wheeled away into the ocean. Leaning back on a wall, the man turned and stared directly at me. I'd been expecting that, so I'd already slunk down against the recliner, tilting my head as though dozing. I watched him through slitted eyes. The man ghosted a smile. I'd have missed it in the subdued lighting if I hadn't got a flash of saliva on teeth.

He shifted his gaze. Out of his line of sight I was already mid-text to Rink.

GET HERE FAST. TROUBLE.

I hit the send button just as the man turned away and walked along the coast path. His black hair shone in the lamps along the path, so I could make out his progress beyond the wall to Jorgenson's garden. I blinked and the man was suddenly crouching on the wall like some unearthly bat. Next instant he was down in the garden and he paused to check his pockets. When next he moved it was as if a snake had sprung out of a coil, fast but sinuous at the same time. Then I couldn't see him because of the angle and the obscuring foliage.

Keeping low, I moved to the edge of my balcony. The lights above the entrance door spilled across Jorgenson's terrace, making for faux-daytime. Then came a noise like a sharp cough and the garden went dark.

As soon as it did, I was on the move. But not without hearing four rapid shots from a silenced handgun, and the smashing of glass.

Going back through my apartment would take too long. I swung over the edge of the balcony and jumped to the terrace below. Harking back to my parachute-days, I tucked and rolled, absorbing the impact, and came up with my SIG levelled towards Jorgenson's house. Then I moved forward. Further down the garden, only the shrubbery marked the boundary, but here close to the entrances a small wall had been erected to offer privacy to occupants sitting on the terrace. I had to shift a terracotta pot containing some fern-type plant. Then I vaulted the wall and landed in Jorgenson's property.

There was another dull thud, then the bang and rattle of something clattering down a staircase. I stepped into the foyer just as the man I'd watched outside raced up the stairs. The big man who'd called Marianne inside earlier was dead. A telephone was still in his hand, but he'd ripped the cord loose as he'd died. Another man sprawled on the floor and his blood decorated the walls and made a crazy pattern on the shattered mirror.

What the fuck have I got myself into this time? I wondered. I couldn't take time to ponder the bad luck that had cast its hand my way. Marianne was up those stairs. Who this killer was I had no idea, but whether or not Marianne was the target she wouldn't get out of this situation alive if I stood there trying to figure out the age-old question.

The killer was already out of sight. Another gunshot, then muffled talking. I swung onto the stairs and saw another corpse. A young woman with half her head gone. This angered me more than any amount of slaughtered bodyguards. It also told me the killer wouldn't pause to put a bullet through Marianne as well.

Silent as possible, I made my way up the stairs. The killer and someone I took to be Jorgenson were conversing in low tones. I wasn't concerned about what was said—the threat in the killer's voice was enough to keep me moving.

On the landing now, I moved along the hall. A thick carpet beneath my rubber soles ensured silence and I was able to move directly to the bedroom door without raising the alarm.

There I readied my gun. Listened.

Jorgenson's voice came sharp and clear now. Anger born from fear. "You touch either of us, you'll be hunted down," he promised. "They won't stop. You'll be hounded constantly and when they get you they will make you hurt!"

"They?" the killer asked. "Who are these they you have so much faith in? They will have to find me first. If I don't want them to find me, they never will."

Self-conceited, over-confident bastard, I thought. I stepped into the room behind him. "They already have," I said.

Should have kept my mouth shut. Self-conceit and over-confidence can get anyone killed.

The killer spun and fired even before I'd done gloating.

His bullet missed me. Only just. But it made me flinch and my return fire missed him as well.

Sometimes sudden violence can have a strange effect on the senses. As adrenalin spurts through the system, you can experience a startling bending of reality so that everything around you seems like a slow-motion, hyper-clear shot on a 3D screen. Really it's your mind racing as it seeks the options for flight or fight, overtaking the responses of the machine that the engine of the brain powers.

There was an overriding sense of déjà vu even as I pulled the trigger again and saw the material of the man's suit jacket trail in the wake of the bullet's passing. Unfortunately there was no blood. Missed the fucker a second time. Then he was lunging to one side, and he was shooting across his body at me. Throwing myself into the room, I fired off a volley of five rounds. Unlike his silenced pistol, my SIG roared like Thor's battle cry.

I was here on the knight errant's quest to save a damsel in distress. I wouldn't be much good to her if I ended up dead.

Swinging round into a sitting position, I levelled my SIG on the killer.

He must have had an equally important reason to live, because he fired back. Burning cold creased my right shoulder. It wasn't a debilitating hit, in fact, having been shot before, I realised that the bullet had barely grazed me. It was enough to draw my aim though, and my return fire went over his head and struck the doorframe as he vaulted back into the landing. The clatter of his feet down the stairs resounded through the house.

Pretty certain he wasn't going to return to the room in the next second or two, I searched for Marianne. She was unhurt, but still in a state of near collapse. Jorgenson was in a duck's crouch of his own, ass almost touching his heels.

"You okay?" I asked, my words for both of them.

Receiving nods from both, I rolled over on my front, swinging to cover the door. "Jorgenson," I said. "Get over here."

Jorgenson blinked at me, half rose from his crouch. Then he sunk down again. Not sure about staying there, but not wanting to approach me either.

I snapped at him, "If you want to get out of here alive, you're gonna have to do what I say. Now get the fuck over here!"

When I came here it was with the understanding that I might have to kill Bradley Jorgenson. It's funny how fate plays out sometimes. The arrival of this would-be killer had changed the dynamics of my mission. In my mind, Bradley had been someone to be loathed, someone to be put down with all the regret of shooting a rabid dog. And yet here I was, offering to be his protector.

"Are you armed?" I asked him.

He shook his head.

"What about him?" I jerked my head towards a man folded over a desk.

Jorgenson's eyes teared up. He shook his head sadly.

"Make sure," I ordered him. "He could be carrying."

"He isn't," Jorgenson said. "That's my father. He abhorred violence. He was a man who only wanted to stop pain."

Noble, I thought, but misguided. Someone who makes their billions from military contracts can't throw the moral card when challenged over their source of income. He could say what he wanted, but Daddy Jorgenson had as much to do with causing pain as curing it.

"Check," I said.

Rising up, I crept over to the door. Keeping low, I bobbed my head round the frame, then back inside again. I didn't see the killer, but he was likely still in the house. When I glanced round, Jorgenson was gently patting around inside his father's jacket. He was looking at me and his eyes were full of disgust.

"Anything?"

"Nothing," he spat, moving away quickly.

"Get Marianne," I told him. "Take her over there."

Jorgenson helped Marianne up. She looked shaky, but unhurt. On rubber legs, she allowed Jorgenson to lead her past the dead man to the far end of the room. Her eyes swooped, like birds chasing insects at dusk, never still, never in one place.

"Do you know that man?" I demanded. I snuck a look around the doorframe, noticing a play of shadows from below.

"No," Jorgenson said. "And I don't know you. Who the hell are you?"

Surprisingly, it was Marianne who offered explanation. "He's Joe. He's here to help."

"You've no idea why he wants you dead?" I asked.

No reply. When I looked, Jorgenson was holding Marianne to him, his hands cupping her head against his chest. Marianne was sobbing into his shirt. The picture of young love. It didn't look much like Marianne had ever suffered at his hands. Maybe she'd only traded one lesser terror for another.

There'd be time for resolving the Jorgenson problem later. Right now there was a far greater danger to Marianne's welfare. The killer was downstairs and he was up to no good.

"Is there another way out of here?" Studying the windows, I decided that we could smash one of them and climb out. It would be a fair drop to the ground but we were all capable of it. What I didn't like was the idea of the killer waiting for us, picking us off from below as we clambered from the window.

RINK HOW FAR AWAY.

My text was hurried. Thankfully I received his reply in seconds, but it wasn't what I wanted to see.

FIFTEEN MINS.

Not soon enough. The killer wasn't going to wait that long.

I heard a clatter and dull thump from below us.

"What's he doing?" Marianne asked.

I'd been thinking the same thing. Sounded like he was in the kitchen.

MEET US SOBE, I sent to Rink.

In her schoolgirl guise, Marianne might not have been much help in these circumstances. But as the sleek trophy Jorgenson had made of her, perhaps there was something she could bring into play.

"Marianne, you have perfume in here?"

Marianne stared at me as if I was mad. In all honesty she wasn't too far off the mark. "Perfume?"

"Good stuff. Concentrated."

She nodded, pulling free from Jorgenson's embrace. She avoided the dead man, taking a wide berth, and went to a credenza. Pulled open a compartment and grabbed at bottles of scent. Judging by the brands and designs of the bottles, she handed me the makings of a bomb worth thousands of dollars.

I again snatched a look, checking that the killer wasn't sneaking back along the landing. The sounds from below reassured me he was still being industrious in the kitchen area. For a second I considered leading Marianne and Jorgenson out of the bedroom, taking our chances on getting down the stairs while he was busy with whatever the hell he was doing. He'd hear us, though, and would nail us as we came down the stairs.

When I turned back to the bedroom, Jorgenson had joined Marianne beside me.

"This better not be what I'm thinking," Jorgenson said to me. His head shake was pure denial.

"We have to make a diversion; otherwise we aren't going to get out of here alive." I began unscrewing tops off the perfume bottles. "Find me something larger than these. That wine bottle over there will do."

"But my father . . ." Jorgenson croaked.

"Your father is already dead," I pointed out. "But I'm pretty sure he'd want you to live. Now go and fetch me the fucking bottle."

Then I stepped out onto the landing and peered over the railing. The killer immediately shot at me, and I ducked back. I unloaded five bullets directly through the floor. Not really an attempt to hit him—the wooden joists would probably sap much of the velocity of the rounds—but it was enough to force him back into the kitchen.

Two could play at the same game. The killer's bullets

drilled upwards, lifting tatters of carpet in front of my eyes. I jumped back into the room. Good enough, I thought, I'd got his attention. Plus he was using the kitchen for cover.

"Empty the perfume into the wine bottle, and get me some sort of rag for a fuse," I whispered to Marianne. She understood my train of thought and nodded. She turned to the bottles I'd set on the floor.

Jorgenson brought the wine bottle. He walked slowly, and his eyes never left the still form of his father. His father was a sick man, dying from cancer as I recalled, but I don't think that Jorgenson ever expected to be cremating him so soon.

"If there was any other way," I said, by way of apology. His face was set in stone. There'd be no consoling him. Not at that moment. It'd be pointless trying, so I turned away from him, concentrating on keeping the killer at bay.

Behind my back Jorgenson sobbed for his murdered father. It was enough to make him step over a precipice.

The stupid son of a bitch swung the bottle and smashed it over my skull.